As Fate Would Have It

Moira Leigh Macleod

As Fate Would Have It

tellwell

Tellwell Talent
www.tellwell.ca

ISBN
978-0-2288-6387-8 (Hardcover)
978-0-2288-6385-4 (Paperback)
978-0-2288-6386-1 (eBook)

A Brief Recap

The Year With No Spring

LILY AND ED:

Lily and her children are being held captive at The Roachville Pines by Dan McInnes (AKA Barry Sheppard) when she meets, Ed Baxter, a guest at the motel who unexpectedly finds her in distress. After meeting Sheppard, the man he assumes is Lily's husband, Ed makes inquiries of an RCMP colleague, who in turn engages Gordon Dunphy of the Glace Bay Police Department.

While Ed and Gordon investigate their suspicions Barry Sheppard is actually Dan McInnes, a one-time, dirty cop currently wanted for the attack on well-known artist, Myrtle Munroe, Lily finds McInnes trying to rape her young, co-worker, Anne. McInnes is stabbed during the altercation, flees, and is later helped by a Mi'kmaw elder who is unaware the man he is treating attacked his grandniece. Once he recovers, McInnes, who stole thousands of dollars from Lily when they first met, is anxious to get the money and move on. His efforts to get to his hidden stash are thwarted, however, when Ed spots him in the area. McInnes, once again on the run, hides out at an abandoned fishing camp, where Henri Gehue, Anne's father, finds him, ties him to a tree, and cuts off his genitals.

With the help of an anonymous tip, Lily finds the money McInnes had hidden and returns to Glace Bay to give it back to Mabel and Stanley. Ed, now living in Cape Breton, accompanies Lily to Glace Bay where she meets Victoria Donnely and immediately recognizes her as the daughter she gave up for adoption. Lily then returns to New Brunswick and begins seeing Anne's father, Henri Gehue, unware he killed Dan McInnes.

Ed buys a house in Cape Breton and pursues a relationship with Amour, Victoria's mother. Ed and Lily remain close.

Mabel and Stanley

Mabel and Stanley's marriage hits a rough patch when Mabel refuses to tell him why her close relationship with Mark has cooled. Mabel, however, remains steadfast, unwilling to divulge Alice's shameful secret that she slept with her husband's brother, and that Matthew is Mark's child.

Stanley eventually solves the mystery after Alice lashes out at Mark. Both Mabel and Stanley worry Mark might have also put two and two together. Mark returns to Halifax but, some months later, pays Mabel an unexpected visit, asking her if he is Matthew's father. Mabel acknowledges he is, imploring him to leave things be. Mabel doesn't tell Alice about Mark's visit, or that she confirmed he was Matthew's father.

Mabel and Stanley welcome their third child, Liv.

The Cast of Characters You've Met Along the Way

Leading Roles

Mabel (Adshade) MacIntyre – As a young girl, Mabel survived the tragic loss of her mother (Ellie) and spent her teen years with an alcoholic, abusive man (Johnnie Adshade) whom she assumed was her father. Poor and uneducated, she landed her dream job baking bread at Cameron's Store. After a series of traumatic events, including almost freezing to death in a coal shed, her rape at the hands of Johnnie's friends, and a corrupt murder investigation led by a dirty cop and an ambitious prosecutor, Mabel eventually discovers her mother's secrets. Smart, strong, and resilient, she marries Stanley McIntyre, has three children and turns a small, neighbourhood bakery into one of the town's most successful enterprises.

Stanley MacIntyre – A former boxer, coal-hauler, and long-time friend of James and Margaret Cameron, Stanley found Mabel near frozen to death at the bottom of a coal shed. Charged with the death of Johnnie Adshade, Stanley was prepared to face the death penalty rather than expose a secret he knew would bring Mabel shame. After being rebuffed on numerous occasions, he eventually convinces Mabel to marry him and opens a successful construction company where he employs Dirty Willie, a man he accidentally left brain damaged after a sparring match. He also hires, Lily, a young mother down on her luck, who later robs him and flees town. Despite being urged to do so, he refused to involve the police.

Johnnie Adshade - The alcoholic, abusive man who married Mabel's mother, **Ellie**. Found dead in a ditch under suspicious circumstances, Johnnie's death led to Stanley being charged with his murder, and James Cameron being charged as an accomplice. Johnnie, who hated his wife's childhood friend, James Cameron, died before learning James was his half-brother.

James and Margaret Cameron. James Cameron and **Percy McPherson** were childhood friends of Mabel's mother, Ellie, whom they lost touch with when they served overseas during WWI. Ellie, knowing she was dying and that she couldn't trust her husband, Johnnie, to do right by

Mabel, contacted James out of the blue to ask that he manage a small sum of money she set aside for her daughter and that he keep an eye out for her wellbeing. Years later, James, feeling guilty for breaking his promise to his dying friend, hires Mabel over his angry wife's objections, causing more friction in their already troubled marriage. Margaret, bitter over the loss of their only child, was initially suspicious and jealous of Mabel, but eventually warms to her and the young Toth boys left orphaned after their father jumped to his death. Margaret would later die of a stroke, and her devastated husband, of a bad heart.

Dan McInnes (AKA **Barry Sheppard**) – A corrupt, ambitious Sergeant who went to jail for trying to frame Stanley for the murder of Johnnie Adshade. McInnes was later sentenced a second time for brutally attacking Mabel. After his release from Dorchester, he returns home to live with his aunt, Gladys Ferguson, who, along with his late uncle, raised him as a boy. Seeking revenge on Stanley, whom he blamed for ruining his life, McInnes engages a former cellmate, **Lenny Slade** to kidnap Mabel and Stanley's young son. After Lenny and his sister, **Sylvie Sheppard**, are discovered to have taken the child, McInnes flees to Quidi Vidi, Newfoundland. Broke, bitter, and with a mangled hand, he once again returns home, where he attacks Mabel's neighbour, Myrtle Munroe; skipping town as the police began to close in on him. He meets Lily in a bus station on the mainland and soon discovers that, like him, she is on the lam, and with a pile of stolen cash. Posing as Sylvie's dead brother, Barry Sheppard, he holds her and her three, young children captive at the Roachville Pines Motel in New Brunswick, until Ed Baxter and Gordon Dunphy discover his true identity. Once again on the run, McInnes is tracked down by the aggrieved father of a young Mi'Kmaw girl he tried to rape. He was found tied to a tree with his genitals cut off.

Amour Donnely – Johnnie Adshade's sister, married her first husband, **Roddy**, as a young girl and moved to Boston. Their cold, sexless marriage ended with Roddy killing himself while awaiting trial for a sexual assault against a colleague's young son and suspicions he was responsible for the murder of David Greene, the homosexual son of a Jewish cobbler. Amour then married, **Michael Donnely.** After adopting **Victoria**, Amour and Michael spend time in London, England, before returning home. In 1948, Michael was tragically killed in a mine accident while investigating complaints the mine was unsafe.

Victoria Donnely—Adopted daughter of Amour and Michael. Victoria and John Toth formed a special friendship after the unexpected death of her father, Michael. Victoria frequently babysits the MacIntyre children.

Luke, Mark and John Toth – three brothers orphaned as children. Mabel and Mary Catherine babysat the boys before their father committed suicide. James and Margaret Cameron, who lost their only child, James Jr., to the flu, would form a special bond with the boys. Luke, who served as a gunner in WWII, suffers post-war trauma. He married, Alice, the former girlfriend of his younger, skirt-chasing brother, Mark, a bartender in Halifax.

Lily – turned out of her home as a pregnant teenager by her strict Catholic parents, Lily gave up her child and married, Chester, nine years her senior. Suspicious of Lily's relationship with Father Gregory, Chester beats the popular, young priest to death in a fit of jealous rage. Rumoured to have been romantically involved with Father Gregory, Lily is also blamed for his death and she and her children become the target of the town's wrath. Scorned and broke, Stanley hires Lily to work at his construction company. Lily, trying to protect her tormented children, betrays him and cleans out the company's bank account. She meets Dan McInnes (Barry Sheppard) while she and the kids are fleeing town. McInnes soon discovers she is on the run and holds her captive with the threat he will report her to the authorities if she refuses to do his bidding. She meets, Ed Baxter, the man who eventually helps her and her children escape their captor, while living at the Roachville Pines and working as a chambermaid.

Ed Baxter – A civilian member of the RCMP and a regular visitor to the Roachville Pines, Ed misplaces his glasses and returns to his motel room where he discovers Lily sobbing. After another chance meeting, Ed is convinced Lily is in an abusive relationship. After meeting Barry Sheppard, he enlists the aid of Frank Miller, a colleague with the RCMP, to investigate Sheppard's background. With the help of Gordon Dunphy, they soon confirm Barry Sheppard is Dan McInnes, a suspect wanted for the assault of Myrtle Munroe. Ed then moves to Cape Breton where he becomes close friends with Gordon and his wife, Charlotte, and where he develops a relationship with Amour Donnely.

Kenny Ludlow – Known for getting into mischief and finding trouble without looking, Kenny is head over heels in love with Victoria Donnely. Along with his fellow *Blackheads* and long-time friends, **Tommy Simms** and **Harley Woodward**, Kenny was charged with the assault on Myrtle Munroe that the authorities later determined was the work of Dan McInnes.

Supporting/Recurring Roles

Mary Catherine – Mabel's long-time friend, Mary Catherine converted to Judaism and married **Sam Friedman**, a lawyer who defended Stanley during Johnnie Adshade's murder trial. She and Sam have three children, **Irwin, Lydia, and Judith Devorah**.

Alice - Works at the bakery with Mabel and married Luke Toth. Lives in the apartment above the store with Luke and her son, **Matthew.** She previously dated Luke's younger brother, Mark.

Myrtle Munroe – Mabel's bald, eccentric neighbour is like a second mother to Mabel's and Stanley's children. She used to sell preserves around town, but recently found considerable success selling bright, playful watercolours. She was viciously attacked by Dan McInnes during a botched robbery.

Ted Collins– A retired officer with The Glace Bay Police Force, Ted was instrumental in proving Stanley's innocence during the Adshade trial, and later helped Stanley and Mabel reunite with their kidnapped son. He lost his first wife, **Muriel**, to cancer. He later married **Judge Kennedy**'s widow, **Gloria**.

Gordon and Charlotte Dunphy - A captain with the Glace Bay Police Department, Gordon moved up the ranks despite the corrupt efforts of the local police commission and Crown Prosecutor. One of the good cops, he was prepared to testify on behave of Stanley during his murder trial, and stuck up for Kenny and his friends when they were wrongfully charged with attacking Myrtle Munroe. Despite having strong feelings for Mabel, Gordon married Charlotte, a nurse at St. Joseph's Hospital.

Lenny Slade and Sylvie Sheppard – Lenny, an ex con, was enlisted by Dan McInnes to kidnap JC, Mabel and Stanley's two-year-old son. Lenny's mentally disturbed sister, Sylvie, is happy to welcome the child into their home, believing her husband, Barry Sheppard, who has been missing for years, will return home and they will be a family. She is unaware Lenny shot her husband and that he is buried not far from her home.

Yvonne and Giles LeBlanc- Friends of Ed Baxter and owners of The Roachville Pines, they hired Lily as a chambermaid and let her, her kids, and Dan McInnes live in the motel in exchange for a reduced wage. Childless, they formed a deep bond with Lily and her children.

Fred Clarke – Long-time supervisor at Stanley's company, S&M Constructions. Married to **Aggie**.

Billy Guthro and Eddie Lynch – Johnnie's drinking buddies. Billy rapes Mabel, and he and his simple-minded friend, Eddie, set fire to Stanley's barn killing his ponies. They later allege they heard Stanley threaten to kill Johnnie.

Mannie Chernin – the corrupt, politically-ambitious Crown Prosecutor.

The Chief – a wise, Mi'kmaw elder who tended to Dan McInnes' stab wounds after his sons found McInnes passed out in his truck.

Henri Gehue –A giant of a man who lives with his daughter, Anne, and his elderly mother, **Nukumi.** After learning McInnes tried to rape Anne, he tracks him down and kills him. He begins to date Lily, but never tells her he killed McInnes, or that he was the one who sent the note telling her where to find the money McInnes had taken from her.

Rosie – A rough-around-the edges fixture behind the Woolworth's lunch counter, Rosie was let go to make way for the manager's niece. On the day of the opening of Michael's Manor, Rosie offers to help in the kitchen when the whistle blows, signaling there is an accident at the mine. Her husband, **Bernie**, was one of the victims. Amour later hires Rosie and Dirty Willie's sister, **Sandra**, who also lost her husband in the mine accident.

Father Gregory—A handsome, young priest, bludgeoned to death by, **Chester**, Lily's jealous husband.

Gladys Ferguson — She and her late husband raised Dan McInnes from the time he was a young boy. Gladys defended her corrupt nephew against every charge until it was clear he robbed her. She had an intense dislike for Mabel and Stanley, blaming Mabel for taking a job at Cameron's store she felt she was entitled to, and blaming Stanley for McInnes fall from grace.

Mother and Father – Kenny Ludlow's exasperated parents.

Ten-After-Six – A former trapper boy who worked with the pit ponies, **Peter Boyd** can't stand up straight. He walks at an awkward angle with his head down, earning him the nickname of Ten-after-Six. Peter, who works part-time for Stanley, supplements his wages with the money he finds while on his walks.

Clair Romano – Stanley's first love. Engaged to be married, Clair's father put a stop to the wedding believing Stanley was not good enough for his daughter. After many years of living away, Clair returns to Cape Breton at a time when Stanley's and Mabel's marriage is in crisis. Although Clair is anxious to rekindle their romance, she eventually realizes Stanley will never leave Mabel. She goes back to Halifax, returning briefly, where she attended the opening of Michael's Manor and met Owen, Michael Donnely's brother-in-law. Clair and Owen married soon after and live in Halifax.

Lizzie MacNeil — A well-known spinster and busy-body, Lizzie is always plastered in gaudy makeup and traipsing about in skin-tight clothes and six-inch heels. A clerk with the town's Records Department, her curiousity led to the discovery James Cameron and Johnnie Adshade were half-brothers.

Cameo Appearances

Willie Morrison (AKA Dirty Willie) – As a young boxer vying for a national title, Willie suffered a serious brain injury during a sparring match with Stanley. He now works for Stanley at S&M Construction.

Corliss – Alice's father, Corliss lost a leg in the mine and is now a part-time employee at Cameron's Store.

Bessie – An older, big-busted widow Mabel hired to help at the bakery.

Mary Mack – a young, clumsy employee at the bakery who is always late for work.

Carol — Ed Baxter's late sister.

Big Dick and Little Dick – Two Glace Bay police offers with the same first and last names; one very large in stature, the other very small.

Judge Cummings – an old friend of Ed Baxter's, Lily discovered a young man leaving the judge's motel unit in the middle of the night. His marriage fell apart after it came to light his wife, **Wanda**, was cheating on him.

Geezer – The town drunk. While not from Glace Bay, Geezer practically lives at the town jail, where Gordon Dunphy and his fellow officers make sure he has something to eat and a place to sleep.

Curtis – Son of the late Judge Kennedy and his wife, Gloria, Curtis is a law student at Dalhousie.

Charlie— Sam Friedman's young law clerk.

As Fate Would Have It

Friday, June 27

Victoria walked down School Street feeling blue. She had hoped to catch up on John's news, but he was in and out of the store within minutes, stopping just long enough to ask how she was before dashing up to the apartment to get ready for rugby. They used to be inseparable, spending almost all of their free time together. Now, he barely acknowledged her. She wondered if he was still seeing Marjorie, or if he had moved on. He was certainly handsome enough to have any girl he wanted. She darted across Pit Street and headed down Quarry Road, thinking she'd call Kenny when she got home and tell him it was over. She liked Kenny well enough, and he certainly made her laugh, but he was way too serious. She was approaching Holy Cross Church when she saw an older woman trip and fall hard to the ground. "Oh no," she whispered, charging forward. She stopped to let a truck pass and watched as a man she assumed was the fallen woman's husband, appeared at her side.

"Is everything all right?" Victoria asked, running toward them.

"My wife took a tumble."

"I'm fine. Just twisted my ankle, that's all," the injured woman said.

Hector MacDonald pointed. "Jeanne, you're bleeding." He took a hankie from his pocket and was about to press it against her bloody chin when she snatched it from him.

Victoria looked back toward the row houses across the street. "I can ask someone to call an ambulance."

"No," Jeanne said firmly. "I'm fine. I just need a moment to collect myself," she said, dabbing at her chin.

Hector touched his wife's shoeless foot. "Jeanne, I think she's right. It might be broken."

The thin, grey-haired woman slowly moved her foot from side to side. "It's not broken. Probably a slight sprain."

"Are you sure, Jeanne? You took quite a spill. I can drive you to St. Joseph's...have someone check you over."

Jeanne held her arm out to indicate she needed help standing. "It's nothing a good cup of tea and some ice won't cure. Help me up," she insisted.

Hector got to his feet and reached down, placing one hand under her arm. Victoria took the other. "Not too fast," he cautioned, as Jeanne slowly straightened up, standing unevenly and leaning into her husband for support.

Victoria opened the passenger door. "Here, sit a bit...get your bearings," she said, helping Jeanne sit sideways in the front seat.

"Hector, take the dishes down to the kitchen," Jeanne said.

"The dishes can wait."

"No, they can't! We're here now. There's no need to make a second trip."

Hector knew not to argue. He unlocked the door to the church basement, then removed a large box from the trunk of the car. "For tomorrow's church supper," he said to Victoria. He nodded toward his wife. "Would you mind waiting with her while I drop these off? Won't take a minute."

"Not at all," Victoria said, running ahead and holding the basement door open. Hector stepped in front of her, stopped, and stared. "Sorry, for a moment there you reminded me of someone." He adjusted the box against his chest. "Thank you, dear. I won't be a second."

Victoria smiled. "You're welcome." She picked up Jeanne's shoe and handed it to her. "Might be a while before you get to put it back on, your ankle is quite swollen."

Jeanne examined her husband's blood-stained hankie. "That's what I get for being careless...not watching where I was going." She pointed. "Would you mind getting my purse?"

Victoria saw the tan bag resting in the high, dry grass at the edge of the dirt lot. She gathered up the prayer beads dangling over the side, tucked them back inside, and snapped the small purse shut. She placed it next to Jeanne. "There you go."

Hector returned. "Let's get you home," he said to his wife. "Can you swing your legs around?"

"Of course I can. I'm not an invalid," she said sharply.

Hector helped her sit forward and shut the door. He smiled at Victoria. "Can I give you a lift somewhere?"

Victoria pointed. "Thanks, but I live on Hillier Street…just a few minutes away." She smiled at Jeanne. "Hope you feel better soon."

Victoria watched the elderly couple drive off and was about to head home when she spotted a thin, black cord in the grass. She reached down and picked it up. A pair of horn-rimmed eyeglasses dangled from one end. She closed the arms over and looked in the direction of the departing Chrysler. "Hey!" she hollered, waving them in the air as the car drove out of sight. She'd leave them in the church basement next to the dishes. She turned the knob and pushed on the door, but it didn't budge. She tried a second time, again with no luck. She decided to hang them on the door knob. She was urging the tip of the unattached arm into the small loop at the end of the cord when a bunch of kids came barrelling down the street on their bikes. They turned into the parking lot, one pedalling at top speed before slamming on his brakes and sliding sideways, kicking up a shower of dust. Better not leave them here, she decided, draping them around her neck. *I'll call Father O'Handley when I get home and tell him I have them.* She blessed herself. *Then I'll call Kenny.*

Hector hung up the phone, poured Jeanne's tea, and put it on the small table next to the couch. He reached down and lifted the bundle of ice off of her red, swollen ankle. "I wish you'd let me take you to the hospital. I'm not convinced it's a sprain."

"Trust me, it's not broken," she said, once again moving it back and forth. "What did Dot say?"

"Brian's going to drop the crutches off when he gets home from work. How's the chin?"

Jeanne reached for her tea. "It's just a scrape. Stop hovering over me like I'm near death and pass me my purse." Hector picked it up off the chair and handed it to her. Jeanne unsnapped it and removed her rosary. "I don't see my glasses. I was sure I put them in my purse."

Hector looked around their sparse living room, then the kitchen. "Do you think they fell out when you took your spill?"

She raised her eyes to the ceiling. "Probably upstairs on my dresser."

Hector stopped at the top of the stairs, his heart beating faster than it should from such a short climb. He shook his head, lamenting the feeble state of his aging body. He looked down the hall to the master bedroom, wondering where the years went, a thought that occupied his mind more and more of late. He turned to his left and pressed his palm against the door he was forbidden to enter. He looked back over his shoulder, then placed his hand on the doorknob.

"Are they there?" Jeanne hollered.

Hector quickly removed his hand. "I'm still looking," he yelled back, dropping his head, and letting his arm fall to his side. He entered the bedroom he and Jeanne shared for almost forty years, checking the dresser and Jeanne's bedside table, before moving down the hall to the bathroom. He checked the drawers of the vanity. "I don't see them," he called out, and headed downstairs.

"Check the bathroom!"

He stepped off the landing. "I did. They're not there," he said, looking down the hall at the yellow owl-shaped clock above the kitchen sink. He checked his faithful Vertex military watch, then looked back at the big-eyed, ceramic bird staring at him. *Stupid thing can't even tell time. And she paid full value for it. She never pays full value for anything.* He entered the living room and looked around. With the exception of images of Jesus, the Virgin Mother, and the pope, the cream-coloured walls were bare. *This place is so goddamn depressing.* He massaged the back of his neck, wondering why we was feeling so out of sorts. "They're not upstairs. They must have fallen out of your purse when you fell." He picked up his car keys, hoping a change of scenery would lighten his mood. "I'll go there now so I can get back before Brian gets here with the crutches. Need anything before I go?"

Jeanne looked down at *The Post* resting on her lap. "Hand me your glasses," she said, holding out her hand.

Hector reached in his breast pocket and passed them to her. "Don't try and get up while I'm gone. I won't be long."

Hector pulled into the church lot, smiling nostalgically at the youthful antics of the neighbourhood kids playing ball hockey. He shut the engine off, thinking about a recent meeting of the church council. A number of the more vocal church elders put a motion forward to prohibit local youths from gathering on church property for any purpose not sanctioned by Father O'Handley or the council president. Several argued in favour of the motion, citing a good number of the youth spotted on the premises were from Protestant families. Others, including Jeanne, had taken offence to reports wayward youth were frequently heard swearing, taking the Lord's name in vain, or spotted behind the church with girls of ill repute. In the end, Hector was glad Father O'Handley convinced the more hard-nosed members to think of the church grounds as an extension of the church itself. '*We are all sinners. And God welcomes everyone into His home. If we turn them away as children, they will surely not come to us as adults.*'

Hector stepped out of the car and waved. "Hi, guys," he hollered. Some waved back, but most ignored him all together. He reached the area where Jeanne had fallen and carefully began to push the high grass aside with his foot.

A young red-headed kid sped toward him, skidding to an abrupt stop. "Lose somethin?" he asked, straddling a bike he had long outgrown.

"My wife lost her glasses."

The kid let his bike fall to the ground and got down on his hands and knees. He began patting the grass. "Ya sure they're here?"

"I think so. You go to Holy Cross?" Hector asked.

His young helper sat back on his heels. "Do I look like a friggin Micky? Any reward?"

Hector smiled and put his hand in his pocket. "Fifty cents. So, what's your name?"

"Tipper."

"Really?"

"*Yeah...really.*"

More and more boys approached, traipsing through the tall grass in search of the missing glasses. "Thanks, guys, but I don't think they're here after all," Hector said, thinking that if they were, they'd soon be shattered under foot. "They must be back at the house. But I appreciate your help," he said, urging them to go back to their game. He pulled Tipper aside and slipped him the fifty cents.

Tipper peeked at the two quarters in his hand. "What's this for?"

Hector smiled. "For trying," he said, going back to his car. He was about to start the car, but instead sat back and watched Tipper rejoin his friends. He smiled, thinking how blissfully indifferent they were to each other's religion, wealth, or social status, then dropped his head. Won't be long before life beats the innocence out of you, he thought. He lifted his head, adjusted the rear view mirror, and looked at his dull eyes and grey hair. "Older, but really no wiser. Just a lot more cynical," he whispered. He continued to watch the boys for a few more minutes, then sat up, gripping the steering wheel. Tipper was on his bike, hurtling toward the opening between two pit boots, when he suddenly pulled up on his handlebars and leaned back; his front wheel spinning in the air. The goalie jumped out of the way at the last minute, landing hard on ground.

Tipper sailed through. "He scores!" he yelled, pumping his fist in the air.

"Fuck you!" the shaken netminder screamed, jumping to his feet, and brushing the dust off his pants. He picked his hand-made goalie stick off the ground and hurled it in the air, barely missing Tipper's head.

Tipper threw his bike down and angrily rushed forward, punching his fist into his chest. "Oh yeah! Ya wanna piece of me, you bag a shit! C'mon! Put em up, ya fuckin pussy!"

Hector stepped out of the car. "Tipper! Guys! Take it easy!" He felt his chest tighten. "Tipper, slow down, son. Tip...Tip," he gasped, struggling to suck the warm air into his heavy lungs.

Stanley hung up the phone.

"Who was that?" Mabel asked, crawling on her hands and knees to stop Liv from scurrying away.

"Luke. Mark's coming home."

Mabel closed her eyes. "*Oh?*" she said, setting her squirming, naked baby down on a towel.

"He's bringing his girlfriend."

Mabel pulled the open safety pin from between her teeth and expertly fastened the side of Liv's fresh diaper. "Must be serious, he never brought anyone home before. When are they arriving?"

"Tonight."

Mabel reached in her apron pocket for the second safety pin, thinking Alice was going to be livid. "Where are they staying? With John home from college they barely have enough room to breathe as it is."

"Don't worry, apparently Alice put her foot down...said there was no way they were staying with them. Luke got them a room at the Broughton Inn."

Mabel screwed up her face. "That drafty old place?" she said, fastening the second pin. Liv quickly rolled onto her belly and crawled away.

"I guess that's all Mark can afford," Stanley said.

Mabel got to her feet. "Too bad Amour's redoing her guest rooms. She would have gladly put them up." She gave her husband an exasperated look. "I don't blame Alice for putting her foot down. Hard enough living with the truth, let alone having it stare you in the face. And I can't imagine Mark wanting to stay there either...pretending to be the doting uncle. It's a wonder he can look his brother in the eye." She shook her head. "What a mess."

"We could put them up," Stanley said.

"*Us*?" Mabel said. "Where would *we* put them?"

"In JC's room."

Mabel looked surprised. "Mark and his girlfriend...in the same room?"

Stanley dipped his chin and smiled at his wife. "Yes, Mabel. I'm gonna take a wild guess and say they're sleeping together."

"So, we put JC on the couch?" Mabel asked.

Stanley looked down at his feet, picked Liv up, and nosily nuzzled her neck. "JC can stay with Myrtle. He's there half the time as it is." He waited for Mabel to consider his suggestion.

Mabel picked up Liv's soiled diaper. "I had hoped to get a few hours to put my feet up and read a good book. I guess I better strip the bed and run to Mendelson's. I assume we're only talking a couple of days?"

Stanley shrugged. "I'm sure it's just for the weekend. Mark will have to get back for work. Oh, I forgot to tell you, Fred and Aggie put their place up for sale. They bought a piece of land across the street from their son."

Mabel took Liv from her husband and set her on her lap. "So they're moving to Truro, after all. Aggie must be over the moon. I know how much she missed her grandchildren. We'll have to do something special for them. Maybe dinner at the manor. When is Fred's last day?"

Stanley shrugged. "Not sure...he wants to sell the house before he finishes up."

Mabel pointed. "Pass me that."

Stanley handed her Liv's top. "I'm going to miss him. He's been with me from day one." He pressed his lips together. "I'm thinking about asking Harley to take on some of his duties."

"*Harley*?" Mabel said surprised. "Is he ready?"

"I think so. He's a good worker and smart as a whip. I throw some measurements at him and he'll tell me right off...'We need forty two-by-fours, twelve sheets of plywood...at least four pounds of four inch nails.' And he's usually bang on. Hell, I've been at this business for years and I still need to work it out on paper. Besides, I know he could use the money. His father is waiting to see a surgeon in Halifax."

"There, then, stop thinking about it and just do it. Now, call Luke and tell him Mark and his girlfriend can stay with us."

Hector sat in the car with his hands and head on the steering wheel.

"Hey, old man. You okay?" Tipper asked. He turned back to his friends. "D'ya mind?" he said, shoving one of the guys hanging over his shoulder. "For Christ sakes, give us some friggin space." He looked back at Hector. "Want me to get ya an ambulance...fetch the priest?"

Hector shook his head. "No ambulance...and no priest. I'm not going anywhere just yet. Though I doubt it won't be long." He coughed and reached in his pocket for his hankie, before realizing he had given it to

Jeanne after her fall. He motioned for Tipper to step away from the door and spit a thick mouthful of dark phlegm on the ground.

Most of the boys decided they'd seen enough and went back about their business.

Tipper screwed up his face. "Jesus, man, that don't look so good. Anyways, I just meant I could get the priest to drive ya home, cause I doubt yer gonna let me."

Hector leaned back against the seat. "You got that right. How old are you, anyway?"

Tipper drummed his hands on the roof. "Old enough to handle this old bucket of bolts. So, what's wrong with ya? Bad heart?"

Hector shrugged. "Probably. Bad lungs for sure. Black Lung to be exact."

"So, ya want me to drive ya home or not?"

Hector smiled and nodded toward the ball hockey game that was back in progress. "What happened to the goalie?"

"That sook. Probably home, sittin on his mommy's lap...bawling his friggin eyes out." Tipper bent down and picked up the goalie stick; the blade loosely held to the shaft by a nail. "But I got myself a new stick." He pushed the tip of the blade, sending it swaying from side to side. "Just needs a cupala nails." He pointed. "One here. And one here...and it's as good as new. Sure ya don't want me to drive ya home?"

Hector started the car. "Thanks, Tipper. I think I'm okay now."

"Yeah, well good luck." He patted his pants pocket. "Oh, and thanks again for the coins."

Hector drove home knowing his health was failing and that, soon, even the simplest of tasks would prove too much for his coal-coated lungs. Mowing the grass, shoveling snow, cleaning the windows, routine jobs that he was once eager to tackle, were now onerous, stressful tasks he dreaded. He knew Jeanne was loathe to hire someone to help out, insisting it was good exercise and that the money could be put to better use, but he also knew he had no choice, he needed help. *I wonder what Jeanne would think of my feisty new friend?* He pulled in the driveway. "That's it, I'm doing it anyway. To hell with her."

Victoria dialled the number, thinking it wouldn't be fair to break up with Kenny over the phone. I have to tell him in person, she decided. "Hi, Kenny. Mom told me you called."

"Yeah, *Hour of Glory* is playing at The Russell. It's supposed to be really good. I was thinking we could grab a bite at The Grill and go to the seven o'clock show."

Victoria rolled her eyes. "Actually, I'm really tired. The kids ran me ragged today. I thought I'd just lay low…curl up with a book."

Kenny's heart sank. She can't back out, not tonight, he thought. He reached in his pants pocket and ran his thumb over the sharp corner of the small, white box he was anxious to give to her. He had waited long enough. He couldn't wait any longer.

"You still there?" Victoria asked.

"Yeah, I'm here. Just really disappointed, that's all," he sulked, wrapping the phone cord around his hand. "I already gave the guys the brush off," he lied. "But I guess if you'd rather be alone, I could stay home with Ma and Da."

Victoria tilted her head back, closed her eyes, and sighed. *Why does he always make me feel so guilty?* "Okay, I'll go. But Ed's coming by any minute to take a look at my resume, so I can't go to The Grill."

Two hours later she was sitting in the theatre with her arms folded across her chest, thinking about how much she hated war movies.

Kenny nudged her. "Licorice?" he asked, holding the bag in front of her.

"No thanks."

"Ya sure? It's real good," he said, sticking his finger in his mouth. "It's not stale, like last time," he mumbled, before removing his finger and examining the black goo under his nail.

Victoria suppressed a gag. She looked over her shoulder when she heard the familiar voice. John was standing in the aisle with Marjorie Steele at his side, whispering his apologies. "Sorry," he repeated, as legs were lifted or pressed to the side to let him and his pretty date edge past.

Victoria turned back to the unlit screen. "The movie should have started by now," she said impatiently. The words were barely out of her mouth when the lights dimmed. She looked up at the hazy, narrow beam of blue light shining from the projection room, then at the black flecks dancing across the white screen; waiting for the images to appear. The theatre suddenly went completely dark. "*Now what?*" she said, exasperated. The lights came back on to a chorus of groans. Movie-goers began stomping their feet and chanting, "Weiner! Weiner! Weiner!"

"It'll only take a sec. See, there's Weiner now," Kenny said, pointing to the stout, bald man running up the side aisle with his flashlight in hand. "He'll have it fixed in no time," Kenny yelled over the growing din. His teeth were completely black.

It was a scene Victoria would normally find hilarious, but not tonight. "Your teeth," she said flatly. "They're black."

Kenny ran his finger across his front teeth, then bared a ridiculous, toothy grin. "Better?"

Victoria shook her head in disgust. The house lights once again dimmed and the screen lit up a second time. The silhouette of a flattened popcorn box sailed past the bright screen to cheers of approval. "Finally," she said.

They weren't five minutes into the movie when Victoria felt Kenny's fingertips making circular motions on her upper arm. She wanted to scream at him to stop and tear out of the theatre, but instead leaned away, hoping he'd take the hint. Kenny removed his hand. Thank God, she thought, only to feel it on the back of her neck. She flinched. "Don't," she whispered harshly.

"*What?*"

"It's...it's...distracting."

Kenny nodded and pulled his arm away, thinking she was in a shitty mood and must be on the rag. *God, don't let it be her period. Not tonight,* he silently prayed.

As much as Victoria hated war movies, and as anxious as she was to put Kenny and the night behind her, she didn't move when the ending credits began to roll, fearing she would run into John and his date.

Kenny stood up and glanced back at the line of people waiting for him to move out of their way. "Ya comin? We're holding everyone up."

Victoria looked over her shoulder to make sure the coast was clear, then stepped into the aisle. Kenny smiled and grabbed her hand. Victoria's first instinct was to yank it free and run for the exit, but she didn't. Let it go, she thought, the night's almost over and I'll soon be free of him.

They were in the car heading down Commercial Street when Kenny suddenly turned up Brookside. "What are you doing?" Victoria asked.

"Just takin a little drive."

"Kenny, I'm tired. Take me home."

"It's not even eight-thirty. I promise we won't be long," he said, smirking. He turned down Dominion Street, passed the church, then took a sharp left onto Emery Street.

Victoria knew he was heading to the slag heaps. "Forget it, Kenny. Take me home."

"Aaah, c'mon," he said, slowly pulling in behind a huge mound of black rock and shutting off the engine. He touched her hand. "I got ya something."

Victoria turned her head and looked out at nearly a dozen other cars, thinking the town would soon be experiencing a mini baby boom. It's now or never, she decided. *I have to tell him it's over.*

Kenny reached under the seat, retrieved a flashlight, and set it on the dash. "Close your eyes."

Victoria quickly turned to face him. "*What?*"

"Close your eyes," he repeated.

"Kenny, we need to talk."

"We will. But first you need to close your eyes," he insisted.

Victoria sighed loudly and did as he asked. "What are you doing?"

"You'll see," he said, adjusting the light. "Okay, you can open them." A small, white box with Lighter's Jewelers embossed in gold across the top was sitting in the palm of his outstretched hand.

Victoria's eyes widened in horror. She put her hand over her mouth, thinking he had lost his mind. Kenny was grinning from ear to ear, his still-black-stained teeth making him look ghoulish in the shadowy light. "Just a little something I thought you'd like toooo…try on?" he asked, raising his eyebrows.

Victoria took the box from him and slowly removed the lid. Her mouth fell open as she stared down at the thin, paper packet sitting on top of a small square of cotton batting.

Kenny's heart was pounding as he waited for her to say something. "Do you know what it is?" he asked nervously.

Victoria nodded, unable to think of what to say.

"Well?" he asked. "Want to give it a go?"

Victoria threw the box at Kenny's head. "Take me home! I mean it Kenny! Right this minute!" she demanded. "Or, I swear to God, I'll get out and walk."

"Okay! Look, I'm sorry. I just thought—"

"That's it, Kenny, you just don't think at all! Are you crazy! Hell, what made you think I'd ever do that with you? I don't even like you that much!" she scoffed. "In fact, I was going to tell you tonight that we're done. It's over. I don't want to see you again. Ever! And forget about driving me home, I'll walk." She put her hand on the handle.

Kenny quickly reached across and held the door shut. "No, please. I'll take you home."

They were turning back onto Dominion Street when Victoria let out a loud sigh. "God, I hate this. Look, Kenny, I'm sorry about what I said. I do like you. You're a nice guy. But, well...I don't like you in that way. To be honest, I never have. I should have told you right from the start."

Kenny looked heartbroken. "I get it. It's okay. It's just that we've been datin for so long...almost nine months and I just—"

"Kenny, I was away at school for most of that time. Honestly, we went out...what...maybe five or six times? Look, I'm sorry...I don't know what else to say."

"No need to say anything else. I get it."

They drove the remainder of the way in silence; Kenny dying inside, the disappointing turn of events made worse by the fantasy night he had played out in his mind over and over again; Victoria, repulsed by what had just transpired, and horrified by the mean words that spilled out of her.

Kenny pulled in front of the manor and smiled sadly at the girl of his dreams.

Victoria smiled back. "I'm sorry, Kenny. I really am." She squeezed his arm. "Are you okay?" He nodded. Victoria got out. She turned when she reached the front door and waved goodbye, curing herself for letting Kenny think he ever stood a chance. Her mother and Ed were standing by the doorway when she entered.

"How was the show?" Amour asked.

Victoria headed directly upstairs. "I hate war movies. Oh, and I just broke up with Kenny," she said, without looking back.

"Are you okay?" Amour called out.

"Better than Kenny," Victoria said, disappearing out of sight.

"We're almost there. Are you doing okay?" Hector asked.

"I'm fine," Jeanne said, grateful she only had two steps to go. When they got to the top step, Hector passed his wife the second crutch. Jeanne tucked it under her arm. "It's going to take time to get used to these things, especially on the stairs," she said, walking down the hall to the bathroom. "My nightgown's hanging on the back of the bedroom door. Grab it for me please?"

Hector placed the floor-length flannel nightdress on the vanity. "I turned down your bed. I'm gonna close things up. I won't be long." He went downstairs, locked the front door, and reached under the shade of the floor lamp. He was feeling for the cord when he spotted the picture of Jeanne leaning in and kissing his cheek. It was their wedding day. *God, we were so young. So happy. So in love.* "Hard to believe," he whispered sadly. He looked at the other photos on top of the upright piano.. There wasn't a single picture of another living soul. They were all gone. Dead, buried, and mostly forgotten. He picked up a picture, ran his finger over the top of the dusty frame, and began to well up. He walked to an armchair in the corner of the dimly-lit room, sat down heavily, and looked down at his mother's sepia face. "You were a wise woman. You said time was fleeting and warned me to use it wisely. I wish I had listened to you. I squandered so much of it...made so many mistakes," he whispered sadly.

"You alive down there?" Jeanne called downstairs.

Hector lifted his head. "I'll be right up," he said, standing and putting his mother's picture back in place. He once again reached under the lamp shade when his eyes locked on the picture above the high-backed chair in the corner. In contrast to the more popular images of a handsome, bearded Jesus dressed in white and surrounded by a beautiful orange glow, this one was stark and gruesome. His eyes were lifted skyward, and His head was tilted back and to the side. Blood trickled down from His crown of thorns, and His mouth was contorted in pain. Hector had looked at this same picture a thousand times over the years, but he never once saw it in the same light as he did at this moment. The familiar image now left a new, almost sinister impression upon him. He wondered if it was just because he was not feeling himself lately. He heard the toilet flush and wiped his eyes. "God help me," he said, turning the lamp off.

He mounted the creaky stairs, paused briefly outside the forbidden room, and continued to the bathroom.

Jeanne waited impatiently in the bedroom for her husband to join her. "What's keeping you? I need you to turn off my light," she hollered down the hall.

"I'm coming," Hector said, shuffling into the cramped room with the yellowing, flowered wallpaper. He bent down and kissed his wife's cheek, turned her bedside lamp off, and climbed in his own bed. He closed his eyes, hoping he would wake free of the nagging sadness that gripped him throughout the day. The image of the pretty young girl who had come to their aid came to mind. He turned his head toward Jeanne. "So, I'll go to the manor first thing tomorrow and pick up your glasses. It was very nice of that young lady to go through the trouble of calling Father O'Handley. Not everyone would bother, you know. Maybe you could write a little note to thank her for all her help?" He waited for her to answer. "Jeanne, dear, did you hear me? I was asking if you—"

"Yes, I heard you. Now be quiet, I'm trying to pray."

Ed draped his overcoat over his arm. "Thanks for supper."

Amour smiled. "My pleasure. And thanks for giving Victoria a hand with her letter. With any luck, she'll be teaching this fall." She looked up to the top of the stairs, then back at Ed. "I hope she's all right. I liked Kenny. He made me laugh." She chuckled. "Sometimes when I'm not so sure he meant to." Her voice became more serious. "Honestly, I sometimes get the impression Victoria still likes John Toth. They were always so close. Inseparable, really." She shrugged. "Anyway, that's when they were kids. They're all grown up now."

Ed leaned in and kissed Amour's cheek. "I wouldn't worry about her if I were you. She's smart and beautiful. Won't be long before another young man comes calling. I'll see you tomorrow night." He opened the door to leave, then quickly stepped back inside.

Amour gave him a curious look. "Forget something?"

"It's Kenny. He's still out there. Just sitting in his car."

Amour pulled the door forward an inch and peeked out. "Poor guy. He was pretty smitten. He must be heartbroken."

Ed nodded. "I'll check on him."

Amour reached over and squeezed his arm. "Thank you. And drive carefully. It's getting pretty foggy out there."

Ed rapped on the passenger window and opened the door. Kenny's head shot up. "Hey there. You okay, bud?"

"I guess so."

Ed got in and closed the door. "Young love...it's never easy."

Kenny shrugged. "She said she doesn't want to see me no more."

Ed smiled and nodded. His jaw dropped when he spotted the small white jewelry box in Kenny's hand. "Jesus, Kenny, you didn't propose or—"

Kenny sat up. "Hell no! Do I look crazy!" He shoved the box in his pocket.

"Oh, okay. I just saw...I thought it might be a ring," Ed said.

"No way! I mean...maybe someday. But, shit, I still live with my parents. I gotta get established first."

Ed nodded his relief. "Kenny, I know it's hard to believe, but you're young. You'll get over this. Trust me, the heart—"

"Ain't nothin to get over," Kenny blurted. "I figure it's just that time of the month. She's been in a pissy mood all week. She'll see the error of her ways."

Ed smiled. "Who knows, maybe you're right. But you can't sit out here all night." He puckered his mouth and squinted. "It doesn't look good. Makes you look desperate. Go home and get some sleep," he said, reaching for the door handle.

"So, are ya gonna propose to Victoria's mom?" Kenny asked.

Ed turned back toward Kenny. "*What?*" he asked, surprised by the question.

"Are ya gonna pop the question...take the big dive...drink the poison?"

Ed smiled. "Victoria's mother and I are good friends, that's all."

Kenny laughed. "Bullshit! Ya can't kid a kidder. I see the way ya look at her. Everybody does." Kenny wiggled his fingers at the side of his head. "Ya get all moony-eyed when yer round her. Hell, even Victoria said she figured you were about to drop down on one knee."

Ed turned his mouth down and tilted his head. "I had no idea I was under such scrutiny…or that my intentions were the topic of so much speculation."

"So, what's keepin ya? Ain't like yer gettin any younger?"

Ed popped the door open. "Take care of yourself, Kenny. Oh, and a word of advice, don't grovel. Don't go driving by the house or seeking out opportunities to run into her. I did that once and ended up with a shiner," he said and stepped out.

Kenny laughed. "She smucked ya?"

Ed dipped his head back inside. "No, her brother did."

Kenny nodded toward the house. "Don't worry. Won't be me doin the grovellin. You wait. She'll come round."

"Take care, Kenny."

"Yeah, you too."

Ed was standing next to his car when Kenny pulled onto Hillier Street, his headlights cutting through the misty, grey air. If only I had half your gumption, Ed thought. He was about to open his door when he heard Kenny gun the engine. He looked up to see Kenny plow through the intersection and fishtail onto South Street; his red tail lights quickly disappearing behind the thick fog.

Amour appeared at the window and waved. Ed took a deep breath, thinking it was getting harder and harder to leave. He smiled, waved back, and got behind the wheel of his Buick Roadmaster. "You're right, kid, I'm not getting any younger," he whispered. "Time to put up or shut up."

Mabel looked up at the clock, then removed the roasting pan from the oven. "I thought they would have been here by now. I'm just going to assume they had supper."

"Don't worry about them. They likely stopped somewhere along the way," Stanley said. He opened a beer. "Sure you don't want one?"

"I'm sure. How many beer has John had?"

Stanley shook his head. "He's a grown man for goodness sakes. He can handle it." There was the sound of a car door closing, then a second.

"There they are now," he said, putting his beer down. "Hey, Luke! John! They're here."

Mabel stood inside the door, thinking about the last time she had spoken to Mark. It was more than three months ago. He had come home to help a friend whose girlfriend was moving to Halifax and surprised her with a visit. She remembered thinking he was sick. His face was gaunt, and his clothes, loose on his once-muscular frame; the cost, she had thought, of a troubled mind. He had come to confront her about his suspicions, which she reluctantly confirmed. She quickly blessed herself, silently praying that Mark would continue to keep his word and never lay claim to his brother's child.

Stanley pushed the door open so Mark and his girlfriend could enter.

Mark hugged Mabel. "Thanks so much for putting us up." He turned to his girlfriend. "This is Antoinette...Toni Moody. Toni, this is Mabel."

Mabel smiled at the pretty strawberry blonde gripping her purse. "Nice to meet you, Toni. How was the drive?"

Mark put an overnight bag down. "We ran into heavy rain in St. Peter's, then hit thick fog the last ten miles or so. You could barely see the nose on your face."

Mabel pulled a chair out for Toni. "Here, have a seat. Are you hungry? I made a pot roast."

"No thank you. We ate," she said shyly. "I packed up some sandwiches for the drive."

John and Luke entered, each carrying a large suitcase. Mabel stared at the two bags, then at Stanley standing in the doorway, looking sheepish.

"Where should we put these?" Luke asked.

Stanley pointed down the hall. "Upstairs in JC's room." He turned to Toni. "How about a beer?"

"No thank you."

"I will," Mark said.

Stanley opened the fridge, bent down, and reached in to get Mark his beer.

Mabel put her hand on his back. "Bottom shelf," she said. She lowered her voice to a whisper. "Just a couple of days, you say."

The men quickly retreated to the living room, leaving Mabel and Toni alone in the kitchen. "Here," Mabel said, holding her arms out.

"Let me take your coat." Toni stood, slowly unbuttoned her knee-length coat, and slipped it off her shoulders; her tight-fitting dress, clinging to her swollen belly. Mabel tried not to outwardly react to the surprising discovery. She hung Toni's coat in the back entrance and returned to the kitchen. "How about some tea."

"That would be nice." Toni put her head down. "I figure I'm about five months along," she said, unsure of how her news would be received.

Mabel smiled. "And how are you feeling?"

"Better. First few months were pretty hard. I had to quit my job. I was a telephone operator."

"I'm sorry to hear," Mabel said, wondering if Mark would do right by her and the baby. She opened the fridge. "You must be excited about becoming a mom?"

"To be honest, I'm scared to death. With me and Mark out of work, I worry about how we'll make ends meet."

Mabel closed her eyes. "Mark's not working?"

"Oh, I just assumed you knew. That's why Mark wanted to come home. He said it'd be cheaper to find a place to live and that he had some good connections."

Mabel put a plate of squares on the table. "Yes, I imagine it's quite expensive to live in the city." She returned to the stove to get the teapot. "Are you from Halifax?"

"Waterville. It's in the Valley...the Annapolis Valley."

"And your parents, do they still live there?"

"Yes, with my younger brother, my uncle, and grandfather. They have a small farm."

Mabel wasn't sure if she should ask, but decided it was bound to come up at some point. "Are they excited about the baby?"

Toni dropped her head. "Actually, I haven't told them. Truth be told, they don't even know I have a boyfriend. But I know they wouldn't be happy." She looked up at Mabel and shrugged. "They're Baptist."

Luke and Mark entered. "We're switching to rum. So, how are you ladies getting along?" Mark asked.

"We're getting along just fine. Congratulations," Mabel said.

Luke gave Mabel a quizzical look, then turned to his brother. "*Congratulations*? What for? Don't tell me, you're engaged?"

Mark nodded toward Toni. "We're having a baby."

Luke stared at Toni's baby bump. "What the hell!" He pulled Mark into a bear hug. "Why didn't you say something?" he asked excitedly. He rushed to Toni and kissed her cheek. "Hey, John! Stanley! Get in here! Mark's gonna be a daddy," he hollered into the living room.

Stanley leaned against the counter and put his arm over Mabel's shoulder. "Told you they were sleeping together," he whispered.

John, like Luke, was visibly excited by the unexpected news, slapping Mark on the back and offering his congratulations. Luke poured a round of rum and held his glass in the air. "You wait," he said to Mark, "there's nothing better than being a father."

Mabel and Stanley smiled at one another, each knowing what the other was thinking; each struck by the bitter irony of Luke's excitement over news his brother was going to be a first-time dad. Mabel dropped her head, the pang of guilt she felt in betraying Luke never sharper than at this moment.

Toni beamed, delighted their news was so well received by Mark's brothers. She looked at her hosts. Stanley was sipping his drink, and Mabel was staring down at her feet. Neither seemed to be enjoying the moment. She looked back at Mark. He was dabbing the cuff of his shirt against the corner of his eyes and laughing awkwardly. Toni's heart fell and her smile faded. There was something about Mark's smile. It didn't look natural. It looked forced. And his tears, she thought, didn't appear to be tears of joy. They looked more like tears of regret.

"*What the hell, Kenny! Are you crazy! Jesus, you're an idiot*!" Tommy screamed into the phone.

Kenny put his head in his hand. "What do ya mean? You were the one eggin me on…always goin on about *you and Sally*...how she can't wait to tear yer friggin clothes off. Hell, weren't you always raggin on me…askin what was takin me so long?"

"Yeah, but I didn't mean Victoria. I meant…I don't know…maybe Doreen Burke or Betty Reynolds? They're more likely to put out for ya. Victoria ain't that kinda girl. Sounds to me like you're screwed."

"I wish," Kenny said.

"Well, one thing's for sure, ya don't stand a chance of gettin back with her now. That train left the station for good."

"Whadaya mean, the train left the station? She'll come around, you wait," Kenny sulked.

Tommy laughed. "*Ya think*? Jesus! Ya put the rubber in a jewelry box for Christ sakes!"

"Nah, that wasn't it. I think she was on the rag. She was in a shitty mood all week. And I shouldn't have taken her to a war movie. I'll give it a week or two. Like they say, abstinence makes the heart grow fonder."

"*Absence*, you idiot! *Absence*!" Tommy shouted.

Kenny momentarily held the receiver away from his ear. "Jesus, ya don't have to scream."

"Look, if ya want, I can ask Sally if Doreen will go out with ya."

Kenny thought about it for a moment. "She the one with the big tits?"

"Yeah." Tommy waited. "*Well*?"

Kenny pictured Victoria's heartbroken reaction when she found out he was seeing another woman. "Yeah, why not."

"Good. I'll call Sally tonight and get back to ya."

"Hey, Tommy."

"Yeah?"

"So, how long before ya think Doreen will go to the slags with me? Yeah, I know. Yes to the rubber…no to the jewelry box. Thanks. Oh, and call me back as soon as ya talk to Sally. You know it! Yep, I'm already as horny as a ten-point buck." Kenny put the receiver down, stood, and did a little dance. "*Yes!*" he said, pumping his fist at his side and twirling around. "Ma," he said meekly. "When did you get home?"

"Around the same time as the train left the station," she said, her arms folded across her chest.

Mabel sat at the side of the bed and squirted a small dab of Jergens hand lotion onto her palm. "Well, that was awkward. I couldn't wait for the night to end," she said, rubbing her hands together. "How did you find Toni?"

Stanley climbed under the covers. "She seems nice enough. Why?"

"I mean, how did you find her mood?"

"Hard to tell. Why, what are you getting at?"

Mabel shut the bedside lamp off and crawled in beside him. "One minute she seemed happy as a clam, the next, as if she were about to burst into tears."

"I didn't notice."

"You're a man. Trust me, her mood changed. I think she saw what I saw."

"And what did you see?"

Mabel laid her hand across Stanley's stomach. "I saw a man who wasn't happy with his circumstances."

"You mean the baby?"

"No, I don't think it's the baby. I think it's something else. I think it's his conscience. As long as Mark was in Halifax he didn't have to look his guilt in the face. Now that he's here, he can't escape it."

Stanley rolled over to face her. "Then why move back home?"

"I think they're in dire straits...both out of work, with a baby on the way. And from what Toni tells me, they couldn't turn to her parents for help. They don't even know about Mark, let alone the baby. Anyway, I'm pretty sure Toni picked up on Mark's reaction when Luke and John were congratulating him on news about the baby. He looked so...so uncomfortable. I wanted to run off screaming, so I can only imagine how Mark felt. And poor Toni. I honestly saw her face fall. It was as if somebody flicked a switch. She probably thinks he's not happy about the baby."

"Better she thinks that, then discover her boyfriend fathered his brother's child. Anyway, there's nothing we can do about it."

Mabel plumped her pillow. "Do you think they'll get married?"

"I think Mark's first priority is getting a job. He's hoping to get a desk job...so he can put his schooling to use, but there aren't too many of those jobs around here. Anyway, I can keep him busy for a while...at least until something better comes up."

"Did you mention it to him?"

"No, I thought I'd talk to you first."

"Of course you should offer him a job. Why wouldn't you?"

Stanley turned and gave her a look. "Last time I offered him a job without talking to you, you nearly took my head off."

"Oh, yeah," Mabel said, thinking back to the turmoil Alice's secret had once caused their marriage.

Stanley leaned in and kissed her forehead. "I'll talk to him in the morning. Goodnight."

"Goodnight. Oh, and one more thing."

"What's that?"

"Can you give Mr. Bruffatto a call...see if he has an apartment for rent?"

"Uh-huh. Goodnight."

"Good. And the sooner the better. Oh, and maybe tell Mark you'll give him an advance on his wages...you know...so he and Toni can get settled in before the baby arrives. And I'll gather up some baby clothes, bedding, and dishes. I'll call Mary Catherine and Charlotte to see if they have any old baby clothes they can spare. And the baby will need a cradle and some toys. And I'm sure Amour must have some things she no longer—"

Stanley glanced over his shoulder. "Go to sleep."

Mabel smiled. "Sorry." She flipped onto her back and stared at the ceiling. *Alice is going to hit the roof when she finds out Mark is moving back to town. She'll likely do everything possible to steer clear of him, but there's no way she'll be able to avoid him forever. Luke has always been tight with his brothers. He'll want to have lots of family gatherings. I wonder if they're as close as they are because they grew up as orphans. It had to have brought them closer together. Luke must have felt the weight of the world on his shoulders, being the oldest. Dear God, they've all suffered enough. Please don't let Luke find out what happened. It will destroy him.*

Mabel rolled over. "Damn," she silently whispered, wishing Alice never told her Mark was Matthew's father. It was a secret she had hoped to take to her grave, but that was not to be. She closed her eyes, picturing the day Mark showed up at the house, drunk. He picked Matthew up and held him in the air. '*Ah, there's my boy... my beautiful boy...my handsome little man,*' he had said, unaware he was holding his own child. Alice had heard enough. She grabbed the baby from Mark. '*Shut up! Shut up! Shut up! He's not your boy,'* she had screamed; her angry outburst so sudden and surprising, it eventually led both Mark and Stanley to the truth. The only saving grace, Luke was not present to witness the revealing scene.

Mabel opened her eyes. *God, if Alice finds out that Mark knows he's Matthew's father, there'll be hell to pay.*

Mark stood beside the bed. "You okay? You've been so quiet," he asked Toni.

"I'm fine. Hard to get a word in edgewise with you and your brothers." She watched him strip down to his underwear. "I'm surprised they didn't know about the baby?"

"Why is that?" he asked, pulling the covers back and crawling in bedside her.

"I dunno, I just thought you would have told them our news when you called to say we were coming."

Mark chuckled. "That's the kind of news you share in person. So, what do you think of Mabel and Stanley?"

"They're nice. I feel badly for putting their son out of his room... making him stay with the neighbour."

Mark pulled the blanket up over his bare shoulder. "JC doesn't mind. He loves staying with Myrtle. She spoils him to death."

"Mark, do you think you'll find work soon? I'd like to know we'll have a place of our own before the baby comes."

"You worry too much. We'll have our own place in a couple of weeks," he said, disappointed Stanley hadn't offered him a job.

Toni picked up Mark's hand and placed it on her belly. "Wait." She moved his hand to the right and pressed down. "There, feel that?"

Mark smiled and nodded. "Active little guy, isn't he?"

"Or she."

"Yes, or she."

Toni turned her head to face him. "Mark, you are happy...about the baby, right?"

Mark leaned on his elbow. "Of course. *Why*, what are you getting at?"

"I just thought…well I thought you didn't seem yourself tonight…you know, when Luke and John were celebrating our news…you just didn't seem happy. In fact, I thought you looked awkward…even sad."

Mark smiled down at her. "So, *it's true.*"

"*What's true?*"

He laughed. "Expectant mothers get all emotional. Toni, your hormones are just acting up, making you act…a little…irrational. You know I'm happy about the baby." He bent down and kissed her. "Now stop worrying about everything and go to sleep."

Toni reached over and turned the lamp off. "I love you. Goodnight."

Mark rolled away from her. "Me, too. Goodnight."

Mark laid awake in the dark, wishing he could follow his own advice. Wishing he could stop worrying. Wishing he could fall asleep. He listened to Toni's shallow breathing. He couldn't get the image of Luke holding up his glass up and smiling proudly. '*You wait. There's nothing better than being a father,*' he had said. If you only knew, Mark thought. He reached over and grabbed his watch off the bedside table, holding it an angle to catch the light coming in from the moon-lit window. It was going on three. He flopped back down. Toni stirred. He reached over and touched the end of her hair, splayed across her pillow. *What a mess I made of things. God, I'm sorry.*

Saturday, June 28

Hector put Jeanne's tea in front of her. "I'll go for your glasses after I do the dishes."

"No need to make two trips. We can pick them up when we go to the church supper."

"But you'll need them before then."

"I'll wear yours. You look tired. Did you sleep okay?" Jeanne asked.

"Not the best. Actually, I was thinking we could skip the supper. No one will expect us there with your ankle and—"

"We're going!" Jeanne said firmly. "I haven't missed one in over forty years and I'm not about to start now." She placed her hand on her crutches and leveled her tone. "And I have these."

Hector sat across from her. "I met a young man at the church yesterday. Calls himself Tipper." He hesitated for a moment. "Polite young man. He helped me look for your glasses. Anyway, I was thinking we could hire him to do some chores around the yard."

Jeanne picked up her tea cup. "Not this nonsense again. We've already been over this a million times. It's a waste of good money and you could use the exer—"

Hector suddenly pushed his chair back and stood up. "No Jeanne!" he said with authority. "I'm too tired…too old. I need help keeping up with things."

Jeanne was surprised by her mild-mannered husband's sharp tone. She blew on her tea and looked out the window at the paint peeling away from the sill, another project her husband never seemed to get around to. *Maybe he's right; maybe we could use some help.* "This young man, is he trustworthy?"

Hector was surprised she was open to the idea. "Yes. He's young, but eager. And I'm sure he wouldn't expect much by way of compensation."

"Fine," she said, dismissively flicking her wrist. "But I don't want him in the house…looking to use the bathroom, or asking for something to drink. And not a penny more than fifty cents an hour."

Hector smiled. "Great, I'll talk to him." He walked into the living room and opened a drawer in the buffet. His eyes, once again drawn to the picture of Jesus. *Why, after so many years, am I only now seeing it in such a disturbing light?* He returned to the kitchen with a note pad and pen, and placed them next to his wife.

Jeanne looked up at him. "*What's this?*"

"Remember, last night, I mentioned you should write a little thank you note to the young lady who helped us after your fall…found your glasses? Father O'Handley said her name is Victoria Donnelly. Her mother runs Michael's Manor on Hillier Street. Her father was killed in Twenty Six a few years ago. Remember, the brakes gave out on the rake and slammed into the coal face?"

Jeanne pushed the note pad forward. "At least let me finish my tea."

Mabel was feeding Liv when Toni entered the kitchen. "Good morning. How did you sleep?" she asked.

Toni smiled. "Great, thank you. So, this is Liv?"

"It is."

Toni pulled a chair out from the table and sat down. "She's beautiful. She has your eyes…and mouth."

Mabel laughed. "Hope she doesn't have my mouth. Stanley says it can be pretty salty at times." She opened the cupboard. "Tea or coffee?"

"Tea, please." Toni picked up Liv's spoon. "Do you mind? I could use the practice."

Mabel smiled. "Fill your boots."

Toni dipped the spoon into Liv's small bowl. "I can't believe I slept so late. I didn't even hear Mark get up."

Mabel poured Toni's tea. "He's out in the barn with Stanley and the kids. I was thinking that after you have your breakfast, I'd show you around town. What do you think?"

"Sure, I'd like that. And if it's not too much trouble, maybe we can stop by Luke's. I'd like to meet Alice and Matthew." Toni ran the spoon under Liv's chin to scoop up the runny porridge. "Funny, Mark is always talking about his brothers, but he barely mentions Alice. Whenever I ask about her, he just says *she's nice*. If I'm going to be living here, I might as well make a friend or two. I know we're close in age, so I'm hoping we'll hit it off." She looked at Mabel. "Do you think we will?"

Mabel knew there was no chance Toni would get her wish. If anything, she would be getting a frosty reception from the woman she hoped to befriend. "I don't see why not," she lied. "I'll give her a call...see if it's a good time to stop by."

There was a loud rap on the screen door. Toni put her hand over her chest.

Mabel chuckled. "That's my neighbour, Myrtle. She has a habit of sneaking up on people."

Myrtle entered and placed a mason jar on the counter. "JC forgot your jam," she said. She turned to the young woman feeding Liv.

Toni looked up at the tall woman with the toque pulled down above her eyes. "Hello."

Myrtle checked out Toni's swollen belly. "You're pregnant."

Mabel smiled at Toni, then at Myrtle. "Myrtle, this is Antoinette Moody. But she prefers to go by Toni."

"Toni's a boy's name," Myrtle said bluntly. "So, Antoinette, are you a miss or missus?"

Toni looked away. "Miss."

"Me, too," Myrtle said. She turned to Mabel. "That fresh tea?" she asked, before playfully sticking her tongue out at Liv. She then plopped down next to Toni and pointed. "How long before ya drop the kid?"

Toni didn't get a chance to answer. Amour, Victoria, and Mary Catherine charged through the back door. The kitchen was soon a noisy hive of activity, with introductions and the rapid small talk that follows an awkward discovery. Unlike Myrtle, Toni knew the most recent arrivals were trying to avoid any mention of her obvious condition. She smiled nervously with her arm over her belly, a habit she recently fell into, as if it would protect her unborn child from the disapproving eyes of others.

Mabel leaned against the sink, sipping her tea. Toni looked in her direction. Mabel's eyes were soft and reassuring. *It's okay*, she mouthed.

Toni stood, arched her back, and rubbed her belly. "I'm at that point when I need to pee every ten minutes."

Mary Catherine laughed. "Every ten minutes! You wait! I could barely leave the bathroom. I used to say Devorah was dancing on my bladder.

That's *Dev..or..ah*… with a *V*. She's my youngest."

Amour placed her hand on Toni's belly and smiled. "So, how far along are you?"

Despite Jeanne's objections, Hector was in his car and on the way to see Father O'Handley. He could have waited until supper before going for her glasses, but he was anxious to talk to Tipper. He turned into the parking lot, happy to see a game of shinny underway. He stopped and got out, surveying the raucous gathering. He was disappointed there was no sign of the brash young man who made such an impression on him. He was returning from the Glebe House with Jeanne's glasses when he saw Tipper tear in on his bike, with one hand on the handle bar and the other holding his goalie stick.

Tipper pulled up beside him. "Hey, old man. See yer still standing."

Hector laughed. "And I see you fixed your stick."

Tipper held it in the air. "Good as new."

"I was hoping to run into you," Hector said.

Tipper straddled his bike. "Oh, yeah. Why's that?"

"How would you like to earn a few dollars? I need someone to help out with some chores around the house. Mow the lawn, a little painting… maybe do a little shoveling when the snow comes."

"How much ya payin?"

Hector shrugged. "How does forty cents an hour sound?"

Tipper screwed up his face. "Sounds like you can do better. How about seventy-five?"

"Sorry, young man, that's more than I can afford," Hector said. He started to walk away.

Tipper put the butt of his goalie stick flat on the ground and flicked a small rock into the air. "Okay, how about fifty cents."

Hector turned and smiled. "Deal." He opened his car door and handed Tipper a piece of paper with his address and phone number.

Tipper looked at it and shoved it in his pocket. "So, when do I start?"

"Weather permitting, Monday at ten. If it rains, Tuesday at the same time. Oh, and no cursing. If my wife hears you swearing, she'll chase you off the property. What's your phone number?"

"Don't got one."

"No phone?"

"Nope."

"What if I need to reach you?" Hector asked.

Tipper pointed to the row houses at the top of Pitt Street. "Guess you'll have to come to the house. I live in the second one on the left."

Hector nodded. "Well then, I guess I'll see you Monday at ten."

Tipper leaned forward and pushed down on the balls of his feet, propelling his bike forward. "Yep. Ten o'clock, if it ain't friggin rainin."

Hector drove off. He had one last errand before heading home and starting lunch. He headed up South Street, made a left onto Hillier Street, and turned into the manor. He was about to knock on the door when a car pulled up.

Amour stepped out from the passenger side. "Hello. Can I help you?"

Hector turned and smiled. "I was looking for Victoria...Victoria Donnely." He held up a small envelop. "A thank you note for her help yesterday."

Victoria leaned across the front seat. "Oh, hi. How is your wife feeling?"

Hector ducked his head in the window and smiled at the kids piled in the back seat, then at Victoria sitting behind the wheel. "She's doing better, thank you. I just stopped by the Glebe House and picked up her glasses. Just wanted to make sure you knew how much we appreciated your help," he said, passing her the note.

Victoria smiled. "Honestly, there was no need."

Mary Margaret twisted about in the backseat and elbowed her brother. "Get off of me," she screamed.

JC gave her a shove.

Victoria turned sharply. "Settle down, or there'll be no park." She turned back to Hector. "They can be a handful from time to time. Anyway, it was very sweet of you to go through all this trouble. Give your wife my best." She put the car in drive. "I better get going before they kill one another."

Hector stepped back from the car. "Thanks, again," he said and watched her drive off. He turned and smiled at Amour, deadheading a planter at the entrance. "You have a beautiful property."

Amour beamed. "Thank you. We love it here."

"And your daughter is very kind...and beautiful."

"Thank you. I think so, too. I'm very proud of her."

"Is she still in school?"

"She just graduated from Normal School. She's hoping to get a teaching job in September."

Hector nodded. "I'm sure she'd make a marvelous teacher." He walked to his car and opened the door. Yesterday, he thought he saw the resemblance, today he was sure of it. He looked back at Amour. "Have a good day."

Amour smiled and waved. "You, too. Bye now."

"Yeah, well I can't. Cause Ma heard me talkin to you on the phone, *that's why.* Yeah, she had a puss on her that would stop a friggin clock. Tell me about it. She heard everythin. Yeah, that too. And that was before I told her about me and Victoria. Yeah, she blames me. Said she knew Victoria would end up dumpin me. Yeah, I know. She really liked her. Said I wasn't gonna do any better. Anyway, I gotta start bikin to work...not allowed to have the car anymore. Yeah, and how the hell would that work? *Hey, Doreen, wanna go to the slags? Great, hop on the back of my friggin bike.* What? I never thought about the brook. Think she'd go for it? Okay, okay! Relax! Give me her number. I'll get her to meet me downtown. With any luck, I'll run into Victoria. She'll lose her friggin mind when she sees me with a new girl on my arm. Yeah, well I think you're wrong. She'll come around. Frig off. Just give me the friggin number." Kenny opened the drawer of the telephone table and removed a pencil. "Yeah, I'm ready." He quickly jotted down Doreen's number. "Got it. Look, I gotta go. I wanna call her before Ma gets home. Yeah. Thanks, bud."

Kenny hung up and looked out the window to make sure his mother wasn't on her way home. He picked the receiver back up, dialled the number, and waited. "Oh, hi. Is Doreen there?" He could feel his heart speed up. "Doreen, it's Kenny...Kenny Ludlow. I'm good. Look, I was talkin to Tommy and—Yeah, he told me. So, I was wonderin if you'd like to go out with me? Great. Tonight. Perfect. How about I meet you at the fence?" Kenny pressed his eyes closed. "Sorry, I can't pick you up. I got no wheels...engine troubles. Yeah, sorry. It should be back on the road before too long. Okay, does six o'clock work? Great. Yeah, see ya there."

Mother came through the door as Kenny was hanging up. "Who was that?" she asked.

"Tommy," he lied.

She looked at him from the corner of her eye. "What are you two cooking up now?"

"Nothin!"

"Better not be." She pointed down the hall. "If you need the bathroom, ya better jump in before your father gets home. Oh, and I ironed your green shirt. It's hangin in your closet."

Kenny screwed up his face. *Why did she iron my shirt?*

She pointed to his pants. "You can wear your brown cords."

He laughed. "What are you talkin about? Where am I supposed to be wearin my green shirt and brown cords?"

"What do you mean, *where*? To the church supper."

"I thought that was next week."

"Well, it's not. It's tonight and we have to be at the hall in less than an hour."

Kenny shook his head. "Sorry, I got other plans."

Mother's head shot up. "What plans?" she asked sternly.

"I'm gonna meet Harley and Tommy...shoot a cupala games of pool," he lied again.

Mother sneered. "Your plans just changed. You're coming with me and your father! I promised Sister Agnes Paula you'd set up the tables and chairs. And you'll need to put the hall back together after everyone leaves. Now, get up to your room...get changed and washed up."

Kenny knew better than to argue. He went upstairs, changed, and quickly returned to the kitchen, hoping his mother would leave so he could call Doreen and postpone their date. He watched her ice three carrot cakes; her annual contribution to the church gathering. "Is that what you're wearin?"

Mother looked down at her shift. "Why, what's wrong with what I'm wearing?"

"Nothin. Just thought you were gonna get changed, that's all."

"It's perfectly fine," she huffed. "I'll be in the kitchen all night, dishing up supper for everyone else."

Father charged through the back door and rushed past them. "I know I'm late. I just need ten minutes."

Kenny closed his eyes. He wouldn't be running into Victoria with a new girl on his arm, or unbuttoning Doreen's blouse in the high grass along the brook. No, he'd be stuck in a musty old church basement, making small talk with hairy-chinned old women, and sitting down to a plate of stinky cod cakes and cold beans.

Father returned. "All set?"

Mother placed the cakes in a shallow box. "One of you take these to the car. I just need to fix my hair and put on some lipstick."

Kenny glanced at the clock. Doreen would be leaving soon. "I'm gonna take my bike, I'll meet you guys there."

Father picked up the box and thrust it at Kenny's chest. "Get in the goddamn car! You're coming with us."

Mabel and Toni put the grocery bags on the kitchen table. "The town is bigger than I expected," Toni said. "I thought it would be much smaller."

Mabel peeked in one of the bags and removed a flat of eggs. "It's small in some ways, but not in others. Size-wise it's quite big, with lots of sprawling neighbourhoods surrounding the eleven pit heads, but most people know one another." She chuckled. "Unfortunately, lots of folks make it their business to know everyone else's. Won't take long before you figure out who they are."

Toni passed Mabel a box of Oxydol. "But you like it here, right?"

"I can't imagine living anywhere else. The good far outweighs the bad. And I certainly couldn't imagine living in a big city like Halifax."

"I'm sorry I didn't get to meet Alice today," Toni said.

Mabel opened a cupboard door, pressed her eyes together, and thought of the call that ended with Alice in tears. Alice was adamant she had no interest in getting together with Toni. She also let Mabel know, in no uncertain terms, her feelings about Mark being back in town. Mabel turned back to Toni and smiled. "You'll meet her soon enough. She works every other Saturday, so when she gets a day off she spends it with Matthew."

Mark came through the back door, tilted his head, and grinned mischievously at Toni.

Toni chucked. "What's that look for?"

"Didn't I tell you not to worry?"

Toni's mouth fell open. "Oh, my God. Did you find work?"

Mark nodded. "Stanley offered me a job."

Toni looked from Mark to Mabel and clapped her hands together. "I can't believe it!"

"And that's not all," Mark said. "He found us an apartment. Right downtown. Above the Co-op. It's small. One bedroom. But it'll do for now...till we find something more permanent. Even has a sofa and a sideboard. We just need a bed and —"

Toni ran to Mark and threw her arms around his neck. "Thank God."

Mark laughed. "Thank Stanley. Oh, and Mabel."

Toni looked at Mabel with tears in her eyes. "I don't know what to say. We can't thank you enough."

Stanley entered. "I see Mark shared the news."

Toni rushed to the door. "I'm....we're so grateful. I can't believe it. I was afraid the baby would come and we'd have no money...no place to live." She leaned in and hugged him. "Thank you so much."

Stanley laughed. "We're happy to help."

"So, when do we move in?" Toni asked Mark.

"Monday morning."

Mabel reached into one of the grocery bags and removed a ham wrapped in butcher paper. She smiled, thinking of the time she stuffed the toe of Johnnie's pit boot with the same scented paper and headed off to Cameron's store in the middle of a snowstorm. She was cutting through MacLeod's field when their German Shepard viciously attacked her, ripping off Johnnie's boot, and angrily tearing the soft pink butcher paper to shreds. She would have frozen to death if Stanley hadn't found her in the coal shed. She looked at her husband, hunched over the sink, washing his hands. Stanley winked at her. Mabel put the ham on the counter, walked up beside him, and rubbed his back. "Thank you," she said.

Stanley chuckled. "What for?"

"For everything," she whispered.

Kenny was setting up the long wooden tables, pissed he wasn't going to be sowing his oats, when Victoria came down the basement stairs. "What the hell," he muttered. He pushed a chair aside and walked toward her, smiling. "Miss me already?"

She chuckled. "Kenny, I didn't even know you were here. Father O'Handley asked if I'd help serve. Here, hold this," she said, handing him a pastry box and taking off her sweater.

Kenny laughed. "Yeah, sure."

Victoria took the box back. "Trust me, I'm not here to see you." She turned and walked away.

Kenny put his hand on her arm. "I'm sorry, I know I was outta line. It's just...well ya—" He laughed nervously. "What can I say, I'm a guy." He leaned in and whispered in her ear. "Ya do things to me." Victoria pulled her arm free and headed for the kitchen. Kenny jumped in front of her. "Look, I understand. We can take it slow. As slow as you like." He crossed his heart. "Promise."

Victoria shook her head. "Sorry, Kenny. It's not going to happen."

Kenny pointed to the entrance. "Maybe we can go for a walk after we finish up? Talk about our little misunderstandin."

Victoria smiled. "Kenny, there's nothing to discuss. We're not getting back together. Period!"

Kenny's heart sank as he watched her disappear into the kitchen. He momentarily dropped his head. When he looked up, his mother was approaching him. "Damn," he whispered.

"Victoria is here," she said.

"Yeah, Ma, I saw her."

"*Well*?"

"Well what?" Kenny asked sharply.

"Well, did you talk to her?"

"Yeah, I talked to her."

Kenny's mother was getting angry at her son's failure to be more forthcoming. She pulled him aside. "I don't know what you did to that poor girl. I only hope you didn't let those filthy images in those vulgar magazines you and Tommy look at put any crazy ideas in that—" She made a fist and knocked him hard on the head. "Empty shell of yours."

Father approached. "What's going on with you two?" he whispered loudly.

Mother smiled at several parishioners walking within earshot and spoke under her breath. "Kenny did something to sweet Victoria."

Father turned to Kenny. "What did you do?"

Kenny's mouth fell open. He raised his shoulders and held his arms off to the side. "I didn't do a darn thing to her. I swear," he pleaded. "Ma just thinks—"

His father cuffed him off the head. "Don't talk back to your mother."

"But I didn't talk back—"

He got another swat on the head. "And don't talk back to me."

Kenny had had enough. "I'm outta here," he huffed, storming up the steps.

Father was about to charge after him, but Mother pulled him back. "Let him go. There's no point in chasing after him. He'll just ruin the night for everyone else."

Amour tied her plastic rain hat under her chin. "Can we swing by the church and check on Victoria? It's raining cats and dogs out there and she didn't take her raincoat."

Ed looked at his watch. "Of course. We've got plenty of time. I told Gordon we'd be there for eight," he said, taking her by the hand.

They ran through the pouring rain to Ed's car and drove the five minutes to Holy Cross Church. People were piling out of the basement entrance and quickly scattering in all directions. Ed shut the engine off. "Wait here. I'll get her," he said, opening the door and stepping out. Amour lost sight of him under the torrent of water beating down on the windshield. He's a fine man, she thought. *So considerate of everyone.* She put her head down, once again, struck by a powerful wave of guilt; guilt for letting him believe they had a future together, and guilt for wanting it. She opened her purse, pulled out a hankie, and pressed it against her eyes. "I'm sorry, Michael," she whispered. *I know you'd like him. I think you'd be good friends.*

The back door suddenly flew open. "It's crazy out there," Victoria said.

Ed jumped in the front seat. "Whew! We might have to sit for a while and let this pass."

Amour looked back at her daughter. "I'm glad we came for you. You would have been soaked to the bone by the time you got home."

"Actually, I had a drive, but I'm glad you came."

"Oh?" Amour asked. "Who was that?"

"You know that man who stopped by the manor with the thank you note, he and his wife offered to drive me home."

Ed looked back over his shoulder. "Is that the couple I saw you talking to? She was on crutches."

"Yes, that's Jeanne…the lady who fell in the parking lot. I found her glasses. Oh, and Kenny's parents offered to give me a drive, but that would have been way too awkward. I'd rather swim home."

Ed looked in the rear view mirror. "Jeanne's husband looked familiar. What's his name?" he asked Victoria.

"Hector MacDonald."

Ed glanced at Amour and shrugged. He then looked back at Victoria. "I'm sure I met him somewhere. Where do they live?"

"Maple Avenue, just past the tracks on the right. Jeanne asked me to stop in for tea."

Ed watched the rain stream down the windshield and thought of a similar day almost two years earlier. He had driven Lily to town so she could return the money she had stolen from Stanley, but there was no one home, so they drove to Maple Avenue and parked across the street from a modest, two-storey home. It was where Lily had taken her first steps, and, where as a pregnant teenager, she was shown the door and told never to return. Ed closed his eyes, recalling the image of Lily's father standing beside his Chrysler with an armful of groceries, staring at the unfamiliar car idling on the side of the road.

"Ed, we should get going," Amour said. "The rain seems to be letting up and I don't want to keep Gordon and Charlotte waiting." Ed put the car in gear. Amour smiled. "You looked like you were lost in thought. What were you thinking?"

"I was thinking about the last time I remember this much rain. It was the day of the mine accident."

Amour nodded. "Yes, the same day I had the grand opening for the manor. One minute we were celebrating a wonderful occasion; the next, we were mourning the dead," she said sadly.

Victoria leaned forward and touched her mother's shoulder. "Just like the day we lost Daddy."

By the time Kenny reached the Commercial Street Bridge, his shirt was clinging to his body and his pants were hanging low on hips. *Screw you, Victoria. You're just a hoity-toity bitch. And screw you too, Ma. Nothin I ever do is good enough.*

A car suddenly stopped and the passenger door flew open. "Hey, asshole! Get in!"

Kenny jumped in the front seat and ran his fingers through his wet, stringy hair. "Holy shit! The friggin skies just opened up. Thought I was gonna drown out there. Where you comin from?"

"Sally's. I just dropped her and Doreen off."

"So, I guess I won't be goin to no brook tonight," Kenny said.

Tommy laughed. "Not unless you were plannin on goin for a swim. One thing's for sure, you ain't gettin lucky."

The two childhood friends drove to the stone chimney above the Cameron Bowl. The mood was solemn as Kenny told his friend about his encounter with Victoria and his fight with his parents.

Tommy reached in the back seat, grabbed two beer, and popped the caps. "Fuck em," he said, passing one to Kenny. "Fuck em all."

They clinked bottles. "Yeah, fuck em all," Kenny repeated.

Tommy laughed. "If we're not gonna get laid, we might as well get drunk."

An hour later, the life-long members of The Blackheads were laughing about their youthful antics: hooking off school, setting Mr. Spencer's car on fire, tormenting Myrtle, and tearing around Bicycle Hill.

Kenny suddenly became quiet. "I think you were right."

Tommy held his bottle to his mouth. "Bout what?"

"Bout the train leavin the station. I don't think Victoria's gonna change her mind."

Tommy shrugged. "Sorry, bud. I know ya liked her a lot."

"Yeah, well I guess she don't feel the same about me."

"Doreen's really nice. And she likes you."

Kenny shrugged. "She don't even know me."

"But she likes what she sees. Just don't go fuckin it up. Remember, ya gotta get em all hot and bothered before you haul out the rubber." Tommy reached back for another beer. "You tossed the jewelry box, right?"

"Yeah. Won't be makin that mistake again," Kenny said, tilting his head back and taking a swig.

Tommy gave him a playful shove. "Good news is, ya won't have to. Doreen's...well...well let's just say she's no Victoria."

Jeanne pulled on the end of a skein of blue yarn and readied her knitting needles.

"What are you making now?" Hector asked.

"Mittens for the Tea and Sale."

Hector dipped his chin and looked over his glasses. "Isn't that in the fall?"

"Yes, the end of October. I've got a lot of odds and sods. I might as well make use of them."

Hector picked his newspaper off his lap. "I dunno, I don't understand why anyone would want to be knitting in the middle of the summer."

"And why's that?"

"Just seems more like a winter pastime."

Jeanne rummaged around in a bag at her side and held up a ball of green yarn. "Do you like this colour?"

Hector shrugged. "It's all right."

"I was thinking about making a scarf for Victoria...you know...just a little something for all her help. Maybe a soft yellow would be better. Oh, I was also thinking about asking her if she'd like to help out with Sunday School. Good practice for a teacher. And I'm sure the school trustees would look favourably upon her for taking such initiative."

Hector smiled at his wife. "I think that's a fine idea, but you should probably speak to Father O'Handley first."

Jeanne scowled at him. "Of course, I'd speak to Father O'Handley first. You don't have to tell me that!" she hissed, roughly unwinding her skein. "Why don't you put the kettle on? I feel like some tea."

Hector nodded. He started to get up, then sat on the edge of his chair and leaned forward. "Jeanne, does Victoria remind you of anyone?"

"What do you mean?"

"I mean—" Hector wasn't sure if he should go on. He swallowed. "Well, she reminds me of Lily."

Jeanne's hand shot up. "Not another word."

Hector shook his head. "Jeanne, dear, I'm only—"

Jeanne put her knitting to the side. "I guess if you're not going to make the tea, I will." She stood, grabbed her crutches, and started for the kitchen.

"Sit down!" Hector ordered harshly. Jeanne stopped and stared down at her husband. He lowered his voice. "I'll get the tea."

Hector waited in the kitchen for the kettle to start boiling. He reached in his back pocket, took out his wallet, and pulled out the small, cracked photo he kept hidden from his wife. He ran his thumb over the tiny image of the young girl sitting on the front step. She had braids and was holding a Bible. He and Jeanne were standing behind her and smiling proudly.

"Why don't you make some bread and molasses," Jeanne hollered from the couch.

Hector quickly put the picture back in his wallet. "One or two pieces?"

"One for me."

Hector put the kettle on the stove, sliced the bread, and ran his knife down the hard butter. He repeated the mindless task until he had shaved off enough butter to cover each slice of the thick, airy bread. My life is a joyless grind, he thought. *Just one mundane task after the other. Get up. Shave. Eat breakfast. Eat lunch. Eat supper. Read the paper. Go to bed.* He opened the larder and noisily shuffled its contents about.

"The molasses is in the larder...top shelf," Jeanne said.

"Found it." Hector removed the sticky lid, poured a liberal amount on the first slice, and watched the thick, black blob pool on top of the cold butter. He moved from one slice to the next, deftly creating the perfect combination of bread, butter, and molasses, just as his mother had shown him. He ran his finger under the rim of the molasses jar to catch the syrupy drips, stuck it in his mouth, and closed his eyes, savouring the sweet reminder of his childhood.

"Hector! What in the world is keeping you? I was hoping to have my bed lunch...not breakfast."

"That was lovely. I'll have to ask Charlotte for her recipe. Do you think I should add it to the menu?" Amour asked.

"What?"

Amour studied her driver. "Are you okay? You don't seem yourself. You've been distracted all evening."

Ed turned up South Street. "It's just work stuff. Nothing serious," he lied.

Amour didn't believe him, but decided not to push the matter. "At least the rain has let up. I worry about you driving home on those dark, wet roads."

"I know them like the back of my hand," Ed said matter-of-factly.

"I suppose you do. Still, I can't help but worry."

Ed looked at her. "Do you?"

Amour laughed. "Do I *what?*"

"Do you worry about me?" Ed asked.

Amour looked puzzled. "What is that supposed to mean? Of course I worry about you. What is up with you tonight? Even Charlotte asked if you were feeling all right."

Ed suddenly pulled over and turned the engine off.

"Now, you're scaring me," Amour said.

Ed could feel his heart quicken. He knew it wasn't the time or place for the conversation he wanted to have with her, but he couldn't help himself. "Amour, I think you know how I feel." He reached over and took her hand in his. "Look, this isn't how I planned it, but I need to know if we have a future together. And I don't mean as good friends who chum around together, then go home to our separate homes…separate beds...separate lives. I love you. And I want to get married." Ed's heart fell when Amour pulled her hand away.

She dropped her head. "I…I don't know what to say. I mean…I wasn't expecting any of this. Honestly, I don't know what—"

Ed put his hand up to stop her from going on. "It's okay. I understand." There was an awkward silence. He leaned against the door. "Can I ask you something?"

Amour looked at him and nodded. "Of course," she said meekly.

He smiled. "Is it me? Or is it Michael?"

Amour reached over and grabbed his hand. "It's neither. It's…it's me. I don't know. I just feel—" She shrugged and shook her head, unsure of what to say.

"Guilty?" Ed asked.

Amour looked away from him. "Yes, I suppose so."

"Amour, I never met Michael, but from all I hear he was one hell of a guy. He had to be… to win you over. Don't you think he'd want you to be happy?" Ed pleaded.

She nodded. "I know he would."

"*See*, so there's no need to feel guilty. And for the record, I know he'll always be a big part of your life. I don't expect you to stop loving him. But, Amour, Michael's not here." He thumped his chest. "*But I am.* And I know he'd be happy for us. Don't you see, in a way you'd be honouring his wishes. So, I guess the only question I have is…do you love me?"

"Yes," she whispered.

Ed was disappointed by her meek response. He rubbed his forehead. "You don't sound so sure."

"Honestly, Ed, I love our time together. And I miss you when you're not around. And Victoria adores you…and my friends, they all love you. It's just a lot to take in. I wasn't expecting this…at least not tonight. I'm sorry, it's just that you've taken me completely off guard."

Ed sat up and drummed his fingers against the steering wheel. "No kidding. Truth be told, I surprised myself. Hell, I had always pictured myself getting down on one knee. And I certainly didn't intend to ask you in my car…sitting on the side of the road." He reached over and squeezed her shoulder. "Just tell me you're willing to give it some thought?"

"Of course."

Ed smiled. "I'm sorry for taking you by surprise. I know you weren't expecting it. And you're right, it's a big decision…a huge decision. I won't pressure you…or rush you. Take as much time as you need."

Amour closed her eyes. "Thank you. I'm glad you understand."

Ed grinned. "But hopefully not too much." He started the car and began to chuckle. "Frankly, I'm relieved you didn't just turn me down flat."

Amour smiled. "Well, it wasn't the most romantic proposal I've ever heard."

Ed leaned across the seat. "Maybe not, but trust me…no one has ever been more sincere," he said and kissed her.

Jeanne looked up from her knitting. Hector was standing in the entrance to the living room holding a tray with their bed lunch. "What is it?" she asked, wondering why he was staring at her. Hector suddenly dropped the tray, grabbed his chest, and fell to one knee. "Hector!" she screamed, tossing her knitting to the side and scrambling to his side.

"I can't breathe," he gasped.

Jeanne pushed the cups and tray out of the way, and put her arm around his back, easing him down on the floor. "Don't move," she said, struggling to her feet and hobbling to the phone. Her hand shook as she dialled the operator. "Please! We need an ambulance right away!" she cried, her voice cracking. "My husband's having a heart attack. Forty-six Maple Avenue. I'll put the outside light on. Hurry!" she begged. Jeanne hung up, put the light on, and rushed back to Hector. He was sitting up with his back propped up against his chair. Jeanne picked his limp hand off his lap and held it to the side of her face. "Hold on, Hec. The ambulance will be here soon."

"Jeanne," he whispered.

Jeanne gently swatted her husband's sticky pant leg. "Shush. Shush. Don't talk," she said, flinging her wrist to free her hand of a sliver of butter. "Everything's going to be just fine. Just stay still and take slow, deep breaths. I'm here and you're going to be just fine. Just fine," she said, the fear in her voice belying her comforting words. She looked at Hector's watch. It had been almost ten minutes since she had called the ambulance. "Is the pain getting worse?" Jeanne asked.

Hector nodded and closed his eyes.

Jeanne heard the siren. "Here that. They're almost here," she said, standing and limping to the front door. "Bring a stretcher," she hollered.

A growing crowd gathered to watch the ambulance attendants load the patient into the dark cabin of the black wagon. Several onlookers hovered close to Jeanne, offering encouraging words. Her neighbour, Dot, handed Jeanne her crutches. "Brian will drive you to the hospital. Oh, and don't worry about the mess. I'll tidy up. I'm afraid the rug might be permanently stained."

Jeanne nodded. "It's the least of my worries." She put the crutches under her arms and headed for the steps. "I just need to grab some things and lock up." Dot helped her inside and up the stairs to her bedroom. Jeanne packed a small overnight bag with Hector's pajamas, slippers, robe, and shaving gear. She then picked her Bible up off the night stand. "I guess that's it," she said, looking around.

Dot grabbed Jeanne's overnight bag, shut the light off, and helped her friend downstairs. "Jeanne, Hector's strong. I'm sure he'll be just fine."

"He better be. I couldn't possibly live without him."

Sunday, June 29

Ed sat on the step and watched the sun come up. He looked at his watch. He needed to speak with Lily, but it was still too early to call. He sipped his coffee, wondering if Amour was any closer to making a decision. "You promised not to rush her. Don't do anything stupid," he whispered. He leaned back on his elbows and chuckled, thinking, if it weren't for Kenny, he probably would never have mustered up the courage to propose. He ran his hand through his hair, wondering how his young friend was doing, then suddenly sat up. Hopefully I haven't spooked Amour and we end up in the same boat, he thought. A black cat dashed across the lawn. Ed leaned forward to see where it ran off to, but it disappeared out of sight. "A black cat. That can't be good," he said and got to his feet. He crossed the street to the shore, picked up a handful of rocks, and began throwing them into the harbour. *I need to get out of town for a while...give Amour some space.* He stretched his arm back as far as he could, firing the last rock a good distance beyond the pier. He wiped his sandy palm down his pant leg, went inside his small bungalow, and flopped down on his bed. He had laid awake all night, unable to settle his anxious mind, but now, in the light of day, he suddenly felt like he couldn't keep his eyes open.

He was in a mourning suit and standing at the altar. Kenny was standing next to him in his underwear and a tee shirt. The music started; soft at first, then ear-piercing. He covered his ears. The double doors at the back of the church slowly opened. The bride gradually came into view, first her head, then her shoulders as she mounted the steps; her veiled face, blackened by the glare of the bright sunlight behind her. Her full silhouette hauntingly appeared in the entrance, then slowly started down the aisle; her halting steps making her journey seem endless. She stopped and turned toward him. Ed lifted her veil and stumbled back. It was Victoria. He looked up at the altar. A black cat was sitting on the credence table licking its paw. He fell to his knees and bent over, once again covering his ears, this time to stop the shrill clanging of the church bells.

Ed opened his eyes, confused by the remnants of his disturbing dream. The phone was ringing. He scurried off the bed, walked into the hall, and picked up the receiver. "Hello," he said groggily. "Oh, hi, Gordon. What's going on?" He started to laugh. "*What*? No, I'm fine. Honestly. No, I'm sorry I had her worried. Just work stuff," he lied. "Yes, I suppose they do. Tell her I'm fit as a fiddle and looking forward to coming back for another great meal. Sure. Yes, I understand. Yes, we'll be in touch. Have a great day and give Charlotte my best."

Ed hung up and glanced at his watch. He picked the receiver back up, dialled the operator, and waited for the connection. "Hey, Rory. How's it going, bud? Yes, it's me. You and your sisters having a good summer? That's great. Is your mother home?" Ed waited. "Hey there. Yes, I'm good. And you? Oh, I'm sorry to hear. But you're okay? What about Henri? I'm sorry, Lily. I really liked him. Yes, no point in dragging it out if it's not going anywhere," he said, hoping he and Amour wouldn't be suffering the same fate. "And how are Yvonne and Giles? That's wonderful." Ed reached into the kitchen, dragged a chair into the hall, and sat down. "Lily, there's something I need to ask you. No. No, I swear it's nothing bad. Is your father's name Hector?" Ed closed his eyes and nodded. "No, it's nothing like that. Actually, it might be a good thing. Lily, I'm pretty sure Victoria has met your parents. At Holy Cross. Your mother had a fall. No, she's fine. Just a sprained ankle. Victoria saw it happen and stopped to help your father get her back to the car. I know. Look, I've decided to take a few days off and head home to the farm. Yes, it's been a while. Tomorrow. Anyway, I was thinking if the timing worked for you, I could stop into Sussex. Maybe we could grab a coffee? *What am I up to today?* Nothing much, why? You're right, I am the boss.

Not like I have to ask permission." He looked at his watch. "Why not. If I leave within the hour, I can be in Sussex before five. Maybe we can swing over to The Pines for supper. My treat. What? Are you sure? No, that would be fine. But don't go through any trouble. Great. Okay, see you soon. Me, too."

"How are you feeling?" Jeanne asked.

Hector sat up slowly. "Better," he said, placing his hand on his chest. "Have you been here all night?"

"Of course. Where else would I be?"

"Did you sleep?" he asked.

"I dozed off and on. I'm fine. Dr. McLellan says you'll need to stay here for a few days. Then, it's complete bed rest for a few weeks. I guess it's a good thing you hired that young man after all."

Hector pointed to her bad ankle. "How are you going to manage?"

Jeanne stood at his side. "Dot's right next door. And I'm getting used to the crutches."

"You should go home. Get some rest." He waved his hand. "No point in both of us being stuck here."

"I'm fine. Besides, I have to wait for Brian to get off work?"

Hector gave her a puzzled look. "*Why*?"

Jeanne smiled. "So he can drive me home. You don't expect me to walk?" she said in a teasing way.

"No, Jeanne, I expect you to call a cab."

Jeanne pulled the bedsheet up to his chest. "Waste of money. And I don't mind waiting."

Hector pushed her hand away and angrily flipped the sheet back. "Call a cab," he said forcefully.

Jeanne looked hurt. "You want me to go?"

Hector stared up at the ceiling. "You must be tired. Go home and get some rest. We can afford a goddamn cab...for Pete's sake."

Jeanne put her husband's unusually harsh rebuke down to a combination of his medication and brush with death. She reached for her crutches. "I suppose you're right." She leaned down and kissed his forehead. "I'll try and get a lift back tonight. Anything you want me to get for you?"

Hector closed his eyes. "Jeanne, I don't expect you to come back tonight. I'll be fine. Look after yourself."

Jeanne walked haltingly toward the door, turned, and smiled. "I'll see you soon."

Hector nodded. I'm living on borrowed time, only I'm not really living, he thought. *I might as well be dead. I wouldn't be feeling so lost… so goddamn useless. I wouldn't feel anything, and I'd rather feel nothing than feel like this.*

"Good morning, Mr. MacDonald. I just saw your wife on her way out. You gave her quite a scare," Charlotte said. "It's so dark in here." She walked to the window and threw the curtains open. "There, that's better." She smiled at her patient. "Everything looks better when the sun is shining."

Hector squinted into the sunlight. "Even the future?"

Charlotte laughed. "Especially the future. You're a lucky guy. You got a warning. Dr. MacLellan said you just need to rest up, change your diet, lose a few pounds…maybe walk a bit more. He said you gained some weight since he last saw you."

"I'm not as active as I used to be. No energy. And I got the Black Lung."

Charlotte walked to his side and put her hand on his arm. "I know. Once you get past the next few weeks, Dr. McLellan wants you to come in for inhalation therapy."

Hector sighed. "And what will that cost me?"

Charlotte grinned. "I'm not sure. Think of it as an investment in your future," she said, handing him two pills and a glass of water. "Do you have children?"

Hector swallowed and passed the glass back to her. "A daughter."

Charlotte smiled. "Me, too. She's thirteen months old and a going concern. Do you have any grandchildren?"

Hector pictured Rory being pushed down in the snow with several older boys piling on top of him. "Yes," he said, his voice cracking. "Four."

Charlotte patted his arm. "Then you better listen to the doctor. I'm sure you'll want to see them grow up and have babies of their own. Now, is there anything I can get you before I check in on Mrs. Ells?"

Hector looked at her through misty eyes. "Yeah." He lifted his hand, holding his thumb and pointer finger a few inches apart. "How about a nice, juicy T-bone streak…around this thick."

Rory sat by the window anxiously waiting for Ed. "He's here!" he yelled and tore outside.

Lily smiled at the excitement in her children's voices. She pushed her hair behind her ears, ran her hand down the front of her dress, and walked to the open doorway. She laughed. The kids were jumping around Ed and squealing, and Yvonne was flailing her arms about, rapidly saying something in French. Ed scooped Laura up and kissed the side of her head. Lily felt a lump rise in her throat. She smiled and waved. "How was the drive?"

"Long, but worth it. I never had a welcome like this before," he said, laughing.

She smiled. "Hope you brought your appetite."

"You know it."

Giles retrieved Ed's bag from the backseat. "Good to see you."

"You, too." Ed pointed to Giles car. "How's my Cadillac?" he teased.

"Still purring like a kitten."

"Okay, kids, let him come inside," Lily hollered.

Ed walked up the steps with Laura in his arms. Rory and Rachael were on his heels, followed by Yvonne, then Giles with his luggage. "Great to see you," he said to Lily, leaning in and kissing her cheek.

"Did you bring us anything?" Laura asked.

"Laura!" Lily chided.

Ed laughed and put Laura down. "What do you think?" he asked, taking his overnight bag from Giles and zipping it open. He removed a paper bag and held it over his head. "Three guesses."

"Hershey bars," Rachael called out.

"Darn!" Ed said, shaking his head. "There's no fooling you guys." He was about to pass the bag to Rory but stopped. "Wait. What does your mother say?"

Lily grinned and snatched the bag from him. "Mother says not until after supper."

They were sitting around the table within minutes; Rory and Rachael relentless in their appeals to eat, so they could have their sweet treat. Lily looked at the smiling faces around the table and felt her heart soar. It was ages since she felt this happy. It was almost as if they were a real family, made whole by Ed's homecoming. She turned to see Yvonne smiling at her. Her neck grew hot. She picked up the gravy boat. "More gravy, Yvonne?"

Yvonne smiled slyly. "Merci."

"Me, too," Rory said.

"And how about you, Ed?" Lily asked.

"Why not," he said, waiting for the gravy to be passed around the table. "It's very good. Everything is. And I told you not to go through any trouble."

Lily picked up her fork. "It wasn't any trouble."

Rory laughed. "Yeah, like we eat like this every night."

Yvonne flicked his ear. "Mind your manners."

The adults lingered round the table after dessert. Ed smiled to himself, grateful Lily talked him into stopping in for the night. Lily had a glow about her as she talked about how well Rory and Rachael were doing in school, and she seemed to love her new job as a secretary with the Department of Indian Affairs.

"Ed," Giles said, "Judge Cummings was asking about you?"

"Oh? How is he?"

"He seems fine. Asked me to say hello for him."

"Make sure you do the same for me," Ed said. "I feel bad for him and his young son." He paused trying to recall his name. "Graham, I think. Yes, Graham. He can't be more than ten. I'm still shocked. I didn't have Wanda pegged as the cheating type."

Lily thought of the night at The Pines when she saw a young man leaving Judge Cummings unit. It was obvious what they were up to. She closed her eyes, recalling her ridiculous plan to extort money from the judge for her silence. "No one really knows what happens in a marriage," she said. "You see a couple and you think they're so in love…that they have the perfect marriage. But no one really knows. Sometimes I think it's the couples who seem the happiest who are the most miserable."

Giles laughed. "*Really*? What about me and Yvonne? Do you think we look happy?"

Lily smiled. "I'm not talking about you. You're the exception. It's obvious you two are nuts about each other."

"Or just nuts," Yvonne said, elbowing her husband. "At least I am for putting up with this fool."

"All right, time for bed," Lily said, holding her hand out to Laura. "That goes for you, too," she said, waving for Rory and Rachael to follow her.

Yvonne started to clear the dishes.

"Sit," Ed said, "I'll do the dishes."

"Nonsense," Yvonne scoffed. "You're the guest of honour."

Giles and Yvonne were tidying up the kitchen, and Ed was opening a bottle of wine when Lily returned.

"Don't worry, it's not Four Acres," he said, reminding Lily of the first time they shared a bottle of wine.

Lily jumped at the sound of the popping cork and laughed. She then put four glasses on the table.

"None for us," Yvonne said. "We've got to get going."

Giles gave his wife a curious look. "No we don't." He picked up one of the glasses. "I'll have some."

Yvonne grabbed the bottle from Ed and quickly poured an inch of wine into Giles' glass. "Drink up and get in the goddamn car." She hugged Ed. "Always love our visits. Don't be a stranger." She pulled on her husband's arm. "C'mon Giles."

Ed and Lily saw them out, took their wine outside, and sat next to each other on the narrow stoop.

"I'm proud of you," Ed said.

Lily playfully nudged him. "And I'm proud of you. Moving to a brand new place…and the boss of what, fifty people?"

Ed slapped his hand over his heart, feigning hurt. "Excuse me!! Fifty seven!" They laughed. "Seriously, Lily, you look wonderful. And the kids, they're doing so well…they had a good year at school and they're meeting new friends. No more bullying, right?"

"No. Thank God."

Ed glanced over his shoulder. "And you have a government job and a lovely home."

"It's just a little bungalow. And the bank owns it…most of it anyway. But I'm working on it. Maybe it'll be mine in another twenty or thirty years."

Ed sipped his wine. "But you're happy?"

Lily let her head fall from side to side as if weighing the question. "I guess. It's kind of like my mortgage." She chuckled. "I'm working on it. What about you?"

"The same. I'm working on it." Ed was about to tell Lily about proposing to Amour, but she suddenly stood up.

"It's getting chilly. Let's go inside."

Ed followed her into the living room and sat beside her on the couch.

"Okay, now that we're alone, tell me about Victoria and my parents," Lily said.

Ed told her all he knew, which wasn't much more than he mentioned on the phone. At times, Lily seemed happy about the unlikely meeting that brought her daughter to her parents' aid; at others, she seemed agitated. "It's not fair. Why do they get to be with her, but I don't? They threw me out for Christ sakes. So much for their sanctimonious bullshit…their… forgiveness. They were the ones who robbed me and my kids…their own flesh and blood…from being a family…a real family. Goddamn them! I wonder what they would do if they knew Victoria was their granddaughter. Do you think they'd have anything to do with her?"

Ed raised his eyebrows. "I actually think they would. People mellow with age…let go of old ideas…old ways."

Lily sat back. "Daddy, maybe. But not my mother. She'd likely chase her out with a broom."

Ed topped up their wine. "I'm not so sure, your mother invited her for tea."

"Yes, but she doesn't know she's my child. My bastard child. And what about Victoria, I wonder what she'd think if she knew they were her grandparents?" Lily asked.

Ed placed the bottle on the table. "I'm sure she'd be over the moon."

"Ed, why didn't you ever tell Amour I'm Victoria's mother? I mean, Victoria knows she's adopted, so why not just tell her?"

Ed took a drink. "Well, first of all, I didn't think you wanted me to. Remember, when you first realized Victoria was your daughter, I asked what you planned to do? If memory serves me correct, I believe you told me you didn't want to do anything. You wanted to leave things just as they were."

Lily nodded. "I know. But I was in a bad spot back then...still reeling from everything that happened. Stealing money from Stanley. Getting mixed up with that bastard, Sheppard or McInnes...whatever the hell his name was. Living in a motel with three young kids. I figured Victoria was better off not knowing. But things have changed. I'm in a much better place now, with a good job and a decent roof over my head. I'm just saying, maybe it's time Amour knew."

Ed leaned back and stared at her. "Would you want to know...if you were in her shoes?"

"Yes, I think I would. Actually, I'm sure I would," she said confidently.

"And you'd tell your daughter?"

Lily thought about it for a moment. "Yes, if I thought she was old enough to understand."

Ed puckered his mouth. "You could be right. But, Lily, you never asked me to tell Amour."

Lily nodded. "I know. And I still think it was the right decision at the time. But, like I said, things have changed. I'd like to get to know Victoria. And I'd like for her to get to know me and the kids. And she's met my parents. It's not fair that they don't know they're related. And if Amour's not open to telling her about me, then that would be that. I'd respect her decision."

Ed raised his eyebrows. "And you think I'm the one to tell her?"

"Yes. I mean, who else? Not like I can just call her out of the blue. I think that would be too—

"Threatening," Ed said.

"Yes, threatening. I think she'd want to hear it from someone she trusts."

Ed shrugged. "Funny, I often felt guilty that I knew and she didn't."

"Then you should have told her.""

Ed gave her a puzzled look. "Well, if I had known you wanted me to, I might have. Honestly, I'm not sure. Unlike you, I'm not convinced Amour would want to know. Mabel told me that ever since Michael died, she's become very protective of Victoria. It's understandable, I guess. It's all the family she has. So, if she found out about you, never mind Victoria's grandparents, I think it's only natural she might feel—" He searched for the word.

Lily smiled. "Threatened."

Ed raised his glass. "There's that word again. And, yes, threatened."

Lily looked down into her glass and ran her finger around the rim. "So, it's not just because I didn't ask...you were protecting her?"

Ed took a sip. "Yes, I guess I was."

Lily's eyes filled up. "From me?"

Ed sat up. "No, not from you...from her fears...as the mother of an adopted child. I dunno, maybe I should have told her."

Lily leaned forward. "It's not too late. Ed, I promise I won't interfere," she said in a pleading tone. "I know Amour is Victoria's mother. And I'd never do anything to hurt her or Victoria. But wouldn't it be wonderful if Victoria could meet her brother and sisters? Doesn't she deserve to know them? And I honestly believe Amour would be okay with things. Who knows, she might even be happy about it."

"Maybe," he said, scratching his thumb nail across his forehead. "Let me think about it."

Lily placed her hand on his thigh. "Thank you! Thank you! Thank you!"

Ed reached for the empty wine bottle. "But, for now, enough with all this...this heavy talk. Let's just relax and enjoy our time together." He stood and held up a finger. "I'll be back in a jiffy," he said, dashing off. Lily sat sideways with her legs tucked under her and reached for her glass. She felt giddy, as much from the prospect Victoria might meet her brother and sisters, as from her handsome companion and the sweet-tasting wine. She heard the back door fall shut and wondered what he was doing.

"Ta da!" Ed said, holding up another bottle of wine.

Lily laughed. "Are you trying to get me drunk?"

Ed twisted the corkscrew. "Why not? We need to let our hair down... forget our troubles...have a little fun."

Ed topped up her wine and sat down beside her.

"God, I missed you," Lily said.

Ed smiled. "And I missed you...*and the kids*."

Lily leaned over and removed his thick-rimmed glasses from his shirt pocket. She turned them over in her hands. "I would never have met you, if it weren't for these," she said, opening up the arms and putting them on. She pushed them up on the bridge of her nose.

Ed grinned. "They look good on you. Really good."

Lily laughed and took them off. "They look better on you." She moved closer, got on her knees, and slid the arms over his ears. She smiled and brushed the hair back off his temples. He looked up at her. She stared down intently, then brought her mouth down to his. Ed closed his eyes, fighting the urge to respond. He moved slightly to one side. "Lily," he whispered.

Lily sat back on her heels. "I'm sorry. It must be the wine," she said. "I'm not used to —"

"Really, it's okay. Honestly, I'm flattered. You're a beautiful, smart woman. It's just that—" Ed stood up and walked to the window. He turned and leaned against the sill with his legs stretched out. "Lily, I asked Amour to marry me."

Lily felt the blood drain from her face. She shifted into a sitting position. "I didn't realize it was that serious," she said flatly. She dipped her head. "God, I'm so mortified."

Ed smiled reassuringly. "There's no need to be."

Lily looked up and brushed away a tear. "I just...I had no idea. I hope this doesn't spoil things between us."

Ed knew it would make things awkward. "We won't allow it to."

Lily nodded. "I'm so sorry. I really am happy for you. Congratulations."

He smiled. "You might be jumping the gun. She's hasn't said yes. Not yet, anyway. That's why I'm here. I figured she needed some time to think about it...and I needed a diversion."

"Why didn't you tell me sooner?" Lily asked. "I mean, I would have never—"

"I'm sorry. When we talked on the phone you had just finished telling me you and Henri broke up. I wasn't about to say sorry for your troubles. Oh, and by the way, I'm madly in love and just popped the question. And I wasn't about to say anything at supper, with the kids and Yvonne and Giles here. Be a little embarrassing if Amour turns me down."

Lily smiled. "She's not going to turn you down."

Ed's heart was breaking for his friend. "I wish I had your confidence."

"I only ever met her that once, but I know she's no fool. Trust me, she'll say yes."

"Can I ask you something?" Ed asked.

Lily nodded.

"I thought you and Henri were happy. What happened?"

Lily reached for her wine glass. "I thought we were. Then I realized, he was still married. He was never going to let her go." She took a drink. "I think it would have been easier to compete against another woman than a ghost. His wife was always there. Every minute, of every hour, of every day. I could see it in his eyes." She dangled her glass in the air. "What can I say, she was a saint...irreplaceable. I knew I didn't stand a chance."

Ed stared down at his feet. He looked up at her tear-stained face and swallowed hard. "I'm sorry."

Lily wiped her hand under her eyes. "It's okay. We parted on good terms. And his daughter still looks after the kids when I'm at work. You remember Anne...the girl the bastard tried to rape?"

"Of course."

Lily laughed. "So much for our fun night. But, then again, there *is* a silver lining."

Ed cocked his head. "*Oh*? What's that?"

"In all likelihood, you'll soon be Victoria's stepdad." She smiled. "And nothing could make me happier."

Ed smiled sadly. "Or me," he said, wondering if his happiness, too, would soon fall victim to a saintly ghost.

Monday, June 30

Lily stared at the bedside clock, her mind jumping from her embarrassing attempt to seduce Ed, to lemon meringue dripping down the wall after one of Dan McInnes' jealous rages, to sitting next to her late husband on the bus as he told her he was pissing blood. It was quarter to five and she hadn't slept a wink. "God, what was I thinking," she muttered. Laura kicked her. Lily gently moved her youngest to the other side of the bed, then laid back down. She needed to pee. She got up, slowly opened her door and tiptoed into the living room.

"You're up early," Ed said.

Lily jumped. "Jesus, you scared me," she whispered.

"Couldn't sleep?" he asked.

"Not really. *You*?"

Ed fumbled around in the dark and turned on the lamp. "Slept great," he lied. He reached for his shirt.

Lily squinted into the light. "Sorry, I know the couch isn't very comfortable."

Ed stood and began buttoning his shirt. He wanted to be on the road before Lily got up, knowing the morning light would only bring her embarrassment into sharper focus. "Couch was fine."

"I'll put the kettle on for coffee," Lily said.

Ed smiled. "Not for me. I thought I'd just hit the road. Get a jump on the traffic."

Lily tilted her head. "*Traffic?*" She laughed. "*In Sussex*?"

Ed chuckled. "You're right. But I'm up now. I should get out of your hair...let you get ready for work...get the kids up."

Lily was crestfallen. "You're not going to say goodbye to them? And it's still dark out."

Ed tucked in his shirt and eased his belt through his pant loops. He smiled. "That's why cars have headlights."

"Ed, I'm so sorry about last night. But at least now I know my boundaries. It won't happen again."

He smiled. "Lily, please. No more apologies. There's no need."

Lily was afraid she wouldn't see him again. "I thought we weren't going to let last night change things between us?" she said, her eyes brimming.

Ed realized he was just making matters worse. He walked around the couch and hugged her. "You're right. Of course I'll stay and say goodbye to the kids. Besides, I'll need a good feed to get me all the way to Bathurst."

Lily closed her eyes, rested her head against his chest, and chuckled. "I'm afraid there's not enough food in Sussex for that to happen."

"Mom?" Rory said from the doorway of his bedroom. "What time is it?"

Lily quickly stepped away from Ed. "It's too early for you to be up. Go back to bed." She looked at Ed and smiled. "Normally, I'd have to haul him out of bed."

They cooked breakfast together. Ed buttered a piece of toast. "Lily, I lied to you."

Lily looked puzzled. "*About what?*"

"I didn't sleep a wink all night."

Lily looked down at the stove. "I'm not surprised. I'm sorry, I don't know what got into me. I think it was the—"

"I'm going to tell Amour," he blurted.

Lily's eyes flew open. "*Really?*"

He nodded. "Yes. I should have told her sooner. Victoria deserves to know. And I can't keep something so important from the woman who might be my wife. It wouldn't be right."

Lily hugged him. "Thank you."

"Now, don't get ahead of yourself. She might not like the idea. If she decides not to tell Victoria, you have to honour her wishes and promise that'll be the end of it."

"Absolutely. I promise I won't ever interfere." She gave him a hopeful look. "But I honestly think she'll be okay with everything. I really do."

They ate breakfast together; any lingering awkwardness from the night before, soon lost in Lily's excited chatter about the possibilities of her family finally being made whole. She smiled at Ed. "I don't know what would have become of me if you hadn't come into my life. I'd likely still be back at The Pines with that monster, cleaning toilets, and cooking on a hot plate."

Ed ran his toast around his plate to sop up his egg yolk. "You're a smart lady, you would have found a way out."

Laura walked into the kitchen and climbed on Ed's lap. "Good morning, Nugget. Have a good sleep?" Ed asked.

"Uh-huh." She ran her hand over his stubbly jaw. "Rory said you're gonna be our new daddy."

"Laura!" Lily said, horrified. She quickly lifted her off of Ed's lap, put her down, and lightly tapped her bottom. "Ed's not going to be your daddy. He's mommy's friend, that's all."

Ed smiled at Laura. "Mommy's right, sweetheart. Your mom and I are just friends...best friends."

Lily took her plate to the sink. *Please, please don't cry,* she silently prayed. "Laura, go wake up Rachael." She rinsed the dishes, fighting back tears. "I better get ready for work. Anne will be here in minute," she said, putting her head down and quickly disappearing down the hall.

"So what do you think?" Mark asked Toni.

Toni peeked into the bedroom. "It's...fine," she said unconvincingly.

"Not exactly the ringing endorsement I was hoping for."

"It's just smaller than I thought."

Mark smiled. "It's only temporary...till we get on our feet. A few months, that's all."

Toni ran her hand down his arm. "Of course. It's fine. After all, beggars can't be choosers." She walked into the bedroom and pushed the curtain aside. "Dear Lord," she said, putting her hand over her mouth.

"What is it?" Mark asked, rushing to the window. He threw it open. "Hey, asshole!" he yelled into the alley. "Screw off."

Toni looked at the paint-chipped radiator. "And I thought it was cat piss I was smelling."

John and Luke entered carrying a solid oak table, a discard from Mary Catherine and Sam.

Toni ran her hand over the top. "It's beautiful. I don't know why they'd just give it to us."

"They bought one of those new Formica tables," Luke said.

"Is Alice going to be home this evening?" Toni asked him.

Luke shrugged. "As far as I know." He ducked his head into the kitchen, then turned to Mark. "I think the table's way too big for the kitchen."

Stanley came in and stepped around the clutter of packing boxes and donated furniture. He looked in the kitchen. "The table's too big."

Mark nodded. "So I hear." He scanned the room, feeling overwhelmed with the task at hand. "Thanks, guys. I think Toni and I can take it from here."

Stanley pulled Mark aside and slipped him some cash. "For some groceries and your first month's rent."

Mark looked at the wad of twenties in his hand. "Thanks. I'll pay you back as soon as I can."

Stanley smiled. "You can worry about that once you're settled in. So, I'll see you tomorrow?"

"Eight o'clock sharp," Mark said.

Stanley tucked his wallet in his back pocket. "Make sure of it. The boys need to be in Gabarus by nine-thirty to get the best pick of lumber."

"I'll be there."

"Thank you," Toni hollered. She sat down on the rust-coloured sofa and toppled to one side. "Whoa!" she said, trying to right herself.

Mark helped her to her feet. "I'll put some plywood under that."

Toni took his hand and held it to her belly. "Feel that?"

Mark smiled. "He's kicking up a storm this morning."

Toni chuckled. "You keep saying *he*. It might be a girl. Hope you're not going to be disappointed."

Mark bent down and picked up a box. "Of course not."

"Good. It's just that I hear most men prefer to have a boy...at least for their first. After that, it doesn't seem to matter so much."

Mark walked away, picturing Luke toasting the news he and Toni were going to have a baby. He entered the kitchen, put the box on the counter, and closed his eyes. "I need to get the hell out of here," he mumbled.

Toni came up behind him and placed her hand on his shoulder. "Everything okay?"

Mark fought back tears. "Just tired," he said. He turned quickly. "I'm gonna take a quick run to Bugden's...pick up some plywood to fix the couch."

"*Now*?"

"Why not?" He grabbed his jacket. "Need anything?"

Toni looked at all the taped up boxes that Mabel, Amour, and Mary Catherine had packed up for them. "I'm not sure. I don't even know what we have."

"Okay, then. I won't be long," Mark said, kissing her cheek and rushing out.

Toni stared into the open doorway, listening to Mark's heavy footsteps rapidly descend into the dark alley below. She surveyed their cramped quarters, then knelt down. She was about to open one of the boxes when she felt a sharp pain. She looked down at her swollen belly. "Hey little one, that hurt." There was another sharp pain. Toni stood awkwardly, then suddenly bent over, gasping. "Mark," she called out weakly. "Mark."

Luke entered the store, tidied up the licorice display at the end of the counter, and peeked into the bakery. Alice was crimping a pie. "Hey, hun."

Alice looked up. "Oh, hi. What's going on?"

"I just got back from Mark's. Toni was wondering if you were going to be home this evening. She'd like to come over and meet you."

Alice went back to her crimping. "Not tonight. I've been on my feet all day and there's still no end in sight."

Luke stepped up to his wife's work table. "If I didn't know better, I'd think you were avoiding her. You're gonna have to meet her sometime."

"Not tonight," Alice said firmly.

Luke looked at Mabel and grinned. "You're working my wife too hard."

Mabel greased the tops of her oven-ready loaves and smiled. "After a day of unpacking, I'm betting Toni will be looking forward to putting her feet up and spending a quiet night at home with Mark," she said, hoping to give Alice an out.

Luke reached over Alice's shoulder, picked up a piece of sugar-coated apple, and popped it in his mouth. He licked his fingers. "You're off on Saturday, right?" he asked Alice.

"Yes."

"Great. How about we have a few folks over Friday night? Mark and Toni will be all settled in by then."

Alice had no intention of doing any such thing. "We'll see," she said matter-of-factly.

Matthew charged in and ran to Luke. "There's my boy," Luke said, handing him a piece of the sugared apple. "Where's Victoria?" he asked. Matthew pointed. Luke carried Matthew into the store.

Victoria was holding Liv and talking to John.

"Victoria," Luke said, "keep Friday night open. We're gonna have a party so Toni can get to know everyone. Tell your mom and Ed." He looked at John. "We'll set the counter up as a bar and you can be bartender."

"I have a date," John said.

"So, bring her," Luke said. He turned to Victoria. "And you can take your boyfriend. What's his name again...Kenny?"

Victoria shook her head. "We broke up."

"I'm sorry," Luke said.

"It's okay. We weren't really serious."

Luke laughed and pointed at John sitting on a stool behind the counter. "Unlike Romeo, here. He's head over heels. Aren't ya, bud?"

"Don't listen to him," John said. "He says that about every girl I date."

Mabel joined them in the store. "Victoria, are you feeling okay? You look a little pale."

"*Really*? No, I'm fine," she lied, wondering if Luke was right and John really was in love with Marjorie.

Mabel took Liv from Victoria. "Good, because Alice and I are running behind on the orders and I was hoping to stay for a few more hours. Do you think you can take Liv home for her nap?"

Victoria pointed to the stroller on the step. "I'd love to, but I don't have the car. We walked."

"I'll drive you," John said.

Victoria smiled. "Are you sure?"

John jumped down from his stool. "Absolutely. I was gonna pick Marjorie up at two. I'll just go a little early. Works for the both of us."

Amour couldn't wait to get rid of the suppertime crowd and climb into bed. She couldn't concentrate, twice mixing up her orders. She entered the kitchen, looked at the clock, and plopped down on a chair. "Will this day ever end?"

Rosie looked over her shoulder. "They all do. And if you're lucky, there'll be another one for you to complain about tomorrow. What's eatin at you, anyways?"

"I'm just tired. I haven't been sleeping well."

Rosie put a dollop of cranberry chutney on a plate. "One more Ploughman's Special. It sure is popular."

Amour pictured Ed pulling a spoon out of his mouth and playfully shaking it at her. *You gotta put Myrtle's chutney on your menu. Make it part of a Ploughman's special. Mabel can make some delicious, nutty loaves and you can pick up some really nice, sharp cheeses at The Creamery. Trust me, it'll be a big hit. There'll be so many people lined up for my culinary invention, you'll want to kiss me.*" Amour smiled, thinking of their last night together. Ed had rarely kissed her on the mouth before, and when he did, it was like what you would expect from a parting friend. Saturday's kiss was different. Not overly passionate, but not perfunctory either. It was warm and serious.

"Amour, the ploughman ain't here to deliver the special. Are you gonna serve it, or do ya want me to?" Rosie asked.

Amour sighed wearily and hauled herself to her feet. "Hold your horses, I'm coming."

Rosie held the plate out to her and grinned. "Good thing it's served cold, cause you sure are draggin your arse this evening."

Two hours later, Amour was at the door saying goodnight to the last of her grateful diners. Rosie came up from behind and handed her a glass.

"What's this?" Amour asked.

"Your sleeping aid."

Amour smiled. "Thanks, but I don't drink alone."

"Good thing for me, you don't have to," Rosie said, pointing to an open quart of whiskey.

The two sat at a table by the window and chatted until the bottle of Jack Daniels was down a third. Amour excused herself, went to the foyer, and returned with Michael's portrait. She placed it on the table and started to cry. "He was a wonderful man. You would have loved him."

Rosie nodded. "I saw him in Woolworth's once. He sure was handsome. Was he good in the sack?"

Amour swatted Rosie's arm. "*What?* I can't believe you just asked me that?" She started to laugh. "But, yes. He was very...very attentive. God, I miss the—"

"Sex."

"I was gonna say intimacy...but okay, that too," she said and laughed.

"My Bernie wasn't no Adonis...not by a long shot...but boy oh boy... he sure could make my eyes roll and my toes curl. Sometimes I think it's the guys who get shortchanged in the looks department that take special care to please their women. At least I always thought Bernie did."

Amour squeezed Rosie's hand. "I'm sorry. I know you must miss him."

Rosie nodded. "So, how is Ed in bed?"

Amour choked. *"Rosie!* I'm not sleeping with Ed. *God, what made you think that!*"

Rosie raised a shoulder. "I just assumed. You're a couple aren't ya? And it ain't like you two are virgins, for Pete's sake. Hell, if Ed came knockin on my door, my drawers would be wrapped round my ankles in no time." She smiled at Amour. "Not that I'm gonna try and steal him away from you or anythin."

Amour grinned. "He is a lovely man. Very considerate."

"And funny," Rosie said.

"And smart," Amour added.

"And handsome."

"He is quite good looking, isn't he…in a different sort of way," Amour said.

Rosie raised her glass. "I'd say."

Amour smiled. "He asked me to marry him," she blurted, her fourth glass of whiskey removing whatever inhibitions she had left. Rosie jumped up and let out a whoop. Amour grabbed her arm and pulled her back down. "Shush! I haven't told a soul. Hell, I didn't even give him an answer."

Rosie laughed. "Amour, there's nobody round to hear us. But you're going to say *yes, right?*"

"I'm thinking about it." She looked down at the painting of her late husband and ran her fingers over the frame. "What if we get married and it's not as good as it was with Michael?"

"Maybe it'll be better," Rosie said.

Amour shook her head. "That's not possible. Michael was the love of my life."

"But you love Ed?"

"Yes, I suppose I do. It's only been a couple of days since I last talked to him and I already miss him."

Rosie smiled. "Amour, I'm not an educated woman. And ya can take my advice for what it's worth. But, you should move on. Maybe it won't be as good as it was with Michael, but what if it's half as good. Wouldn't that be better than nothing? You're what, thirty-nine...forty?"

"Forty-two."

Rosie moved Michael's picture out of the way and reached for Amour's hand. "My point is you're beautiful and still young, with a whole lot of livin ahead of you. Don't spend it alone."

Amour brushed away a tear. "I'm not alone. I have Victoria."

"That's not the same and you know it. Besides, Victoria is all grown up. She'll be glommin on to a man of her own before you know it. And look at Judge Kennedy's widow. She adored her husband. Now look at her. She and Ted are as happy as pigs in shit. Don't go denyin yourself a second chance at happiness. You'll regret it. And trust me, regret's not the companion you want to grow old with."

Amour took a sip of her drink. "I'm still going to think on it. And, Rosie, you can't tell a soul. I probably shouldn't have said anything. I didn't even mention anything to Victoria or Mabel."

Rosie pretended to zip her mouth shut. "My lips are sealed." She looked down at Michael's painting. "Amour, memories can warm the heart, but they're a lousy substitute for a warm body to curl up to. Don't let Ed get away. Make more beautiful memories with another wonderful man. I know my Bernie would want that for me. And I'm pretty sure your Michael would want the same for you."

Amour smiled and stood up. "Oops, I'm a little wobbly." She leaned in and hugged the rough-around-the-edges woman she now saw in a whole new light. "Thank you, Rosie. You were just what I needed tonight."

Rosie smiled. "I think it's the other way around. Despite what you might think, I don't have a lot of friends." She laughed. "None to be exact. Tonight, I feel like I made one for life."

Kenny leaned against the three-foot high stone fence, opened his chip bag, and held it in front of Doreen. "Want one?" he asked, glancing at her cleavage.

"No thanks," she said, pointing to the gum in her mouth and waving to a passing car.

"So, wanna take a walk...go to the brook?" Kenny asked.

Doreen looked at him like he had two heads. "I had to walk almost three miles to get here and you want me to walk to the brook?"

"Oh, right," Kenny said, cursing his parents for taking the car from him.

Doreen waved again. "When's your car gonna be fixed, anyway?"

Kenny shrugged. "A cupala days," he lied.

"What's wrong with it?"

Kenny's mind went blank. "Not sure. I think it's the transmitter?"

A car passed and blew the horn. Doreen waved a third time. "*Transmitter*? You mean transmission."

Kenny laughed nervously. "Yeah, transmission."

"That's likely gonna cost ya a small fortune," she said, acknowledging a fourth car that drove past.

"You're really popular," Kenny said.

Doreen took her gum from her mouth, leaned back, and stuck it on the back of the fence. "This is boring. Everybody's shootin the drag but us." She pointed. "Oh look, it's a Hudson. Nice, eh?"

Kenny nodded. "You sure know your cars."

"My brother's a car fanatic...has magazines lying all over the house. He just bought a Chevy Fleetmaster." She stepped forward and waved. "Hey!" A car pulled over on the opposite side of Commercial Street and the driver rolled down his window. "You headin to Bridgeport?" Doreen asked. The driver gave her the thumbs up. Doreen squeezed Kenny's arm. "I think I'm just gonna head home," she said, pointing at the idling car. "That's my cousin. He'll give me a lift. Save us both the long walk."

"But, I don't mind walking—"

Doreen waited for the traffic to pass and looked over her shoulder. "I'll call ya later," she said, and dashed across the street.

Kenny leaned back against the fence. "Fuck," he whispered, thinking he was never gonna get laid. He held the Scotties bag up to his mouth, tilted his head back, and tapped the sides of the crinkly foil pack. He was brushing the salty crumbs off his shirt when Tommy pulled up.

"Get in."

Kenny crumpled up the chip bag and tossed it at the garbage can. "Damn," he said, coming up short. He was about to pick it up when Tommy laid on the horn.

"Get in the goddamn car!"

Kenny jumped in the front seat.

"Where's Doreen?" Tommy asked.

"She got a lift home with her cousin."

"Any luck?"

"Nope. She ain't never gonna go to the brook with me. I need to get myself some wheels. Hey, maybe I can borrow your car some night?"

Tommy laughed and shook his head. "*This baby*? No friggin way. I saw how you drive."

Mark stumbled through the door, felt for the light switch, and flicked it on. Toni was sitting on a dining room chair, staring at him, stone-faced. Mark could tell she had been crying. He dropped his head. "Shit. Sorry. I can see you're pissed."

Toni stood up. "Looks like you're the one who's pissed. I can't believe you left me here alone in this dump…with all this mess…and not a thing to eat. Is that what I'm in for? You tearing off and getting drunk all the time?"

"Of course not," Mark said meekly. "Look, I'm sorry. I was on my way to get the plywood and I ran into a couple of the boys...some old rugby buddies. What can I say, they dragged me off for a few beers and I lost track of time."

"And where did ya get the money to…to fill your belly full of beer?" she asked through clenched teeth.

"The boys picked up the tab," he lied. He looked around at the unpacked boxes. "I thought you woulda been in bed by now," he slurred.

"What bed? You didn't set it up." She placed her hand on her belly. "And I'm in no condition to do it."

"I'll do it now." He stepped forward and tripped over a box. "Sorry."

Toni followed him down the hall and watched from the doorway. Mark was kneeling on the floor with a side rail in his hand. He put it down, picked up a bracket, and looked sheepishly in her direction. "We're gonna have to sleep on the mattress. I don't have the tools to—"

"You mean *I need to sleep on the mattress*. You can sleep on the goddamn couch."

Mark nodded.

Toni angrily wiped away a tear. "I'm spotting."

"*Spotting?* What's spotting?"

"Bleeding."

Mark scrambled to his feet and approached her. He put his hand on her belly. "Is the baby okay?"

Toni angrily pushed his hand away. "I don't know. I hope so."

Mark stared at her belly. "Is it common? I mean, do a lot of women have this…this spotting?"

"I doubt it."

"Is there a lot of blood?" he asked nervously.

"There's enough," Toni said, her anger and worry growing as she put her worst fears into words.

"Should we go to the hospital?"

"For what?" she hissed. "So they can tell me to go home and put my feet up…and charge us a small fortune. I'll see how I am in the morning." She screwed up her face. "Jesus, you stink."

Mark closed his eyes, cursing himself for screwing up again. He got down on his hands and knees, pushing the bed rails and brackets out of the way. He then pulled the mattress away from the wall, letting it fall with a thud. "I'll get you some bed clothes," he said, brushing past her.

"It's the large box…next to the radiator," Toni yelled.

Mark quickly returned. He spread a top sheet over the lumpy mattress. "I'm really sorry, Toni. It won't happen again."

"Don't make promises you can't keep," she said dismissively. She went to the bathroom and sat on the toilet. "Please, God, don't take my baby from me," she whispered, removing her panties. She pulled the wad of toilet paper from between her legs and tilted her head back. "Thank you," she said, blessing herself. She peed, grateful there was no sign of the spotting. She stopped on her way back to the bedroom. Mark was sitting on the couch with his legs stretched out over a box and his jacket spread over him for a blanket.

"Hey, hun?"

"*What?*" she asked harshly.

"I'm sorry."

Toni started down the hall.

"Oh, and Hun?"

Toni sighed. "*What now?*"

"Can you kill the light?"

Toni slapped at the switch and everything went black.

"Thanks. Goodnight."

Toni didn't respond. She felt her way through the clutter in the narrow hallway, entered the bedroom, and shut the door, trying to remember the last time she felt the baby move.

Tuesday, July 1

Amour rolled over and stared at the undisturbed side of the bed. "I miss you," she whispered. She closed her eyes, picturing Michael sleeping on his back, with one arm over his stomach, and one leg on top of the covers. She ran her hand over the crisp, white pillow sham his head would have rested upon. "I hope you understand," she whispered. "You'd like him. He reminds me of you."

Victoria slowly opened Amour's door and stuck her head inside. "Sorry, I hope I didn't wake you?"

Amour propped herself up on one elbow. "No, I've been awake most of the night. What's going on?"

"Just wanted to let you know I won't be home for supper. John's playing softball, so I'll head straight to the field after babysitting. Oh, and we'll likely go to The Grill after the game...grab a bite there."

"John Toth?"

"Yes."

"So, is it a date?" Amour asked, sounding hopeful.

"No, not a date. He just asked if I'd like to come to his game. Said I'd know lots of people. Oh, and I forgot to tell you, Luke's having a party for Mark and his girlfriend on Friday night. He wants you and Ed to come. Anyway, I'm off," she said, pulling the door closed.

"Victoria?" Amour called after her.

Victoria stepped back into the room. "Yes?"

"Oh, never mind. Enjoy the game," she said, deciding she should give Ed her answer before telling Victoria. She smiled, thinking Ed was a man of his word. He said he would give her time to think things over and he did. But she didn't think he was going to stop calling altogether. She was used to hearing from him at least once or twice a day. She sat up, swung her legs over the side of the bed, and reached for her robe. "Well, Mr. Baxter, I guess I'm just gonna have to call you. I hope you're going to like what I have to say." She went downstairs, picked up the phone, and dialled the number. "Hi, Nancy. It's Amour Donnely. Is Ed available? Time off? The farm? Is everything all right? Oh, good. Did he say when he'd be back? *Next Monday,"* Amour said, the surprise obvious in her voice. "No, no. No, that's fine. Yes, you too."

Amour slowly put the receiver back on the cradle. That's so unlike him, she thought. *You'd think he would have at least let me know.* She turned at the sound of the door opening.

Rosie was smiling from ear to ear. "Good morning," she sang. She walked up and leaned into Amour's ear. "Just want ya to know I haven't told a soul. Sleep well?"

Jeanne rested her crutches against the wall and hopped to the chair. "Your young man came by. I had him dig up the garden. I thought you should be there to help supervise when he starts on the window sills. He worked just short of an hour and a half."

"We'll pay him for two hours," Hector said.

"No, we'll pay him for the time he worked. Not a penny more, not a penny less," Jeanne said firmly. "What kind of lesson would that be teaching him. He'll start to think he can get something for nothing. Remember, train up a child in the way he should go and —"

Hector nodded impatiently and twirled his hand in the air. "I know, I know...even when he is old he will not depart from it," he said, completing one of Jeanne's favourite versus from the Bible.

Jeanne pulled her knitting from a bag. "You couldn't have slept well. You seem irritable."

"You would be too…cooped up in here, watching the paint peel. Honestly, why don't you go home. No point in the two of us being miserable."

"Don't be silly. I can do my knitting here, just as well as I can home. What do you think?" she asked, holding up the beginnings of a scarf. "I decided to go with the yellow. Oh, and I called Father O'Handley. He said that asking Victoria to help with Sunday School was a brilliant idea. And of course he's praying for you. He said he'll drop by this evening or tomorrow morning." She looped her yarn around the needle. "This young man, Tipper. He said he lives with his grandmother and his aunt in the row houses at the top of Pitt Street."

"Yes, I know."

She looked up from her knitting. "I don't remember seeing him in church. And he certainly never participated in Catechism. I would have remembered him with that red hair."

Hector sighed and pushed his bed clothes down. "What difference does it make? He's digging up the garden, not hearing confession."

Jeanne's hands fell to her lap. "*What is wrong with you*? I'm just making conversation, that's all. And you…you snap at me for no reason whatsoever. I know you're not happy being stuck in here, but there's no need to bite my head off."

A nurse walked in and placed Hector's breakfast on his bedside table. "Good morning," she said, smiling. Hector looked at the two boiled eggs sitting in the white bowl. He picked one up. "It's as cold as ice."

Jeanne stood and took it from him. She cracked it against the side of the bowl and began peeling it. "You've had them cold before and I don't remember you complaining." She smiled at the nurse. "I'm sorry to bother you, dear, but is there any chance you might get me a cup of tea…two teaspoons of sugar with a splash of milk? Oh, and if there's a spare biscuit or scone lying about…with maybe some strawberry jam?" She pointed to her foot. "I hurt my ankle and my drive came for me before I had a chance to have my breakfast."

Mark's head fell forward. He opened his eyes. Someone was knocking on the door. He sat up, his neck stiff from his uncomfortable night on the couch. He tossed his jacket aside and walked barefoot to the door. "Coming," he said, slowly opening the door. "Mr. Bruffatto?"

Mark's landlord was dangling a pair of keys in front of him. "Thought you could use an extra set of keys."

"Great. Thanks."

"I also thought this would be a good time to settle up on the rent."

"Oh, yeah. Come on in. Sorry about the mess. We're still trying to get settled in." Mark picked up his jacket, feeling for his billfold. "Fifty-five, right?"

"Yeah, that's right. Sixty-five starting in September…to cover the cost of heat."

Mark fingered through the bills. Shit, he thought, remembering slapping a twenty on the bar saying the beers were on him. He pulled out the required amount and flipped his wallet shut. "Here you go."

"Thanks," Mr. Bruffatto said, stepping into the hall and waving his rent money in the air. "Love when my tenants pay on time. Keep it up. Oh, and I apologize for coming by so early."

Mark was about to close the door, then pulled it back. "What time is it, anyway?"

Mr. Bruffatto looked at his watch. "Ten to eight."

"Jesus!" Mark said. "Sorry, I'm running late." He closed the door and quickly gathered his socks off the floor.

Toni came out of the bedroom.

"I slept in," Mark said urgently, struggling to get his second sock on. He quickly removed five dollars from his wallet and threw it on top of a box. "You're gonna have to go downstairs to the Co-op and get some groceries. Tell them we live upstairs and ask if they'll let us open an account. Fuck! I told Stanley I'd be there at eight o'clock sharp. The guys will be waiting for me." He jumped up, roughly tucked in his shirt, walked into his shoes, and shuffled toward the door.

"Mark!"

He spun around. "*What?*" he barked.

"I need to go to the hospital. I'm bleeding…a lot."

Stanley was fuming. He gave Mark a job, found him an apartment, and floated him the cash needed to get on his feet, and yet he couldn't even make it to work on time. He looked at his watch. "To hell with this," he said, waving for Dirty Willie to come to the truck. "Jump in. You're going with Fred and Harley." He leaned into the driver's window. "Sorry, guys. I was sure he'd be here by now."

Dirty Willie climbed in next to Harley and leaned forward. "He's hung over."

"Why do you say that?" Stanley asked.

"Saw him at The Pithead."

"Last night?" Stanley asked.

Dirty Willie laughed and elbowed Harley. "Yeah...he had a pretty good bunt on. Bought me a cupala beers."

Stanley shook his head. "You guys might as well get going." He stepped back. "Drive carefully." He waited for them to pull out, then headed up Commercial Street, turning down the dark alley between the Co-op and Woolworth's, and walking up the rickety wooden stairs to the second floor apartment. He knocked and waited, then knocked again. He turned the knob and pushed the door forward. The room was just as it was the day before, with the kitchen table and chairs in the middle of the living room, and packing boxes strewn about, most still unopened. "Mark, you here? Toni?" He began moving boxes to clear a path down the hall to the kitchen when Luke entered.

"I saw you on Commercial Street. Figured you might be heading here."

"Where the hell is your brother?" Stanley snapped.

"He called me from the hospital. Toni had some cramping and bleeding."

"Jesus!" Stanley said, immediately regretting his angry tone.

"Mark tried calling you at the office but there was no answer. He asked me to track you down. Said he hoped you'd understood why he wasn't at work."

"Of course," Stanley said. "Is the baby okay?"

Luke grimaced. "Doesn't look good."

"Christ! What about Toni?"

Luke shrugged. "I'm not sure, but I get the sense they're mostly concerned about the baby. Oh, and I dropped Mabel off at the hospital on my way here. She said she'd call you later if she needs a drive home." He looked around at the mess. "Doesn't look like they made much progress."

Stanley tilted a box to read the writing on the side. "Do you need to get back to the store?"

Luke shook his head. "No, Corliss and John are there."

"Good," Stanley said, tossing the box at him. "This goes in the bathroom."

Mabel reached down and squeezed Mark's hand. "How are you doing?"

He leaned back in his chair and looked up at the ceiling. "I should have taken her to the hospital last night. I wanted to, but she said there was no point."

"Don't go blaming yourself. Sometimes these things happen and there's nothing you or anybody else can do…not even the doctors."

Mark stood when he noticed the young nurse approach. He could tell the news was bleak. She smiled sadly and shook her head. "Mr. Toth, I'm so sorry. The baby didn't make it."

Mark sat down heavily. "What about my girlfriend?"

"She lost a lot of blood, but she'll be fine. We gave her a sedative, so she's sleeping at the moment. Obviously, she'll need lots of support when she wakes up…both physically and emotionally. In the meantime, if you want to go home…collect your thoughts…grab a bite to eat, I can call when she wakes up. It'll likely be a few hours."

"I don't have a phone," Mark said, fighting back tears.

Mabel rubbed his back. "She can call me and I'll come get you."

Mark slowly got to his feet. "What happens to the baby? I mean is there a—"

The nurse smiled. "The hospital will see to everything."

Mark wiped his eyes. "Can you tell me…was it a boy or a girl?"

The nurse looked at Mabel, then back at Mark. She touched his arm, "A boy. I know it's hard, but you're still young. You wait, you'll be a father before you know it." She smiled at Mabel. "I'll leave you two alone. Don't forget to leave your number at the nurses' station."

Mark tilted his head back and brought his fist to his mouth, struggling to keep from breaking down.

Mabel hugged him. "It's okay. Let it go."

"I'm being punished," he cried.

"*Punished?* What are you talking about? Mark, it's not uncommon for complications to—"

Mark stepped back. "You know damn well what I'm talking about," he angrily spat. He ran his sleeve under his nose and looked down the hall. "I need some air," he said, turning, and quickly walking away.

"Mark, I'll come with you!"

He held his arm up to keep her from going on. "No! I need some time alone," he yelled, bursting through the heavy double doors leading to the exit. A startled orderly jumped out of the way. "Hey, buddy, what's your hurry! Slow down, ya friggin jerk."

"Hey, old man, how's it goin?"

Hector smiled and sat up. "Well, this is a surprise. What are you doing here?"

Tipper nodded down the hall. "Gran has an appointment. Figured I might as well tag along...keep on the good side of my boss. Your old lady's not here?"

Hector smiled. "You just missed her. How did you two hit it off?"

"She thinks I'm gonna steal ya blind. She don't take her eyes off me. But ain't no big deal."

"Come, have a seat," Hector said.

Tipper sat down. "So, how long ya gonna be cooped up in here?"

"A few more days. Then, I'm on bed rest for a while."

Tipper nodded. "So, I dug up yer garden. You'll be happy to hear I didn't find a single body."

Hector laughed and pointed. "Pass me my wallet. Top drawer."

"I'm not lookin for my money or nothin. Just makin conversation, that's all."

"Pass me my wallet," Hector repeated.

Tipper opened the drawer and handed it to him.

Hector removed a two dollar bill and passed it to his young friend. He pointed his finger at him. "And not a word to Jeanne."

"But ya only owe me seventy-five cents."

"Think of it as an advance."

Tipper shoved the bill in his pocket. "So, what's next on the list?"

"The foundation needs scraping. Scraper is in the shed. You'll have to root around, it's a bit of a mess in there."

Tipper put his feet up on the bed rail. "I'll find it."

They were arguing over who was the best outfielder, DiMaggio or Musial, when a nurse and an elderly woman stopped in the doorway. The nurse patted the older woman's arm. "There, you're all set," she said, disappearing down the hall.

Tipper spun around. "Hey, Gran. All done?"

"All done."

Tipper stood and leaned into Hector's ear. "It's my gran. She don't see so well," he whispered.

"But I hear just fine," she playfully scolded.

"Gran, this is my boss, Mr. MacDonald."

"Hello," she said, staring straight ahead.

Hector smiled and waved, before realizing his welcoming gesture went unnoticed. "Nice to meet you."

"Thanks for hiring my grandson. You got yourself a good worker. He's a real good boy."

Hector smiled at Tipper. "I have no doubt of that. I'm sure he'll work out just fine."

"All the same, if he gives you any trouble, let me know."

"You can count on it."

Tipper walked up to his grandmother's side. "Okay, Gran, let's get you outta here." He turned to Hector. "Take care, boss." He led his grandmother away, then quickly popped his head back in the doorway. "DiMaggio, all the way!"

Hector chuckled. "Musial!" He adjusted his pillow and laid his head back, wondering if he still had his old baseball mitt, or, if like so many other childhood treasures, it simply vanished; discarded without hardly a thought of the joy it once brought. I'll get Tipper to check the shed, he thought. He closed his eyes, his mind soon occupied by a jumble of foggy images. *He was standing on the shore. The waters were calm and the sun bright. He felt something touch his wrist and looked down. A small child was reaching up, her tiny fingers searching for his hand.* He opened his eyes. Charlotte was holding his wrist and smiling. "Sorry to wake you. Just checking your pulse."

Amour kicked off her shoes and crawled on top of the bed, grateful for a chance to nap before the suppertime rush came through the door. Despite the room being warm, she reached for the quilt at the foot of the bed, spreading it over her feet and bringing it up over her shoulder. Unlike Michael, who would kick the covers off, she needed the weight of a blanket to help her sleep. She closed her eyes, thinking she had no idea what Ed preferred. She rolled over to face the open window. *Why did you go back to Bathurst without telling me? And why haven't you called? It's not like you. And what did Nancy mean when she said you needed to clear your head? From what? Do you think you jumped the gun, made a big mistake?* She rolled back to face the door. *Funny, this time yesterday I wasn't sure I was ready to get married, now I'm worried I won't have the chance.*

The phone rang. Amour threw the covers back, opened the door, and stepped into the hall. Rosie was confirming a reservation. Amour returned to bed, thinking about Rosie's reaction to news of Ed's proposal. *I had too much to drink. I should never have told her. But then, she was so happy that I confided in her.* She pictured Rosie smiling and saying she had made a friend for life. *She can be loud and inappropriate, but she's also a good soul with a big heart. I need to make more of an effort to include her in things, maybe invite her to club.* Amour thought back to the opening of the manor. Rosie was there as a guest, but quickly offered to help when she knew the kitchen couldn't keep up with demand. It was the same day as the accident at Twenty-Six, the same day Rosie became a widow. Amour pulled the quilt up over her head. *Goddamn mine, left us both widows.*

The phone rang again. *If it was Ed, Rosie would come and get me.* She was almost a sleep when she heard the light knock on the door. "Amour. Amour, you awake?" Rosie whispered

"Yes."

Rosie opened the door. "You're wanted on the phone."

"Is it Ed?"

"No, it's Mabel."

Amour pulled the quilt off of her head. "Tell her I'll call back later."

Rosie nodded. "Okay." She walked to the window and pulled the drapes closed. "You'll never get to sleep with all that light pouring in. Can I get ya anything?"

"No."

"All right then. And don't worry about anythin downstairs. Me and Sandra got everythin under control."

"Thank you," Amour yawned. "I'm exhausted. Wake me in an hour," she mumbled.

"Will do. Nighty night," Rosie whispered, pulling the door shut.

Mark stood in the open doorway and dropped his head. The kitchen table was pushed against the far wall with a few unopened boxes tucked underneath, but otherwise the room was free of its clutter. He walked down the hall and peeked in the bedroom. The bed was put together. He entered and flopped down on the mattress. *You'll be a father soon*, the nurse had said. "Fuck!" he screamed. He jumped up and kicked a box, knocking a lamp on the floor and shattering its glass shade. "Goddammit!" He walked into the kitchen, opening and noisily slamming cupboard doors. "Fuck, Luke! Are ya trying to make me feel worse than I already do! Fuck it, I give up!" he said, storming out and bounding down the back steps.

He was sitting alone at a corner table in The Pithead, his choice of drink no longer the frothy ale he liberally consumed the night before, but the double whiskeys he knew would more quickly dispatch his sorrow, anger, and quilt. He watched the regulars he generously treated the night before make their way toward him. "Fuck off," he said, sending them back to their table. He closed his eyes and put his head down. The image of Alice lying on the floor as he climbed on top of her flashed before his eyes. He made a fist and brought it down on the bar. He felt a hand on his back and looked up. Stanley pulled a stool over and sat down beside him.

"What are you doin here?" Mark slurred.

"You weren't at the hospital, or the apartment, so I took a guess."

"Can I buy ya a drink…with yer own money?" Mark asked.

Stanley smiled. "I'm good."

Mark laughed. "Well, I don't know why the fuck you're here. This is where ya come to have a drink…get drunk…drown your sorrows." He picked up his glass and drained it. "Don't seem to be working too good."

Stanley grabbed Mark's arm. "C'mon. I'll take you home."

Mark yanked his arm free. "I ain't goin nowhere."

Stanley stood up. "Look, I know you're upset. No one blames you for that, but it's time to go home. Mabel made you supper."

Mark made a face. "Of course she did. *Miss Goody Two Shoes.* Fuck Mabel!"

"That's enough!" Stanley said harshly.

"No, it's not!" Mark yelled. "Fuck her. Bitch knew I was Matthew's father. But…nooo…she didn't think I deserved to know." He punched his chest. "I'm the kid's father. Me. Fuck her! I had to drag it outta her. Some friend. She never liked me. Always fawned over Luke and John. She never gave a shit about me," he whispered loudly.

Stanley clenched his teeth. "Given the circumstances, I'm gonna let that pass. Now get up."

Mark shoved him. "Fuck you, too. And stick yer lousy job up yer scrawny arse."

The bartender approached. "Might as well go home, bud," he said to Mark. "You're not getting anything more here."

Mark swept his arm across the bar, knocking a glass to the floor. "Place is a shit hole anyway." He pushed Stanley out of the way and stumbled between the tables to the door.

"Don't come back," the bartender yelled. He looked at Stanley. "Bastard owes me thirteen bucks."

Stanley reached in his wallet and handed him two tens. "And bring me a Johnnie Walker. Make it a double."

Amour woke with a start. She looked at the clock on her bedside table, momentarily confused by the time. "Seven-ten," she mumbled, quickly tossing the covers aside. She got up, walked into the hall, and headed downstairs. She stopped mid-way down. Rosie pointed up at her. "There's the lady of the manor, now."

"I was just telling Rosie that was the best lamb I've had in years," one of the guests said.

Amour smiled. "Then I hope you'll come back?"

"Absolutely." He laughed. "If not for the lamb, for the entertainment."

"*Oh?*" Amour said, looking surprised.

"Ain't too bah…bah…bah bad, is it?" Rosie said, laughing at her own joke. She opened the door. "See ya later, guys. Next time you come back, I'll have some new material." She grinned at Amour. "Another happy customer."

"Rosie, I told you to wake me in an hour. It's after seven."

"Didn't have the heart. You were out like a light, drooling and snoring like a snot-nosed baby. Figured you needed the sleep. Besides, me and Sandra took care of everythin. Sandra handled the kitchen and I waited the tables. It was fun. Forgot how much I missed it. Oh, and Mabel called again. I told her you were still in bed. She said not to disturb you."

Amour ducked her head in the dining room. Only two of ten tables were occupied. "Did we have a good night?" she asked.

"Great night. We had a full house up till an hour ago."

Amour nodded. "Thanks for filling in. You can go back to the kitchen and help Sandra clean up. I'll take it from here."

"Did I do something wrong?" Rosie asked.

Amour shook her head. "No," she said, picking up the phone. "I'll be in in a minute, I'm just going to give Mabel a quick call." She watched Rosie walk into the dining room, then began dialling. "Hi. Rosie said you called. Yes, I hadn't been sleeping well. No, it's nothing. What? When? Dear God. How is she? And Mark? God love them. What can I do? Yes, I suppose so. Thanks for letting me know. Good night." Amour hung up and listened to a conversation coming from the coat room.

"At least the food was good. And you can't beat the view. But, I agree, we'll go somewhere else for your birthday."

"You couldn't pay me to come back. Honey, you know I'm no prude. I can take a joke as well as anyone else, but that woman…she's so crude. And that mouth of hers…just filthy." She lowered her voice to a whisper. "What were the owners thinking…hiring the likes of her?"

Amour forced a smile when they entered the foyer. "Have a nice evening," she said, thinking she'd have to remind Rosie that she was no longer behind the counter at Woolworth's.

The husband nodded and quickly ushered his wife out the door. "Goodnight."

Amour was about to enter the dining room when Victoria came in. "How was the ball game?"

"Okay. Any leftovers?"

Amour thought Victoria might have been crying. "I thought you were going to The Grill with your friends?"

"Changed my mind. I guess you heard Mark's girlfriend lost the baby?"

"Yes, I just got off the phone with Mabel. Terrible. Are you all right?"

Victoria shrugged. "John barely spoke to me."

Amour smiled sympathetically. "You did say it wasn't a date."

"I know. It's just…" Victoria shrugged, "I dunno, I miss the way things were. You know what I mean?"

Amour hugged her. "Yes, honey. I know exactly what you mean."

Stanley looked over his shoulder. "Who was that on the phone?"

Mabel sat beside him on the step, her hands wrapped around her teacup. "Amour. I told her about Toni."

"I'm worried about Mark," he said, telling her about their conversation at the Pithead. "The kid's angry."

"It's understandable," Mabel said. "It's like he's lost a second son."

Stanley leaned back on his elbows. "He's not too happy with you. Said he had to drag the truth out of you."

Mabel blew on her tea. "Well it's true, isn't it?"

"I guess. And he told me to shove my lousy job up my arse. Sometimes, I wanna take him by the collar and shake the living daylights out of him."

"It was just the liquor talking," Mabel said. "He's likely gonna wake up with a big head and a ton of regret."

Stanley stretched out his legs. "I doubt he'll remember a thing."

"Maybe not. But there's no point in throwing it back in his face. He's going through a lot. We need to bite our tongues and be patient." She shivered. "It's getting chilly," she said, putting her tea down. She went inside and came back with a blanket wrapped around her.

"I remember being more sad than angry when we lost Gregory," Stanley said.

Mabel smiled. "That was different. We had JC and Mary Margaret to blunt the pain."

Stanley nodded. "I wonder if he and Toni will ever get married."

Mabel thought of Toni curled up in her hospital bed, crying. "Toni's afraid Mark doesn't want to be with her now that she lost the baby. I feel so bad for her...losing a child she carried for five months, and now, lying in a hospital bed in a strange town with no family around to support her. And Mark, well what can I say. I kept telling Toni he was going to come through the door any minute, but, no, he was off getting drunk."

Stanley sat up. "I don't know about you, but I have a sinking feeling there's going to be more than one broken heart before all this is over."

Mabel moved closer to him, raised her arm, and draped her blanket over his shoulder. "I know. Me, too."

Wednesday, July 2

Mark woke face down on the bed with a sharp pain across his forehead and a foul taste in his mouth. He pushed himself up and looked down at the wet stain on the blanket. "Fuck," he said. He got to his feet, stripped from the waist down, and tossed his wet pants and underwear in the corner. He threw his suitcase on the bed and flipped it open. Toni was going to be furious, he thought. And who could blame her. He could vaguely remember seeing Stanley at The Pithead, but not how he got home. He grabbed a clean pair of boxers and a pair of pants, and walked into the living room. The door to the apartment was wide open. "Christ!" He covered his privates, kicked the door shut, then dashed to the bathroom. He began filling the soap-stained tub, and unzipped his shaving kit; dumping its contents onto the counter. His hand shook as he reached for the bottle of Bufferin. He unscrewed the cap, shook four of the bitter-tasting pills onto his palm, and popped them in his mouth. He started to chew. "Fuck!" he said, gagging from the awful-tasting gritty powder coating his tongue. He quickly turned on the tap, cupped his hands, and sucked up a mouthful of ice cold water. He tossed his head back and suddenly remembered shoving Stanley. "Fuck! What the hell did I do?"he mumbled, climbing into the tub and leaning back. "Oh, no," he said, punching the steamy water. He put his head down and wept.

"Mark! Hey, Mark!"

Mark suddenly sat up and ran his hand down his face. "Yeah?"

"You okay?" Luke asked.

"Yeah, I'm in the tub."

"I thought we'd grab some breakfast at Woolworth's. My treat."

Mark cleared his throat. "Give me a minute," he yelled, climbing out of the tepid water. He quickly dried himself off and wrapped a towel around his waist. He opened the door, surprised to see Matthew jumping on the couch.

Luke grinned. "Not like he's going to ruin the springs."

Mark ran a hand towel over his wet hair. "There are none. I'll just be a sec." He entered the bedroom and sat down heavily on the bed. "God forgive me...give me strength," he whispered.

"Mark! What's keeping you? Your nephew wants his pancakes."

Mabel walked down the hall carrying a small overnight bag. She smiled when she saw Charlotte come out of Toni's room. "How is she?" she whispered.

Charlotte scrunched up her nose. "Not great. She didn't get much sleep. Cried most of the night. I'm going to speak to the doctor about prescribing something to get her through the next few days."

Mabel nodded. "Has Mark been by?"

Charlotte shook her head. "No. Hard enough to lose a child, but then to have to do it alone while the father's off God knows where. I could strangle him."

Mabel thought back to the day she and a stranger helped Charlotte up the hospital steps. Blood was running down Charlotte's legs, saturating her white canvass shoes. "I'm glad Toni has you to help her get through this."

Charlotte smiled. "I'm glad she has *you*." She touched Mabel's arm. "You and Stanley will have to come over for supper some evening. Hopefully, we can find a time when Ed and Amour are free. Gordon loves barbecuing."

"I'd love that. I haven't seen the baby in months."

Charlotte smiled. "She's growing like a weed. Just like Liv, no doubt." She looked over Mabel's shoulder. Jeanne MacDonald was slowly walking up the hall. "Let's make sure we get together. Anyway, I better get moving. Good luck."

Mabel pushed the door open. Toni was curled up on her side, holding a tissue to her mouth. She looked at Mabel and closed her eyes.

"Are you up for a visit?" Mabel asked. Toni nodded. Mabel put the small suitcase on the floor. "I brought you a few things. A night dress… some hand cream. Just some things I thought might come in handy."

"Thank you."

"I was speaking with Charlotte…your nurse. She said you had a rough night." Toni sat up. "She's going to talk to the doctor…see if he'll give you something to help you sleep. Your body needs the —"

"Have you seen Mark?" Toni blurted.

Mabel shook her head. "No." She paused. "But Stanley was talking to him."

"Was he at the apartment?"

Mabel looked away, unsure of what to say. "Toni, Mark is having a hard—"

"He was at the tavern, wasn't he?" she said, tearing her Kleenex into tiny pieces.

Mabel nodded. "Toni, give him time. He needed a bit of a—"

"He needed an excuse," Toni said sadly. "He'd rather be anywhere than with me. And we both know how much he loves his liquor." She looked down at the small mound of shredded tissue on her lap. "At least I know where I stand." Her eyes filled up. "I can still get out while I have a chance. Nothing to keep me here, now." She looked up. "Maybe...maybe it's a good thing I don't…" Her lower lip began to tremble. "I don't have a baby to…to care for," she said, her breath catching between sobs.

Mabel hugged her. "Toni, your emotions are raw right now. In a while, you'll start to see things in a different light. Mark is grieving, too. And everybody grieves differently. He'll come around, you'll see," she said, praying she was right.

Toni leaned back against her pillow and stared toward the door.

Mabel turned around. Mark was standing in the doorway, looking sheepish. Mabel touched Toni's hand. "I'll come back another time," she said. She stopped on her way out and hugged Mark. "Be good to her," she whispered.

Jeanne walked in smiling and sat down.

"Where are your crutches?" Hector asked.

"Don't need them anymore." She looked down at her foot. "I strapped it up. How was your night?"

"Let's just say I'm anxious to sleep in my own bed."

"Well, looks like you're gonna get your wish," Charlotte said, putting a pill bottle on Hector's bedside table. "I just spoke to Dr. MacLellan and he said there's nothing more we can do for you here that your wife can't do for you at home." She smiled at Jeanne. "I'm sure you'll be glad to have him back home."

"Of course."

"When?" Hector asked.

"As soon as I give you your marching orders."

Hector was about to get out of bed when Charlotte put her hand on his arm. "Not so fast. First I need to go over your diet," she said, sharing the list of dos and don'ts. "So there you have it. Cut down on your fat and sugar intake, take your medication at the same time every morning before breakfast, and remember, bed rest for the next two weeks. If you have any questions or concerns, just give Dr. MacLellan a call."

"What about stairs?" Jeanne asked.

"Not for a while."

Jeanne looked at her husband. "You'll have to stay in the bedroom."

"You can't be coming up and down stairs with that foot of yours," Hector said. "I'll sleep on the couch."

"But the bathroom is upstairs," Jeanne protested.

"There's an old chamber pot in the basement. That'll do just fine."

"He's lucky to have you," Charlotte said. She helped Jeanne gather up Hector's things and walked them down the hall. She stopped at the nurses' station. "I'll say goodbye here. Good luck. And don't forget, Mr. MacDonald, listen to your wife. She's a smart lady. Do as she says and you'll get to spend lots more time with those four beautiful grandchildren of yours."

Hector kept walking toward the exit. Jeanne looped her arm around her husband's and pulled him into her. "What did you say to her?" she hissed.

"It's nothing, Jeanne. Let's just go home."

Jeanne pulled her arm free and stopped in her tracks. "What do you mean, it's nothing? What did you tell her?" she demanded.

Hector wanted to run back to his hospital bed and put the pillow over his head. He turned and looked at her; her shoulders squared and her mouth puckered in anger. "The truth, Jeanne. I told her the truth."

"Hello!"

"In here," Mabel hollered.

Amour placed a box on the kitchen table.

"What's this?" Mabel asked, flipping the lid back.

"Just some clothes Victoria and I packed up for Toni. We're hoping Stanley can drop them off."

Mabel removed a sweater and held it up. "This is lovely. It looks like it's never been worn."

"I only wore it once. I bought it in Boston." She shivered. "Reminds me of Roddy."

Mabel nodded and removed a flowered blouse. "I should have asked for first dibs."

"If there's anything you—"

"I'm kidding. I'm sure Toni will be delighted. *Tea*?"

Amour nodded. "How is she?"

Mabel shared her concerns about Toni and Mark. "I'm not sure they have a future together. Mark still has some growing up to do." She looked at her friend. "You seem distracted?"

Amour smiled. "I am, a little," she said, telling Mabel that Ed had left for the farm without telling her and that she hadn't heard from him in four days.

Mabel poured their tea. "That doesn't sound like Ed. Did he mention anything was troubling him?"

"Not exactly," Amour said.

Mabel put the teapot back on the stove and chuckled. "*Not exactly? What does that mean?*"

Amour grinned. "He proposed."

"Proposed!" Mabel screamed. "When?"

"Saturday."

Mabel grabbed her hand, looking for a ring. "And you're just telling me now!"

Amour pulled her hand back. "There's no ring."

Mabel's shoulders fell. "Why not?"

"It just happened so suddenly...when we were driving home after having supper with Gordon and Charlotte. He didn't plan on asking me, it just came out of the blue. And it's just as well he didn't have a ring. I didn't give him an answer."

Mabel's eyes widened. "Why not?"

"I don't know. Honestly, I've been all over the map. This morning I woke up and I was worried he had a change of heart. Right now...I dunno...I'm not so sure. There's no question I miss him, but, truth be told, I'm a little ticked off. He promised he wouldn't pressure me, but that's exactly what he's doing...disappearing without a word. It's like he's provoking me...punishing me for not immediately saying yes."

"Amour, you know that's not the case. Ed wouldn't do that. He's just giving you some space...time to think."

"So why did he just up and leave...not even call? Damn, I'm such a wreck. And then there's Michael. My head tells me he'd be happy, yet I can't help it...I feel guilty just thinking about it. Oh, hell, I don't know what to think."

Mabel sat across from her. "Maybe you're thinking too much. It's not unusual to have doubts. We all do."

Amour looked surprised. "*Really?* I didn't...not when Michael proposed."

Mabel closed her eyes and nodded. "Still, given the circumstances it's only natural you would—"

JC charged through the back door, followed by Mary Margaret and Myrtle.

"Slow down!" Mabel hollered.

"Myrtle, why are you back wearing that godawful toque?" Amour asked.

"Cause my wig's coming undone. Doesn't fit right anymore."

Amour laughed. "You got lots of money, buy yourself a new one."

"Why? I'm not goin anywhere special."

"But you might," Amour said.

"Why, you getting married or something?"

Harley tapped on the door jamb.

Stanley looked up from his paperwork. "What's up?"

"Some guy is here to see you."

"Tell him to come in."

Mark appeared in the doorway, looking chastened. "Luke tells me I owe you an apology."

Stanley sat back and pointed. "Sit down."

Mark pulled a chair over. "I guess I said some pretty horrible things. I'm sorry, I was drunk and honestly don't remember a thing. I didn't mean any of it. It was just the booze talking," he said, sitting down.

"How's Toni?" Stanley asked.

"Sad about losing the baby. Pissed at me. Can't really blame her. I fucked up."

"Yeah, you did."

"I'm sorry."

Stanley gave him a skeptical look. "You've got a lot of anger in you and the liquor doesn't help. But, under the circumstances, I might have gone on a bender myself."

Mark nodded. "So, do I still have a job?"

"That depends."

"On what?" Mark asked meekly.

"On if you stay on the straight and narrow... show up for work on time...no booze through the week." Stanley pointed his finger in Mark's face. "And you never again call my wife a bitch."

Mark dropped his head. "You know I love Mabel. I have no idea what possessed me—"

Stanley held his hand up to keep Mark from going on. "Oh, and The Y is looking for someone to work with a couple of the younger boxers. Nothing serious…hold the punching bag…a little sparring."

Mark hunched his shoulders. "I don't know anything about boxing."

Stanley leaned forward. "But you can fight, can't you? Or was that just all talk…you cleaning the clocks of all those rowdy patrons at the Seahorse?"

Mark smiled. "I can hold my own."

Stanley nodded. "Good."

Mark shrugged. "But fighting is a lot different than boxing."

"You'll learn," Stanley said. He pulled a notepad from his desk drawer and scrawled down a number. He ripped the page free and handed it to Mark. "Call Mackie. He'll show you the ropes."

Mark took the paper. "I don't have a phone."

Stanley got to his feet. "Then stop by The Y on your way home."

"Thanks. And thanks for putting the apartment in order. I appreciate it." Mark stood and started for the door. He turned back. "Oh, I almost forgot, when do you want me to start work?"

"First thing's first. Get Toni home and settled in, then we'll talk."

Mabel threw her robe over the chair, pulled the covers back, and smiled at Stanley. "I have some wonderful news."

"I thought you were bursting at the seams." He put his hand behind his head. "What's up?"

Mabel crawled in beside him. "Ed proposed," she said, grinning from ear to ear.

Stanley's eyes widened. "I hope you told him you were married."

Mabel laughed. "Well, if I wasn't, he'd certainly be on my list."

Stanley gasped. "*You have a list*?"

Mabel curled up next to him and rested her hand on his stomach. "A short one."

"Who else is on that list?"

Mabel lightly slapped his stomach. "I hope she says yes."

Stanley looked surprised. "She hasn't given him an answer?"

"No."

"Why not?" Stanley asked.

Mabel shared her brief conversation with Amour, telling him not to mention it to anyone. "So, how was your day?"

"Mark came by. He was pretty contrite. We had a good chat. Anyway, he agreed to lay off the booze and to help Mackie train some of the younger boxers."

Mabel lifter her head off of Stanley's shoulder and looked up at him. "Didn't Mackie ask you to help out?"

"Yes."

"Perfect, you and Mark can do it together. It will be good for the both of you. Mark could use your guidance and you could use the exercise."

"Not going to happen," Stanley said with authority.

"How come?"

Stanley pulled his arm from under her head. "I haven't stepped foot in a ring in years. And I'm not about to now. Besides, I'm busy enough with work." He kissed her forehead and turned off the lamp. "Goodnight."

Mabel knew the guilt that ate at Stanley after he accidentally left Willie Morrison brain damaged continued to have as much of a hold on him on this night as it did on the night it happened, over twenty years ago. She rolled onto her back, thinking nobody seemed to escape the grip of guilt. *Me, Stanley, Alice, Lily, Mark and now, Amour, whose only fault was falling in love for a second time.* She closed her eyes and smiled, thinking about Ed. He didn't look anything like Michael, but in many ways he reminded her of him. *Amour loves, Ed. I'm sure of it. It would be a shame if she turned him down because she felt she was being disloyal to Michael.* She turned her head and looked at Stanley, sleeping on his side. *And what would I do if something happened to you. I couldn't possibly love anyone as much as I do you.* She kissed her finger tips and touched the back of his head. "Don't you ever die on me," she whispered. She rolled over and pulled the covers up, thinking about Mark, his anger and his drinking. *It must be agonizing playing uncle to your son and living with the guilt of betraying your brother.* She looked at the clock. It was after ten. *Maybe I should have told Alice that you know you're Matthew's father.* She was still awake at five o'clock; her own guilt, and fear of what was still to come, denying her any sleep.

Stanley sat up, surprised to see her awake. "It's early. Go back to sleep."

"If only that was possible," Mabel said, pulling the covers up over her head.

Three Days Later

Sunday, July 6

"Hi, Ed. Yes, we just got back. Mom wanted to go to the late mass. She's upstairs. Oh, just a sec, there she is now," Victoria said, passing the phone to her mother.

"You're back," Amour said flatly, still angry at him for not telling her he was leaving town.

"I just got in the door. Haven't even taken off my jacket."

"It's just past twelve. You must have left in the middle of the night, or driven like a maniac?"

Ed laughed. "I left at five. I stayed in Sussex last night."

"At The Pines?" Amour asked.

"No, at Lily's."

"Oh," Amour said, growing angrier by the minute.

"I've missed you. Anyway, I was hoping to come by this afternoon?"

Amour wondered what he was up to. "Aren't you tired from the long drive?"

Ed sat down. "Not really," he said, deflated by her answer. "But if you're not—"

"No, it's fine," she said, anxious to give him a piece of her mind.

"Okay then. I'll just wash up." He looked at his watch. "Should be there by two. It's a nice day to take a walk on the beach."

Amour looked past the dining room to the grey water in the distance. "If it doesn't rain."

"Of course. So I'll see you shortly," Ed said.

"I'll be here," Amour said and hung up. She looked down at the phone. *First, he left without even calling, and now he tells me he spent the night at Lily's. He's trying to make me jealous, trying to force my hand. Well, to hell with that. I'll make up my own mind, when I'm damn good and ready. And right now, mister, you're on shaky ground.* She looked up at Michael's portrait. "You would never have played such stupid, childish games," she whispered. She walked into the kitchen and began filling the kettle. *What were you thinking, staying at Lily's overnight? She's got young kids, for God's sake. Or maybe they weren't even there. Maybe she shipped them off for the night. I don't trust her. Not one little bit. What the hell am I thinking? She's always been trouble. She probably did sleep with Father Gregory. I wouldn't put it past her. And she knows you and I have been seeing one another. It's like she's trying to break us up. She's up to something, that's for sure. And I won't have it.*

Ed turned the water on and stepped into the shower. He placed his palms against the wall, dropped his head, and let the steamy water wash over him. *You sounded cool. You never even said you missed me, or that you were glad that I'm home. You sounded flippant.* "Well, old man, you might already have your answer," he mumbled. He finished showering, dried off, wrapped a towel around his waist, and entered his bedroom, reminding himself not to read too much into their phone conversation. *Carol always said I worry too much.* He looked in the mirror, then down at the small gold band on his dresser. He picked it up and held it between his thumb and index finger, wondering if Amour would agree that its sentimental value outweighed its worth. He put it back on his dresser and began combing his hair. *I guess I'll find out soon enough.*

Hector was lying on the couch, staring at the hideous picture of Jesus. It was the last thing he saw at night and the first thing he saw in the morning. He closed his eyes, vowing that as soon as he was on his feet he would replace it with something more soothing. He heard the back door open. "That you, Jeanne?"

Jeanne appeared in the entrance to the living room. "Have you been up at all?"

"Briefly."

She looked at the empty chamber pot at the foot of the couch. "Were you upstairs?"

Hector sat up. "I took my time."

"Still, the doctor said—"

"Jeanne, two hours ago you were suggesting I go to mass with you and Dot. How did you think I was gonna get up the church steps...on the wings of a snow white dove?"

"God wouldn't strike you down on the way into His house."

"Oh, but he would for dumping my piss into the toilet?"

"There's no need for that," she said, turning on her heels and heading for the kitchen.

Hector listened to the drawers being roughly pulled open and the noisy rattling of plates. "How was church?" he asked, hoping to soften her mood.

Jeanne sliced a tomato in quarters. Have patience, he's not himself, she thought. "The choir wasn't very good today. Never is when Sister Jean Michael isn't there. Oh, and Gladys Ferguson died."

Hector sat up. "Who's Gladys Ferguson?"

"You know...from Steele's Hill...worked at Woolworth's. Larger woman."

"Doesn't ring a bell," he said, standing and folding his blanket. He looked up to see Jeanne standing in the doorway holding a bread knife.

"Her nephew was that disgraced police officer. The man who attacked the painter near the bridge."

"Dan McInnes," Hector said.

"Yes, that's it," she said, returning to the kitchen.

Hector tossed the blanket on the footstool "He was murdered. I heard he was found tied to a tree with his genitals cut off."

Jeanne put her husband's plate on the table. "Your lunch is ready."

Hector looked down at the wafer-thin slice of ham and the fat tomato wedges meant to sustain him for another four hours. "No need to worry about me having another heart attack, I'm just gonna starve to death," he said, reaching for a slice of bread. "Where's the butter?"

Jeanne sat down across from him. "You can have butter with your supper."

Hector looked at his wife's sparse plate. "I'm the one on the diet, not you. You don't have to deprive yourself on my account. You're already as thin as a rail."

"Well, I'm not going to make it any harder on you than it already is." She cut her ham with her fork. "I saw Victoria at mass today. She's going to come to Sunday School next week. Oh, and I spoke to Father O'Handley. I asked if he might put in a good word for her with the school trustees."

Hector nodded. "That's good."

There was a knock on the door.

"Who can that be?" Jeanne asked.

"It's probably Tipper."

"What's he doing here?" she scoffed.

"He's gonna clean out the shed."

Jeanne glared at her husband. "On a Sunday?"

Hector shoveled the ham in his mouth and pushed his chair back. "Uh-huh. And we're going to listen to the Red Sox game." He grinned. "They're playing the Yankees." He walked out on the back step, telling Tipper he'd be out shortly and to get started on the shed.

"You're supposed to be on bed rest," Jeanne protested.

Hector assured her Tipper would be doing the work while he got some fresh air. He finished his lunch, grabbed the transistor radio from the top of the fridge, and joined his young friend out back.

"You want me to take everything out of the shed?" Tipper asked, placing a box of odds and sods on the ground.

Hector opened a lawn chair and pushed down on the arms. "Might as well. I have no idea what's even in there. Most of it's probably just junk."

"What about this?" Tipper said, reaching in the box and holding up a dusty pint of whiskey. He put the bottle to his mouth, pretending to chug it.

Hector looked back at the house, then quickly at Tipper. "Give me that!" he said, snatching it from him.

Tipper laughed. "*What*, yer old lady don't know you drink?"

Hector hid it behind his back. "Mind your business," he said and winked.

Jeanne finished the dishes and sat down to her knitting. She smiled at the muffled chatter in the backyard. The boy is good for him, she thought. She heard a happy yelp, set her knitting aside, and peeked out the window. Tipper was wildly dancing around, punching his fist in the air. She smiled, thinking he wouldn't be much older than Lily's boy. She closed her eyes, trying to remember what her grandson looked like. He was no more than four the last time she had laid eyes on him. She would never have known it was her grandson had Hector not slowed to a crawl with his eyes fixed on Lily and the boy. Lily was down on one knee, tying his shoe laces. The fair-haired boy had his small hand on his mother's back. Jeanne put her head down, remembering the boy staring into the car as she and Hector slowly made their way up Main Street. She pressed the back of her hand against her wet eyes, thinking it was the same day she began to notice a change in her husband's behaviour; when he became more distant, more sullen...old. She heard another loud cheer and looked up. Hector was on his feet, laughing, and pointing at his downcast helper. She let the curtain fall shut, walked into the kitchen, and poured two glasses of Iron Brew. She opened the back door and stepped out. "Who's winning?"

"The friggin Yanks," Tipper said. He pressed his eyes shut. "Sorry."

Jeanne walked down the steps and passed him a glass. "Do you use that kind of language in front of your grandmother?"

Tipper shook his head. "No, maam," he lied, thinking his grandmother's colourful language would make a sailor blush.

"Then don't use it here."

"Sorry."

She passed Hector his glass and leaned into his ear. "Don't forget, we're paying him by the hour."

Amour was weeding the flower beds when Ed turned in the driveway. She waited for him to get out of the car, got off her knees, and gave a quick wave.

He approached. "Want some help?" he asked, smiling.

Amour brushed the dirt from her pants. "I'm all done. I just spent the last hour and a half on my knees."

Ed grinned. "I'd be happy to get down on one." He leaned in and kissed her cheek. "It's been a long week."

Amour nodded. "You got that right," she said coolly. She started up the steps. "Something to drink?"

"Sure," Ed said, following her inside.

"Something cold, or tea…coffee?" she asked.

Ed sat at the table. "I get the feeling you're sore at me?"

Amour opened the fridge door. "Right again. So what is it, something hot or —"

"Do you want to tell me?" Ed asked.

Amour put a bottle of Coke on the counter and turned to face him. "I don't appreciate being toyed with."

Ed screwed up his face. " *Toyed with?* Amour, I'm sorry, I don't know what you're—"

"Leaving without telling me. Not even a heads up. I'm not a moony-eyed teenager who…who'll be pressured into—"

Ed stood and held his hands up. "Whoa, hold on s sec. I'm not pressuring you into anything. Actually, I left so I wouldn't be tempted to jump in the car and start singing outside your window. And for the record, I called you on Sunday before I left but there was no answer. "Then I called again, first thing Monday morning. I left a message with Sandra. If you don't believe me, ask her."

Amour looked down at her feet, embarrassed she didn't give him the benefit of the doubt before pouncing. "She must have forgotten to tell me," she said contritely.

Ed approached her. "So, we're good?"

Amour gave an encouraging smile.

They took their drinks out back and sat across from each other in the gazebo. Amour told him about Toni losing the baby and Victoria's plans to start teaching Sunday School. "It was Mrs. MacDonald's idea...the woman who fell and hurt her ankle."

Ed took a swig of Coke, thinking Amour had given him the perfect opening to tell her Lily was Victoria's birthmother, but Amour seemed out of sorts, quieter than usual. He'd wait and see how the afternoon played out. "So, I trust Kenny hasn't been hanging around," he said.

"No, not that I'm aware of. I think Victoria would like to get back in John's...John Toth's...good graces. They used to be so close...then...I don't know, they just grew apart. So how are Lily and the kids?" she asked, still annoyed that Ed had spent the night at her place.

Ed shrugged. "Good. Rory and Rachael had a good year at school and Lily likes her job. She bought a small, two-bedroom bungalow. It's nice... has a big yard. I'm really proud of how she turned her life around." He smiled. "And that little Laura, she's something else."

Amour nodded. "Must have been quite crowded, I mean two adults and three kids in a small bungalow?"

Ed tilted his head. "What are you getting at?"

"Nothing. Just an observation. I mean, isn't The Pines just around the corner?"

"It is, but I wanted to spend some time with the kids. And it's a lot easier for me to go to them than to have Lily pack them up and take them to the motel. And in case you're wondering, she has a couch...a very comfortable couch that I slept on...both nights."

"*Both nights?*" Amour repeated, surprised by his revelation.

"Yes. I stayed there last Sunday...on my way to the farm."

Amour dropped her head. "And whose idea was that? Yours or hers?"

Ed thought about it for a moment. "Hers, I guess. I mean I called her on Sunday morning and told her I was going to head to Bathurst the next day...I thought we could grab a coffee on my way through...and she said why not come now. I had no reason not to, so I packed up and headed out. It was all very spontaneous." He tilted his head and smiled. "And all very innocent." He laughed. "What's going on, anyway? I feel like I'm being interrogated."

"I don't trust her," Amour blurted.

Ed felt himself get defensive. "And why is that?"

"*Why is that?*" Amour repeated harshly. "For one, how about all that money she stole from Stanley. She almost ruined his business."

Ed leaned forward. "Amour, Lily paid every cent of it back. Do you know how much courage that took? If Stanley and Mabel can forgive her, I don't know why—"

"And what about her and Dan McInnes? Oh, and the priest? Seems to me she seeks out trouble and loves to play the victim. She might have you, Stanley, and Mabel fooled, but I see her for what she is…a conniving little…slut," she seethed, her words carrying more venom than she intended.

Ed stared at her with his mouth open. He had never seen this side of her. "I can't believe you. Yes, she made some mistakes…big ones. She'd be the first to admit it. But Amour, she's a good soul who'd do anything for her kids. She's trying her best and—"

Amour stood up, as angry with herself for saying things she really didn't mean, as she was with Ed for dismissing her concerns and defending Lily. "I don't want to talk about this anymore."

Ed looked up at her. "She's a friend, that's all," he said, picturing Lily leaning in and kissing him.

Amour stepped down from the gazebo. "I haven't been sleeping well lately. I'm going to take a nap."

Ed followed her to the back door. "Amour, I'm not sure what to say. I did nothing wrong. Neither did Lily."

Amour stomped off. "Go home," she hollered.

Ed watched her disappear into the dining room. He put his hand in his pocket and pulled out the ring his sister Carol had bequeathed him in the hope he would one day give it to his future wife. "Well, sis, looks like you're not gonna get your wish after all," he whispered sadly.

Mark helped Toni to the couch. "It's not perfect, but at least you won't sink to the floor."

Toni looked around the tidy apartment. "You've been busy."

Mark took Toni's things to the bedroom and placed them on the bed. He opened the paper bag the nurse had handed him on their way out. "What's with all the pads?" he asked.

"I'm still bleeding."

Mark appeared in the doorway. "Is that normal?"

Toni shrugged. "It's just a bit. They said it should stop in a day or two."

Mark went back inside. "Mabel sent over a casserole and some fresh rolls for supper," he hollered.

Toni smiled. "She's been so sweet. Helping us get settled, checking in on me every day...and now, bringing us food."

Mark came out carrying a box and set it down beside her. "And Amour sent these over. Said to keep whatever you want and give the rest to Goodwill. Oh, and we won't need any jam or chutney for God knows how long. Myrtle stocked the cupboards."

Toni reached in and pulled out a blouse. "Everyone's been so good to us...with all the furniture, food, and clothing."

"Want some tea?" he asked.

"Sure."

Mark went to the kitchen and started filling the kettle.

"Mark?"

He turned the tap off. "What?"

"Don't you find it strange I never heard from Alice? I mean, I know we never met, but she's your sister-in-law for goodness sakes. I mean, if the situation were reversed and she lost a baby, I would have reached out to her by now."

Mark turned on the stove. "Luke said she's been really busy at the bakery," he lied. He pressed his eyes tight. "And when she's not working, she's busy with Matthew."

"Mabel works and has three kids...she somehow managed."

Mark opened the cupboard and removed two cups. "Don't forget they were planning to have a party for us."

"*Alice and Luke*?" Toni asked.

Mark peeked his head in the doorway. "Yeah. Remember, last Friday."

Alice shook her head. "You didn't tell me that."

"Sure I did."

"No, I'm sure you didn't," she said firmly, knowing she would remember any outreach by Alice. "Still, you'd think that—"

"Want a raisin tea biscuit?" Mark asked, anxious to change the subject.

"No thanks. I think I'll take a bath. I'll have my tea later." Toni started the water in the tub and went to the bedroom.

Mark was in the kitchen buttering a slice of bread when he realized the water in the tub was still running. "Toni," he hollered. "Toni." He put his knife down, walked past the living room, and pushed the bathroom door forward. "Shit!" he said, quickly turning the water off. He walked down the hall. "Toni, you left the water running. It nearly over-flowed," he said, entering their bedroom.

Toni was sitting on the edge of the bed clutching a small, crocheted blanket and crying. Mark looked at the box Mary Catherine had dropped off. He quickly put it out of sight, then sat down beside her. "I'm sorry," he said, wrapping his arm around her shoulder. "I meant to get rid of that."

Toni nodded. "It was a boy, you know."

Mark cleared his throat. "Yeah."

"I know it's been hard for you, too. And even though you said it didn't matter, I know you wanted a son." She ran her hand underneath her eyes. "I miss him."

"I know," Mark said.

"We should give him a name."

Mark swallowed hard. "I'm not sure that's such a good idea. I mean, isn't it better if we just put it behind—"

Toni turned to face him. "How can you say that? I carried our baby inside of me for five months. And he wasn't an...an *it* that we can just put behind us. He was our son and he deserves a name."

Mark knew she was in a fragile state and didn't want to add to her anguish. "Did you have a name in mind?"

Toni smiled. "Duncan, after my father. And Alexander, after my grandfather."

"Duncan Alexander," Mark repeated softly. "I like it. But maybe... maybe we should save that name in case...in case—"

"In case we have another son*?*" she asked.

Mark nodded. "Yeah. It's a nice name. A strong name."

Toni smiled sadly. "Don't you think the baby deserves a nice name? He's already been cheated out of so much."

Mark smiled. "You're right."

Toni put her hand on his leg. "If we have another boy, we can name him after your father."

Mark shook his head. "I don't think that would—"

"Oh, right. Your nephew's name is Matthew. Did your father have a second name?"

Mark felt like he was ready to explode. "I don't know." He stood up. "Why don't you get in the tub? I'll bring you some tea." He picked up the box marked *Baby Toth* and put it in the hallway outside their apartment, then brought Toni's tea into the bathroom. He set the cup down on an overturned box beside the tub. Toni entered, wearing a robe. Mark rubbed her back. "I told Mackie I'd stop in The Y for a bit...set up the schedule for the week. I won't be long."

Toni looked surprised. "But you'll be home for supper?" she asked, disappointed he would leave her so soon after she got out of the hospital.

He gave a reassuring smile. "You won't even know I'm gone."

Hector entered the kitchen holding up a baseball glove. "Look what Tipper found," he said, smiling.

Jeanne pulled her hands from the soapy dish water and quickly dried them. "I thought that old thing was long gone."

Hector pulled out a chair and sat down. "I need some shortening to soften it up," he said, pushing the stiff sides together.

Jeanne took the can of Crisco down from the cupboard and put it on the table. Hector was about to scoop it out with his hand when she slapped his arm. "Don't you dare," she said, opening a drawer. "I suppose you're going to give it to the boy?"

Hector smiled. "I am, along with an old sled he found buried under a mountain of junk. I just need to fix one of the runners."

Jeanne passed him a spoon. "He's doing quite well for himself, isn't he? I mean, getting all that stuff, plus a good wage for a boy his age."

Hector slapped a blob of Crisco into the mitt, stuck the spoon back into the can, and looked up. "After all these years, sometimes I just don't get you," he said sadly. He shook his head in disgust. "You'd give anything to the church, but yet you begrudge the poor kid a few things you didn't even know we had."

Jeanne dropped her arms at her side. "That's not what I mean and you know it. I just made an observation, that's all. I don't have any qualms about giving the boy a few old toys," she said with a dismissive flick of her wrist. "And, yes, I will happily give to the church all that I can. It's called being a good Catholic."

Hector got up and pushed his chair back under the table. "Or a fool," he said under his breath.

"What did you say?" Jeanne snapped.

"Nothing." He walked past her into the living room, then turned back to face her. "And, Jeanne, the boy's name is Tipper. *Tipper.*"

Jeanne was doing the dishes and thinking about her husband's troubling mood swings. She remembered Charlotte telling her that heart attack victims often exhibit noticeable changes in behaviour and that it was nothing to be overly concerned about. And while Hector's mood swings did seem more pronounced since his heart attack, Jeanne knew he hadn't been himself for some time. She ran her dishrag around the rim of a teacup, picturing Hector laughing at Tipper as they listened to the ballgame. The boy is good for him, she thought. *I have to make more of an effort.* She dried her hands and stood in the doorway to the living room. Hector kept his eyes down, massaging the now partially pliable glove.

"You're right. I should be kinder to the…to *Tipper*," she said contritely.

Hector looked up, surprised by his wife's concession. "He's a good kid, Jeanne. And he could use a male influence in his life."

"Well, he won't find any better," she said and smiled.

Hector looked down into the glove that brought him so much joy as a boy. "I'm not so sure about that."

"I am," Jeanne said, tearing up. She cleared her throat. "Will Tipper be coming by tomorrow?" she asked.

"He's going to mow the lawn…if it doesn't rain."

Jeanne nodded. "Well, if he does come by, maybe he'd like to come in and have lunch with us."

Hector smiled. "I'm sure he'd like that. And, Jeanne, thank you. It means a lot."

Mark was putting the donated box of baby things in the trunk when he spotted the neck of a quart of whiskey sticking out from under an old blanket. Not today, he thought, it's Toni's first night home and I have work in the morning. He slammed the trunk down and walked down the dark alley toward the sunlit street beyond, stopping briefly to look up at his bedroom window. Naming the baby just makes it harder on everyone, he thought.

He stepped onto Commercial Street. Apart from a few people sitting on the stone fence fronting St. Agnes church, the town was deserted; the shuttered stores and legal drinking establishments leaving the less faithful with little choice but to spend the day at home with their families.

Mark crossed the street and walked up the steps of St. Agnes. He knew it wasn't the church of his faith, but it didn't matter. He pulled on the heavy door and looked down the aisle, the sun pouring in through the stain glassed windows casting bright bands of colour onto the shiny backs of the varnished pews. He sat down in the pew closest to the door and looked at the huge pipe organ on the altar, surprised there was no image of Christ on the cross. He closed his eyes and tried to pray, but his mind was full of jumbled thoughts. Making love to Alice in the back of the store. Luke slapping his back and toasting the news he was going to be a father. Toni standing in the cluttered apartment telling him the bleeding was getting heavier.

There was a loud bang overhead. Mark opened his eyes, turned sideways, and looked up at the choir loft.

An older man descended the side stairs. "Sorry if I disturbed you. I dropped a box of hymnals." He held up a gnarly hand. "Arthritis."

Mark stepped into the aisle. "That's okay. I was just on my way out."

The old man smiled. "Hope you found what you were looking for."

Mark puckered his mouth. "I'm afraid that'll take more than one visit."

"Our doors are always open."

Mark walked back out into the warm sunlight, thinking he'd likely get more satisfaction from hitting a seventy-pound bag than he would from prayer. He walked the short distance to the two-story, brick building on the corner of MacLean and Commercial streets, put the key in the lock, and pushed the door open. He turned the lights on, walked up to the punching bag, and took a few quick jabs. He hit it slowly and softly at first, then harder and faster, until his wet hair clung to his forehead and his arms felt like they were on fire.

"What's eatin you?" Mackie hollered from the doorway.

Mark's head shot up, sweat dripping off his nose and chin. He grabbed the bag to stop it from swaying and ran the back of his arm across his face. "Thought I'd take advantage of the quiet," he panted.

Mackie slid a duffle bag off his shoulder, pulled out a hand towel, and tossed it at him. "Your hands are bleeding. If you're gonna go at it that hard, ya should tape them up."

Mark ran the towel over his face. "I got carried away."

"Maybe I'm training the wrong guy. Ever think about stepping into the ring?"

Mark chuckled. "I do my fighting on the street, not in a ring."

Mackie shrugged. "That's fine…if ya want to end up in the slammer." He pointed to the ring. "But that's where you earn respect. And who knows, if you're good enough, you might even make some serious money."

Mabel sat on the park bench watching the kids play tag.

"Push over," Amour said.

Mabel looked up. "What are you doing here?"

Amour smiled. "I needed to talk to you. Stanley told me where to find you."

Mabel scooted over. "Everything okay?"

"Not really," she said, telling Mabel about her conversation with Ed.

Mabel listened without interruption.

"I admit I over-reacted. But I couldn't help myself, it annoys me to death. And what if the shoe were on the other foot and I stayed with…I don't know…some guy friend…it'd be a scandal. Anyway, I said some pretty awful things, especially about Lily." She grimaced as if in pain. "I called her a slut. What do you think, is Ed convinced I'm a witch?"

Mabel kept her eyes on the kids. "I think you better call him. First, you beg forgiveness, then you ask where he wants to have the reception."

Amour laughed. "I know I need to apologize, but, after today, I'm not so sure his offer is still on the table …or that I'm ready to say yes."

"You're ready," Mabel said matter-of-factly.

Amour looked at her. "Don't you find his relationship with Lily strange? I mean they write all the time… and I know he calls her. And it's not as if she's hideous to look at. And who invites a guy to stay the night at their tiny little bungalow unless they have something on their mind?"

"A good friend," Mabel said. "Amour, you're jealous."

"*What?*"

"You heard me," Mabel said impatiently. "No one has more reason not to trust Lily than me or Stanley. But she did what she did to protect her kids. And she paid us back."

Amour nodded. "I know."

"And I bet that if you were in her shoes, you would have done the same thing."

"*Steal thousands of dollars?*" Amour huffed. "*I don't think so!*"

Mabel faced her. "You know damn well you'd do anything short of killing someone to protect Victoria."

Amour chuckled. "Okay, I'll give you that. Actually, I wouldn't even rule out murder."

Mabel jumped to her feet. "Mary Margaret! Stop kicking your brother. Mary Margaret!" She sat back down and looked at Amour. "I swear that kid is going to be the death of me." She smiled at her friend. "Amour, do you know how lucky you are? Think about it. Ed is a good man with a big heart. And he's a loyal friend. And you know as well as I do, there's not a ton of them wondering around this side of the causeway waiting to be snatched up. As for Lily, Ed didn't propose to her, he proposed to you. Do you think he's that ruthless that he's sleeping with Lily on the side while he's waiting for you to give him an answer?"

"No, of course not."

"Well then, it's time to shit or get off the pot. Call him, apologize, and start planning your wedding."

Amour leaned back. "You're beginning to sound like Rosie."

Mabel looked surprised. "*Rosie?*"

Amour shrugged. "I told her Ed proposed. I didn't intend to, but then she introduced me to Jack Daniels...next thing you know, I'm pouring my heart out." She gave Mabel a pained look. "You're not mad are you?"

Mabel shook her head. "*That you told Rosie?* Of course not."

"I just mean, I'd normally come to you first."

"Don't worry about it. I'm not the least bit put out. You have room in your life for more than one friend. Just like you have room in your heart to love more than one man."

Amour touched Mabel's hand. "Rosie is very lonely, you know. She told me she had no friends. Could have knocked me over with a feather. I thought she would have had a ton of friends, she's so…outgoing."

Mabel smiled sadly. "It must be hard, especially after losing Bernie. You know, sometimes I think it's the people who appear to be the happiest…the most outgoing…who are the loneliest."

Amour nodded. "I think you're right. Anyway, I was thinking we should invite Rosie to club. What do you think?"

"I think that's a great idea. And what about Toni? She's got no one but Mark."

"Does she play cards?" Amour asked.

"I don't know. Is she doesn't, we can teach her."

"There'd be too many of us for Tarabish," Amour said.

Mabel smiled. "Well, we'll play something else. You talk to Mary Catherine. I'll talk to Myrtle and Alice."

Amour laughed. "Good luck with Myrtle. She's won't be happy if she thinks we won't be playing Tarabish."

Mabel nodded, thinking it wasn't Myrtle she was worried about. It was Alice.

Ed popped open a beer, took it outside, and sat down on the front step, feeling drained from the long drive and dispirited from his conversation with Amour. *She basically accused me of being unfaithful.* He shook his head and took a drink. *Maybe we don't know each other that well, after all. I thought you liked Lily and appreciated how far she had come. I guess I was wrong.* He batted away a fly. "Damn," he whispered, wondering how he was ever going to talk to Amour about Lily being Victoria's mother. *It's clear she doesn't like her. Hell, she called her a slut.* He took another long drink. *I should never have told Lily I would tell Amour. God, she was so excited. I should have kept my big mouth shut, minded my own damn business.*

The phone rang. Ed got up wearily and went inside. "Hello." He ran his hand across his forehead. "Lily. Yeah, trip was good. I got in just after one. Oh, sorry. No, I got cleaned up and went to Glace Bay. Actually, I just got back around ten minutes ago. No, no answer yet. Disappointed? Yeah, a little." He kicked at the floor. "Patience has never been one of my virtues." He laughed. "I'm not sure about that. Yes, I know. No, I'm afraid I never got the chance. It just wasn't the right time. Yes, I will." He laughed again. "Yes, I guess neither one of us is very patient. I know you're anxious. Me, too." Ed pinched his eyes closed. "I will, I promise. It was great seeing you…and the kids. Yes, I'll call the moment I have anything to report. Yes, I promise. Oh, and thanks again for putting me up. Likewise. And you know it works both ways. If you and the kids want to come this way, you always have a place to stay. Yes, you too. Bye now."

Ed put down the phone and went back outside. I'm beginning to think neither one of us is going to be happy with Amour's answer, he thought. He sat on the top step. *But I promised you I'd tell her, and I will.* He drained the last of his beer and went inside for another. He had two more after that, then went to his bedroom and laid on top of the bed with his hands behind his head. He closed his eyes, his mind flashing from images of Amour's reaction after he told her he had spent two nights at Lily's, to Lily's surprising kiss. The kiss was nice, he thought, wondering if Lily was just caught up in the moment, or if there might have been more to it. *Don't go reading anything into it. It was just the wine. But, I gotta admit, you're a smart, beautiful woman. And, despite everything you've been through, you've never given up.* Ed rolled onto his side. *Funny how I never really thought of you in the romantic sense until now. Why is that? Probably because of how we met. You were such a mess. I knew it had to have been a bad relationship. Wonder what would have happened if we met under different circumstances.* He opened his eyes. "Don't be ridiculous," he said and sat up. He ran his hand through his hair. *What am I doing? I'm only thinking about you because I'm ticked off at Amour. She had no right to call you a slut.* He looked down the hall, through the screen door. There was a bright, orange ribbon of sunlight reflecting off of the flat water in the harbour. He got up and pushed the door forward. He had one foot down when he heard the loud hiss and immediately stepped back inside. The black cat was back, baring its menacing fangs, and arching its bony back.

Toni was curled up on the couch reading when Mark came through the door. "Smells good."

She closed her magazine and tossed it at her feet. "I was beginning to worry."

"Sorry, Mackie came by and we got talking." Mark picked up the magazine and sat down. "Anything interesting in here?" he asked, fanning the pages.

"Some—Oh my God," she said, grabbing his hand. "*What happened*?"

Mark pulled it back. "I took advantage of the punching bag."

Toni ran to the bathroom and started opening drawers. She returned with a jar of petroleum jelly. "Give me your hand," she said, smearing it over his bloody knuckles. "Now, the other," she said, repeating the application. She jumped back up. "We need to cover them. Do we have any gauze?"

"Under the sink."

Toni wrapped his second hand. "Mark, the nurse told me you talked to her about Duncan."

Mark looked confused. "What are you talking about?"

Toni's eyes filled up. "I mean, about the funeral."

"Funeral?" Mark said, pulling his hand away. "I didn't talk to anybody about *a funeral*. I just asked what would happen with the baby and they told me the hospital would take care of things." He stood up. "Is supper ready?"

Toni smiled. "But what does that mean...they'd take care of things?"

"Goddammit, Toni, how the hell am I supposed to know! It's not like I've been through this before." He waved his arm in the air. "I assume they buried him somewhere."

"Without telling us? Without us there?" she whispered.

Mark looked at the floor and curled his hands into fists. "I can't do this. I need some air," he said, grabbing his jacket and storming toward the door.

"Mark, please don't go!" Toni pleaded. "I'm sorry, it's just...Mark! He was our baby...your son." The door slammed shut. "Mark!"

Monday, July 7

Ed was returning to his office after a meeting with his staff.

"Here you go," Nancy said, handing him his messages. "Call the top one first." She grinned. "She seemed anxious to talk to you."

He sat behind his desk, dialled and waited. "Hi there. No it's fine. I just got back from a meeting." He looked at his watch. "Besides, it's almost lunchtime. I'm glad you called. I was beginning to think I'd never hear from you again. *Last night?* I was home all night. You must have called while I was down on the shore. So how are you? Yes, I'd like that. What time? Yes, I can leave from here. Can I bring anything? You sure? Okay, see you then. Oh, and Amour? Oh, never mind, it's nothing. Yes, I'll see you soon," he said and hung up.

Ed shuffled through the other messages, then tossed them aside. He wasn't sure where he stood with her; if she was inviting him to supper to say things were over between them, or to say yes to his proposal. *Or, maybe, it's neither. Maybe she just needs more time.*

He walked out and smiled at Nancy. "Off to lunch," he said. He got in his car, but didn't go to the Maple Leaf Restaurant for the daily special like he normally did; he headed for home. He'd pick up the ring and take it with him, just in case.

Ed pulled in the yard and immediately went to his bedroom. He opened the small wooden box on his dresser and spotted the silver tie clip Lily and the kids had sent him for his birthday. He touched it and smiled, thinking of Laura climbing on his lap and asking if he was going to be her new daddy. He then picked up his late sister's ring, put it in his pocket, and entered the kitchen. He put the kettle on and stood at the counter eating the remains of a two-day-old pie directly from the pastry box. He held up a large forkful. "Lemon Meringue, your favourite," he said, picturing Lily sitting across from him in the diner. He chuckled and took a mouthful. *You couldn't wait to get rid of me. And you were so jumpy… evasive. I knew you were in some kind of trouble. Little did I know how much. God knows, why I ever got involved. It was like I had no choice. Like someone was pushing me toward you. Whatever the reason, I'm glad I did. I can't imagine my life without you and the kids. Amour is dead wrong. She has no business talking about you like that. She barely knows you. She doesn't see what I see. God, maybe getting married isn't such a good idea after all.* Ed took another bite and shook his head. *Who in the hell am I kidding.*

The kettle started to whistle. Ed poured the hot water into a cup, added a teabag, and watched as spidery, ribbons of amber slowly seeped out. He waited for the water to turn a dull brown and took a sip. I should stop by Cameron's on my way to Amour's and pick up a pie for dessert, he thought. *I'll get your favourite as a peace offering.* He wiped his mouth. *Hmmm, I'm not even sure what that is.*

Jeanne stood on the back step. "Lunch is ready."

Hector got up from his lawn chair. "C'mon, Tipper. Let's see what feast awaits us."

Tipper was surprised he was being invited in for lunch. And as hungry as he was, he wasn't keen on sitting down to eat with the boss' old lady. "I think I'm just gonna work through lunch. Hopin to finish up early so I can meet up with the boys for a game of ball."

"Nonsense, Jeanne's already got a plate set out for you. You can leave after lunch and finish up tomorrow."

Jeanne smiled at Tipper when he came through the door. "Bathroom's upstairs. Down the hall on the right."

"Oh, I'm okay," Tipper said. "Don't need to go. My Gran says I can hold my piss…I mean my bladder… better than a miser's fist round his first dollar."

Hector put his hand on Tipper's shoulder. "She means for you to get washed up."

"Oh, yeah," Tipper said, disappearing down the hall.

Jeanne looked at her husband. "You need to talk to him about that foul mouth of his."

Hector washed his hands in the sink. "He's nervous."

Jeanne put a plate of bread on the table. "What does he have to be nervous about?"

"*You.* You can be pretty intimidating." Hector dried his hands. "Don't be too hard on the boy."

Tipper came downstairs and stood in the doorway waiting to be told where to sit.

Jeanne pulled out a chair. "Sit here. Do you like blood pudding?"

Tipper shrugged. "Blood pudding," he repeated, thinking it sounded disgusting. "Not sure."

Jeanne put their plates down.

Tipper looked at his full plate, then at theirs. He leaned into Hector. "How come I got so much?" he whispered.

"Because Hector has a bad heart and needs to watch his diet. Eat up before it gets cold," Jeanne said.

"So, you live with your grandmother and aunt," Jeanne said.

Tipper popped a round of blood pudding in his mouth and nodded. "Uh-huh."

Hector grew increasingly frustrated with his wife as she peppered their young guest with one question after the next. By the time lunch was finished, Jeanne knew his aunt worked for the coal company, his grandmother had a condition that left her almost totally blind, and his father disappeared before he was born.

"And what about your mother?" Jeanne persisted.

"Gran said Ma got on the bus to visit a friend in Sydney and never came back." He laughed. "Apparently she jumped off the bus, hopped on a train, and headed straight for a place called *see you later alligator.* Ain't no big deal. I don't remember her anyways." He smiled and ran his sleeve across his mouth.

Hector stood up and looked at his wife. "Are you finished?"

Jeanne held up her tea cup. "Not quite."

"I'm not talking about your tea," Hector said with a tone. He looked at Tipper. "Go catch up with the boys. I'll see you tomorrow."

Tipper started to collect his dishes. Jeanne touched his arm. "Leave them. I've got all day."

Hector saw Tipper to the door and returned to the kitchen. "I'm going to lie down."

Jeanne looked up from her tea. "Are you feeling okay?"

"Never better," he said sarcastically.

"What do you mean you and Tommy got a place?" Mother asked.

"We got a place…off Union. Amelia Street. It's nice."

"And how do you plan to pay for rent and still save for college?"

"Mr. Swartz asked if I wanted to stay on. I'll go to college next year."

Father tapped his pipe against his ashtray. "That's what ya said last year."

Mother pointed her paring knife at Kenny. "So you wanna be selling furniture off the back of a truck for the rest of your life, is that it?"

"No, Ma. It's only temporary. I'm gonna go to college, just not right away."

"Does this have anything to do with that girl I hear you and Tommy whispering about? What's her name…Doreen?"

"Nooo. Look, it's time I got a place of my own. I can't live here forever."

"You know folks are gonna talk," Father said.

Kenny shrugged. "Bout what?"

Father dipped his chin and looked over his glasses. "Bout you and Tommy shacked up together."

Kenny laughed. "I'd be living with another guy if I went to college."

"That's different," Father said.

Kenny looked up at the clock. "Damn, I gotta go. I'm meeting Tommy and the owner at the house."

"Will ya be home for supper?" Mother asked.

"No. Gonna meet up with some of the guys," he said and left.

Mother angrily sliced her carrots. "I don't like it. Not one little bit. God knows what shenanigans he and that Tommy will get into with no one keepin an eye on them. Next thing you know, he'll have Doreen or some other skanky thing knocked up...and be delivering furniture for the rest of his life."

Father lit his pipe. "Well at least you'd get your wish and he wouldn't be headin to the pit with me."

Mother turned to face him. Her eyes full. "And what am I going to do all day, with nobody to pick up after?"

"Aah, now Mother. It's not like he's moving to California. He'll be less than a mile away. And you know darn well he'll be popping in every other day, looking for a home-cooked meal, or askin you to wash his dirty underwear."

"Still, it won't be the same," Mother sulked.

Father reached for her arm and pulled her onto his lap. "You'll still have me."

Mother nodded sadly. "You know what I mean. The house will be so quiet."

Father grinned. "But it does have its upside." He put his arm around her waist and kissed her cheek. "Whenever you get frisky, we won't have to creep upstairs. You can have me right here...on the kitchen floor and scream yer friggin lungs out."

Mother elbowed him. "Stop with your foolishness."

"Now, Mother, you know ya can't get enough of me," he said, loudly chomping at her neck.

Mother laughed and stood up. "Go way with ya...ya horny old fart."

Mark grabbed his lunch can and looked down at the dirty, frayed bandage covering his hand. He wondered if Toni would offer to wrap his hands in fresh gauze, or if she'd be too angry. She was asleep when he in crawled in bed after midnight and when he crawled back out to go to work. He jumped down from the truck. "Thanks, Fred. See you in the morning." He climbed the stairs and entered the apartment, bracing himself for the cold shoulder and sharp tongue he knew he was about to receive. "Oh, well, I asked for it," he muttered and opened the door. Toni wasn't in the living room as he had expected. He peeked in the kitchen. "Toni?" There was no answer. He looked in the bedroom. Toni was curled up on her side. "You awake?" he whispered. "Toni, I know you're mad. Look, I'm having a hard time dealing with things, too. I don't know. All this talk about the baby...it just makes me crazy. I just think it would be better for the both of us if we move on...put things —"

"I'm not good," she said weakly.

"What?" He crouched beside the bed and was immediately struck by how pale she was. "Are you all right?"

Toni's eyes were closed. "Wa...water."

"Okay." Mark went to the kitchen, poured a glass of water, and returned. He put the glass on the floor. "Here, let's sit you up," he said, tossing the bed covers back. "Jesus!" he said, looking down at Toni's blood-soaked night gown. He scooped her up. "Okay, don't worry. I'm going to take you to the hospital. You're going to be all right. Hold on," he said, entering the living room and fumbling for the door handle. "Hang on," he said, as they made their way down the steps, through the alley to the back parking lot. "Hey," he screamed to one of the bag boys from the Co-op. "Get the door." He laid her down in the backseat. "Everything will be okay." He jumped behind the wheel, trying to steady his hand so he could get the key in the ignition. He looked over his shoulder. "Hold on. You're going to be okay," he repeated, tearing out of the parking lot. He sped up Main Street, ignoring the stop signs, pulled in front of St. Joseph's, and quickly gathered Toni in his arms. He charged through the entrance. "Help! I need help!" he hollered.

A nurse hurried toward him. "This way," she said, pointing to a room.

Mark put Toni down on a bed. "She lost a baby... a few days ago. I came home from work. And she was just lying in bed...full of blood. Is she gonna be all right?" he asked frantically.

The nurse looked at his blood stained shirt and gauzed hands. "Let's have the doctor take a look. You said your wife just gave birth?"

Mark looked confused. "Yes...well no. She lost the baby. It was dead."

The nurse took Toni's pulse and smiled. "Yes, it's still a birth. A stillbirth."

Mark looked to the door. "Are you gonna get the goddamn doctor or not?" he asked angrily.

The nurse slowly pulled a white sheet from the bottom of the bed and tucked it around Toni's shoulders. "Take a seat. I'll be back shortly." She smiled. "*With the doctor.*"

Mark stood over Toni. She was shivering and her lips were white. She opened her eyes. "Am I going to die?" she whispered.

He leaned down, brushed her hair back, and kissed her forehead. "No...no, of course not. You're gonna be just fine. The doctor's on his way."

Toni eyes fell shut. "Bury me with our baby," she whispered.

Mark pinched his eyes close and cleared his throat. "No, sweetheart," he said, tears streaming down his cheeks. "You're not going to die. You can't die."

Ed passed Amour a pastry box and looked into the dining room. "No dinner guests?" he asked, taking off his jacket.

Amour smiled. "Just you. I closed things up for a few days. Sandra's gone to Antigonish for her niece's wedding, and the dining room needs a good scrubbing." She held the box up. "I told you not to bring anything."

"You know I can't come empty-handed."

"I know you can't drive by Cameron's bakery," she said and laughed. "What is it anyway?"

"Pie. Lemon meringue."

"Oh?"

"Not your favourite?" Ed asked.

"It's fine. But for the record, I prefer cherry."

Ed smiled, thinking her response suggested they'd be sharing more desserts. He followed her past the dining room into the kitchen. "Smells good."

"Just stew," she said, grabbing a spoon. She pointed to the counter. "I thought we'd pour ourselves a drink and go out back."

"Sure." He held up a bottle. "Vermouth or Jack Daniels?"

"Vermouth."

Amour tapped the spoon on the side of the pot. "I was wrong," she blurted.

Ed smiled, grateful for her apology, but still anxious about what the night might bring.

"I said some things I didn't mean, especially about Lily. I know she's had a hard go of things and that she loves her kids." She closed her eyes. "I guess I was just surprised when you said you had spent two nights at her place."

Ed walked to the stove and handed Amour her vermouth. "We all say things we regret. I'm just glad you didn't mean what you said about her. She really is a good person." He kissed Amour's forehead and walked to the door. "Let's just forget about it."

They took their drinks to the gazebo; the residual awkwardness from the tension of the night before lifted with the help of the alcohol and a noisy family gathering next door. Ed fought the urge to pull the ring from his pocket and get down on one knee. It's up to her now, he thought, listening to her describe her plans to renovate the kitchen. Once again, he began to feel discouraged. That's the sort of thing you'd plan with your husband, he thought.

Victoria came through the back door. She smiled and waved. "Hi, Ed." She stepped up onto the gazebo and tapped Ed's leg. "Push over."

Amour took a sip of her drink. "I thought you weren't coming home for supper?"

"I'm not staying." She grinned mischievously. "Just wanted to share my news." She clapped her hands together. "I got a teaching job," she squealed.

Amour stood and hugged her. "That's wonderful, honey. I'm so proud of you."

Ed held up his glass. "I'm not surprised. Congratulations."

Victoria threw her arms around Ed's neck. "I couldn't have done it without you. They loved my cover letter. Oh, and Mrs. MacDonald spoke to Father O'Handley. And he spoke to some other folks, and the next thing you know, I'm a teacher at Holy Cross Elementary."

Ed nodded. "The same Mrs. MacDonald who fell outside the church?" he asked, picturing Lily's excited reaction after he told her he would tell Amour she was Victoria's birthmother.

Victoria smiled. "Uh-huh. Same one."

"Oh, I forgot to ask. How is Mr. MacDonald doing?" Amour asked.

"Good, I think. He's out of the hospital," Victoria said. "I'll know more in a few minutes. I promised Mrs. MacDonald I'd tell her the moment I heard from the board. Then, I'm going to The Grill to celebrate with the girls."

Amour looked at Ed. "Funny how things work out. If Victoria hadn't stopped to help her after her fall, Mrs. MacDonald wouldn't have a clue she was looking for a teaching job."

Ed nodded. "What happened to Mr. MacDonald?"

"He had a heart attack," Victoria said.

"But he's okay?" Ed asked.

Victoria shrugged. "I guess. He's out of the hospital."

"You should take a little something to Mrs. MacDonald to thank her for all her help," Amour suggested. She looked at Ed and scrunched up her nose. "Maybe your pie? Unless, of course, you're set on having it for dessert?"

Ed shook his head and smiled at Victoria. "Absolutely, take the pie."

Victoria peeked at Ed's watch. "Shoot," she said, jumping to her feet. "I better get moving. Thanks for the pie, Ed," she said and ran off.

Ed looked out at the grey water in the distance, thinking about the strange twists of fate that brought him to this place, at this time. If he hadn't lost his glasses he would never have become friends with Lily, and he would never have met Amour. And if Victoria hadn't found her grandmother's glasses, they would likely have never met. He dropped his head.

"A penny for your thoughts?" Amour asked.

Ed smiled. "Do you believe in fate?"

Amour chuckled. "Where did that come from?"

Ed leaned forward with his elbows on his knees. "Just curious," he said, wondering if this was the right time to tell her Lily was Victoria's birthmother.

"I'm not sure. Why, do you?"

"Yes."

Amour sipped her drink. "Do you think it was fate that introduced us?"

Ed nodded. "I have no doubt of it."

Amour grinned. "Then, I guess we were meant to be together."

Ed sat up and tilted his head. "What are you saying…I mean, is that a *yes*?" he asked excitedly.

Amour smiled and nodded. "Yes…it's a yes."

Ed jumped down from the gazebo, swung his arm in the air, and let out a whoop. The neighbours turned and looked in his direction. He pointed to Amour. "She said yes," he hollered, waving to the distant well-wishers holding up their beers and cheering his news.

Amour laughed. "Ed! What are you doing? We haven't even told Victoria."

He jumped back onto the gazebo, got down on one knee, and took her hand. "Sorry, I got carried away." He reached in his pocket. "It might not look like much," he said, sliding the plain, gold band with a tiny, solitary diamond onto her finger. "But it's been in my family forever. Carol left it to me." He glanced skyward, then back at Amour. "You've made her very happy." He smiled. "You've made us both very happy."

Amour looked down at the modest ring, then laid her hand on the side of his face. "Maybe I do believe in fate after all," she said and kissed him.

"How did Mark make out today?" Mabel asked.

Stanley could smell the booze off Mark the moment he showed up for work, but saw no point in worrying Mabel. "He put in a good day. And I ran into Mackie today. He wants to train him."

"You mean as a boxer?"

"Yep. Said he's a little awkward on his feet, but that he more than makes up for it with speed."

Mabel lifted Liv out of her highchair and passed her to Stanley. "I had a very unpleasant conversation with Alice today. I wanted to invite Toni to join us at club. She said that if I did, she'd drop out. It's maddening." Mabel clenched her teeth and shook her fists. "Sometimes, I could just… just strangle her. She won't even meet the poor girl. I have a half a mind to tell Alice that if that's what she wants, so be it …she can leave."

"You're not going to do that, and you know it," Stanley said.

"I know. But it's crazy. Alice is only postponing the inevitable. She can't avoid her forever. And poor Toni. God knows what she thinks of Alice."

Stanley bounced Liv on his knee. "If you were in Alice's shoes, you might feel the same."

Mabel shot him a look.

Stanley chuckled. "*What?* I'm just saying it would be really hard on her. But I agree. It's not like she can avoid them forever. It's a small town and he's her brother-in-law for Pete's sake."

Mabel put their plates in the sink. "Exactly my point, but she refuses to listen to reason. And I'm caught in the middle...making excuses for Alice, or worse, lying. Trust me, I'm not going to be doing that forever."

The phone rang.

Stanley set Liv on the floor. "I got it." He picked up the receiver. Mabel was filling the sink with water when he returned. He put his hand on her shoulder. "That was Mark. He was calling from the hospital."

Mabel turned off the tap. "What is it?"

"It's Toni."

Mabel brought her hand to her mouth.

"Mark had to rush her to the hospital. I guess she was in a bad state when he got home from work. Apparently she lost a lot of blood. She's in surgery. They're doing a hysterectomy."

"Oh dear God," Mabel said, blessing herself. She quickly dried her hands. "You'll need to get the kids ready for bed," she said, tossing the dish towel on the counter and untying the back of her apron.

"Mabel, she's in surgery. They're not going to let you see her tonight," Stanley protested.

Mabel pulled her apron over her head and thrust it at him. "Maybe not, but at least I can be there for Mark."

Victoria backed out of the driveway and gave one last wave. She was glad she had stopped in to personally thank Jeanne for her help in getting the teaching job, but felt badly she didn't have time to stay for tea and some of Ed's pie. She would come back another day. She drove down Brookside

Street, thinking about the circumstances that brought them together. *If I hadn't been there when Jeanne fell, I likely wouldn't have gotten the teaching job. Such a nice, old couple. Poor Mr. MacDonald, though. He didn't look well.* Victoria pictured him sitting up when she came into the room. He had smiled, yet he looked sad, almost as if he wanted to cry. She turned down Park Street. *I wonder if they have any children or grandchildren. I didn't see any pictures suggesting they did, but then I wasn't there very long.* She glanced over her shoulder. A woman was walking with several small children in tow. Victoria smiled, thinking she might be looking at her future students. She was on Union Street looking for a parking spot when she saw John and his girlfriend enter The Grill. "That hurts," she whispered, pulling up to the curb, getting out, and entering the restaurant. She stood in the doorway looking for her friends. John waved. She pretended she didn't see him. *Shit, he's coming over.*

"Meeting someone?" John asked.

"Oh, hi. Yes. I'm meeting Bea and Ellen. I thought they would have been here by now."

John pointed to the booth. "Sit with us till they come."

"No, I'm fine."

John took her by the arm. "C'mon, before Marjorie starts to think you don't like her."

"Hi there," Victoria said, scooting in across from the pretty blonde.

Marjorie smiled. "Hello."

Victoria looked at John with a pained expression. "I heard Mark's girlfriend lost the baby. I'm very sorry."

John nodded. "Thanks. I haven't seen him in a couple of days. Luke says he's pretty broken up." He pointed. "Look who the cat dragged in."

Victoria looked toward the door. Kenny was looking for a place to sit. Oh, no, she thought, watching him look their way. She quickly turned and smiled at John. "I got a teaching job."

"Wow! That's fabulous. Congratulations. Where at?" John asked.

"Holy Cross."

Marjorie smiled. "What grades?"

"One to five. Anyway, that's why I'm meeting Ellen and Bea. We're celebrating—" She felt a presence at her side and looked up.

Kenny smiled at her. "Hey, guys. How's it goin?"

"Good. How about you?" John asked.

Kenny sat next to Victoria. "Couldn't be better. I'm having a party at my new place on Friday night. Hope you guys can come?"

"You got a place of your own?" John asked.

"Me and Tommy. Eighteen Amelia Street. Can ya make it?"

"I can't. I've got plans," Marjorie said.

Kenny turned to Victoria. "What about you?"

Victoria smiled. "I don't think so," she said, thinking she wasn't about to give Kenny the idea she might be interested in getting back with him.

"Why not?" John asked. "C'mon, it'll be fun. I can pick you up."

Victoria assumed if Marjorie wasn't going, neither would John. She suddenly became more interested. "Okay, why not."

Kenny saw Tommy and Sally come in and head for a booth. He smiled and waved. "I gotta go. So, I'll see you guys Friday night." He sauntered up to his friends and plopped down, excited by the prospect he still had a chance of winning Victoria back.

"What's up with you?" Tommy asked. "Ya look like the cat that swallowed the canary."

Kenny grinned. "Nothin. Oh, by the way, I thought we'd have a little party Friday night. Show off the new digs."

Amour and Ed cuddled on the sofa in the upstairs parlor. "Let's do it tomorrow? We can call the Justice of the Peace and have the ceremony outside by the gazebo," Ed said.

Amour gave him a playful poke. "How about a nice fall wedding. Maybe at Mabel's and Stanley's cottage in Pleasant Bay. It would be beautiful, with all the leaves changing. What do you think?"

Ed reached for his glass. "You're sure you don't want a church wedding?"

Amour closed her eyes, thinking of the day she married Roddy. "Absolutely not," she said firmly.

"And I can't convince you to elope?" Ed asked.

"Michael and I eloped," she whispered sadly. "It needs to be different."

Ed nodded. "I was just hoping it would be sooner than the fall."

"It's not that far off. Just a few months. And it will be amazing, you'll see. Besides, you'll need time to sell your place."

Ed turned down his mouth. They hadn't discussed where they would live. "So, you're not going to run the manor after we're married?"

Amour sat up and looked bewildered. "What do you mean? Of course I am."

Ed raised his eyebrows. "You mean we're going to have strangers in our home at all hours of the day and night?"

Amour laughed. "Why not? You'll get used to it. And you meet some pretty interesting people." She leaned back into him. "Besides, it's my livelihood."

"But you won't have to work. I have a good job…and I've set aside a considerable—"

"But I like what I do. I could never give up the manor."

Ed smiled and nodded. "We'll figure it out."

Amour looked up at him. "We've got so much to consider. What about your best man. Are you going to ask one of your brothers?"

"No. It wouldn't be fair. Who would I choose? And it's too far a drive for a thirty minute ceremony. I'd like to ask Gordon."

Amour smiled. "Perfect."

Ed looked down at the black-rimmed glasses poking out of his shirt pocket. "If I didn't go back to my motel room to look for my glasses, I would never have met Gordon, or you."

"It's that fate thing again," Amour said and laughed.

"I believe it is. Think about it. I lost my glasses…such a random, insignificant little thing. People lose things every day and never give it a second thought. And yet, I misplace my glasses and look at all of the wonderful things that have happened. Lily got her life back, her kids are happy, and we're about to get married." Ed sipped his drink. "I assume you're going to ask Victoria to be your maid of honour?"

"Of course. But I'd also like to ask Mabel. Why don't you ask Stanley?"

Ed nodded. "I'd like that," he said, thinking now was the time to tell her Lily was Victoria's mother. "Amour, I think there might be more to this fate thing than you realize. I mean…the way Victoria met the MacDonald's and—"

Amour sat up. "I think that's her now."

Victoria walked into the room, surprised to see her mother snuggled up bedside Ed. "Oh, hi," she said, feeling a bit embarrassed. She smiled. "Sorry, am I interrupting?" she asked, laughing nervously. Amour and Ed stood up and smiled. Victoria's eyes darted from one to the other. "What's going on?"

Ed looked at Amour, then at Victoria. "I hope it's okay, but I asked your mother to marry me."

Victoria squealed, ran to him, and threw her arms around his neck. "*Okay?* Of course, it's okay! It's fabulous! And it's about time!" She stepped back and looked at her mother. "I mean, you did say yes, *right?*" Amour beamed, held up her hand, and wiggled her finger to show proof of the pending nuptials. "And I thought getting a job was the best news of the day," Victoria said. She hugged her mother. "Mom, I'm so happy for you. And I know Daddy would be, too. He'd loved Ed as much as we do. I know he would."

Tuesday, July 8

Mabel tiptoed into the bedroom, feeling about in the dark for the chair in the corner.

"I'm awake. You can turn the light on," Stanley said.

"Sorry I'm so late."

Stanley turned on his bedside lamp and blinked into the light. "What time is it?"

"Just past eleven."

"How are they doing?"

Mabel kicked off her shoes. "Not good. Mark is beside himself. The doctor said Toni will be okay, physically at least. They're giving her transfusions. They let Mark in to see her for a few minutes. He said she was as pale as a ghost and unresponsive. Opened her eyes a couple of times, but that was it. To be expected, I guess...she just come through major surgery and was pretty doped up. I feel so badly for her."

"And Mark, too," Stanley said.

"Yes, of course. His heart is broken. But as hard as it is for the father, it's twice as bad for the mother. The mother feels...she feels like it's her fault."

Stanley leaned on his elbow and pinched the corners of his eyes. "That's crazy. It's no one's fault."

Mabel smiled sadly, thinking there wasn't a day that went by that she didn't feel guilty about falling down the icy steps, going into early labour, and losing Mary Margaret's twin brother. "Kids go down okay?" she asked.

"All but Mary Margaret."

Mabel stripped down to her slip and pulled the covers back. "I'm too tired to look for my nightgown," she said, crawling in beside him. She leaned over and kissed him. "I'm exhausted. Goodnight."

Stanley shut the light off. "Goodnight."

Mabel looked over her shoulder. "Oh, I told Mark you wouldn't expect him at work tomorrow."

"Good. Not like I'd be down a man. He's barely worked a full day as it is."

Mabel sat up. "He hasn't had much of a choice. He and Toni have been through so much."

"I know, I know. I'm glad you told him not to come in." Stanley shifted his pillow. "Oh, and Amour called about an hour ago."

"What did she want?"

"Said for you to call her first thing in the morning. Goodnight."

"Must be important. Not like her to be calling so late. Did you tell her about Toni?"

"Yes, of course. She said she'd send some food over. Goodnight," he said a third time, this time as an appeal.

Mabel rolled onto her side, thinking about Toni lying alone in the hospital. She was so excited to become a new mother, and, now, she was left barren and bereft. It would be a lifetime sentence of pain and inescapable loss. Everyday sightings: a mother pushing a stroller, or a child playing in the park, would be a gut wrenching reminder of one of the saddest days of her life. And as each year passed, her eyes would be drawn to a child that would be the same age as the child she lost. Mabel closed her eyes, thinking about her own children and how she couldn't imagine life without any one of them. She smiled, thinking of the night she drove home from club and Stanley was standing in the doorway holding Liv, and JC and Mary Margaret were waving from the window. It was a sight that gripped her with breathtaking sharpness, but one born of joy, not heartbreak. She began to pray, giving thanks for her blessings, and asking God to give Toni and Mark the strength to get through the painful days ahead.

She woke several hours later with Stanley hovering over her. She sat up. "*What?*" she asked, looking around the dimly-lit room.

"You were talking in your sleep...calling out for Gregory."

Mabel nodded and slumped back down on her pillow. She put her arm over her forehead. "Bad dream."

"You okay?"

Mabel nodded. "Yes, sorry. Go back to sleep."

Stanley turned the light off. "Goodnight."

Mabel recalled the images of her disturbing dream. *Gregory, her stillborn son, was alive. He took his twin sister's tiny hand in his and walked with her to the edge of the cliff. They both turned and smiled, then jumped to their death. Just like the day of the fire when Mabel thought she had lost JC to the ocean below, she was overtaken by grief and screaming up at the sky.* Mabel threw the covers back, momentarily sat on the side of the bed, then got up.

"Where are you going?" Stanley asked.

"I can't sleep." She reached for her robe. "I'm going to make some tea."

"But it's not even four o'clock."

"The kettle works as well at night as it does in the day," she said. She walked down the hall, quietly opening doors and peeking in at her sleeping children. She then went downstairs, entered the living room, turned the lamp on and stared up at the image of her mother flanked by her father and James Cameron. She smiled, searching her mind for one of the few memories she had of her mother. It was a beautiful spring day and they were in Pleasant Bay. Her mother had picked her up, put her on a stool, and pointed out the kitchen window. *Look. See there. When the snow melts and the ground warms up, that's where we'll plant our cherry trees. The cherry blossoms will be beautiful. And when the berries come, we can make cherry pies. Lots of pies. We'll have so many cherry pies, we'll have them for breakfast, dinner, supper and dessert. Won't that be fabulous? We may not have a lot, but we have each other and we live in the most beautiful part of the world. Remember, Mabel, always count your blessings.* Mabel wondered if the memory was real, or whether it was contrived in her youth and embellished over time; her mind's way of coping with great loss. She turned to see Stanley coming down the stairs. She quickly brushed away a tear. "What are you doing up?" she asked.

He smiled and put his arm over her shoulder. "Tea is always better with company."

Ed took his coffee out to the front step and looked at his watch. He'd wait until eight-thirty before calling Lily at work. He smiled as a flock of small seabirds darted along the shore. God I love this place, he thought. He took a sip, thinking he'd soon be waking up to a different view. *Jesus, I don't know what Amour's thinking, guests coming and going all hours of the day and night. I'll have to walk through a crowded dining room to get to the goddamn kitchen. Maybe she'll have a change of heart.* He stood up and went back inside, thinking he seemed to be the only one making concessions. He picked up the receiver, called the operator, and waited for the connection to be made. "Lily? It's me. Yes, I know. I was going to call you last night but thought it might be too late. Look, I know you're busy. I won't keep you long. No, it's not that. I wanted to let you know that your father had a heart attack. No, no. He's all right. He's at home with your mother. I'm not sure. Victoria told me. Anyway, I thought you should know. *What? A stroke? When?* Will he be okay? Thank God. Yes, of course. Yvonne must be worried sick. I can only imagine. It'll be hard for her to care for him and manage the motel. *Selling*? Yes, I guess that makes sense. Yes, I'll call her tonight. Well, not all bad news." Ed looked up at a small spider scurrying across the ceiling. "Amour said yes. Thank you. Last night. No, no date. Probably sometime in October. She wants to have a fall wedding. I'd love if you and the kids could come. And hopefully Giles will be better by then. But I'd certainly understand if you can't make it. It's a long drive." Ed laughed. "No, I'm not trying to dissuade you. Oh, I almost forgot. Victoria got a teaching job. Holy Cross. Your mother helped her get it. I guess she spoke to the parish priest and he put in a good word with the trustees. I think she's seen them a few times. I know she was there yesterday. She brought them a pie as a thank you for helping her get the job. No, I haven't spoken to Amour yet. I had planned to talk to her last night, but well—" Ed looked down at his feet, searching for the words. "It didn't seem like the right time. No, I will. I won't be seeing her today, she's playing cards tonight. But hopefully within the next few days. Lily, I know you're anxious for everyone to know, but...well, Amour might not be so keen on the idea. I just don't want you to get your hopes up and—" Ed chuckled. "Yeah, I guess it's too late for that. I'll do my best. Yes, I promise. And I'll call Yvonne. No, I appreciate it. Give my best to

Giles and say hi to the kids. Thanks. Yes, I miss you, too." He hung up and reached for his suit jacket.

The phone rang. "What did you forget?" he asked, laughing. "Oh, it's you. No, I wasn't expecting to hear from you so early. No, I thought it was Lily calling me back. Yes, we just hung up. Why?" Ed had to think quickly. "Uh, she called to tell me Giles had a mild stroke," he lied. "No, I think he'll be fine. *Why*? Really? That was quick. What did he say? Great. No, I understand. Of course not. What date is that? October fourth. The weekend before Thanksgiving? No, that's fine. And they don't mind having it at their cottage? I guess that's that, then. Of course, I understand." Ed closed his eyes. "I know. Hard to ask one without the other. I just thought maybe we'd do it together. No, I'm not upset. I'm glad you're excited about the wedding. Yes, I told Lily. *What did she say.* She said she was happy for us. No, I won't forget to call Gordon. Love you, too." He hung up. Despite insisting otherwise, his conversation with Amour left him feeling unsettled. He was glad she was anxious to share their good news, but felt it wasn't her place to ask Stanley to be his groomsman. That's a guy to guy thing, he thought. *Funny how up until she said yes, she could do no wrong. Now, all of a sudden, I'm seeing all these things that make me wonder. Christ, it hasn't even been twenty-four hours. Way too soon to be getting cold feet.*

Luke nodded for Mark to step into the hallway. "You should go home and get some sleep. Clean yourself up. I'll sit with her for a few hours," he whispered.

Mark ran his hand over his bristly chin. "You sure?"

Luke nodded. "John's got the store covered." He held up a pocket novel. "And I came prepared."

Mark hugged his brother. "I'll be back before noon."

Luke smiled. "No rush," he said, entering the room and sitting in the chair next to Toni's bed. He looked at her lying curled up on her side, grateful that she was asleep and he didn't have to search for the reassuring words he knew would ring hollow. He opened his book to a dog-eared page and began reading, unware that Toni was awake, her mind tormented by thoughts of her stillborn son and her future with Mark.

Toni rolled over so Luke couldn't see her face, wishing she had died on the operating table so she could be buried with her son. *I have nothing left. I'll never be a wife, mother, or grandmother. There'll be no joy-filled celebrations. No christenings, no birthday parties, no weddings. Those special moments have been buried with my baby boy.*

Charlotte walked in and smiled at Luke. "She's still asleep?" she whispered.

Luke nodded and pointed to her breakfast tray. "And she still hasn't eaten."

Charlotte walked around the side of the bed and looked down at her patient. Toni's cheeks and pillow were wet. She looked back at Luke. "Perhaps you can wait outside for a bit? I'm going to get her washed up for the day."

"Sure. I'll be in the waiting room," he said.

Charlotte waited for him to leave. "Toni," she said. "Toni, dear, I know you're awake. You really do need to eat. Can you open your eyes for me?"

"I'm not hungry. And I don't want any visitors. I want to be left alone."

Charlotte pulled a chair over and sat beside her. "I know, dear. And I know you must be dying inside. But Toni, I promise things will get better. But first, you need to eat…build your strength up." She waited for Toni to say something. "Would you like to talk to someone, perhaps the hospital chaplain? I could ask—"

"No," Toni said harshly.

"Toni, I lost a baby as well, but I'm not going to pretend to know what you are going through. I can't imagine how agonizing this is for you. But you're young and you have your whole life ahead of you. And there are lots of children who need—"

Toni suddenly rolled onto her back and pointed. "Get out! Get the hell out!" she screamed, startling Charlotte.

Charlotte quickly stood. She went to touch Toni's shoulder. "I'm sorry if I upset—"

"Get out! Get out! Get out!" Toni screamed, batting Charlotte's hand away.

Luke and several nurses appeared in the doorway. Charlotte smiled and walked toward them. "Let's leave her be for a while," she said, pulling Toni's door closed. She looked at one of her co-workers. "Is Dr. Morrison doing rounds this morning?"

"Yes."

"Tell him we need to up her dosage of Phenobarbital." She looked at Luke. "It's a drug that will help her cope with her—"

Luke nodded. "I know what it is," he said, thinking about the little, blue pills he took to calm his nerves.

Charlotte smiled. "It's not the ideal course of action. I'd prefer she talk about her feelings. Maybe talk to the chaplain, or a doctor that specializes in emotional trauma, but she's not keen on the idea."

Luke's eyes widened. "She likes Mabel. Maybe she'll talk to her."

Stanley pulled in front of Cameron's. "You look exhausted."

Mabel rubbed her forehead. "That's because I am. I have half a mind to skip club tonight. I'm not in the mood, especially with what's going on with Toni and Mark."

"Well, do it. The girls will get along fine without you."

Mabel sighed. "I can't. It wouldn't be fair to Amour. She's going to tell them about the wedding. She'll want me there." She opened the door. "Hopefully I can get away early and grab a nap. Shake this awful mood I'm in. Maybe you should, too?"

Stanley raised his eyes and grinned. "Are you suggesting what I think you're suggesting?"

"Nice try, but no. I'm just saying you didn't get much sleep either," she said, stepping out and closing the door. She entered the store, stopped briefly to speak to John, then joined Bessie and Alice in the bakery. "Good morning," she said flatly, without her usual smile. She picked up the stack of phone-in orders and quickly sifted through them. "I don't care if the mayor himself calls, don't take any more orders. We'll be lucky to get through what we have. I'll look after the bread orders. You two can handle the rest."

Bessie and Alice immediately detected something was wrong and exchanged glances. "Everything okay?" Alice asked.

"Everything's just tickity-boo," Mabel said with a hint of sarcasm. She tied her apron in the back and began readying her baking station, hoping to complete the bread orders by two so she could head home. She glanced at Alice and felt herself bristle. "John said Luke is at the hospital."

Alice greased the inside of her cake pan. "Yeah, he went to give Mark a break."

"Your husband's a good man," Mabel said.

Alice smiled. "So, how is she doing?"

"Her name is Toni!" Mabel yelled, slamming a wooden spoon down and snapping it in two. "And how the hell do you think she is! She lost her baby and can never have another!"

Bessie put her head down.

Alice looked up with her mouth open. "Mabel, I'm sorry. I just—"

Mabel closed her eyes and tried to slow her breathing. "No, I'm sorry." She smiled at Bessie who looked as if she were about to burst into tears. "Bessie, I apologize. I didn't mean to…to frighten you. And that goes for you too, Alice. There's no excuse for my behaviour."

John appeared in the doorway. "What the heck is going on?"

Mabel began untying her apron. "I lost my temper. I need some fresh air. Again, I'm sorry for the outburst." She left the bakery and was about to cross School Street on her way to the brook when she heard John calling her name. She turned around to see him waving her back. She took a deep breath and walked toward him.

"Luke is on the phone. He wants to speak with you. Said it's about Toni."

Mabel rushed into the store and picked up the receiver. "Luke, is Toni all right? Oh, thank goodness. I thought things might have taken a turn for the worse. Well, of course. It's just, well I'm not sure I'll have any more luck than Charlotte. Yes, I suppose so. Actually, I'll come now. No, Alice and Bessie can look after things. No, that's fine. I'd prefer to walk. It'll give me time to collect my thoughts."

"Mabel!" Stanley hollered upstairs. "Amour is waiting out front."

"I'm coming," she snapped, rushing down the stairs with her pumps in her hand. She threw them on the floor and quickly stepped into them. "I'd rather be soaking in a hot tub and climbing into bed."

Stanley passed Mabel her coat. "Try and have some fun."

Mabel kissed his cheek and ran to the car.

Amour immediately picked up on Mabel's flat mood. "What's wrong? You don't seem yourself."

Mabel started telling her about her visit with Toni. Amour passed Myrtle's driveway. "Aren't we picking Myrtle up?" Mabel asked.

"She had an appointment in town...said she'd meet us there."

"Anyway, Toni's heartbroken, and Mark is like a lost soul."

Amour shook her head. "God love her. Maybe I should talk to her? You know, tell her about adopting Victoria and how it changed my life."

Mabel nodded. "I think that's a good idea, but not just yet. Charlotte says there giving her medication to help her cope, but that she's likely not ready to open up and talk about her feelings. I just wish she'd start eating." She rolled her window down. "Are we picking up Alice?"

"Oh, I thought you knew. She's not coming...said she's not feeling well."

Mabel dropped her head, knowing that wasn't the reason. "That's not it. She's mad at me."

Amour looked surprised. "*What for?*"

Mabel shifted in her seat. "I lost my temper with her today. I apologized, but I don't blame her for being angry with me. It was my fault."

Amour turned down Kind Edward Street. "I can't imagine. What did Alice do that got you so riled up?"

Mabel smiled. "Nothing really. It was just all stupid. Totally my fault," she said, careful not to divulge too much for fear it would lead to more questions. "Excited about telling the girls your news?" she asked, hoping to change the subject.

Amour stopped in front of Rosie's and put the car in park. "Of course. Especially Myrtle. There's Rosie now."

Rosie climbed in the back seat. "Hello, ladies. Can't tell you how happy I am to see you. Really appreciate you inviting me to join your club. Got us something special for the occasion." She leaned forward and passed

Mabel a deck of cards. "I thought we'd play with these. Go ahead, open em up," she said, grinning.

Mabel took the deck from her, shook the cards into her hand, and started to chuckle.

Amour glanced over at Mabel. "What's so funny?"

Mabel held up the king of hearts.

Rosie laughed. "Wait till you see the jack of clubs. He got a dong on him a mile long. She reached into her bag. "Oh, and I'm assumin you'll all be up for a snort or two," she said, holding up a quart of Johnnie Walker.

The kitchen was soon abuzz as Mary Catherine poured the tea, Myrtle unwrapped a plate of egg salad sandwiches, and Mabel arranged a tray of sweets.

Amour smiled at Mabel. "Excuse me, ladies. Ladies!" she repeated more loudly. Everyone stopped what they were doing and turned toward her. "I have some news," she announced.

Mary Catherine looked at Amour's hand and squealed. "Oh, my God, you're getting married!"

There were hugs all around as everyone celebrated the exciting news. Myrtle sat down. "When's the big day?"

"October fourth. The weekend before Thanksgiving…at Mabel's and Stanley's in Pleasant Bay. It will be small, but of course you're all invited."

"I'll be there with bells on," Rosie said. She reached in her tote and held up the bottle of Johnnie Walker. "This calls for a toast."

Mabel looked at Myrtle, surprised her reaction was so muted. She approached her. "Wonderful news, don't you think?"

"Yes, wonderful news," she said flatly.

Mabel smiled. "I thought you'd be more excited?"

"I'll believe it when I see it," Myrtle whispered.

Mabel laughed. "Why would you say that?"

"Just a feeling. Remember…I'm a witch."

Rosie handed Mabel and Myrtle their drinks and called for everyone's attention. "I'm so excited to be here with you gals…to be part of your club. Thanks for invitin me. And I'm really glad I get to congratulate my beautiful friend on her engagement to the man of *my dreams*," she said, elbowing Mabel and winking. Everyone, but Myrtle, laughed. "I gotta tell ya, if Amour didn't say yes, I'd be bangin on Ed's door." She grinned.

"I'd be bangin something, fer sure." Again, everyone but Myrtle laughed. "Anyway, cheers to the happy couple."

After a million more questions about the proposal and the wedding they gathered in the living room. Mary Catherine tossed a deck of cards on the table. "I'll sit out the first game. Then we'll draw jacks."

"Do you mind?" Rosie said, holding up her pack. "I brought my lucky cards."

Mary Catherine shrugged. "Sure."

Amour and Mabel huddled together with their hands over their mouths, waiting for Mary Catherine's and Myrtles' reactions. Rosie passed out several low cards, trying not to laugh as she waited to flip up a face card. Finally, she dealt Mary Catherine the king of spades.

Mary Catherine stared wide-eyed at the shocking image of a smiling king holding a huge penis in his hand. "Holy Shit," she said, pointing. She burst out laughing. She picked it up and brought it close to her face. "Oh my God! It's Sam," she said to gales of laughter.

Mabel nudged Amour and nodded to Myrtle sitting stone-faced.

Rosie roared with laughter. "Oh, and ladies, those aren't spades. Look more closely, they're vaginas." She started sifting through the other cards. "And wait till you see the jack of clubs."

Myrtle leaned over the table and quickly gathered Rosie's cards into a pile. "I don't know about the rest of you, but I came to play Tarabish, not look at filth!"

The room went quiet.

"Of course," Rosie said meekly. "Sorry, I just thought it might be fun to—" She looked at Amour. "I'm sorry," she said, struggling to hold back tears.

Despite efforts to put the awkward moment behind them, the joy of the night was lost as Rosie became unusually quiet, and Myrtle maintained her frosty demeanour.

Mabel entered the kitchen and passed Mary Catherine several plates.

"What the hell is eating Myrtle?" Mary Catherine whispered.

Mabel shrugged. "I'm not sure. I feel bad for Rosie. I doubt she'll come back."

Amour entered. "Rosie decided to walk home." She winced. "She said she was sorry for ruining the night."

Mary Catherine's shoulders fell. "It wasn't Rosie's fault," she whispered.

"No, it was mine," Myrtle said, approaching from behind.

"I didn't say that either," Mary Catherine protested.

Mabel smiled. "Let's just call it a night. No one meant any harm."

"I think I'll walk, too," Myrtle said. She smiled. "Sorry I spoiled things for everyone. What can I say, I forgot to take my bitch pills this morning."

"*Myrtle*," Amour objected. "I'll drive you. I'm taking Mabel home, I might as well drop you off, too."

"Thanks, but it's a nice night. I want to walk," she said and left.

Mabel was at the door about to leave when Mary Catherine told her to wait, disappearing briefly, before returning with Rosie's cards. "Wouldn't want Sam or the kids to find them. Give them to Amour so she can get them back to Rosie."

Mabel put them in her purse. "Thanks again," she said, waving from the step. She climbed in beside Amour. "Well, that was quite the night."

Amour put the car in drive. "I know. And what the hell is wrong with Myrtle? She was so mean to Rosie. Do you think she's feeling okay?"

Mabel pictured her wooden spoon snapping in two. She looked over at Amour and smiled. "It's probably nothing. We all have our off days."

Wednesday, July 9

Mabel entered the bakery, surprised Alice's station was clean and she was nowhere in sight. "Good morning, Bessie," she said, removing her coat.

"Morning," Bessie cheerily replied.

"Where's Alice?"

"Luke just popped in…said she's not feeling well. Mary Mack is on her way."

Mabel nodded, suspecting Alice wasn't really sick, but rather still upset with her for her outburst. "I was hoping to tell her the good news."

Bessie smiled. "*Oh?*"

Mabel looped her apron over her head. "Amour and Ed are getting married."

Bessie beamed. "That's wonderful. I like that young man." She started to laugh. "And he sure likes us. Don't know anyone who comes here more often than him. And he doesn't gain an ounce."

Mabel smiled. "Bessie, I want to apologize. I'm really sorry about yesterday. I was way out of line."

Bessie looked up from her kneading. "Oh, that's okay." She laughed. "Believe me, I've been known to break a few wooden spoons in my day, too."

Mabel was peeling apples when she suddenly stopped. She put down her paring knife and quickly cleaned her hands in her apron. "I'll be back in a minute," she said to Bessie and entered the store. John was waiting on a customer. She smiled and climbed the stairs to the apartment. She walked down the hall to what was once James' and Margaret's bedroom and felt her chest tighten. The door was closed. She tapped lightly. "Alice, are you all right?" She waited. "Alice?"

"I'm not feeling great."

"Can I get you anything?"

"No, I'm okay."

"Alice, I'm sorry about yesterday. I don't know what got into me."

"It's okay. I understand."

Mabel dropped her head. "We missed you at club. Amour shared some exciting news. She and Ed are getting married."

"That's great. I'm happy for them."

Mabel looked up. "All right then. I hope you feel better soon. Let me know if you need anything."

"I will."

Mabel hesitated, then started toward the stairs. She stopped outside of what was now Matthew's room. The door was ajar. She pushed it open and peeked in. It was the room she had stayed in after James and Stanley found her in the coal shed. She entered and let her finger tips rest on the small, wooden rocker that had once belonged to James' and Margaret's son. She sat on the side of Matthew's bed and thought of Toni. Her circumstances were heart wrenching, but at least she didn't experience the love of a child that would be taken from her, like Margaret. Mabel fixed the pillow behind her head, stretched out, and closed her eyes, thinking about how cold Margaret was when they first met. It would take time before she would eventually come around and they would become as close as a mother and daughter. Images of Margaret began flashing before her. Margaret handing her a beautiful pair of boots and telling her it was time for her to go home to Johnnie. Margaret and James waltzing at Amour's bistro. Margaret lying in bed with Luke and his brothers curled up at her side as she read *Smokey the Cow Horse*.

Mark picked up the magazine he had just put down and once again idly flipped through the pages. He looked up to see Toni, lying on her side, staring at him. He tossed the magazine aside and smiled. "You're awake?"

"I wasn't asleep," she said flatly.

"Oh, I just assumed...your eyes were closed. Are you feeling any better?"

"I want to go home."

Mark smiled. "Well, that's good. And I want you to come home, but I'm not sure they're gonna let you out just yet."

Toni turned onto her back and stared up at the ceiling. "I want to go home...to Waterville."

Mark laughed nervously. "*Waterville?* You mean for a visit?"

"No, I mean to stay."

Mark reached for her hand, but Toni quickly pulled it away. "Toni, the doctor said it's gonna take time for you to come to grips with—"

"I want to go home," she said more firmly.

Mark wasn't sure what to say. "I think you'll start to feel better in a couple of days. And...well, you'll start to see things in a better light. Charlotte said—"

"I want you to leave," she said softly.

"What?"

"Go home," Toni repeated.

Mark smiled. "Toni, I'm not going anywhere. I'm gonna stay for as long as—"

Toni suddenly turned her head toward him and pointed to the door. "Get out!" she seethed.

Mark recoiled. "*Toni?*"

Toni's face contorted. "Now! Leave! Get the hell out of here!"

Charlotte appeared in the doorway. "Mark, can you give us a few minutes?"

Mark looked at Toni, then started for the door. He stopped beside Charlotte. "I'm sorry. I didn't mean to make her so upset," he whispered.

Charlotte smiled and squeezed his hand. "Wait outside. I won't be long," she said and closed the door. She walked to the window. "Hard to get your rest with the light pouring in," she said, pulling the curtains over. "And I'll make sure you're not disturbed until it's time for lunch. How does that sound?"

Toni turned onto her side and pulled the sheet over her head. "I don't want lunch. I don't want supper. I just wanna die."

Charlotte sighed. "I don't blame you. And I'm not gonna lie. You have a long, hard road ahead of you. But you'll go on and you'll get through this." Toni didn't respond. "I'll check back before too long. In the meantime, get some rest. You've been through a lot and your body needs time to heal." Charlotte stepped into the hall expecting to see Mark. She went to the nurses' station. "The young man that was visiting Miss Moody, did you see where he went?" she asked a young candy-striper.

She pointed to the exit. "I assume he left."

Charlotte nodded. "We sometimes focus so much on the mother, we forget the dads are hurting just as much. Hopefully he's all right."

Mark got into his car and leaned over the steering wheel, sobbing. He sat up at the sound of an incoming ambulance, wiped his wet face, and pulled away. He'd head to The Y and take his anger out on a punching bag. He parked behind the Co-op, walked through the alley to Commercial Street, and waited for the traffic to pass. He looked to his left, then started walking. He pulled on the heavy wooden door, walked into the smoky room and sat down heavily.

"What can I get you?" the bartender asked.

"Johnnie Walker...bring the bottle."

Harley knocked on Stanley's door. "Gordon Dunphy's on the phone. Said he needs to talk to you."

Stanley pushed his chair back and walked out to take the phone. "Hey Gordon. How are you? Great news about Amour and Ed. Yes. Looking forward to it. We'll have to plan a bachelor party. *What? Iggies?* Jesus Christ. Is he all right?" Stanley looked at his watch. "Christ, he must have started early. Is he being charged? Thanks for doing that. No, I'll deal with the damages. Did you call Luke? *Oh?* No, never mind. It doesn't matter. I'll come now."

Gordon met Stanley at the front desk and led him downstairs to the jail. "I guess he got pretty belligerent and started mouthing off to some guys from New Waterford. He sucker punched one of them. Broke his nose. Then, all hell broke loose. But he held his own. Anyway, Big Dick convinced them not to press charges. Said it wouldn't do much for their reputations…three guys against one and they come out on the losing end."

Stanley stopped outside the cell he had occupied after he was charged with Johnnie Adshade's murder. He smiled at Gordon. "I like what you did to the place."

Gordon laughed. "Amazing what a new coat of paint can do."

Geezer appeared at his cell door. "Hey, bud. Got a smoke?"

Stanley patted his pockets. "Sorry."

"What's for supper?" Geezer asked Gordon.

"Stew."

"I had stew for lunch," Geezer protested.

Gordon laughed. "I'll talk to the chef. Wouldn't want you to start looking for new accommodations." He looked at Stanley, then pointed at Mark splayed face down on his cot.

"You know he and his girlfriend lost a baby and they can't have any more," Stanley said.

Gordon nodded. "Charlotte told me. I know how I felt when we lost the baby. Anyway, at least I knew we could keep trying and, lo and behold, we got lucky." He slid the cell door open, stepped over a puddle of vomit, and shook Mark's shoulder. "Mark, wake up. Stanley's here to take you home. Mark, c'mon bud. Time to get up."

Mark rolled onto his side and briefly opened his eyes. "I don't feel so good," he slurred.

"You don't look too good, either," Stanley said, grabbing him under the arm and helping into a sitting position. "That's quite the shiner."

Mark started to lie down again, but Stanley stopped him. "Oh, no you don't," he said, straightening him back up. "You're coming with me."

Stanley laid Mark down in the back seat of his car and closed the door.

"Are you gonna be able to get him up to his apartment by yourself?" Gordon asked. "He's like dead weight. I can follow you…give you a hand."

"Thanks, but I'm not taking him to his apartment. He's coming home with me. I want to keep an eye on him...have a little chat when he sobers up." Stanley was about to get behind the wheel when he stopped. "Oh, by the way, did Mark mention why he wanted you to call me and not Luke?"

"He just mumbled something about being a miserable brother and asked for you." Gordon shrugged. "I was surprised. I always thought they got along pretty well. Apparently not."

Stanley nodded. "Thanks," he said, getting in and starting the car. He looked over his shoulder at Mark passed out in the back. *I know you were talking about yourself, not Luke.*

Mabel woke with a sore neck, confused by her surroundings. She quickly sat up, wondering how long she had been asleep. She stood, walked into the hall, and looked back toward Alice's bedroom. Her door was still closed. She started down the stairs.

John was replenishing the cigarette display. "Have a good sleep?" he asked.

Mabel was surprised by his comment. "I nodded off. What time is it, anyway?"

John looked at his watch. "Quarter after three."

"*Three!*" Mabel repeated, shocked she had slept most of the day. "Why didn't someone wake me?"

John nodded into the bakery. "The ladies figured you needed the sleep."

"Bessie and Mary Mack must be run ragged," Mabel said, quickening her pace. She entered the bakery. "*Alice*," she said, surprised to see her.

Alice spun around. "You're up."

"So, you're feeling better?" Mabel asked.

Alice nodded. "Yes. How about you?"

"I didn't mean to fall asleep. And I certainly didn't mean to sleep the day away."

Bessie closed the oven door. "You must have needed it."

Mabel laughed. "I guess I did." She walked up to Alice. "Everything good?"

Alice assured Mabel that the orders were in hand, suggesting she should head home early. It didn't take much convincing. Mabel gathered up her things and left for home, thinking her unplanned, six-hour sleep left her feeling sluggish, not refreshed. She'd walk to town and get the bus from there. She got about fifty feet down School Street when she stopped. She looked back, then began retracing her steps, walking past the bakery.

She was halfway up Dominion Street when she stopped and pushed on the heavy, wrought iron gate leading to the graveyard. She grimaced at the sound of the loud, grating sound. She slowly closed it over and began following the winding graveled pathway, lamenting the sorry state of many of the gravesites. Perhaps there was no one left to maintain them, she thought. Or maybe, over time, the visitors became less frequent as the dead became a distant memory. She stopped at the headstone of a small child, picked up a discarded cigarette pack, put it in her purse and continued toward the Red Maple that Stanley had planted shortly after James had died. She smiled at its beauty. The sun was shining through the branches, casting rays of light onto the three well-kept graves below. James and Margaret would be pleased, she thought, getting down on her knees and reading, as she always did, the words on the three headstones. She blessed herself and closed her eyes. *You're never far from my thoughts, but, today, you've been occupying them. Probably because I was in the apartment. Every time I climb those stairs it brings back a flood of memories. Reminds me of how blessed I was to have you in my life. God knows where I'd be if not for you, your love, and generosity. I struggle every day to live my life as you did yours, and to be kind to others. But lately, I've found myself faltering…growing impatient…judging. I pray I can overcome my shortcomings and become a better person. And I can always use your help. Mark and his girlfriend, Toni, lost their son; a heartache you both know too well. And Toni just had a hysterectomy. I pray she will recover in body, mind, and spirit, and that, someday, she'll experience the kind of joy you found in Luke, and the boys. Anyway, I needed to visit you today. You settle my mind…help me feel better. Thank you for everything you did and continue to do for me. I'll come back again soon. Love and miss you dearly.*

Mabel stood, kissed her finger tips, and laid them on Margaret's headstone, then James'. She then bent down and laid her hand on top of the small granite tablet with the engraved lamb. "Rest peacefully, sweet child. And please watch over my beautiful boy."

"Look, I know you're hurting. And I don't blame you for wanting to drown your sorrows. But, Mark, Toni needs you right now. Ya gotta get your shit together." Stanley put another cup of coffee in front of him. "Can I ask you something?"

Mark stared blankly into his cup.

"Are you planning to marry her?" Stanley asked.

He shrugged.

"Do you love her?"

Mark sighed and shook his head. "I thought I did. I mean, I thought we'd get married once we got settled and I got steady work."

"And now?" Stanley asked.

"And now it doesn't matter. She doesn't wanna have anything to do with me. I think she blames me."

Stanley sat down. "That's crazy. What happened to Toni had nothing to do with you. It was a tragic—"

Mark's head shot up. "She's right. I wasn't there for her when the bleeding started. She was asking about the baby's funeral. I asked her to stop, but she kept at it. I couldn't help it, I got mad and stormed out...left her alone. When I got home, she was in bed. Then I got up to go to work without talking to her. She was probably bleeding the whole time. If I had stayed with her instead of going off and getting drunk, maybe she wouldn't have had to have her womb cut out," he said, stifling a sob.

Stanley leaned forward and squeezed his shoulder. "Mark, these things happen. You can't blame yourself. That's the last thing Toni needs right now. You need to be strong for—"

"God's punishing me," Mark blurted.

"*What?*"

"God's punishing me for screwing Alice...for betraying my brother."

Stanley leaned back. "Mark, that's nonsense."

"It's true," Mark insisted. "Pretty sick sense of humour, eh? Gives me one son I can't have, then another he snatches away before he takes his first breath."

The front door opened. Mabel sat on the landing of the stairs and kicked off her shoes. "Stanley," she called out.

Mark quickly wiped his tear-stained face.

"We're in the kitchen."

"I was surprised to see the car out front," she hollered, putting her purse on the floor. She could see the back of a man slumped over the table. "If I knew you were leaving work early I would have had you pick me up," she said, entering the kitchen. "Oh, Mark, it's you. I was wondering who Stanley was— Oh my God! What happened to you? Were you in a fight?"

Amour held the spoon up to Ed's mouth. "So Giles will be okay?" she asked.

Ed sipped the hot broth. "Oooh, that's good," he said, smacking his lips together. He took two bowls down from the cupboard and put them next to the stove. "Yes, I think so. Yvonne says he'll need physical therapy, but that the doctors are optimistic he'll make a full recovery."

Amour ladled the soup into a bowl. "I set a table in the dining room. It's more romantic." She laughed. "Might as well enjoy it while it lasts. We'll soon be an old married couple and the romance will be out the window."

Ed kissed her neck. "Never," he said, picking up his bowl. He waited in the dining room for her to join him, wondering whether he should tell her about Lily before or after they eat. He smiled as she approached. "If you keep cooking like this, I'll gain fifty pounds by the time the wedding rolls around."

Amour sat down. "You can afford to put on a few more pounds. You're too thin."

The mood was happy and light as they ate dinner, drank wine, and discussed plans for the wedding. Ed, suddenly became quiet. He turned his head and looked out at the ocean. Amour studied his handsome profile, reminding herself how lucky she was to have found love a second time. She wondered what he was thinking. "Not having second thoughts I hope?"

Ed smiled. "Not a chance. But there is something I need to talk to you about."

Amour looked perplexed. "Sounds serious. You're not going to tell me you're already married," she said, grinning.

Ed wiped his mouth with his napkin and leaned back in his chair. "Actually, it's about Victoria."

"*Victoria?* What about Victoria?"

Ed leaned forward and put his hand over hers. "It's nothing bad. Nothing bad at all. In fact, I'm hoping you'll be pleased with what I'm about to tell you."

Amour laughed nervously. "Well, stop teasing and just tell me."

Ed smiled and squeezed her hand. "She has siblings...half-siblings. Three in fact. A brother and two sisters."

Amour pulled her hand free and squared her shoulders. "And how would you know that?"

Ed's mouth was dry. "Amour." He paused. "Lily is Victoria's birthmother."

"Lily? *Stanley's Lily*?" Amour laughed, as if the suggestion was preposterous. "Where in the world — *Who told you that*?"

"It's true. Lily knew right away...the moment she set eyes on her. And if you saw pictures of Lily when she was younger, there's no denying the resemblance. There's no question about it. God, I can even see it now. Amour, this is —"

Amour angrily pushed her chair back and stood up. "What are you up to? I don't believe a word of it. It's not true! It can't be! Lily's a thief...a liar and a—"

"Don't go there again," Ed warned. He dropped his head, then slowly stood up. "Amour, I have no reason to lie about this. I swear it's true. I had Frank Miller, my friend with the RCMP, ask around. Victoria's birthdate is the same as the child Lily gave up, and she was adopted from the same orphanage. You said you always celebrate May eighteenth as Victoria's second birthday...the day you and Michael took her home from the orphanage. That's the same day Lily's child was adopted. Amour, I'm sorry you feel this way." He was about to touch her arm.

She flinched. "Don't touch me!"

Ed laughed in disbelief. "*What*?"

"You heard me!" she snapped.

Ed dropped his arm at his side. "I thought you might see this as good news...that you'd want Victoria to know her brother and sisters. But it's your call...no one else's. You can tell her if you want, or you can just go on as if nothing has changed. But you should also know, Jeanne and Hector MacDonald are Lily's parents...Victoria's grandparents."

Amour spun around and stared. "That's nonsense."

Ed shook his head. "No, Amour. It's all true. Why would I make it up? And if you don't believe me, I'm sure Frank will be happy to come and talk to you."

Amour walked to the window. "So, that's why they helped her get the job," she scoffed. "They're just trying to get in her good graces...worm their way into—"

"Amour! Stop! They're not trying to do anything of the sort. They don't even know. Lily hasn't spoken to them in years. Not since she got pregnant with Victoria. They have no idea they're even—"

"How long have you known?" Amour demanded.

"About Lily?"

"Yes."

Ed took a deep breath. "I've known for a while. Look, I thought about telling you, but I didn't think it was my place to—"

"*To what*?" Amour seethed. "To tell me you were in cahoots with Lily to take my daughter from me!"

"Don't be ridiculous!" Ed said, regretting his angry tone. He leveled his voice. "No one is taking Victoria away from you. It's just that she has a family she's never met...grandparents that she's visiting with no idea who they are. Amour, she's not going to stop loving you because—"

"How long have you known?" she repeated.

Ed shook his head and sighed. "Since the day Lily came to give Stanley his money back."

Amour spun around and glared at him. "That was two years ago! The day we met!"

Ed nodded. "Amour, Lily knows that it's totally up to you if you tell Victoria. If you don't want to tell her, Lily promised she'd stay away...not interfere. In fact, she was prepared to let everybody carry on without telling a soul. But once Victoria met her grandparents ...I don't know... she asked me to talk to you...see if you'd be agreeable to the idea of—"

"And how did Lily know Victoria met her grandparents? You just said they haven't spoken in years."

"I told her."

"Of course you did! You tell Lily about Victoria meeting her grandparents, but, nooo, you don't tell me anything," she hissed between clenched teeth. She batted away a tear. "Lily knew damn well I'd have to tell Victoria. She's a grown woman, for God's sake...she can make up her own mind who she wants in her life. So, I guess her father will be the next one to come knocking on my door."

"Now you're being ridiculous," Ed said, exasperated. "Lily hasn't seen or heard from him in years. She doesn't even know where he lives." Ed closed his eyes. "So, you're going to tell Victoria?"

"What choice do I have!" Amour fumed.

Ed hoped she would see his sincerity. "I'm sorry I didn't tell you sooner. But, I'm glad you finally know." He went to hug her, but she stepped back.

"Secrets don't make for a happy marriage," she said, roughly pulling off her engagement ring and holding it out to him.

Ed looked stunned. "You can't be serious?"

"Take it," Amour insisted.

Ed shook his head. "Amour, I'm sorry. Honestly, I didn't think it was my place. I'm sorry I didn't tell you sooner. I don't know what to say."

Amour slammed the ring down on the table.

"Amour, I love you. Please don't do this. Amour!" he pleaded.

"You can see yourself out," she said and headed for the stairs.

Ed followed her to the landing and watched her scurry upstairs and disappear out of sight. He called her name several times, then turned to leave. He was heading for the door when he looked up at Michael's portrait. "She sure doesn't make it easy, does she?" he whispered.

Thursday, July 10

Mark had promised he would lay off the booze, but Mabel wasn't hopeful. She greased the tops of her rolls, worried about what was to become of him and Toni. He was like a broken man, with nothing to lose, she thought.

Corliss poked his head into the bakery. "Amour is here."

Mabel looked up. "*Amour*?" she said, surprised. "Well, tell her to come in."

He winced. "She's a little upset. Said she'd wait in the car."

Mabel quickly slid her rolls into the oven, closed the door, and went outside. She opened the car door and immediately knew Amour had been crying. She climbed in and hugged her friend. "What's wrong?"

Amour reached in her pocket for a tissue. "The wedding is off."

Mabel stared in disbelief. "*Why*? What happened?"

"Lily happened...that's what happened," Amour wailed.

"Lily?"

Amour proceeded to tell her about Ed's revelation.

Mabel was as shocked by the news that Lily was Victoria's birthmother as she was by the news that Amour ended things with Ed. "I can't believe it. I mean, I did see a resemblance, but never in my wildest dreams did I ever think they were related. Have you talked to Victoria about Lily and her grandparents?"

Amour shook her head. "Not yet."

"But you're going to?"

Amour blew her nose. "Of course. Tonight." She started to laugh. "I hope she's happy about it, because I know she's going to be heartbroken when I tell her about Ed. She was so excited about the wedding."

Mabel nodded and smiled. "Amour, do you think you might be being too hard on Ed?"

"*Too hard!* How can you say that? He's known for two years and never said a word! How could I ever trust him again?" She blew her nose. "You know, I've never really understood his relationship with Lily."

Mabel knew Amour was upset and didn't want to make things worse. She squeezed her hand. "They're good friends, that's all."

"Well that just goes to show how bad his judgement is. I know you like her, but you gotta admit she just jumps from one mess to the next. She's trouble. Thank God Victoria's nothing like her."

Mabel dropped her head, thinking Amour wasn't being fair to Lily. "I don't know what to say...or do, for that matter."

Amour wiped her wet cheek. "Can you come over this evening... be there when I tell Victoria? I mean, I'll tell her myself, but I'd love if you can be there for moral support." She smiled. "If not for Victoria, for me."

Mabel rubbed Amour's leg and smiled. "Of course."

"And Lily sent you pictures of the kids, right? Maybe you could bring them along, so Victoria can see—" Amour started to sob. "The...the family I took her away from."

Mabel put her arms around her. "Amour, you didn't take Victoria away from anyone. You rescued her from the orphanage and God knows what else. Victoria loves you. And she's going to love you even more, if that's possible, for introducing her to her brother and sisters."

Amour sat up and tilted her head back. "And her mother...*and grandparents*."

"The woman who gave birth to her, not her mother," Mabel corrected. She shook her head in disbelief. "I still can't get over all of the strange coincidences. Lily meeting Ed. Ed moving to Cape Breton and meeting you. Victoria stopping to help her grandparents, completely unaware of who they were. Honestly, you could write a book."

Amour dropped her head. "Ed says it's fate."

Mabel nodded. "I think he might be right. One thing is for sure, it's no accident. Seems to me there's a higher power at work...one that wants all of you to come together as a family. And, I'm pretty sure I know who's behind it."

Amour looked confused. "What do you mean?"

Mabel smiled. "I'm saying I think Michael might have a hand in things. He wanted Ed to find you...and he had Lily make it happen."

Mark stood in the doorway of Toni's room, surprised to see her sitting up and eating. He tapped lightly on the door, unsure of what kind of reception he was in for. "Can I come in?"

Toni looked up. "What happened to you?"

Mark smiled and touched his black eye. "I was sparring with one of the guys at The Y," he lied. He bent down and awkwardly kissed her cheek. "You're looking better. How are you feeling?"

Toni idly tore at the crust of her bread. "I'm ready to go home."

Mark wasn't sure if she meant to the apartment or Waterville, but knew not to ask. "It's good that you're eating," he said. He pulled a chair over to the side of the bed.

Toni shrugged. "It's not because I want to," she said, pushing her tray to the side. "The nurses tell me it's the only way out of this damn place."

Mark nodded. "You need to get your strength back. How's the pain?"

Toni stared into his eyes. "Which one? The one in my belly, or the one in my heart?"

Mark put his hand over hers. "Both, I guess."

Toni's lower lip began to quiver and her eyes filled up. She turned her head away and looked out the window. "I never told you this before, but when I first found out I was pregnant...I wasn't happy about it. I even thought...I thought about getting rid of it," she said, choking back tears. "I thought we needed more time to get to know each other...to have some fun without the worries of bringing up a kid. Then, I felt the baby move and everything changed." She shook her head. "Didn't matter that we were piss poor. Didn't even matter that we weren't married. Everything would work itself out." She turned back to Mark. "And it almost did." She smiled sadly. "Almost," she whispered.

Mark sat down and put his head in his hands.

Toni placed her hand on the back of his head. "I don't expect anything from you. You owe me nothing."

Mark raised his head and ran the back of his hand under his nose. "What are you talking about? I'm not going anywhere. You just need time to get strong…stronger," he said, his breath catching in his chest.

Toni brushed away a tear. "I won't do it to you. I won't let you throw away any chance you have of becoming a father."

Mark tilted his head back, her words reminding him of his betrayal and the cruel twist of fate that would haunt him forever.

"All finished with your lunch?" a young nurse asked cheerily. Her face fell when she looked at Toni, then Mark. "I'll come back later," she said sheepishly.

"No," Toni said. "My visitor was just leaving."

Mark looked at Toni with tears in his eyes. "I don't want to go. I want to stay with you."

"No, Mark. It's time to go."

The nurse picked up Toni's tray. "I see you didn't eat much of your lunch. If you want to get home to your handsome, young man, here, you're going to have to do better than that."

Mark squeezed Toni's hand. "I'll come back this evening."

"I'd prefer if you didn't." She smiled. "I need some time alone."

Mark nodded and kissed her forehead. "Don't give up on me. I promise I can do better," he whispered.

Toni didn't respond. Mark turned in the doorway and waved. Toni raised her hand off her belly, smiled, and mouthed *goodbye*.

Mabel paced back and forth in front of the store, anxious to share Amour's news with Stanley. He barely came to a stop when she jumped in the front seat. "I was calling. Where the hell were you?" she asked.

"I was out on a job. Why, what's wrong?"

"Lily is Victoria's birthmother and the wedding is off."

Stanley laughed and put the car in park. "*Oh, is that all*? And here I thought you might have some big news to share. Have you been drinking?"

Mabel scoffed. "Of course not!"

"Well, nothing would surprise me."

"What's that supposed to mean?" Mabel grumbled.

He stared at her. "I was looking for the car keys this morning and found an empty pack of cigarettes in your purse."

Mabel looked confused. "Oh, that. I picked that off a grave while I was at Greenwood Cemetery. I forgot to throw it out."

Stanley nodded. "And what about the cards? Did you find those at the graveyard too?"

Mabel screwed up her face. "What cards?"

Stanley dipped his chin and gave her a look that suggested she wasn't fooling him.

"Ooooh, those cards." Mabel rolled her eyes. "Those are Rosie's. She brought them to club…as a joke."

Stanley squinted. "I'm starting to wonder about that club of yours."

Mabel slapped his arm. "Smarten up. Did you hear what I said? Lily is Victoria's mother and Amour called off the wedding. Ya know, I thought I saw a resemblance, but I never once considered Lily could be her mother," she said, filling Stanley in on the details of Amour's conversation with Ed. "Ed should have told her sooner, but I still think Amour is over-reacting. I mean…calling off the wedding seems a bit much, don't you think?"

Stanley leaned against the driver's door. "She was probably just thrown off by the news. She'll come around."

Mabel shook her head. "I'm not so sure. She's pretty upset. I don't understand why Ed didn't tell her sooner."

Stanley started the car and pulled onto School Street. "I dunno, I'm not so sure I would have."

"What are you talking about? Of course you would have."

He made a face. "Think about it. Ed knew Amour for quite a while before they started seeing each other. Was he supposed to tell her before they started dating? I don't think so. Why would he? By the time they became a couple, the damage would have been done. And it's certainly not the sort of thing you just blurt on your first date." He glanced at Mabel.

"Like, *pass the butter. And, oh yeah, I've been meaning to tell you, I know your daughter's real mother."*

"Actually, he did tell her over supper," Mabel said.

Stanley turned down Pitt Street. "And didn't you just tell me Lily was prepared to let sleeping dogs lie… until what…a few days ago?"

"Yeah. Apparently she changed her mind when she found out Victoria met her parents."

"Well then, as far as I'm concerned Ed was right to keep his mouth shut. At least until Lily gave him the green light to talk to Amour."

"So, what if Lily hadn't? Are you saying it would have been okay for Ed to marry Amour and never tell her?"

Stanley pursed his lips.. "That's a whole other kettle of fish."

"It's the whole secrecy thing that's got Amour so mad. She said she could never trust him again."

"That's too bad." Stanley said. "Cause he's a real nice guy."

When they pulled up the driveway, Victoria was sitting on the front step with Liv on her lap, and JC and Mary Margaret at her feet.

Mabel touched Stanley's leg. "Look," she whispered. "See the resemblance? God, it's so obvious."

Stanley shut off the engine. "You see it now because you know to look for it."

"No, I see it because…because it's there," Mabel insisted. She stepped out of the car and smiled. "How was your day?" she asked Victoria.

Victoria handed Liv to Stanley. "Let's just say, I'm glad to see you," she said with a chuckle.

"I'm sure you're anxious to get home. I just need to duck inside for a minute. Then, I'll drive you home," Mabel said, entering the house in search of the photos Lily had sent to her. When she came back outside a few minutes later, Stanley, Victoria, and the kids were standing in the entrance to the barn.

"I put a meat pie in the oven," Mabel said to Stanley. She gave the kids a quick kiss. "All set?" she asked Victoria.

They were barely out of the driveway when Victoria began excitedly rattling on about the wedding.

Mabel felt the seven minute drive across town would never end, as Victoria excitedly asked her what colour dress would be best for a fall wedding, and whether she should wear her hair up or down. She pulled into the manor and shut the engine off, relieved she managed to avoid telling Victoria the wedding was off. "Your mother has the property looking so beautiful," she said, gathering up her purse.

"Mabel, do you like Ed?" Victoria asked.

Mabel laughed. "Of course I like Ed. He's a wonderful man. Why would you ask that?"

Victoria shrugged. "I don't know. It's just you don't seem very excited about the wedding."

Mabel smiled. "I'm sorry. It's not Ed. I've just been preoccupied lately…with Toni and Mark…the bakery."

"Thank God. For a moment there I wasn't so sure. I'm really happy for Mom. She'd never admit it, but I know she's been really lonely since Daddy died."

Mabel nodded. "Well, let's not keep her waiting. Let's go see what delicious creation she's cooked up for supper."

"Oh, I didn't realize you were staying for supper. That's great! Hopefully Ed's coming, too. We can nail down some of the wedding details. If the weather is nice enough, I think we should set up the bar in the backyard. That way we'll have more room inside for serving the food. What do you think?"

Ed was about to open the back door when he thought he heard something. He leaned over the railing with his ear cocked, then walked down the steps. He got down on his hands and knees and looked through a narrow opening under the back step. It was dark, but he could see movement. A tiny head tuned in his direction. Then another. He leaned in. "Hello, kitties," he whispered. "You guys okay under—" A paw suddenly slashed at his face. Ed jumped back as their protective mother hissed her displeasure. "Okay, okay," he said, sitting back on his heels and holding his hands up as if at gun point. "I get the message." He got to his feet and brushed the dirt off his knees. "You're not the only angry mother I know," he said. He went inside, dropped his briefcase on the floor, and opened the fridge. He grabbed two beer and a bottle opener, took them to the front step, and sat down. He looked at his watch, deciding it was still too early to call. He loosened his tie, opened a beer, and held his bottle in the air. "Congratulations, old man, you take the prize for the shortest engagement in history." He took a swig, thinking about his conversation with Amour. *You're right. I should have told you sooner. Anyway, too late now. You won't even take my calls.* He leaned back and closed his eyes, feeling the evening sun on his face, and thought of Carol, always looking out for the stray cats on the farm. *You preferred cats, and I preferred dogs.* He smiled, thinking it was one of the few things they didn't agree on. He looked up at the sky. "I know you're disappointed. So am I," he said sadly.

He finished the first beer and opened the second, wondering if it wasn't all for the best. *At least I won't have to give up this place.* He shook his head and chuckled. *Who am I kidding, I'd give it up in a flash.* He checked his watch a second time, went inside, and started dialling.

"Hey, Rory. How are you? That's great. Wow, a home run! I'm really proud of you. Yes, is she there?" Ed waited. "Oh, hi. Hope I gave you time to get settled in from work. Good. Yes, I have news. I told her. To be honest, she was shocked. It was a lot to take in." Ed picked the phone up off the table, stepped over the long cord, walked to the front door, and looked out at the beads of condensation dripping down his sweaty beer bottle. "Yes, she's going to tell her. She didn't say. No, I'm sure it won't be too long. Yes, of course I told her about your parents. Same thing, shocked. As far as I know, your father is still doing well. *Will I be there when she tells Victoria*?" Ed pinched his eyes. "I don't know. I doubt it. Because she'll likely prefer to tell her herself. No, we didn't discuss it. It didn't come up. No, I won't be seeing her tonight. No, nothing is wrong," he lied. "I took some paperwork home with me, that's all. No, I'm not lying, and, no, she's not mad at me." Ed listened as Lily expressed concern he wasn't being completely honest. He tilted his head back. "Yes, I'd tell you if anything was wrong. Listen, I talked to Yvonne. Yes. She said things were looking good. Yes, he was very lucky. Great. Give them my best. Yeah, I better get going. Yes, I'll call the moment I hear anything else. I know you do. You're welcome. You, too."

Ed hung up and put the phone back on its table. He started to walk away, then turned back. "Goddammit," he said, picking the receiver back up and dialling.

"Oh, hi. Is that you, Mabel? So, I assume Amour has told you the latest. How is she?" Ed's head fell. "That's good. *Me?* I could be better. No, really, I'm fine." He chuckled. "At least Stanley doesn't have to wear that monkey suit. I know. But not nearly as disappointed as I am. I don't suppose she'll talk to me? *Oh?* Is she telling her now? I'm glad. Victoria deserves to know. Yeah, me too. And I'm glad you're there with them. I know they count on you for support. Can you let me know how things go…how Victoria took the news? Thanks. Yes, I'm sure it will go well. Thank you, Mabel. I appreciate it. Oh, and could you tell Amour I called. Thank you."

Mabel hung up and looked up to see Victoria and Amour coming downstairs. It was obvious they had both been crying. Mabel hugged Victoria. "How are you?"

"Honestly, I'm not sure. I went upstairs thinking I was an only child and came down with at least three siblings." Victoria held up Mabel's photos of Lily and the kids. "It's a lot to take in. And I can't believe Jeanne and Hector are my grandparents. I mean, it's kind of freaky don't you think?"

"It's fate," Mabel said, smiling.

Victoria turned to her mother. "And I sure didn't expect to hear the wedding was off," she said sadly.

"It wasn't meant to be," Amour said.

"Mom, Ed's a great guy. He just got caught up in things. He'd never deliberately hurt you. He adores you." Victoria looked at Mabel. "Tell her she's being crazy," she pleaded.

Mabel smiled at Amour. "She's right, you know. That was Ed that just called. He's worried about you."

Amour held up her hand to indicate she had heard enough and walked down the remaining steps to the landing. "Let's eat."

Mabel looped her arm around Victoria's. "Give her time, she'll come around," she whispered.

"Oh, no she won't," Amour said defiantly.

They sat at the kitchen table discussing the remarkable sequence of events that brought them to this point. Amour smiled as Victoria shared her excitement about meeting her new family, but Mabel knew she was dying inside; worried her relationship with her daughter would change now that she discovered her new family, devastated by her break up with Ed, and embarrassed she would have to tell everyone the wedding was off, just two days after she announced it was on.

Amour excused herself to answer the phone.

Victoria leaned forward. "I have so many questions, but mom's so emotional. I didn't want to make things harder for her," she whispered.

Mabel nodded. "I know. It's a lot to fathom. And your mother has a lot going on right now."

Victoria looked into the dining room to make sure her mother was nowhere in sight. "I know Lily stole a ton of money from you and Stanley," she whispered. "And mom says that's not all. She said she has a bit of a checkered past. I mean, I want to meet Rory and his sisters…my sisters," she corrected, "but I'm not so sure I want to have anything to do with Lily. I mean, her own parents don't want to have anything to do with her."

Mabel re-filled Victoria's tea. "Your right, Lily stole from us. But not because she was greedy. She was desperate…desperate to get out of town and give her kids a better future…somewhere where they wouldn't be tormented to death." She put the teapot back on the stove. "Remember the day you first met her…that's the day she came home to return the money she had stolen. Every penny, plus interest. Victoria, that took courage… real courage. Lily's been through a lot. But she's finally on her feet and doing well. And, one thing I know for certain…she'd do anything to protect her children. Trust me, she's not a bad person. Quite the contrary. And, as for your grandparents…what can I say. They're deeply religious. They couldn't accept she got pregnant out of wedlock. And they weren't alone in their thinking. Lots of people from their generation felt the same. Hell, lots of people still do. I'm sure your grandparents are lovely people, but I also think they were wrong to throw Lily out. Think about it. She was just a kid...younger than you are now. I think they ended up punishing themselves as much as they did her." Mabel put her hand on Victoria's shoulder. "And look at all they missed out on."

Victoria smiled. "I have no regrets." Her bottom lip started to quiver and she started to get teary. "I couldn't have asked for a better mother or father. But it's just not Lily's past I'm worried about, I don't want to hurt Mom, especially now that she and Ed have called it quits."

Mabel took a sip of her tea. "Victoria, I've known your mother for as long as I can remember, and believe me, nothing that makes you happy could ever make her sad."

Victoria nodded. "That day at your place…when I first met Lily and Ed, I couldn't figure out why she was staring at me and asking so many questions. *What grade I was in? What I wanted to do after I graduated?* I mean I had just met her. I guess she knew as soon as she saw me."

"She did."

"Yet she walked away from me a second time."

Mabel smiled. "She saw you were happy and well cared for. She probably didn't want to upset the apple cart."

"What are you two cooking up?" Amour asked.

Mabel leaned back in her chair. "We're talking about Ed… and how much we like him. That wasn't him calling again, was it?"

Amour sat down next to Victoria. "No. It was Myrtle. She's been asked to exhibit her paintings at an art gallery in Halifax."

"That's wonderful," Mabel said. "When?"

"The fall. She didn't give them an answer. She told them she needed time to sleep on it."

"But why?" Victoria asked incredulously. "It's such a wonderful opportunity."

Mabel smiled. "That's just Myrtle. She hates to be the centre of attention." She looked at Amour. "Did you tell her about Ed and —"

"No. The timing didn't seem right," Amour said. She turned to Victoria. "Speaking of timing, it's totally up to you when you want to reach out to your…to Lily. And I know you're anxious to tell your grandparents, but given Mr. MacDonald's health issues, I think it's best if we wait a couple more weeks. Let him fully recover."

Victoria cringed. "I don't know that I can wait that long."

Amour smiled. "You've waited this long, you can wait a little longer. Maybe we can use the time to put a photo album together for them."

Victoria shook her head. "I still can't believe it. I hope they'll be happy…I mean, maybe they'll feel the same about me as they do about Lily…and they won't want to have anything to do with me."

Mabel smiled. "I'm sure they'll be over the moon."

Victoria looked at her mother. "Mom, I'd like Ed to be with us when we tell them."

Amour shook her head. "Absolutely not. There's no need for him to be there."

"You're not being fair. If wasn't for Ed, I'd never know they were my grandparents. And he can tell them about Lily and the kids. Who knows, maybe he can help everyone come together as a family."

"No," Amour repeated.

Mabel looked at Amour. "I think Victoria has a point. At least give it some thought."

"I gave it all the thought it deserves," Amour said firmly.

"But Mom!" Victoria protested.

Amour slapped her hand down on the table. "Enough!" she said, abruptly pushing her chair back. She began pacing. Mabel and Victoria exchanged nervous glances. "I'm sorry. I'm tired and my head feels like it's about to explode," Amour said. She looked at Mabel. "I know you mean well, but I'd really appreciate it if you would stop hounding me about Ed." She turned to Victoria. "And that goes for you, too." She kissed the top of Victoria's head. "I'm sorry. I'm off to bed. Goodnight."

Victoria put her head down, shocked by her mother's sharp rebuke. "I don't think she's ever going to forgive him."

Mabel smiled. "She'll come around. Have faith."

Victoria shook her head from side to side. "I'm not so sure. She can be pretty stubborn."

Mabel chuckled. "Yes, she can be stubborn. But, that's not the issue. Your mother is scared."

Victoria looked puzzled. "*Scared*? Scared of what?"

Mabel picked up her cup. "Scared she can't trust her own feelings. Look, I agree with her. Ed should have told her sooner. But I also think she's over-reacting. He made a mistake. Yes, a big one...but that's all it was...a mistake. And your mother's no dummy. She knows darn well he didn't deliberately set out to deceive her. She feels guilty...like marrying Ed would be a betrayal of your father."

"But Dad would love Ed...and he'd want Mom to be happy. I know it!" Victoria insisted.

Mabel nodded. “I agree. She loved your father so much, she just can’t help herself.” Mabel dipped her chin. “And to be honest, I think she’s also worried about losing you.”

Victoria laughed. “That’s just ridiculous! That could never happen.”

Mabel smiled. “Maybe not, but just like you with Lily, your mother needs time to come to grip with things. Trust me, everything will work out. Fate wouldn’t have gone through all the trouble of bringing everyone together...Lily and Ed...Ed and your mother...you and your grandparents... without seeing things through to the end. He’s got more up his sleeve, I’m certain of it.”

Victoria shrugged. “Or, maybe he figures the rest is up to us.”

Friday, July 11

Victoria sat on the front step and watched her mother weed the flower bed. "Looks great," she hollered.

Amour smiled and waved. "Are the girls picking you up?"

Victoria shook her head. "No. Remember, Kenny's having a few friends over. John is coming for me," she said, thinking her mother was showing signs of forgetfulness since her breakup with Ed.

Amour stood and removed her gardening gloves. "John Toth?"

"Yes." Victoria saw John's car turn down Hillier Street. "There he is now," she said, jumping to her feet. She waved to her mother and bounded down the steps. "Bye."

Amour stood and waved. "Have fun."

Victoria was about to jump in the front seat when she suddenly stopped. Her heart sank. Marjorie was sitting beside John and pointing to the back seat. Victoria climbed in back, the excitement of the night replaced by a sense of dread at the thought of fending Kenny off, as opposed to sharing her exciting news with John.

Marjorie looked over her shoulder. "Change of plans. Decided I'd come after all."

Just as Victoria had feared, the night was turning out to be a disaster. Every time she turned around, Kenny was either hovering over her, or leering at her. John, on the other hand, was nowhere to be seen. Victoria surveyed the rowdy crowd. Most of the partygoers were drunk, with several passed out, and another puking off the back step. She was getting up to leave when Harley elbowed his way toward her.

"Hey, you. Having fun?" he asked.

Victoria smiled. "No. I was just about to head home."

"By yourself?"

Victoria nodded.

Harley downed his beer. "C'mon, I'll walk with you. I wanna get out of here before the cops show up."

Kenny spotted Harley walking out with his hand on Victoria's back. He jumped in front of them. "Where are you guys goin?"

Harley looked over his shoulder. "Home."

"But it ain't even nine-thirty. Party's just gettin goin."

"Are you crazy? The place is nuts. Besides, I'm beat. I worked all day," Harley said.

"Me, too," Victoria said. "But thanks for inviting me."

Kenny grabbed Harley's arm and roughly pulled him to the side. "You plannin on walkin her home?"

Harley pulled his arm free. "Yeah, what's it to you? She's not your girlfriend anymore."

"Don't mean it's cool for you to just jump right in there."

Harley shook his head. "Relax, I'm just keeping her company, that's all." He looked up to see Tommy coming downstairs with Sally trailing behind.

Tommy looked at the sea of wall-to-wall people. "What the fuck," he said, scanning the room for Kenny. He spotted him in the kitchen and pushed his way through the packed hallway. "Jesus, Kenny. Who the hell are all these people? Christ, we're gonna get the fuckin boot. Landlord told us no parties."

Kenny shrugged. "I figured you invited them."

"I don't even know half them," Tommy screamed. He pointed his finger in Kenny's face. "This was your friggin idea." He spun around as a scuffle broke out behind him, then turned back, grabbing Kenny by the collar. "Ya better hope the goddamn cops don't show up, or you'll be movin back in with mommy and daddy before ya know it. Now, shut the goddamn place down! Now!" he yelled, shoving Kenny and storming off.

Harley looked at Kenny and laughed. "Good luck with that."

Kenny stood on a kitchen chair. "Hey, guys," he hollered, waving his arms in the air, desperate for the attention of the noisy crowd. He tried several times to quiet the raucous partygoers, with no luck. He looked toward the back door. Harley and Victoria were fighting their way out, as new arrivals were pushing their way in. Kenny's head dropped, nothing was going as planned. He looked up. "Hey!" he screamed at the top of his lungs. "Everybody out! Party's—" He closed his eyes as something came flying at his head.

When he came to, he was lying on the couch with Tommy and Sally looking down at him. He touched his swollen cheekbone and licked his fat, bloody lip.

"Ya took a boot to the face," Tommy said.

Kenny sat up. "What?"

"Someone threw a boot at you. Here, put this on your lip," Sally said, handing him a cold cloth.

Kenny looked into the kitchen. "Fuck, the cops are here."

"Yep," Tommy said, resisting the urge to strangle his friend.

Kenny rested his head in his hand. "Jesus, are we getting charged?"

Tommy nodded toward Big Dick who was showing some of the partygoers out the door. "Not sure. We're lucky it's him and Little Dick. They're usually pretty good."

"Who called them?" Kenny asked.

Tommy shrugged. "Probably one of the neighbours. Anyway, we're likely gonna get the boot and lose our first month's rent. Who the hell did you tell, anyways? Half of New Waterford is here."

"I only told a few people. I guess word just spread."

Big Dick entered the living room and kicked the feet of a guy passed out in the corner. "Hey, buddy. Wake up, party's over. Time to go home." The guy stirred, then rolled over on his side. Big Dick approached Kenny and pointed. "You won't be able to see out of that eye in about an hour."

Kenny touched the side of his face and flinched. "We just asked a few folks over to see our new place. We don't even know half the people who showed up."

Big Dick pointed to a bottle on the floor. "Where'd the moonshine come from?"

Tommy and Kenny both insisted they had no idea who brought it and that they only bought a couple of flats of beer.

Little Dick came through the front door. "I put three of them in the wagon. All from Bridgeport. Oh, and someone ran into Edna Marsh's fence."

"We'll fix it," Tommy eagerly offered.

Big Dick flipped open his notebook.

"You're not gonna charge us are ya?" Kenny asked.

Big Dick stopped writing and looked at his partner. "What do you think?"

Little Dick shrugged. "Well, we got illegal possession and underage drinking."

Big Dick nodded. "And don't forget damage to private property."

Tommy tucked his hands under his armpits and tilted his head back. He wanted to kill Kenny.

Kenny let his head fall forward. "I swear to God. Things just got outta hand. People just showed up outta nowhere." He looked up with tears in his eyes. "Please! Please! Please, don't press charges." He looked at Tommy. "We could lose our jobs."

Big Dick flicked his notebook shut. "Yer right. No need to put you through all that, especially since you boys already did time for a crime you didn't commit."

Tommy sighed. "Yeah, that's right."

"Thank you! Thank you! Thank you," Kenny said, his right eye now almost completely closed over.

Big Dick smiled. "Besides, when your parents find out, I'm sure they'll decide on an appropriate punishment."

Kenny's face dropped. "You're not gonna tell our parents, are ya?"

Big Dick shook his head. "No." He smiled. "I'm not...you are."

"I'd rather be locked up," Kenny said.

Big Dick looked at his partner who was grinning from ear to ear. "Let's get out of here." He turned to leave, then stopped and pointed at the guy in the corner. "Where does he live?" he asked Tommy.

Tommy shrugged. "No clue."

Big Dick bent down. "C'mon, bud. You might as well come with us... ya can keep Geezer company for the night," he said, effortlessly throwing him over his shoulder.

Kenny, Tommy, and Sally waited for them to leave, then looked around at the mess.

Sally pointed. "Someone tried to peel the wallpaper off." She picked up a cigarette butt. "And you're gonna have to replace the rug, it's full of cigarette burns."

Tommy held his hand out to her. "C'mon, let's get outta here."

Kenny's mouth dropped open. "*What?* You're not gonna help me clean up?"

"Your party, your mess," Tommy said.

"Hey," Kenny called out. "Where's Doreen?"

Sally put her jacket on. "Oh, she left an hour ago…with Jerry Bigelow."

"*Jerry Bigelow*?"

Sally shrugged. "What the hell did ya expect? Not like you were payin any attention to her."

Saturday, July 12

Amour stood on the ladder with her back to the door. "Is that you, Rosie?"

"No, it's me," Myrtle said, putting a bucket on the floor.

Amour started down the ladder. "I wasn't expecting to see you."

"Rosie said you were scrubbin down the dining room, thought I'd help."

Amour was surprised to hear Rosie and Myrtle were talking to one another after the rough start they got off to the night of club. "*Oh*?"

Myrtle held the door open. "She and Mabel are just grabbing some stuff out of the car."

"Mabel's here, too?" Amour said.

"Yep, and Mary Catherine's on her way."

Rosie and Mabel entered with buckets, rags, and a box of cleaning supplies.

"Well, this is a pleasant surprise," Amour said.

Mabel smiled. "Many hands make light work."

Amour assigned everyone a task, then pulled Mabel aside. "Did you tell them the wedding was off?"

Mabel shook her head. "No, that should come from you."

Amour nodded. "I'll tell them when we stop for lunch. Oh, and what the heck is going on with Myrtle and Rosie?"

Mabel smiled. "I guess they ended up walking home from club together. You'd swear they were long lost friends. They seem to be getting along like two peas in a pod."

Victoria entered the dining room. "What can I do?"

"You can help me with this box," Mary Catherine yelled from the doorway.

Two hours later, the drapes were outside airing, and the ceiling and two walls were washed down. Amour prepared lunch and listened to the chatter, grateful for Mabel's efforts to change the subject whenever anyone mentioned Ed or the wedding. She closed her eyes, dreading the thought of breaking the news to her friends, especially so soon after announcing the engagement. "They'll think I'm a fool," she muttered, placing a plate of sliced tomatoes and cucumbers in the centre of the table. She stepped into the doorway. "Lunch is ready, ladies."

The large kitchen suddenly appeared small as everyone lined up for tea and to fill their plates with an assortment of beautifully arranged sandwiches. Amour leaned against the counter and watched her hungry crew settle around the table. Mabel was looking at her, smiling, and subtly nodding her encouragement.

Mary Catherine sat next to Victoria. "Aren't you joining us?" she asked Amour.

"No, you guys go ahead. I had a big breakfast," she lied. She took a sip of her tea and put her cup down. "I'm so lucky to have you as my friends," she said, her voice cracking.

Rosie grinned. "We're lucky to have you."

Amour smiled. "I'm glad you're all here, it's easier to tell you all at once."

Myrtle leaned in to Mabel. "Here it comes," she whispered.

"Ed and I aren't getting married after all."

Mary Catherine's mouth fell open. "*What?*"

Amour closed her eyes. "The wedding is off. It was all a big mistake."

Mary Catherine stood up and hugged her. "Are you all right?"

Amour nodded. "I'm embarrassed. I feel like a fool. But, it's all for the best."

"Don't be ridiculous," Mary Catherine insisted. "You have nothing to be embarrassed about."

"What happened?" Rosie asked.

Amour joined them at the table. "Let's just say, he's not the man I thought he was. But all is not lost." She looked at Victoria. "Go ahead, sweetheart, tell them your news."

It was after four by the time Mabel, Rosie, and Myrtle loaded up the car to head home. "Rosie's coming to my place," Myrtle said, once again surprising Mabel. "I'm gonna give her painting lessons."

Mabel looked in the rear view mirror and smiled at Rosie. "That's wonderful. I'm glad you ladies are hitting it off. I gotta say, I wasn't expecting it," she said, starting the engine and pulling away.

"The world is full of surprises," Myrtle said flatly.

"No kidding," Rosie said. "I still can't believe Amour ditched poor Ed and that Victoria met her grandparents. The whole thing is really strange, if you ask me."

Mabel glanced over at Myrtle. "How did you know they wouldn't go through with the wedding?"

"I told you, I'm a witch."

Rosie leaned forward and put her hand on Myrtle's shoulder. "You knew they wouldn't get married?"

Mabel turned to Rosie. "That's what she told me."

Rosie's eye's widened. "Maybe I'll get you to take me home after all."

Mabel laughed. "Don't worry, Rosie, she's a good witch." She looked at Myrtle, sitting stone-faced with her familiar toque pulled down over her forehead, staring straight ahead. "Myrtle, what's wrong?"

Two Weeks Later

Tuesday, July 29

Jeanne put her purse over her arm and spotted the key on the table. She picked it up and closed the door.

"Tipper," she hollered from the step. "Hector forgot his key so I can't lock up. He'll likely be back from the hospital within the hour. I'll need you to keep an eye on things for me."

Tipper got off his knees and brushed his hands free of the grass he was pulling away from the side of the shed. "Okay."

Jeanne descended the steps and smiled at Dot waiting in her car. She slid in beside her neighbour of twenty three years and held up the house key. "I'm worried about Hector. He's been so absentminded lately. He forgot his key, *again*," she said, putting it in her pocket.

Dot backed out of the driveway. "I don't know why you bother locking your doors. Nobody's gonna rob you."

"Tell that to Mrs. Jessop."

Dot laughed. "That wasn't a real robbery. It was her good-fer-nothin son-in-law. Nobody in these parts is gonna break into your place in the middle of the day."

"Better safe than sorry," Jeanne huffed.

"So, how's Hector feeling?" Dot asked.

"Better. He's been going for his inhalation therapy. Seems to have helped a bit with the coughing. Oh, and he lost twelve pounds. You know, Dot, I think the boy has been really good for him. I mean, he helps when Hector gets in one of his dark moods. They like to listen to the ballgames together...talk sports. And I think Hector is good for the boy. Here, let me give you some money for gas, before I forget," she said, opening her handbag and removing her change purse. "He has no father, ya know... *or mother.*"

"Yes, you mentioned," Dot said.

"And his grandmother is practically blind."

"Good thing for him he found you and Hector. I'm sure you're a big help to him."

Jeanne opened her change purse, removed several quarters, then began pushing the loose change around with her finger. She noticed her house key wasn't there. She started to chuckle. "Looks like Hector's not so absentminded after all. It's my key. Do you mind if we go back so I can lock up?"

Dot shook her head. "Jeanne, dear, I don't know what you think you have that's worth stealing?"

"It would give me peace of mind, that's all. But, if it's too much trouble, never mind," she sulked.

Dot put on her signal light and pulled into Saint Anthony's parking lot. She laughed. "No trouble, just all bother," she said, turning around and heading back to Maple Avenue.

"Thank you. You're a good friend," Jeanne said. "I'll treat you to an orange pineapple ice cream on the way home."

Mark looked at Toni's thin frame and pale complexion, wondering if it was too soon for her to be leaving the hospital. "Can I give you a hand with that?" he asked, as she folded a nightgown and placed it in her small suitcase.

"No," she said meekly.

Mark smiled. "Well, one thing's for sure, you don't need to worry about cooking for quite a while, the fridge is full. Everyone's been dropping off food. Mabel, Amour, Mary Catherine, Myrtle...Alice."

Toni stopped what she was doing and looked up. "*Alice?*"

"Yes, she sent over a ham...and a card."

Toni went back to her packing.

Charlotte entered carrying several pill bottles. "So, here are your pills. Instructions are as indicated. If you have any questions, just check with Dr. Morrison's office." She held up one of the vials. "The Phenobarbital will need to be re-filled in a few days. Just take the empty bottle to Ferguson's." She placed them in the pocket of Toni's suitcase and touched her arm. "I'm sure you'll be glad to get home to your own bed."

Toni nodded. "Thank you," she said flatly.

Charlotte scanned the room. "So, you have everything?"

Toni snapped her suitcase shut. "I have nothing," she whispered.

Charlotte glanced from Mark, who looked completely lost, to Toni who was staring blankly at the grey wall. She walked up behind Toni, put her hands on her shoulders, and her mouth to her ear. "Remember, one day at a time. I promise it will get better."

Toni grasped the handle of her suitcase.

Mark jumped up. "I'll get that," he said, taking it from her.

Toni walked into the hall.

Charlotte smiled at Mark. "It's not going to be easy. You need to be there for her. Make sure she takes her medication and no heavy lifting. And, Mark, her whole world has been turned upside down. Be patient."

Mark smiled and nodded. "Thanks again for all your help."

Charlotte followed him out of the room and watched him run down the hall to catch up with Toni. He tried to take her hand, but Toni quickly pulled it way. Charlotte tilted her head back. "God help them," she sighed.

Tipper dropped the paint brush on the grass and walked around to the back of the shed. He started to unzip his pants, then stopped. The neighbour who lived behind the MacDonald's was in her backyard, weeding her garden. "Great," he mumbled, rounding the shed. He looked up to the top floor of the two-storey house and closed his eyes, picturing Hector reciting Jeanne's rules. *Don't step a foot inside the house unless she invites you in or there will be hell to pay.* "When ya gotta go, ya gotta go," Tipper whispered. He glanced back at the neighbour, then dashed up the back steps. He threw the door open and ran upstairs and down the hall. He quickly unzipped his pants, sighing as he relieved himself. He walked into the hall and looked to his right. Hector and Jeanne's bedroom door was open. He poked his head in and checked it out. *Twin beds. What's up with that?* He went back downstairs and entered the living room. He walked over to the upright piano and lifted the lid, exposing the yellowing, chipped keys below. He pressed his finger down and made a face. "Definitely needs a tune up," he said, closing the lid. He looked at the black and white pictures sitting on top. "Scary looking bunch," he mumbled, trying to remember if he flushed the toilet. *Shit, I can't remember.* He ran back upstairs and stopped outside the one room he hadn't checked out. He turned the knob and pushed it open. There was a twin-sized bed and a small wooden desk. The curtains were closed, and apart from a home-made cross made of withered palm leaves, the walls were bare. "Weird," he said, slowly pulling the door shut and heading to the bathroom. "Good thing I friggin checked," he said, wrapping toilet paper around his hand and wiping the seat. He dropped the soggy paper in the bowl. *Old bat woulda had my balls in a wringer.* He pushed the handle down and watched the yellow water swirl around and disappear with a swoosh.

Jeanne looked down at the dirt on her floor, then peered out the kitchen window for any sign of the boy. She heard footsteps overhead, looked up at the ceiling, and clenched her jaw.

Tipper was halfway down the stairs when he saw her standing on the landing, glaring up at him. He turned and pointed over his shoulder. "I was just...just using the —"

"Get down here, this minute!" she seethed.

Tipper swallowed hard and slowly approached her. "I'm sorry. I had to pee. I couldn't hold it any—"

Jeanne quickly grabbed him by the collar, dragged him into the living room, and slapped her hand down hard on the coffee table. "Empty your pockets."

Tipper looked confused. "*What?*"

"You heard me! Empty your pockets."

Tipper put his hand in his pocket. "I was gonna relieve myself outside, but...but your neighbour was in her garden," he said, removing his hand and dropping thirteen cents on the table.

Jeanne pointed. "And the other!"

Tipper reached into his second pocket and put two bottle caps, a book of matches, and a five dollar bill down.

"Where did you get the five dollars?" she demanded.

Tipper closed his eyes. "My grandmother gave it to me," he lied.

"Don't you dare move," Jeanne warned, rushing upstairs.

Tipper looked at the front door, momentarily frozen by fear. "Fuck this," he whispered. He was at the door when Jeanne reached the landing. "Get back in here you miserable, little thief. We've been so good to you and you stole from us," she said, cuffing him off the side of the head.

Tipper bent down and held his arms over his head to defend himself from another blow. "I just used your bathroom. I didn't take nothin. I don't steal," he pleaded.

"Don't lie to me you little—" she said, striking him a second time. "I knew you were trouble the moment I laid eyes on you."

"What the hell is going on!" Hector shouted.

Jeanne spun around. Hector and Dot were standing behind her; Hector glaring angrily at his wife, and, Dot, wide-eyed with her hand over her mouth.

Jeanne pointed at Tipper. "Your little...little helper, here, stole from us."

"I did not," Tipper cried.

"I caught him upstairs and made him empty his pockets." She looked at her husband. He was staring down at the floor and rubbing his forehead. "Look!" she said, pointing at the table. "That's the five dollar bill that was on your dresser," she said smugly.

Hector raised his head. "I gave it to the boy," he said wearily.

"*What?* What do you mean, you gave it to him?" Jeanne huffed.

Hector walked up next to Tipper and put his arm around his shoulder. "This morning. I gave it to him this morning."

Jeanne looked from her embarrassed friend to her angry husband and smiled nervously. "I don't believe you. Why would you pay him before he did the work? We always pay when the job is done," she said firmly.

"I gave him the goddamn money!" Hector screamed, causing Jeanne to step back. He gathered up the bottle caps, matches, and loose change, and handed it to Tipper. "Go, get in the car. I'll drive you home." He then picked up the five dollar bill, balled it up, and tossed it at his wife's feet. "For the church," he said. He started to follow Tipper out, stopped, removed the picture of Jesus from the wall, and smashed it against the arm of the chair. He dropped the disturbing image and busted frame on the floor and walked over it.

Jeanne closed her eyes at the sound of the crunching glass and brought her trembling hand to her mouth. "Hector," she whispered hoarsely.

He turned back, looked at his wife of thirty-nine years, and shook his head in disgust. "I'll be back in a couple of hours…for my things."

Ed picked up the phone. "Lily, is everything all right? Look, I get it. But, Lily, you need to give them time." He dropped his head, exasperated. "No, as far as I know she hasn't gotten in touch with your parents. Mabel said they're giving your father time to recover from his heart attack. No, I haven't talked to her in a while. *The last time*? Honestly, if you must know, it's been a couple of weeks. Lily, the wedding is off and we're no longer seeing each other. *Why*? I guess she doesn't love me. Actually, I'm pretty sure she's not ready to let her late husband go. Same sort of thing that happened between you and Henri, I guess. No, it has nothing to do with you or Victoria," he lied. "I swear. She just had second thoughts. Better that I know before the wedding, right? Yes, a blessing in disguise. No, I'm good. Work has been keeping me busy." Ed closed his eyes, desperately wanting to change the subject. "So, how's Giles?" he asked, interrupting Lily's persistent questioning about the reason for the breakup and his emotional state. "Great. I'll have to give them another call. And how are the kids? Rory hit anymore home runs? Tell him I'll get him and his sisters a Hershey bar for every one he hits. No, I don't think you should call Amour. No, Lily, just let it go for now. Remember, you promised not to interfere. I know. Mabel told me Victoria's anxious to reach out to her grandparents. It will happen soon enough. Okay. And, yes, you and the kids, too. Lily, please don't push things too quickly, you might end up setting things back. Good. And don't worry, if I hear anything more, I'll let you know right away. Yes, I miss you guys, too. Okay, take care. Bye."

Ed hung up, relieved he finally told Lily the wedding was off, but feeling guilty for lying about the reason. I had no choice, he thought. *No need to make her feel responsible for my mistakes. God, why didn't I tell Amour sooner?* He picked up the receiver, wondering if he should call Amour one more time. He let it dangle above the cradle as he weighed the pros and cons, then slowly put it back down. She knows how to reach me, he thought.

Ed looked up to see his secretary standing in the doorway. "It's Arnie's fiftieth birthday. A few of us are taking him to the Silver Rail for a few drinks. Wanna come along?"

Ed removed his glasses. "Thanks, Nancy. I think I'll pass. But wish him a happy birthday for me."

Nancy's face fell. "Are you sure? You look like you could use some fun."

Ed nodded. "I'm sure. But thank you."

"Okay. Next time for sure, promise?"

He smiled. "I promise."

Hector stumbled through the front door and plopped down on the couch. He was kicking off his shoes when Jeanne entered from the kitchen.

"I'm glad you're home. I was beginning to worry," she said.

Hector looked up but didn't say anything.

"I'm sorry. I should never have struck the…Tipper," she said contritely.

Hector put his shoes together and set them to the side. "No, Jeanne, you should never have accused him in the first place," he said sadly.

"You're right, I shouldn't have. As I said, I'm sorry. I'll apologize to him first thing in the morning."

Hector leaned back. "No you won't. He's not coming back."

Jeanne nodded. "I guess I can't blame him." She made an effort to smile. "I'll fix things, I promise. I'll go see him in the morning…tell him I was wrong. He'll come back." She waited for Hector to say something. "Hec, I'm truly sorry. I over-reacted. I just thought—"

Hector angrily pointed at her. "That's just it, Jeanne, you think too goddamn much! And ya know, it's always the worst," he seethed.

"I don't know what to say. I'm trying to apologize," she pleaded. "Tipper knew the rules. He wasn't supposed to be in the house without—"

Hector scrambled to his feet and angrily pointed upstairs. "He had to have a piss! A piss!"

Jeanne jumped.

"A goddamn piss," he said, clenching and unclenching his fists. He leveled his voice. "Christ almighty, Jeanne, the poor kid never caught a break. Then you…you ruin the one good thing that's happened to him… *and to me for that matter*…since God knows when."

Jeanne sat down heavily on the chair next to the piano and looked down at her lap.

"Ya know why I gave him the five dollars?" Hector asked.

"No," Jeanne whispered.

"Because he said he was saving up for something special. I thought it must have been a new bike…the one he has is way too small for a boy his size." Hector felt a lump in his throat. "But that wasn't it. Ya know what it was, Jeanne?" he asked harshly.

Jeanne looked up, her face tear-stained. "No."

"A mattress. A goddamn, friggin mattress. And not for himself, Jeanne." Hector welled up. "For his blind grandmother. He had it on lay-away," he said hoarsely, and sat back down. "Honestly, Jeanne, I don't understand you anymore," he said, sounding defeated. He shook his head. "I'm not sure I ever did."

Jeanne removed a tissue tucked inside her sleeve and blew her nose. "I know you're angry. You have every right to be. And I know you've been drinking, but please, Hec, do you have to take the Lord's name in vain?"

Hector laughed. "Oh, God forbid I offend your precious Catholic sensibilities," he hissed. "And what a grand, God-fearing, forgiving woman you are," he said sarcastically.

Jeanne stared in disbelief. "What is that supposed to mean?" she asked indignantly.

"You know damn well what I mean," he barked. He waved his arm around. "Look at this place. We're surrounded by pictures of dead people. It's like a goddamn mausoleum." He grabbed a picture frame off the piano and stared at the grainy images. "Not a single picture of the living. Hell, I don't even remember half of them. Everybody else we know has pictures of their children or grandchildren on display. But no, not us!" He tossed the picture on the couch.

Jeanne held the balled up tissue to her mouth. Hector crouched down in front of her and put his hands on her knees. "Jeanne, if we're lucky we've got…what…maybe ten, fifteen years left," he said calmly. "I'm tired of going through the motions. I'd rather be dead and buried than live my life the way I have for the past eighteen years. I miss her. And I want to spend whatever time I have left with my grandchildren." He started to cry. "Jeanne we were wrong. We were so wrong."

Jeanne dabbed at her wet nose. "Hector, we've already been through this. She gave us no choice. She knew it was a sin to—"

Hector looked at her sadly. "Jeanne, she was so young. She made a mistake. Hell, I know at least two other girls on this street who made the same mistake. We should never have made her leave. She's our flesh and blood for God's sake. That's the real sin, Jeanne…it wasn't Lily having a child out of wedlock, it was us for turning our backs on her."

"She disgraced us. And what about that…that mess with Father Gregory?" Jeanne argued.

Hector ran his hand down his face and shook his head. "Jeanne, you've always been too quick to judge…and too slow to forgive. With Lily…and now Tipper."

Jeanne was about to protest, but was afraid she would further aggravate her husband.

Hector slowly got to his feet. "And as far as all that talk about Lily and Father Gregory, I'll give the benefit of the doubt to my daughter over all those ugly gossips looking for a scandal around every corner." He smiled sadly. "Jeanne, I know Lily hurt you. She hurt me, too. But, Jeanne, if God be our judge…and some day he will… I expect he will judge us more harshly for failing to forgive, than he will Lily for bringing an innocent child into the world."

Jeanne dropped her head. Hector turned to leave. She grabbed his large, rough hand. "I'm sorry. Please, Hector. I'll do better. I promise! Please, Hec! You're not going to leave are you?" she cried, her eyes pleading for the answer she needed to hear.

Hector placed his hand on the side of her wet face. He felt his heart would break into pieces. He smiled down at her. Despite all of her flaws, she was the only woman he ever loved. He would give her one more chance. After all, he thought, if I expect her to forgive others, I need to forgive her. "No, Jeanne," he said softly. "I'm not going anywhere. I have nowhere else to go."

Ed dumped a can of beans into a pot, thinking he should have gone to the Silver Rail and ordered a steak. He heard a car door and went to the window. Amour's car was in the driveway. He ran to the back door and quickly pulled it open. His heart fell when he saw Victoria step out.

"I hope it's all right that I stopped by unannounced," she said.

Ed smiled. "Of course. I'm always happy to see you."

Victoria leaned over the front seat and removed a pastry box. She held it up. "Mabel said she hasn't seen you lately. Thought you might like a reminder of what you're missing out on."

Ed grinned. "Haven't had reason to drive to town lately." He walked down the steps and took the box from her. "Pie?" he asked.

"Strawberry and rhubarb…straight from the oven."

They entered the kitchen. "Want a beer?" Ed Asked.

"If you promise not to tell Mom," she blurted, before realizing what she had said.

Ed laughed and opened the fridge. "Not like that's gonna happen anytime soon."

"Sorry, I didn't—"

"Don't worry. So how is she?" Ed asked, putting the beer on the counter.

"Honestly, I think she's miserable. I know she misses you. She's just being stubborn."

Ed poured Victoria's beer into a glass. "Actually, she's right. I should have told her sooner."

"Then just tell her that."

"I tried. She said she no longer trusts me." He handed Victoria her glass. "Does she know you're here?"

"God, no. She'd kill me. She thinks I'm with my girlfriends."

Ed nodded. "C'mon. Let's sit out front."

They sat on the top step, discussing the breakup, the remarkable turn of events that brought Victoria to her grandparents, and Lily and the kids. Victoria leaned back and squinted up at the sky. "Mom is going to invite the MacDonalds to lunch on Saturday so we can tell them. Can you come? It's at noon."

"Is that your idea, or your mother's?"

Victoria smiled. "Mine."

Ed looked surprised. "And did you ask her if it would be okay?"

"Of course," Victoria said, thinking technically she was telling the truth. She did ask. She held her breath hoping Ed wouldn't press the issue, forcing her to lie.

"And you want me there?"

"That's why I'm here. If it wasn't for you, I'd never know they were my grandparents. And you can tell them about Lily."

Ed took a swig of his beer. "Then, I guess I have no choice," he said, excited about the prospect of seeing Amour again. He leaned back on his elbows. "I almost joined Nancy and a few of our co-workers at the Silver Rail for a few drinks. Glad I didn't. I would have missed your visit."

"Nancy, your secretary?" Victoria asked.

Ed nodded.

Victoria tilted her head. "She's very pretty."

Ed raised his eyebrows. "I guess. If you like those curvy, long-legged types."

Victoria gave him a serious look. "Ed, don't give up on Mom. I know she loves you."

Ed noticed a group of kids huddled together on the side of the road. He pointed. "Wonder what they're up to?"

"Oh, it's a dead cat. I saw it when I was pulling in."

"Jesus," Ed said, jumping off the step and heading across the street. He pushed his way through the small gathering and roughly grabbed a stick from a kid stabbing at the belly of the pure black cat. "Okay, boys, leave her be." He hurled the stick onto the shore. "Show's over. Go on," he said, shooing them away.

Victoria walked to the edge of the property and waited for Ed to cross over. "Do you know who owns it?"

"She's been living under my back step. Just had a litter. Come with me," he said, walking around the house. He got down on his hands and knees, reached under the step, and pulled out one kitten, then another.

Victoria knelt down beside him. "Oh, no. They're not moving. I think they're dead," she said, tearing up.

Ed laid on his side to extend his reach and pulled out a third kitten. He smiled. "This one's alive," he said, handing the tiny black and white ball of fur to Victoria. He reached in again. "I think there's one more," he said, blindly patting the cool, damp earth. He pulled the last of the litter out and gently cradled it in the palm of his hand. It mewed weakly. "I don't suppose your mother would want a couple of kittens?"

Victoria shook her head and wiped away a tear. "She's not fond of cats. Poor little things, left with no mother."

Ed stood up. "Their mother wasn't really a friendly cat. Hated me. I actually named her Nasty. Wonder what she'd think if she knew I was going to take care of her babies."

Victoria held her tiny kitten up to her face and nuzzled its small, pink nose. "You're going to keep them?"

"It's not like I have much choice. They wouldn't last another night without their mother."

Wednesday, July 30

Jeanne stood at the kitchen sink and looked out the window. Hector was bent down, picking up the paint brush Tipper had left on the ground. He removed a blade of grass from among the stiff bristles and entered the shed. *I made a mess of things. He's so dispirited.* She sat down at the table, grateful the weather cooperated and Hector wasn't cooped up inside, adding to the disquiet that carried over from the night before. She sipped her tea thinking it would take time for things to return to normal. I have to do better and not rush to judgement, she vowed. She rested her chin on her hand, picturing the last time she had spoken to her daughter. Lily was sobbing and begging for forgiveness. She threw her arms around her father's neck and buried her wet face in his chest. *Daddy, I'm so sorry. Daddy,* she had called out, over and over again. Hector pried her arms free and stepped back. *Listen to your mother,* he had said coldly. Jeanne closed her eyes. She could still remember the awful thud of Lily's suitcase hitting the steps as she dragged it behind her. She waited for her daughter to come downstairs and opened the door. *Go and take your shame with you.* Lily picked up her suitcase and stepped out, turning back one last time. *I have nowhere to go,* she had said, her breath catching between sobs. Jeanne dropped her head as she thought back to the harshness of her final words to her daughter. *You should have thought of that before bringing a little bastard into the world.*

The phone rang. Jeanne walked down the hall and picked up the receiver. "Hello. No, everything's fine. I know. He came home just after six. Yes, he's staying. At least for now. Thank you, Dot. You're a good friend.

Town? I'd love to. Twenty minutes. Yes, I can be ready. I'll meet you out front." Jeanne hung up and started flipping through the phone book. She picked the receiver back up and dialled the number. "Oh, hello, I'm calling to inquire about a lay-away. A mattress. My name? Well, it's not in my name. The last name is O'Dell. I'd like to pay the balance owing and have it delivered. How much? Twenty-seven and fifty. Yes. So, if I come down in about an hour and pay it off, it'll be delivered today? And you have the address? Great. I'll be there shortly."

Jeanne put the phone down and returned to the kitchen. She rinsed her cup and watched from the window as Hector dipped his brush into the paint and slapped it on the side of the faded shed. He looked like he had aged five years since his heart attack. He's right, she thought, our time on earth is coming to an end. She wondered where Lily and the grandchildren were, then shook her head. "What difference does it make," she mumbled, thinking back to the warning from Deuteronomy. *No one born of a forbidden union may enter the Assembly of the Lord. Even to the tenth generation, none of his descendants may enter the assembly of the Lord.* Jeanne picked up a dish towel and ran it around the inside of her cup. Those words seem so harsh...so unforgiving, she thought. *Why would God blame an innocent child? That doesn't seem right.* She opened the cupboard and put her cup away. "No point in dwelling on the past. It is what it is," she whispered.

Mark walked down the dark alley and climbed the back steps, dreading the thought of another tortuous night with Toni in their dreary apartment. He sighed and opened the door. "I'm home," he called out, peeking in the kitchen. He put his lunch can on the floor. "Toni! You here?" He walked down the hall. *Christ almighty, she's back in bed.* He tapped lightly on their bedroom door. "You awake?" He waited for an answer, then quietly pushed the door forward. Toni was curled up in the fetal position with her back to him.

"Toni," he whispered. "You okay?"

"Fine."

It was the same answer he got every time he asked. "I heard Mabel and Myrtle stopped by earlier."

"Yes."

"How did that go?"

"Fine."

Mark wanted to put his fist through the wall. He closed his eyes, remembering Charlotte's advice. *It won't be easy. You'll need to be patient.* "Look, it's a beautiful day. I was thinking we could go for a drive. Maybe to Mira. We can grab something to eat along the way."

"You go."

Mark sat at the bottom of the bed. "I'm not going without you. Please, Toni? I need this. It will do us both some good."

Toni suddenly flipped her blanket back and sat up. "Fine."

Mark was surprised by her response. "Great," he said. "Just give me a sec to clean up."

Mark leaned over the sink, cupped his hands, and splashed cold water on his face. Hopefully the drive will do her some good and she'll start going out more, he thought. He grabbed a towel and pressed it against his face, wondering if the pills were finally taking affect, or if the passage of time had begun to blunt the sharpness of the pain. Maybe it's both, he thought. Whatever the reason, he was grateful to escape the deadly quiet of their dreary apartment for a few hours. He tossed the towel in the sink and leaned into the mirror, touching the faint trace of yellow under his eye. He felt a sudden pang of guilt as the image of the young man holding his busted nose flashed before him. *I fuck everything up.* He looked down at the brown cigarette burns in the linoleum floor near the toilet, remnants from the previous tenants. *What a fucking dump.* He grabbed his tee shirt, quickly pulled it over his head, and opened the door. Toni was sitting on the couch, holding a piece of paper.

Mark smiled. "What's that?"

"The bill from the hospital," she said flatly.

Mark took it from her. "That's okay, I get paid this week." He unfolded it and looked at the balance owing. Thirteen dollars. He then read the line to the left. Burial costs for baby Toth, DOD – 1952/07/01. Mark folded it over and shoved it in his back pocket. "I'll take care of it. All set?"

Toni stared straight ahead. Mark leaned down and put his hand under her arm. "C'mon, let's go."

Toni slowly got to her feet. Mark walked her to the door. She suddenly stopped. "I'm sorry. I can't."

Mark's head fell. "Toni, please don't do this. You're killing me!"

Toni turned, went back to their bedroom, and closed the door.

"Fuck this," Mark mumbled, kicking his metal lunch can across the room and storming out. He tore down the back stairs to the foul-smelling alley below. He stopped under their bedroom window and looked up, then continued toward the bright sunlight ahead. *I'm trying, Toni. I'm fucking trying.*

Ed pushed his foot down on the shovel and maneuvered the blade to lift up the edge of the sod. He repeated the effort several more times, tracing out a sizable rectangle. He then grabbed the heavy, green carpet of grass, yanked it free of its stubborn roots, and tossed it aside. He reached down and took a swig of beer, then returned to his digging, dropping the moist earth into his wheelbarrow. He finally let the shovel drop and looked at Nasty and her kittens, lying motionless on an old towel. He grabbed both ends of the towel and gently laid it in the hole. He got down on his knees, placed the kittens closer to their mother, and pulled the edges of the towel over their heads. "Don't worry, Nasty, I'll take care of your babies," he whispered, felling a sudden wave of sadness. He quickly refilled the hole, put the sod back in place, and sat down on the grass. He looked at the two tiny kittens curled up together in their shallow cardboard box. "I guess you guys need names," he said, scratching their small heads. He looked up to see the familiar car slow down, turn left, and then take a sharp right into his driveway. He stood and held his hand up to block the glare of the sun. "What the hell," he whispered.

The back door suddenly flew open and Rory charged toward him, followed by his sisters; each eagerly seeking his attention. He picked Laura up. "Well, this is a surprise," he said.

Lily lingered near the car. "Hopefully a pleasant one."

Ed mussed Rory's hair. "A wonderful surprise." He pointed. "Are you returning my Cadillac?" he asked, grinning.

"Giles thought it would be more trustworthy than my rusty, old heap."

"How is he?"

Lily smiled. "He's doing really well. Hardly know he had a stroke."

"Mommy," Rachael excitedly hollered. "Look, kittens. Can we pick them up?"

Ed nodded and put Laura down. "Sure, just be careful."

Rory picked one up. "What's his name?"

Ed laughed. "I haven't decided. I'm not even sure it's a *him*. Maybe you guys can help me name them?"

Lily looked at the wheelbarrow and shovel, then at the dirt around the raised sod. "The mother?" she whispered.

Ed leaned into her ear. "And two babies. Glad you didn't come any sooner."

Lily apologized for showing up unannounced, telling him she had started her vacation and that it was just a spur-of-the-moment decision.

"You must be tired after the long drive. Let's get you guys settled in," Ed said, heading toward the car.

Lily grabbed his arm. "Oh, we're not staying. I reserved a room at the Isle Royale. The kids were just so excited to see you they insisted we stop here first."

Ed shook his head. "Nonsense! I stayed with you, you're staying with me."

"But, you have work and—"

Ed held up his hand. "No buts about it. Besides, I could really use the company."

Amour held up a strand of hair and checked for any sign of grey. She then leaned into the mirror and ran her hand under her eyes. "I look tired," she mumbled. She turned off the bathroom light, entered her bedroom, and climbed in bed. She shut the bedside lamp off, hoping her exhausted body would will her troubled mind to sleep. It didn't. She couldn't stop thinking about her angry exchange with Victoria after learning she had paid Ed a visit and invited him to lunch with the MacDonalds. She sat up and punched her pillow. Dammit, Victoria, she thought, you had no business going behind my back. She laid back down, picturing her tearful daughter pleading with her to be reasonable, then throwing her hands in the air and storming out.

They had had arguments in the past, but nothing like this. Amour pinched the corners of her eyes, wishing she hadn't told her daughter to shut up. *Maybe she's right. Maybe I am being unreasonable. What harm would it do if Ed came? It's not like we would be alone together.* She thought about how excited Victoria was when they told her they were getting married. *Hell, she hugged Ed before she hugged me. And she made it clear, even if Ed was no longer a part of my life, he'd always be a part of hers.*

Amour turned the lamp back on, opened the drawer of her bedside table, and removed the engagement ring that had belonged to Ed's late sister. She had been meaning to mail it to him, but never got around to it. She held it under the light. It belongs in his family, she thought. *I'll give it back to him on Saturday.* Her chest tightened when she realized Ed might end up asking another woman to wear it. *I wonder if he'd ever marry Lily.*

There was a light tap on her door. "Mom?"

Amour quickly put the ring back in the drawer. "Come in."

Victoria slowly pushed the door open. "I'm sorry."

Amour sat up and smiled. "Me, too. Did you have supper?"

Victoria nodded. "Harley and I went to The Grill, but I didn't have much of an appetite."

Amour nodded. "I should never have told you to shut up."

"And I shouldn't have asked Ed without speaking to you first."

Amour patted the bed. "Come, have a seat."

Victoria climbed onto the bed and curled up on her side. "I'll call Ed in the morning and tell him not to come."

Amour smiled. "That won't be necessary. You were right, I overreacted. It's all right if he comes."

"Are you sure?"

Amour nodded.

Victoria closed her eyes. "I miss Daddy."

Amour felt overwhelmed by her daughter's unexpected expression of loss. She pulled her into her. "I know. I do, too."

"And I can't help it, I miss Ed," Victoria said. She waited for her mother to say something. She lifted her head and looked up at her. "Mom, are you worried about losing me?"

"A little," Amour said hoarsely.

"Is it because of Lily?"

Amour nodded. "Maybe just a bit. I'm used to having you to myself. And ever since your father died, it's been just you and me, kid. But I think it's also because you're all grown up...always on the go with your friends and about to start a career. Next thing you know, you'll be getting married and moving out, and I'll be an old lady prowling around this big, old place by myself."

Victoria rested her head on her mother's shoulder. "Nobody could ever replace you. You'll always be my mother."

Amour tilted her head back, tears pooling in her eyes.

"Mom, I just want you to be happy. I saw how miserable you were after Daddy died. Then Ed came into our lives and I felt like you were your old self again. Mom, he's heartbroken. And I know he feels awful about how he handled things. I also know he'd never do anything to deliberately hurt you or me." She looked up at her mother. "He loves you. Please, give him another chance?"

Amour ran her hand under her wet nose. "Okay, honey. You've made your case. Let's not talk about his anymore tonight. It's been a rough day and I'm mentally and physically exhausted."

Victoria sat up. "I understand." She smiled. "Mom, I may be all grown up, but there are some things I still miss." She raised her eyebrows. "Can I sleep with you tonight?"

Amour touched the side of Victoria's face and smiled. "I'd like that. I'd like that a lot."

Lily entered the kitchen. "What are you doing? I said I'd do the dishes."

Ed reached up to put the plates away. "It only took a minute. Kids go down okay?"

"Yes, thank you. I honestly didn't plan on descending on you like this."

Ed smiled. "Don't worry about it. Like I said, I'm happy for the company."

Lily folded the dry rag. "Are you doing okay?"

Ed nodded. "Hanging in there." He opened the fridge. "I'm afraid I don't have any wine. Would you like a beer?"

"Sure."

"Grab your sweater and I'll meet you out front."

Lily sat on the step and took a deep breath, thinking about the last time she had been here. It was when she came home to give Stanley his money back. She remembered how terrified she was to face her former boss, thinking that if it hadn't been for Ed, she would have chickened out, hopped on the bus, and returned to Roachville. Thank God he convinced me to do the right thing, she thought. *If I had left, I would never have found Victoria.*

Ed came out, passed her a beer, and sat beside her. "I love the way the lights from across the harbour glisten on the dark water."

"It's as pretty at night as it is in the morning," Lily said. "I was just thinking about the last time we sat out here. Remember? It was the day we went to see Mabel and Stanley and I saw Victoria."

Ed nodded. "Hard to forget. Same day as the mine accident."

Lily smiled. "You're a beautiful soul, Ed Baxter."

Ed tilted his head back and laughed. "And why would you say that?"

Lily leaned forward with her elbows on her knees. "It's true. You care about people. And you know the difference between right and wrong. Look at everything you did for me. God, you didn't even know me and yet you went out of your way to help. And you're so good with Rory and the girls."

Ed smiled. "They're great kids. And their mother's pretty special, too."

Lily closed her eyes. She felt like her heart was about to split in two. *If only they had met sooner, under different circumstances.* "Ed, you need to fight for Amour. You need to go see her. Tell her how miserable you are without her."

Ed leaned back. "That obvious, *eh*?"

Lily nodded. "Afraid so. Every now and then, when you let your guard down, I see it. It's written all over your face."

Ed took another drink and began picking at the corner of his beer label. "I'm going to see her on Saturday."

Lily looked surprised. "That's wonderful."

Ed shrugged. "It was Victoria's idea," he said, telling her about their plans to meet her parents at the manor. "I would have told you sooner, but didn't want you to get your hopes up."

Lily teared up. "That's okay. I'm just happy it's going to happen."

Ed put his arm around her shoulder. "Don't worry. Everything will work out fine."

"I hope so. I think Daddy will be happy. After Chester went to jail for killing Father Gregory, he used to send me money. Not much...ten or fifteen dollars. At least I think it was him. There was no note or anything. Just the money in an envelope. My mother, on the other hand, is another story." Lily leaned forward and looked back at him. "Are you going to tell Victoria and Amour I'm here?"

Ed took a drink. "Yes."

"So, maybe there'll be a chance for us to get together?"

Ed nodded. "Maybe. But, Lily, you know it's not up to me."

Lily dabbed at her eyes. "I know. I promise not to pressure anyone." She smiled. "Anyway, I'm glad you're going to see Amour."

Ed shrugged. "I doubt it will make any difference."

Lily laughed through her tears. "Then she's crazy and doesn't deserve you." She shook her head. "I don't get it. I mean one minute you're engaged and the next you're not. Why the sudden change of heart?"

Ed leaned back on his elbows. "You know what they say...it's a woman's prerogative to change her mind."

Lily stared at him. "Ed, you'd tell me if I had anything to do with it, *right*? I mean, she's not mad because you didn't tell her about me? Because, if that was the case, I don't know...I'd die. I would never want to get in the—"

"Lily, stop!" Ed sat up. "I told you, she just had a change of heart. It's been known to happen, you know."

Lily looked up at the sky and pulled her sweater around her. "It's been a long day and it's getting chilly. And you have work in the morning."

Ed helped her to her feet and followed her inside. Lily walked down the hall. "I'll put Rory on the couch," she said, quietly opening the bedroom door. Rachael was on her belly, with her hand dangling above the box with the kittens. And Laura was sideways in the bed with her legs over Rory.

"Leave them be," Ed whispered. "Take my bed. I'll sleep on the couch."

Lily pulled the door closed. "Absolutely not! I'll take the couch," she said forcefully.

They argued back and forth, until Ed finally conceded, fearing Lily was so adamant she might wake up the kids and head off to the hotel.

Ed pointed to the bathroom. "You go first. I need to lock up."

Lily came out of the bathroom to see Ed putting a sheet on the couch. She grabbed his arm. "I can do that," she said, nudging him out of the way.

Ed passed her a pillow case. "I'll be gone before you wake up, so if you wouldn't mind feeding the kittens. I put the stopper on the counter."

"Of course."

"Well, goodnight."

Lily smiled. "Goodnight. Thank you."

Ed turned the light off and crawled in bed, grateful that his unexpected visitors lightened his otherwise dreary day. He smiled as he pictured his old Cadillac turning in the driveway and Rory and his sisters charging toward him. He loved being around them and seeing them happy, especially after knowing what life was like for them when Dan McInnes was around. He rolled over, thinking he willingly gave up on the idea of having children when he got involved with Amour. He'd have to satisfy himself with being an uncle to his nieces and nephews, and spending time with Lily's kids. He was drifting off when he thought of the night Lily surprised him with a kiss. He opened his eyes. Up until then, he never considered she might be thinking of him as anything other than a friend. I wonder, he thought, if things had been different and I never met Amour would our friendship have evolved into something more. He propped himself up on his elbow, chopped his pillow, and laid back down, "Don't go there," he sighed.

Lily laid awake, recalling the first time she had seen Ed. She closed her eyes, thinking the tall, thin stranger who walked into her life two years ago, certainly wasn't the kind of guy who would immediately turn heads. But then, the more you got to know him, the better looking he became. She pictured him sitting across from her in his thick, black glasses as she pointed out her children playing on the lawn outside the diner. It was at one of the lowest points in her life, and she barely knew him, yet, he somehow managed to help her forget her troubles. Lily turned onto her back and stared up at the ceiling. I wonder, she thought, if we met at a different time, under different circumstances, would we have ended up together. *Oh, for God's sake, he's in love with another woman.* She let out a loud sigh. "Let it go," she whispered.

Thursday, July 31

Hector walked down the hall thinking the inhalation therapy was a waste of money. Imagine paying for air, he thought, shaking his head. He looked up and smiled. "What are you doing here?"

Tipper got off his chair and started walking toward him. "Hey, boss."

"Are you here with your grandmother?" Hector asked.

"No. I knew you'd be here for that thing they do to your lungs. Thought I'd come by and thank you."

Hector looked confused. "*Thank me? For What?*"

"For the mattress. Gran's over the moon." He laughed. "Thing is, though, we can't get her out of the friggin sack."

Hector smiled. "I'm glad to hear your grandmother likes her new mattress, but I didn't have anything to do with it."

"*Yeah, right.* I know it was you."

"Honestly, Tipper, I swear…it wasn't me."

Tipper turned down his mouth. "Well, it wasn't my friggin fairy godmother."

Hector smiled. "I'm pretty sure it was Jeanne."

Tipper screwed up his face. "Yer old lady?" He laughed. "More likely my fairy godmother."

Hector laughed. "I think that's Jeanne's way of apologizing. She feels terrible for accusing you of stealing from us. She told me she was going to put things right."

"You told her about the lay-away?" Tipper asked.

"Yes."

Tipper looked down at his feet. "Holy shit, she musta felt really bad. I owed almost twenty-eight dollars. Thought I'd still be paying it off this time next year."

Hector stifled a laugh. "Look, I got a start on the shed. But it's gonna need a second coat. So whadaya say, interested in coming back to work?"

"You shittin me?"

Hector shook his head and wagged his finger at his young friend. "No, but you keep swearing like that I might change my mind."

Tipper grinned. "No problem, boss. And no more cursin, I promise. And I swear to God, I won't set foot inside your house again." They started to walk down the hallway. "You sure yer old lady is gonna be okay with me comin back?"

Hector looked at his watch. "I'm sure." He put his hand on Tipper's shoulder. "You hungry?"

Tipper laughed. "I'm always hungry. Gran said I have two hollow legs and a... *in...in...say...*" He shrugged. "say something-or-other appetite."

Hector laughed. "Insatiable."

Tipper looked impressed. "That's it!"

"Well then, let's go to The Grill and see what we can do about that. I'm a little peckish myself," he said, feeling the need to celebrate.

"Any chance I can get a hotdog?" Tipper asked excitedly.

Hector smiled. "You can have two. And how about a chocolate shake?"

Tipper skipped in front and spun around, facing Hector and walking backwards toward the exit. "*Seriously*? He pumped his fist. "Holy shit... two dogs *annnd a friggin shake*."

"Mom, where's the beach?" Rory asked.

Lily stopped at the top of Dominion Street. "I'm just taking a little detour," she said and turned right.

"I gotta pee," Rachael said.

Lily looked over her shoulder. "You'll just have to hold it," she said, turning left and slowing to a crawl as she passed the modest, brown house. The shingles on the roof were curling at the corners and the lattice around the front step needed to be replaced. You're showing signs of wear, she thought.

Rory pointed out the window. "Who lives there?"

"That's the house I grew up in," Lily said sadly.

"Wow, it's really nice," Rory said.

Lily closed her eyes, thinking Rory would say the same thing about any place that wasn't a cramped motel unit, his home for so much of his young life. She sped up, turned into a driveway, and backed out. She was driving back down Maple Avenue when she saw the oncoming car put its signal on to turn in the yard. She was a few feet away when the driver stopped, his eyes following the beautiful, black Cadillac as it drove past. Lily's heart was pounding. I wonder if he saw me, she thought.

"Mommy, I can't hold it much longer," Rachael pleaded.

"Hold on. We're just a few minutes away." Lily turned onto Brookside and up School Street, racing past Cameron's Bakery and down to Quarry Road. She glanced over her shoulder. "How are you doing, honey?"

Rachael was sitting with her hands between her legs and a pained expression on her face. "How much longer?"

"Two minutes, I promise. Rory, put your towel under Rachael's bum." She turned down South Street. "See, there's the beach."

Lily pulled over on the side of the rode and shoved the car in park. "Rachael, quick! Go! Run to the water!"

Rachael opened the door, but she didn't make it to the water. She stood beside the car and let go. Lily rounded the back of the car and watched the pee stream down her daughter's legs and pool around her small, pink sandals. Rachael started to cry. Lily hugged her. "It's okay, honey. We can go in the water and wash it off."

"I peed my pants," she said, sobbing.

Lily smiled at an older couple returning from the beach with their towels slung around the back of their necks. "Rachael, it's not your fault," she whispered. "It's Mommy's. I should have come straight to the beach."

Rory put his hand on his sister's shoulder. "It's all right, Rach. I peed my pants before, too."

Rachael wiped her eyes. "Really?"

"*Really*."

Lily quickly gathered up their things, took Laura by the hand, and followed Rory and Rachael as they walked through a narrow path that cut through the high grass to the sandy beach beyond. Rory grabbed Rachael's hand and walked knee-deep into the water. He squatted. Rachael followed her brother's lead, then quickly shook her hand free and ran back to shore.

Lily laid a blanket on the warm sand, feeling an overwhelming sense of love for her young son. You will be a wonderful, caring man, and a fabulous father, she thought. She got down on her knees to straighten the corners of the blanket, then sat back on her heels and cried.

"It's freezing cold," Rachael said.

Rory came behind her. "It's not that cold, Rach." He looked at the tears running down his mother's face. "Mom? What's wrong, Mom?"

Lily looked up, wiped her face, and smiled at her pale, thin-framed boy. "Nothing, sweetheart. Nothing at all. I just got some sand in my eyes."

Mark sat between Fred Clarke and Dirty Willie with his lunch can on his lap. Willie started punching the air. "Gonna go to The Y. Gonna whip yer ass," he said.

Mark smiled and nodded. "I wouldn't doubt it."

"Gonna whip yer ass," Willie repeated, baring his yellow, crooked teeth.

Fred approached the intersection of Main and Victoria streets. "I'll jump out at the corner," Mark said, hoping to delay his return home by a few more minutes.

"Are you sure? I'm going right past your place."

"I'm sure." The truck came to a stop. "Thanks. I'll see you guys in the morning," he said, urging Willie to move, so he could get out. When Mark stepped out, Willie was bent over, bobbing and weaving with his fists close to his face.

Willie began bouncing on his toes. "Gotta keep yer hands up. Keep yer hands up. Oooooh, gonna whip yer ass."

Mark raised his arm up and leaned away, as if he was afraid Willie was about to throw a punch.

"Willie, c'mon. Get back in the truck," Fred yelled.

Poor, Willie, Mark thought as he watched them drive away. He shook his head, thinking about how Willie's life had changed in an instant. One minute he was vying for a national boxing title; the next, he was lying on the canvass, damaged for life. And it only took one punch.

Mark stopped and lit a cigarette and thought about how generous it was of Stanley to keep Willie on the payroll. It wasn't like Willie was of much help. If anything, he was a hindrance, always getting in the way or messing things up, costing the company both time and money. Yet Stanley never complained. He'd just take Willie aside and gently explain things to him. And he'd have no tolerance for anyone he caught poking fun at Willie, showing more than a couple of his workers the door after they mocked or berated his long-time friend.

Mark walked past St. Anne's church; the black wagon parked below the steps a telltale sign the gathering inside was there to mourn, not just pray. He tossed his butt on the ground and blessed himself without thinking. He looked up at the steeple and squinted into the bright sun, recalling Margaret telling him to always make the sign of the cross whenever a funeral procession drove past. A car pulled up beside him, interrupting his thoughts.

Luke leaned over the front seat. "You on your way home from work?"

Mark smiled at Alice sitting with Matthew on her lap. "Yes."

Luke nodded. "How's Toni?"

"Not bad, I guess. Taking things one day at a time." He pointed at Matthew. "He's getting big."

Luke laughed. "Big and bad...like his uncle."

Alice turned to Luke. "You're blocking traffic."

Luke looked over his shoulder. "They got plenty of room to get by."

Mark smiled wistfully, knowing Alice was anxious to get away. Apart from encouraging her husband to get moving, she barely made eye contact. He wondered if Mabel told her he knew the truth.

Luke pointed ahead. "Guess there's no point in offering you a lift."

Mark shook his head. "No, I'd get there faster on foot."

"Okay. Remember, you and Toni are welcome to drop by any time."

Alice put her hand on Luke's arm. "For God's sake, Luke, people are starting to come out of the church. It's disrespectful," she said impatiently.

Luke put the car in gear, shook his head, and looked at his brother. "We better get going."

Mark smiled at Matthew. "See you later, little man."

Mark watched them drive off, struck by a sudden wave of emotion. Guilt. Sadness. Anger. Shame. Envy. He reached Senator's Corner and looked across Main Street to The Pithead, cursing himself for getting barred from the town's most popular watering hole. He continued past Senator's Corner, thinking if Toni was in bed, as she usually was, he'd make himself supper and go to The Y. He approached the Co-op, turned up the alley, and climbed the steep stairs to the apartment. He opened the door. As expected, Toni was nowhere to be seen. He walked down the hall, surprised to see their bedroom door open. He walked in and saw the note on his pillow. He picked it up, read it, then laid down on Toni's side of the bed. He clutched the note and began to sob. It was written on the back of the hospital's invoice for Duncan's burial.

Rory jumped in front of Rachael. "Your nose is all red."

Rachael touched his arm. "So are your arms."

Lily closed the trunk. "It's going to take an hour to get back to Ed's. If you need to pee, go now." They shook their heads. "All right, jump in," she said, looking over the open field to the back of the manor. It was huge compared to the much smaller homes in the area. She started the car, drove up South Street, and put her signal on to turn right.

"Where are we goin now?" Rory asked.

Lily turned down Hillier Street. "I thought we'd drive down to the cliffs. It's a beautiful coastline," she said, slowing to a crawl as she drove past the beautiful, yellow manor with the white shutters and perfectly manicured lawn.

"It that a castle?" Rachael gushed.

"No, but it's beautiful, isn't it?" Lily said. She drove to the bottom of the street, made a U-turn, and headed back, once again slowing down as she passed one of the loveliest homes she had ever seen. She looked up to see a car coming toward them. It signalled it was turning into the manor. Lily sped up and stopped at the top of Hillier Street. She adjusted her rear view mirror to see who was getting out of the car. Victoria stepped out and waved goodbye to her driver.

Rory leaned forward. “Mom, what are you waiting for?”

Lily pulled out. “I’m just going to make one last stop,” She said, her voice hoarse with emotion. “There’s a bakery just up the road. Do you remember Mabel and Stanley?” she asked.

“I do,” Rory said.

Rachael shook her head from side to side.

“Well, it’s Mabel’s bakery...Ed’s favourite.”

“Can we get a treat?” Rachael asked.

They were back on the road and approaching the turnoff to the Sydney highway when Laura looked at her mother. “I need to pee,” she said, her face and hands covered in chocolate.

“Hold on, honey?”

Laura scooted her bum forward and grabbed the dash. Lily started to laugh. “I mean, hold your pee till we get home.” Laura pinched her eyes shut and grabbed her crotch.

Lily tore in the yard and jumped out. She threw the passenger door open, grabbed Laura’s sticky hand, and ran past Ed. “Sorry, can’t stop.”

Rory and Rachael got out of the car, each carrying a white pastry box smeared with the remnants of their chocolate-coated doughnuts.

“I see you’ve been to my favourite spot. You guys have a good day?” Ed asked, shaking charcoal bricks into his new barbecue.

Rory grinned from ear to ear. “The best.”

“Well, it’s about to get even better. Wait till you try my world famous Bathurst burgers.”

Jeanne sat down on the couch. “I’m looking forward to seeing the inside of the manor. I hear it’s lovely. It was very nice of Victoria’s mother to invite us over.”

Hector looked over the top of his glasses. “What time are we expected?”

“Twelve.”

“I should be back by then.”

Jeanne pushed her needle up through the button hole. "Why? Where are you going?"

"I told Tipper we'd go fishing."

"Well, just make sure you're back in plenty of time to get cleaned up. Can't be going to such a fancy place with you reeking of fish."

Hector shook his head. "I'm not stupid, you know."

Jeanne tugged on the button to make sure it was well secured. "Of course you're not stupid. I didn't mean to imply you were. I just wanted to remind you not to get caught up with the boy and forget the time. I'll lay your grey suit out for you." She snipped and knotted the thread. "I have no idea what to wear."

Hector marked his page and closed his book. "Go buy yourself a new dress."

Jeanne shook her head. "I'm sure there's something suitable in my closet."

Hector stood, pulled his wallet out of his back pocket, and slapped a twenty dollar bill on the table. "For Pete's sake, Jeanne, go buy yourself a new dress," he said forcefully.

Jeanne let her hands fall to her lap. "Hector, I'm worried about you, dear. Ever since your heart attack, I find you've been short with me. At times I feel as if I'm walking on egg shells."

"I know the feeling," he said under his breath.

Jeanne stared at him. "What did you say?"

Hector dismissively flicked his wrist. "Nothing. I'm going to make some bread and molasses."

Jeanne gave him a disapproving look. "I suppose one piece won't hurt you."

Hector returned ten minutes later and placed a tray on the coffee table. "Help yourself."

Jeanne looked at the plate piled high with a half a dozen slices of thick brown bread, covered in hard butter and black molasses. She angrily gathered up her sewing. "Sometimes I think you do things just to annoy me."

Hector took a huge bite and licked his thumb. "And sometimes I do things just because I can."

"Then do as you damn well please. But I'm not going to sit here and watch you kill yourself."

"Not going to have your tea?" he asked tauntingly.

"No. I'm going to bed."

"Suit yourself. Just means more for me," he said, picking up a second piece. He waited for Jeanne to leave, then tossed it back on the plate, thinking it wasn't nearly as satisfying as he had hoped. He picked up the plate, walked into the kitchen, stepped on the foot pedal of the garbage can, and dumped the remaining slices into the trash. He watched the molasses slowly slide off the hard butter and ooze over the potato peelings discarded from supper. "Damned if I do. Damned if I don't," he whispered, thinking Jeanne would likely be angrier at him for throwing them out, than for eating them. He rolled up his sleeve and reached into the trash can, rearranging the garbage to hide his sinful waste from view. He then slowly lifted the ball of his foot and eased the lid down, cursing himself for deliberately tormenting his wife and bringing more grief his way in the morning.

Friday, August 1

Mark opened his eyes and stared up at the nicotine-stained ceiling. He eased his stiff neck forward and winced from the pain, knocking an empty bottle of whiskey onto the floor. He checked the time, slowly got off the couch, and walked to the window. He pulled the curtain back. Rain was noisily pelting off the thin pane and pooling on the inside ledge. There was a bright flash of light. "Thank God," he whispered, knowing the weather meant he wouldn't be working.

He was washing up when there was a powerful clap of thunder and a sudden and sustained torrent of rain. The light flickered, then went out. "Great," he mumbled, thinking he'd be spending the day alone in the dark. He entered the kitchen and opened the fridge. All this food, and it's just going to go to waste, he thought. He pulled out the ham Alice had sent over and cut off a large chunk. He bit into it and looked at the Crisco can on the counter. He tipped it forward and added up the few pennies inside. "Hope you had enough to get you home," he whispered. He picked the carving knife back up, laid the blade flat against his palm, and stared down at it. "You're a total fuck up," he whispered, slowly running the razor-sharp edge across the top of his fingers. He watched the blood bubble up from the deep slits and drip down his hand and onto the floor. There was another loud crash of thunder.

"Jesus Christ! What the hell did you do?"

Mark spun around. Stanley was standing in the doorway, holding a cardboard box.

Mark threw the knife on the counter and quickly grabbed a wash cloth, wondering how long Stanley was there. "I was cutting the ham and…the knife slipped. I wasn't paying attention."

Stanley put the box down and peeled off his wet slicker. "I knocked. I figured you couldn't hear me over the rain."

Mark ran a rag over the blood on the floor, leaving a red, swirly mess. "What the hell are you doing out in this, anyway?"

"I was heading to the office to do some paperwork and Mabel asked I drop this off for Toni," he said, nodding to the wet box. A few jigsaw puzzles…some extra yarn she had about. Things to keep her busy." Stanley pointed at Marks' hand. "You should put some mercurochrome on that."

Mark shook his head and turned on the tap. "Don't have any. Doesn't matter, it's fine," he said, holding his hand and the blood-soaked rag under the running water.

Stanley looked around. "Toni still in bed?"

Mark watched the bloody water swirl down the drain. "No. She's gone."

Stanley walked over, took the wash cloth from Mark, and wrung it out. He passed it back and turned the water off. "Gone where?"

"Home."

"You okay?" he asked, wondering if Mark was being truthful when he said the knife had slipped.

"I will be."

Stanley bandaged Mark's hand. "That should do for now. Grab your jacket?"

"Why? Where are we going?"

"First, we're going to my office. You studied accounting, didn't you?"

"Yeah."

"Yeah, well you can help me get caught up…show off all those book smarts you're always braggin about. Then, when the power comes back on, we'll go to Ferguson's and pick up some mercurochrome and more gauze."

Ed charged through the back door. "Whew," he said, putting a wet grocery bag down on the kitchen table. "It's like a monsoon out there."

"What are you doing here?" Lily asked. "I hope you didn't come home because of us."

Ed removed his coat. "Actually, I did," he said and laughed. "Why should you guys have all the fun?"

Rory charged in. "Ed, did you hear the thunder?"

"I sure did. You're not scared are you?"

"No way, I like thunder," Rory said.

Lily smiled at Ed, suggesting her son might be putting up a brave front.

"Where are your sisters?" Ed asked.

Rory pointed to the living room. "In there with the kittens." He climbed up on a chair, straining to see in the bag. "Watcha got?"

Ed pulled the bag closer so Rory couldn't see inside. "Let's see. I have some sliced bologna…some milk…some coffee…some cheese….aaand..." He reached in and quickly pulled his hand out, triumphantly holding up a small glass jar. "Sooome…mustard!" He chuckled and winked at Lily. "Oh, and a little something for the adults," he said, removing a bottle of red wine.

Rory's face fell. "Is that all?" he pouted.

"Rory!" Lily scolded.

Ed screwed up his face. "*Why*? Did I forgot something?" he asked Rory.

Rory realized Ed was teasing him. He rubbed his hands together. "Hershey bars?"

Ed looked back in the bag. "Well, whadaya know." He handed Rory three bars. "One for each of you."

"Thanks," Rory said. He was about to jump down when Ed stopped him.

"Wait! Not so fast." He reached back in the bag and handed him several colouring books and a pack of crayons. "Okay, now you can go."

"Thanks," Rory said, running to join his sisters.

Ed looked up to see Lily leaning against the counter with her arms folded. "*What?*" he asked.

Lily grinned and shook her head. "You don't have to do that, you know."

Ed smirked. "But I do." There was a bright flash of lightning. "Okay, wait for it," he called out. He began counting, holding up one finger at a time. "One. Two. Three." A huge clap of thunder shook the house. Laura ran in and wrapped her arms around her mother's legs. Lily picked her up, whispered everything would be okay, and kissed the side of her head.

Ed smiled in a way that made her heart swell.

Lily put Laura back down and grinned. "What's that look for?"

Ed shrugged. "No reason." He tossed the cheese in the air, catching it with one hand. "I'm just in a good mood, I guess."

Lily turned around and began rinsing out the sink. "*Oh*? And why is that?" she asked, hoping she might have something to do with it.

Ed stood next to her. "I dunno." He tilted his head. "I've always loved a good thunder and lightning storm."

Lily nodded. "Uh-huh."

"And I have the afternoon off."

Lily smiled. "That would do it."

"Annnd." He held up a small, pink package tied with string. "The bologna was on sale. Ten thin slices for the price of six thick ones," he said and laughed.

Lily chuckled.

Ed grinned, leaned against the counter, and yelled into the living room. "Hey, kids. Who wants one of my world famous Bathurst bologna sandwiches?"

Stanley came through the back door, draped his wet raincoat over the back of a chair, and sat down to untie his boots.

Mabel put her book down. "That you, Stanley?"

"Yes."

"We lost power," Mabel hollered.

"I know. It's out all over town."

Mabel joined him in the kitchen. "Quite the storm."

Stanley put his boots together and set them aside. "Yep. Where are the kids?"

"Liv is down for her nap. JC and Mary Margaret are spending the night at Mary Catherine's."

"Hmmm...and whadaya know...it's Friday."

Mabel laughed. "So you dropped the stuff off to Toni?"

"I dropped the stuff off. Toni wasn't there."

Mabel looked confused. "Where was she?"

"She went home."

"*Home*?" Mabel said, sounding concerned. "You mean to her parents' place?"

"I guess. She left Mark a note saying she was going home."

"When?"

Stanley walked to the pantry and came back with a bottle of scotch. He put it on the table and grabbed two glasses. "Yesterday. Mark found the note when he got home from work."

"But she's not well enough to travel. I mean, she's still so fragile... emotionally. Did Mark have any idea she was planning to leave?"

Stanley put the glasses on the table and opened the scotch. "He said she mentioned something about going home when she was still in the hospital, but that he didn't think she meant it."

Mabel look dumbfounded. "How would she even get to the bus or train station? I mean, she'd have to get to Sydney."

Stanley poured their drinks. "It's not hard. She grabs a cab."

"I guess, but she'd need to have money."

"She would have had the money," Stanley said sheepishly.

Mabel looked at him. "You gave them more money?"

He pulled a chair away from the table and sat down. "I didn't expect Toni to use it to leave town."

Mabel made a face. "Of course you didn't." She picked up her drink. "Do you think we should call the police...maybe Gordon?"

"*And say what?* Hey, Gordon, we know this grown woman who left her boyfriend to go back home to her parents."

"No, to make sure she's okay. Stanley, she's emotionally distraught. What if she does something awful?"

"Mabel, let's not get ahead of ourselves."

Mabel jumped up. "I'm calling Gordon," she said.

Stanley shook his head. "Oh, no you're not!"

Mabel glared at him. "*Oh, yes I am!*" she said defiantly.

"Mabel, the power is out."

Mabel sat back down. "Dammit." She sighed. "So, Mark's okay?"

Stanley took a drink, thinking there was no need to add to Mabel's worries by telling her he suspected Mark had deliberately cut his fingers. "As good as can be expected."

"Is he going to go after her?"

Stanley shrugged. "He didn't say. But, I don't think so."

Mabel bit her thumbnail. "Toni said she was from the Valley, but I can't remember the town. How about going back to Mark's and ask him? I'll try and reach her parents as soon as the phone lines are back up."

Stanley sighed and dropped his head, knowing he wouldn't have a moment's peace until he did as she asked. He polished off his drink and reached for his raincoat. "You know how lucky you are to have me?"

"I do indeed," she said, smiling. "Thank you."

Stanley grinned. "Okay, but don't forget…it's Fri…day."

Tommy reached in his pocket and tossed Kenny his keys. "I swear to God I'll kill ya if ya get so much as a scratch on her."

"Thanks, and don't worry. I figure it'll be parked most of the night. Oh, and I used a splash of your Old Spice."

"No kiddin, I can smell ya from here. Anyway, good luck."

"Thanks again," Kenny said, opening the back door.

"And, Kenny," Tommy called out. "Ya got a rubber, right?"

Kenny patted his pocket. "Yep. And don't worry, it ain't in no fancy box. See ya."

Kenny held the key up to the ignition, his hand trembling from the anticipation of his night with Doreen. "Calm yourself, "he said, backing onto Amelia Street. He looked up to see Tommy watching from the window, gave a wave, and drove off. He slowed to a crawl when he reached the train tracks at the edge of town and turned right toward Bridgeport. "That's gotta be it," he said, spotting the white shed Doreen had described. He stopped and put the car in park. *Jesus, should I go to the door or just blow the horn.* His tongue felt fuzzy. *Fuck, I can't remember if I brushed my teeth.* He cupped his hands, brought them up to his mouth, and blew into them. The back door opened and Doreen stood on the step, waving him in. Damn, I hope I don't have to meet her parents, he thought. He got out and followed her inside.

"I'm not quite ready," Doreen said. She pointed. "Have a seat, I'll be right back."

Kenny sat at the table in the bright yellow kitchen, stretching his neck to see into the dark living room. The back door suddenly opened. Kenny spun around. Doreen's muscular brother entered with a case of beer under his arm.

"Hey, bud. What's your name?"

"Hi," Kenny said nervously. "Kenny...Kenny Ludlow."

"I'm Vinny. So, I guess you're waitin for Doreen?"

Kenny nodded. "Uh-huh."

"That your beast out back?"

Kenny felt his mouth go dry. "My friend's."

"Nice car. I just got myself a Fleetmaster." Vinny effortlessly ripped the beer case open. "Wanna a beer?"

"Better not. Soon as Doreen is ready ... we're headin out?"

Vinny laid the neck of his beer against the edge of the counter and slapped down on his hand, sending the bottle cap flying. He took a swig. "Where are you two headin?"

"None of your friggin business," Doreen said. "C'mon, Kenny, let's go."

Doreen's brother chuckled. "Be good."

Kenny ran his sweaty palms down his pant legs and stood up. "See ya," he said, following Doreen out the door. He sat behind the wheel praying Doreen wouldn't see his hand shake when he put the key in the ignition. He adjusted the rear view mirror, started the engine, and put the car in reverse. "I like your sweater," he said, thinking it made her boobs look bigger.

"Thanks. It's brand new...just got it at Marshal's."

Kenny nodded. "And your brother seems nice."

"He's okay, I guess. He can be a royal pain in the ass at times."

"Oh?" Kenny said. He turned the wheel to the right and began backing into the opening beside the shed.

Doreen pulled her sweater down, exposing more of her cleavage. "Yeah, ya don't want to piss him off. He got a nasty temper."

Kenny swallowed, turned his head to look over his shoulder, and slammed on the brakes. Doreen's head bounced off the dash.

"Oh, Fuck! Fuck! Fuck! Fuck!" Kenny said, shoving Tommy's car in park and scrambling out to survey the damage.

The back door flew open. "What the fuck did you do!" Doreen's brother screamed, tearing down the steps. He shoved Kenny out of the way and looked at his smashed in grill, and his bumper, hanging loosely from one end. "You fucking idiot," he said, pulling at his hair and racing around in circles.

"I'm…I'm sorry," Kenny stammered. "I didn't see it when I drove in."

"That's because it wasn't there…you stupid…blind arsehole!" He came within inches of Kenny's face and poked him in the chest. "What's wrong with you? D'ya even look where you were friggin goin!" he screamed. "You're payin for the fuckin damages, asshole!"

Doreen got out of the car, crying, with blood streaming from her nose and saturating her new, pink sweater.

Vinny walked up to his sister and put his arm over her shoulder. "Jesus Christ! C'mon, inside," he said, leading her up the back steps. "Shit, ya must have given it a good wallop. Ya probably broke the fuckin thing. What a goddamn idiot."

Stanley walked into the bathroom as Mabel was putting Liv in the tub. "What time did the power come back on?"

"About an hour ago. Did you talk to Mark?"

"Yes. Toni's father's name is Duncan and they live in Waterville."

Mabel closed her eyes and sighed. "Of course," she said sadly. "They called the baby Duncan. Why are you so late?"

"I went to see Luke. Thought he should know his brother's in a bad way. I suggested he and John spend more time with him."

Mabel ran the cake of soap over a facecloth and washed Liv's back. "Did you have anything to eat?"

"A couple of two-day-old doughnuts from the bakery."

Mabel stood up. "Want to take over?"

"Do I have a choice?" Stanley asked.

Mabel dried her hands. "You always have a choice." She grinned. "But don't forget, it's Friday."

Mabel went downstairs and dialled the operator. "Yes, I'm looking for a number for a Duncan Moody in Waterville. No, I'm afraid I don't have a street address. Yes, I'll hold. No, that's fine, I'll take both." Mabel copied down two numbers. "Would it be possible for you to connect me to the first number? That's great, thank you." She waited for the connection to be made. "Hello. Is this Mrs. Moody? Oh hi, my name is Mabel MacIntyre, I'm a friend of Toni's...Antoinette's. Oh? No, that's fine, I have that number. No, thank you. You, too." Mabel dialled the second number. She let it ring a dozen times before finally hanging up. She walked to the kitchen, opened the fridge, and removed a meat pie.

"Hello."

Mabel popped the pie in the oven. "Amour?"

"Yes."

"In the kitchen."

"When did your power come back?"

"About an hour ago."

Amour hung her coat on a hook by the door. "Mine is still out. I'm dying for a hot cup of tea."

Mabel filled the kettle and put it on the stove. "You're welcome to stay for supper. I just put a meat pie in the oven and there's plenty, JC and Mary Margaret are at Mary Catherine's for the night." She smiled at her friend. "I'm glad you stopped by. I was going to call you. I have some sad news." Mabel told her about Toni abruptly leaving town and her efforts to reach her. "She's not in a good way. I'm worried about her." The kettle began to whistle. She got up to make the tea. When she returned, Amour was crying. "What is it?" Mabel asked.

Amour apologized. "I'm sorry, I've just been so emotional lately. I start crying at the drop of a hat. And Victoria and I had a huge fight. She said she feels like she's walking on egg shells around me. Anyway, we're good now. But, oh," she sighed, "I feel so...so anxious, so confused." She wiped away a tear and chuckled. "And now I can add selfish to the list. It's certainly nothing like what poor Toni is going through."

Mabel smiled. "Amour, you're being too hard on yourself. You've got a lot going on right now...with Ed and the breakup...and you must be feeling anxious about meeting Victoria's grandparents. You're allowed to feel out of sorts. It's a lot to deal with."

Amour nodded. "Yes, I guess so."

Mabel touched her arm. "But let's face it, I also think you're missing Ed."

Amour reached in her pocket for a tissue and wiped her eyes. "I don't know. One minute I want to pick up the phone and call him; the next I...I wanna wring his scrawny little neck," she said and laughed.

Mabel leaned back against her chair. "Well, if that's not love, I don't know what is. Amour, call him, or better still, go see him. Tell him you were wrong."

Amour's head shot up. "*Wrong?*"

Mabel scrunched up her nose. "Maybe, not wrong. Just tell him you... over-reacted."

"*You think I over-reacted?*" she snapped. "What would you do? He wasn't honest with me. He hid things from me...important things. I can't trust him anymore."

Mabel got up and came back with the bottle of scotch she and Stanley had opened an hour earlier. "I think you need a stiff drink more than you do tea." She looked up to see Stanley walking toward her, carrying Liv wrapped in a towel. She shook her head.

Stanley's shoulder's fell. *What's going on*, he mouthed.

Mabel waved him away and poured their drinks.

Amour blew her nose. "Victoria invited Ed to lunch with the MacDonalds. That's why we had the big fight. She told me that even if I didn't want him in my life...he'd always be part of hers."

Mabel slid Amour's drink in front of her. "Good for her. Amour, just like you want her to be happy, she wants the same for you. She knows you love Ed." She smiled. "So, you're going to see him tomorrow?"

"Yes."

"That's good. Be good to him. He loves you and he's a really good guy. He made a mistake, that's all. Give him a second chance."

They both jumped at a loud rap at the back door.

Myrtle entered and looked at Amour. "I saw your car pull up. Thought I'd come for a cup of—" She noticed Amour's red eyes. "What the hell's wrong with you?"

Amour started to sob.

Myrtle shook her head. "Oh, for Christ sakes, Amour, why don't ya just marry the guy and get it over with."

Kenny drove to the chimney, shut the engine off, and slammed the palm of his hand against the steering wheel. "Tommy's gonna fuckin kill me." He got out and walked around the back to once again survey the damage. He ran his hand over the mangled bumper and looked at the dented trunk. It'll take me a year to pay for the damages to both cars. He walked to the bushes bordering the steep drop-off to the brook below and looked up at the pinkish-purple dusk sky. "Fuck!" he screamed at the top of his lungs. He heard rustling and turned to his left.

A head appeared over the thick alders. "Geeze, B'y. Ya tryin to wake the friggin dead?"

Kenny stepped back. "Sorry, didn't know anyone was—"

"Wouldn't have a cupula smokes, would ya?"

Kenny returned to the car, leaned across the front seat, and opened the glove compartment. He removed a package of Players. When he returned the stranger's girlfriend was getting to her feet and picking grass from her hair. "Here ya go," Kenny said, passing them the smokes.

"I don't suppose ya got a light?"

Kenny patted the front of his pants. "Yep," he said, pulling his hand out of his pocket and leaning forward with his arm stretched out.

Buddy stepped out of the bushes and started laughing. "I'm lookin for a light, not a rubber."

Kenny's head dropped and his shoulder's fell. He started to well up.

"Oh, dear," the girlfriend said, walking up to Kenny and rubbing his back. "It's okay, honey. We all have our bad days."

"Not like me, you don't," Kenny said. "I just smashed my best friend's car. And that's not all. I backed into my date's brother's car...a brand new Fleetmaster."

Buddy pulled the unlit smoke from his mouth. "Fuck, not Vinny's Fleetmaster...Vinny Burke from Bridgeport?"

Kenny ran his hand under his eyes and looked up. "Yeah, why?"

Buddy walked around the back of the car and got down on one knee. "Nasty drunk. Good thing for you he's on the wagon."

Kenny shook his head. "No he's not. He was drinking beer when I was there."

"And he knows you hit his car?"

Kenny nodded.

Buddy got to his feet. "Hope you and his sister aren't too serious, cause if I were you I'd steer clear of her, especially if Vinny's back on the booze." He ran his hand over the dented trunk. "It's not that bad. You'll need to replace the bumper, but Crackie can probably punch those dents out for ya. Probably won't set ya back more than a hundred…a hundred and fifty bucks…two fifty, tops."

Mabel shut the light off and crawled in bed.

"Thank goodness," Stanley said, turning toward her. "I thought they'd never leave."

"I feel so bad for Amour. She's an emotional wreck. And I still haven't reached Toni's parents."

"No answer?"

"No. And I tried three times."

Stanley laid his hand on her stomach and leaned over her. "They're likely out somewhere. Remember, it's Friday night," he said, grinning.

"But what if something happened to her?"

"Well, there's nothing you can do about it at the moment. On the other hand we can—"

"But we don't know," Mabel insisted.

Stanley sighed. "I'm sure she's fine."

"And when was the last time you saw her?" Mabel asked impatiently.

Stanley shook his head. "I don't know. It was before she lost the baby."

"Exactly," Mabel said. "God, I can't imagine. It's hard enough to lose a child, but to be told you'll never be able to have another. And she's so young. I swear, you could see the pain in her eyes and hear it in her voice. And to just up and leave like that. I should have done more to help."

"What are you talking about? You cooked meals…you visited her when she was in the hospital and checked in on her practically every day since. What more could you have done?"

"I don't know, but I'm sure I could have done something. Amour offered to talk to her about adopting a baby, but I discouraged her. I thought it was too soon. Maybe it wasn't."

Stanley kissed her neck. "Why don't you let me help you forget about things for a while?"

Mabel pulled away. "How can you possibly think about sex at a time like this?"

Stanley flopped down on his back. "Trust me, it's no trouble at all."

Mabel gave him a shove. "We'll have Saturday night sex, instead."

Stanley rolled over with his back to her. "I hope you know how lucky you are."

Mabel put her hand on his shoulder. "I'll make it up to you, I promise."

"I heard that before," he said, feigning petulance.

Mabel laid back down, trying to turn off her unsettled mind. "Stanley?"

"What?" he asked sleepily.

"If I don't reach Toni's parents in the morning, I'm calling Gordon."

"Okay."

"And I was thinking, maybe you should call Ed. I know he's hurting, too. I'm sure he'd like to hear from you."

"Okay."

"God, I hope Amour has a change of heart and takes him back."

Stanley punched his pillow. "Mabel, please!"

"*What?*"

"First, I can't get any sex. Now, I can't get any sleep!"

Saturday, August 2

Ed came out of his bedroom and smiled at Lily. "Presentable?" he asked.

Lily brushed a piece of lint off his shoulder. "Very handsome. Are you nervous?"

"A little. And, you?"

"My stomach is in knots. I hope it goes well…for both of us," Lily said.

Ed reached for his keys. "We'll know soon enough."

Lily walked him to the door. "Good luck," she said, running her hand down the back of his suit jacket. She watched him drive off, knowing that the next few hours would be crucial to her future. Victoria was about to meet with her grandparents, and, if things went well, she'd soon meet her brother and sisters. Lily sat down at the kitchen table and brought her folded hands to her mouth. "Mom, it was my shame, not hers. Don't turn her away," she whispered. She closed her eyes. "And, God, please help Ed find the happiness he deserves."

Ed turned up South Street, anxious about what the next few hours would bring. Don't expect too much, he thought. *If she had a change of heart she would have returned my calls. And don't press too hard.* He thought of his conversation with Kenny. *Don't grovel.* He turned in the driveway and looked at his watch. He was fifteen minutes early. He stepped out of the car, his heart racing in anticipation of seeing Amour again.

Victoria opened the door and smiled. "I'm glad you're here. Thanks for coming."

Ed nodded. "Hope your mother feels the same." He kissed Victoria's cheek. "You doing okay?"

"I'm okay. A little nervous."

Ed laughed. "Me, too." He looked into the dining room. "Where's your mother?"

"I'm right here," Amour said.

Ed looked up to the top of the stairs. "Hi there," he said, smiling broadly.

Amour started down the steps, thinking the summer sun suited him. "Hello."

Victoria closed the door. "I gotta finish getting ready," she said, quickly charging upstairs.

"How are you?" Ed asked, as Amour slowly made her descent.

"I'm good." She stepped off the landing and pointed. "I thought we'd eat in the dining room."

Ed followed her. "The flowers look beautiful. Are they from your garden?"

"Yes," she said, feeling rattled in his presence. "Would you like some tea?"

Ed laughed. "Honestly, I'm a bit on edge. I'd prefer a stiff drink."

Amour smiled to herself, thinking at least he wasn't trying to hide it from her. They walked into the kitchen. She pointed to the counter. "Help yourself."

"Can I get you one?"

Amour wanted one, but declined, wanting to keep her wits about her.

Ed poured his drink. "I missed you," he said, with his back to her. He waited for her to say something. He glanced back. She had her head down, folding napkins. "I know I hurt you and I was wrong," he said.

Amour reached in her skirt pocket and felt for the ring.

"I should have told you." He turned and looked at her. "Amour, you have to believe me. It wasn't a deliberate deception, it was poor judgement. I'm asking you to forgive me."

Amour brought the napkins to the table and sat down.

Ed crouched at her side. "Amour, I'm only asking for a second chance. That's all. If your answer is no, I promise that'll be the end of it. I'll leave after lunch, and, you have my word, I'll never bother you again."

Amour thought of how much she had missed him over the past two weeks. No matter how much she tried to deny it, she knew she loved him and wanted him in her life. "Why?" she asked, running her hand over a napkin and folding it over.

Ed looked puzzled. "*Why?*"

Amour avoided eye contact. "Why do you want to be with me?"

Ed smiled. "Because I love you. I feel grounded when I'm with you… and lost, when I'm not. It's hard to put into words. Honestly, it's like…I dunno…it's like fate led me to you. All I know is I believe in my heart we were meant to be together."

Amour laid her hand on the side of his face and smiled sadly. "I feel the same. And I know in my heart you're not the kind of man who'd deliberately set out to hurt anyone. I might have over-reacted. In fact, I was wrong. I'm sorry."

Ed closed his eyes, tilted his head back, and sighed. He sat next to her and took her hand in his. "So, you're giving me a second chance?"

Amour smiled and nodded. "Yes."

Ed leaned forward and kissed her forehead. "We'll take things slowly. No pressure. Just give me time to prove myself."

Amour took the ring out of her pocket. "I won't put it on just yet, but I'll hold on to it."

Ed kissed her hand. "That's all I'm asking."

Amour smiled. "I wasn't happy when Victoria told me she invited you here today. In fact, I was furious. But I'm glad she did," she whispered. "She told me that even if you weren't in my life, she was never going to give you up. So I guess I was stuck with you one way or the other," she said and laughed.

Ed clicked his tongue. "God, I love that kid. And her grandparents will, too. I know it." His expression changed. "Amour," he said, his tone sounding serious. "In the spirit of telling you everything…and leaving no room for doubt…you should know that Lily and the kids are back at my place, right now."

Amour looked surprised. "*Your place?*"

"They came on Wednesday. I had no idea they were coming. They had a room booked at the Isle Royale, but I asked…actually I insisted they stay with me."

"What are they doing here? I hope Lily didn't get ahead of herself, because it's up to Victoria when, or even if, she wants to see her. She wants to see how things go with her grandparents before crossing that bridge."

Ed put his hand over hers. "I know. But, trust me, that's not why Lily's here. I mean she'd love to see Victoria, if that's what she wants, but I swear, she didn't even know about the meeting with your parents. Honestly, Lily didn't come back to interfere or put pressure on anyone. I think she came because I told her the wedding was off and she was worried about me."

Amour pulled her hand free. "Well now, wasn't that sweet of her. I mean, taking time off work, packing up three little ones, and driving hours to get here...to what, hold your hand?"

Ed was afraid any progress he had made in having her change her mind would soon be lost, but he also knew he had no choice, he had to tell her. He, once again, took her hand in his. "Amour, listen to me. Lily made some bad decisions, but she's a good person. And yes, she cares for me, but not in the way you might think. She knows I love you. In fact, she told me to fight for you."

Amour stood up, still not convinced Lily's intentions were pure, but more convinced than ever that Ed was being genuine. She looked at the clock. "Dear Lord, look at the time. The MacDonalds will be here any minute."

Ed got up slowly, once again, feeling deflated.

Amour tugged on his sleeve and smiled. "It's way too hot to be wearing a jacket. Take that thing off." She pointed to the table. "Oh, and you can fold the rest of the napkins," she said, standing on her toes and kissing him on the mouth.

Victoria appeared in the doorway. "Everything okay in here?"

Ed grinned. "Couldn't be better."

Victoria's mouth fell open. "Does that mean what I think—"

"Yes, Victoria, it means your scheming worked," Amour said and laughed. "Now," she said, reaching for a plate of sliced tomatoes, "you can put these on—"

The doorbell rang.

Victoria's eyes widened. "Well, here goes," she said, heading to the front door.

Ed hugged Amour. "Don't worry. Everything will go great."

Victoria opened the door. “Hi, there. C’mon in,” she said, pulling the door forward and stepping back.

Hector and Jeanne entered, each carrying a bag.

Amour and Ed joined them in the entrance. “Hello,” Amour said.

Jeanne smiled. “Hello.” She looked at the large, bright foyer and the wide staircase leading upstairs. “Oh, my. It’s as lovely on the inside as it is outside.”

Amour smiled. “Thank you.”

Hector nodded. “Very nice.” He handed Amour the bag he was holding. “I hope you like trout. It’s nice and fresh. Caught it this morning.”

Amour smiled. “I love trout. Thank you. How are you feeling? Victoria told us you had a heart attack.”

Hector smiled. “Much better. Thank you.”

“And some fresh tea biscuits to go with it,” Jeanne said, handing them to Victoria. “Hot out of the oven.”

“Lovely. Thank you,” Amour repeated. “Oh, this is my…our friend, Ed Baxter,” she said awkwardly. “He’s going to join us for lunch.”

Jeanne nodded, and Hector and Ed shook hands.

Amour and Victoria took Jeanne on a tour of the manor. When they came downstairs, Ed and Hector were sitting in the gazebo drinking Jack Daniels. Amour called them in for lunch.

“Would you care for some vermouth?” Ed asked.

Jeanne put her hand over her glass. “None for me, thank you.”

Hector held up his glass. “I will,” he said to his wife’s displeasure. He then tucked his napkin under his chin. Jeanne kicked him under the table and placed her own napkin on her lap. Hector, quickly followed suit, remembering Jeanne’s etiquette lecture on the drive over.

Everyone was tense. The MacDonalds, uncomfortable in their luxurious surroundings; and Amour, Victoria, and Ed, nervous over what was to come. Only Hector cleaned his plate, grateful that his wife was not about to snatch it out from under him.

Victoria stared at her mother, urging her to get on with things.

“Well,” Amour said, “we’re certainly delighted you could join us for lunch.”

“It was delicious. Thank you,” Jeanne said.

Hector nodded. “Fabulous.”

"We wanted to have you over to thank you for helping Victoria get her teaching job."

Jeanne smile and nodded. "It was our pleasure. Victoria was so helpful to us the day of my fall. And then going through all the trouble of tracking me down so I could get my glasses back. Not everyone would do that, you know."

"It was no trouble," Victoria said. She turned toward Hector who was staring at her in the same unsettling way he did the day they first met. "Honestly, it was no trouble at all," she said, feeling her mouth go dry.

"But that's not the only reason we asked you to come to lunch," Amour said. She took a deep breath. "You see, we have some incredible news to share with you. News that I'm sure will come as quite a—"

"I think I know what you're about to say," Hector interrupted. Jeanne smiled nervously, looking from Amour to her husband. Hector put his napkin on the table and looked at Victoria. "You're the child Lily gave up."

Jeanne's mouth fell open. "Hector, what are you talking about?"

He nodded toward Victoria. "Look at her Jeanne. Don't tell me you don't see the resemblance."

Jeanne looked mortified. "Hector, Amour is Victoria's mother, not—"

Amour touched Jeanne's hand and smiled. "Jeanne, he's right. My late husband and I adopted Victoria when she was a baby." She turned to Ed. "Ed is a good friend of Lily's. He's checked everything out, and it's true. Victoria is Lily's child...your grandchild."

Victoria squeezed her mother's hand.

Hector put his head down and started to cry. Jeanne sat stone-faced. Amour, Ed and Victoria exchanged worried glances, unsure of what to do or say. Hector lifted his head, pressed his napkin into his eyes, and removed his wallet from his back pocket. He placed the creased photo of Lily sitting on their front step in front of Victoria. "The first time I laid eyes on you, I thought you were the spit of her."

Jeanne reached across the table. "May I?" She looked down at the photo and then up at Victoria. "I haven't seen this photo in years. We were on our way to church." She smiled, her eyes watery and sad. "Remember, Dot had that new camera and wanted to take our picture?"

Hector blew his nose. "I remember."

Jeanne looked from Amour to Victoria. "So, I suppose you know the reason we became estranged." They both nodded. Jeanne touched Victoria's hand. "It's not your fault, dear. Your mother...Lily—"

"Jeanne," Hector said, cutting her off. "They said they know," he said softly.

Jeanne nodded. "Of course." She pushed her chair back, rounded the table, and hugged Victoria. "I knew you were a special young lady from the moment we met."

Hector looked at Ed. "So, you know my daughter?" he said, praying Jeanne would take the extra step and welcome Lily back into their lives.

"Yes, we're good friends," Ed said, explaining that he met Lily while she was working at The Pines Motel in Roachville. "She found my glasses. We struck up a conversation and we've stayed in touch, ever since," he said, careful not to give any hint of the horrific circumstances she was in at the time.

Jeanne touched Hector's arm. "How strange. If Victoria hadn't found my glasses, I doubt we'd be here today." She looked at Ed. "And you met Lily in the same way."

Ed smiled. "I guess it was fate."

"It was God's will," Jeanne corrected.

Hector turned to Victoria. "And you and Lily get along well?"

Victoria shook her head. "I only saw her once...two years ago. I didn't find out until recently that she's my birthmother."

Ed smiled. "I was with Lily the day she and Victoria first met. Lily knew right away." He glanced at Amour. "But she also knew Victoria was happy and well cared for, and didn't want to cause any trouble for anyone. But I can tell you, there wasn't a day that went by that she didn't pray Victoria would get to know her brother and sisters."

Amour and Ed filled in more of the blanks, with Ed telling Hector and Jeanne that he realized they were Lily's parents the night of the church supper.

Hector looked confused. "But we never met before. How did you know we were Lily's parents?"

"That day, two years ago when Victoria and Lily met... the same day as the accident at the mine...Lily and I drove to Maple Avenue. Lily wanted to show me where she grew up. We were parked across the street when you and Jeanne pulled in the yard."

Jeanne started to cry. Hector put his arm around her shoulder. "I remember," he said. "It was raining. I wondered what you were doing, just sitting out there...not moving. I had no idea Lily was in the car. So Lily, she's still in this place, Roachville?"

Ed topped up their glasses. "She and the kids moved to Sussex, a few miles away. She's doing really well. Has a good job with the federal government and a nice home in a good neighbourhood. She went to night school and studied French. She's actually quite fluent."

"And the boy, Rory...he's getting along good in school?" Hector asked.

Ed smiled. "Yes. He's very bright and a pretty good baseball player from what I hear. He's also very protective of his little sisters."

"He's no longer being picked on?"

Jeanne looked at her husband, wondering how he would know Rory had been bullied.

Ed shook his head. "No, not anymore." He smiled. "Your daughter is a wonderful mother. She left town to make things better for the kids, and she did. It wasn't easy for her, being a single mother, but she somehow managed. They're all happy, healthy, well-adjusted, and well-behaved kids." Ed chuckled. "And Rachael and that little Laura, they're something else," he said, beaming.

Amour looked at Ed and smiled, knowing Ed wasn't just trying to make the MacDonalds feel good, he meant every word of it. His face genuinely lit up whenever he talked about Lily's kids. He would have been a wonderful father, she thought. The blood drained from her face, the inescapable pain of her infertile womb hitting her with a sudden and breathtaking force.

Ed looked at her with concern. "Jesus, Amour, you're as white as a ghost. Are you okay?"

"I'm a little lightheaded. Must be the vermouth," she lied.

Jeanne leaned into Hector. "It's getting late, we should get going."

Hector was about to object, when Ed spoke up. "Before you go, you should know that Lily and the kids are at my place...in Westmount. And they'll be here for another week." He turned to Victoria. "She'd like to see you, if you are up for it?"

Victoria nodded. "Of course."

Hector looked at his wife. "Jeanne, please, I want to see her. I want to hug all of my grandchildren."

Jeanne smiled. "Hector, we don't even know if she wants to see us?"

Ed nodded. "She does."

"Jeanne, honey, I'm going to do this, with or without you. Please, Jeanne, I need to see my baby," he said, his voice cracking.

Mabel held the phone to her ear. "Please pick up," she whispered. "Hello, is this Mrs. Moody? Yes, my name is Mabel MacIntyre. I'm a friend of Antoinette's. I was hoping to speak with her." Mabel's head dropped. "She's not there. Halifax. I see." She pressed her eyes shut. "Have you heard from her lately? Yes, everyone's busy. No. No, I'm not calling from Halifax. I'm in Glace Bay. Toni...Antoinette and I met at the phone company," Mabel lied. "I wonder, if I left my number, could you have Toni give me a call next time you hear from her. Yes. *849-1123.* Please tell her to reverse the charges. Yes, that would be wonderful. Thank you." Mabel hung up, her concern for Toni growing by the minute. She picked up the phone to call Gordon, but hung up, thinking Toni might have stopped into Halifax on her way back to Waterville. She'd talk to Mark before getting the police involved.

Stanley came through the front door. "I'm gonna get the kids. Toss me the car keys."

Mabel threw him the keys. "Toni's not home," she said, her voice heavy with worry.

"I'm sure there's a good explanation. Look, I was thinking we should pack up a few things and head to Pleasant Bay for the night."

Mabel looked at him like he had two heads. "Did you just hear me? I said Toni's not home."

Stanley dropped his arms at his sides. "Why do you always insist on taking on everyone else's problems like they're your own?"

"And why is it you don't give a damn?" Mabel snapped. She pinched her forehead, immediately regretting her words. "That was unfair. I'm sorry. And I know it's not true. I mean, you've been so good to Mark and

Toni, not to mention Lily…and Luke…and Willie. I'm really sorry. You care as much, if not more, for other people than anyone else I know. I'm just worried something terrible has happened to Toni."

Stanley stared down at the keys in his hands. "Just the same, I think I'll take JC and Mary Margaret to the country for the night."

Mabel wanted to cry. "Stanley, you know I didn't mean what I said."

He puckered his mouth and nodded. "How about pulling the kids' things together. I'll pick up some food along the way."

"Maybe I'll come with you, after all," she said contritely.

Stanley turned his mouth down. "We both know that's not going to work. You'll be totally distracted. You stay and do what you have to," he said. He opened the door and slowly closed it behind him.

Mabel sat down and looked into the living room. Liv was asleep in her playpen. "Your daddy's a wonderful man. I don't deserve him," she whispered, brushing away a tear.

Jeanne stood next to the car. "It's even more beautiful than I imagined. And the view is breathtaking." She opened the door and got in.

Hector reached across the front seat and touched her thigh. "Thank you, Jeanne. It was really good of you to offer to have the reunion at the house."

"Wouldn't be fair to expect Amour to have us over a second time."

"Anyway, I'm really happy you've agreed to see Lily?"

Jeanne put her purse on her lap. "Who am I to question God's will?"

Hector pulled his hand back. "Why in the world would you ever want to? Jeanne, this is our chance to enjoy whatever time we have left with our daughter and grandchildren. I don't care if it's coincidence or divine intervention that's responsible for bringing us all together, I'm just glad it's going to happen." Hector started the car and pulled away from the manor, his joy at discovering he was Victoria's grandfather, and his excitement over the prospect of seeing Lily and his grandchildren, dampened by Jeanne's suggestion that it was something she had to accept, rather than something she was genuinely joyful about.

"It's not a coincidence, it's God's will," Jeanne repeated.

Hector knew not to argue. "Yes, I believe you're right," he said, wondering if it was also God's will that made them turn their backs on their pregnant, teenage daughter.

"We'll go to the early mass tomorrow. I'll need a full day to get the house in order. Oh, and we might as well swing by Mendelson's while we're out…see what's on special."

Hector drove down South Street. "I wouldn't worry about feeding them. I'm sure everyone will be too nervous to eat."

They left Mendelson's and returned to the car. "I was thinking that we should duck in Woolworth's… get a little something for the little ones," Hector said. "We missed so many birthdays and Christmases," he said, stifling a sob. Jeanne shrugged. Hector looked at his wife. "Jeanne, I prayed for our family to be healed. I want things to go well."

Jeanne looked straight ahead without responding.

"Jeanne, are you looking forward to seeing Lily and the kids?"

"It is what it is," she said matter-of-factly.

Hector shook his head. "What the heck does that mean?"

"It means, we'll see how things go. I agreed to the meeting, didn't I? And wasn't it my idea to have it at the house?" she said defensively.

"Yes, you did. I'd just like to know if it's something you want, or something you feel you have to do."

Jeanne turned to face him. "Are we going to Woolworth's or not?"

An hour later, they entered the house. Hector put their bags on the kitchen counter. "I think I'll lie down for a bit."

Jeanne gave him a look of concern. "Are you feeling okay?"

Hector smiled. "Honestly. I can't remember the last time I felt this good. Just a little tired, that's all. Too much excitement, I suppose."

Jeanne put her arm in one of the bags and removed a block of butter. "Or maybe it was the two whiskies and three glasses of vermouth you belted back."

Ed held up the bottle of Jack Daniels. "Well, I think that went very well. Time to celebrate."

Amour stood up. "I'm sorry, I think I'll lie down for a bit."

Ed's face fell. "Still lightheaded?"

"Just a mild headache," she lied.

Ed stood beside her and placed his hand on her back. "Can I get you something?"

"No, I'll be fine." She kissed his cheek. "And I'm sure you're anxious to get home and fill Lily in on how things went. I'll call you later night." She smiled at Victoria. "They're lovely people. And they're obviously thrilled to know you're their granddaughter."

"Thanks, Mom. And don't worry, I'll clean everything up," she said.

"Call me later," Ed called out as Amour walked away.

"I will."

Ed sat beside Victoria. "Hope she's okay," he said, wondering if something upset her.

Victoria picked up the bottle of Jack Daniels and poured Ed a healthy drink. She then poured herself a small one. "It's got to be hard for her. I tried to reassure her...tell her she didn't have to worry about losing me, but I guess it's easier said than done."

"Or maybe she just has a headache," Ed said. He held up his glass. "All in all, it's been a good day. You're soon going to meet the rest of your family." He smiled at the pretty young woman sipping her drink. "I know you've heard a lot of bad things about Lily, but she really is a good soul. She just had a lot of bad breaks. But she's strong and has come through them all."

Victoria picked up the photo her grandfather had left with her. "I do see a resemblance."

Ed nodded. "Lily has a picture of herself just after she started high school...shortly before she had you. Anyway, when you see it, I think you'll see the resemblance is even more pronounced." He watched Victoria study the picture. "What are you thinking?"

Victoria shrugged. "Just thinking about how hard everything was for her, and how easy it's been for me. I mean, I couldn't have asked for better parents...a better life. Living in England. Going to college to become a teacher." She waved her arm in the air and looked around. "And compared to most families, I live in a mansion."

Ed nodded, remembering Rory and his sisters playing outside their motel unit in their tattered clothes. "Lily didn't give you up because she didn't love you, she gave you up because she did...she wanted you to have a better life."

Victoria smiled. "It really is remarkable, isn't it...Lily finding your glasses and me finding my grandmother's?"

Ed chuckled. "Good thing your grandmother and I both have bad eyesight, or none of us would be any the wiser."

Victoria rested her chin in her hand and stared intently at Ed. "I'm so glad you and Mom made up."

Ed held his glass up. "Me, too. But, like I said, I still have a long way to go before I'm totally back in her good graces. Let's just hope I don't screw things up again."

"You better not," Victoria playfully scolded. "I already picked out the dress I want to wear to the wedding."

Mabel stood next to the car with Liv in her arms, regretting her earlier words, and fighting the urge to cry. "Mary Margaret's blanket is in the side pouch of the suitcase." She smiled. "I don't want you to have to turn around and come home in the middle of the night," she said, referring to the time her strong-willed five-year-old was so upset over her missing blanket, she screeched until her father packed her and her brother up and drove home in the dark.

Stanley nodded and shut the trunk.

"Stanley, I fell awful. You know I didn't mean what I said."

Stanley leaned in and kissed Liv's cheek, then Mabel's. "I know. Mabel, it's not so much what you said that hurt, it's...it's what you do. Sometimes you get so invested in everyone else's life, you forget about us." He smiled. "And, no, I'm not talking about missing out on my Friday night sex," he said and grinned.

Mabel smiled sadly. "I don't mean to. I can't help it."

Stanley pulled on the corners of his mouth. "I know. And I get it. You care about your friends. It's one of the reasons I love you so much." He sighed. "But sometimes it can be exhausting. We bought the property in Pleasant Bay so we could have a place to get away as a family, yet we're more than halfway through the summer and we've only been there twice.

Mabel, I'm not asking you to stop being who you are." He smiled. "Besides, it would be pointless. And frankly, I'm not even going to lay this all on you. I'm guilty, too. I guess what I'm saying is...let's try and find more time for each other...for the kids."

Mabel put her hand on his arm. "Don't move. It will only take a minute for me to throw some things together."

"No," he said, shaking his head. "Stay home with the baby...do what you have to. We'll be back tomorrow afternoon." He rounded the car and opened the door. Mabel followed him and poked her head inside. "Have fun and be good. And don't go near the water without your dad."

"Bye, Mom," JC said. Mary Margaret waved.

Mabel put her hand around the back of Stanley's head and kissed him hard on the mouth. "I love you," she said, her eyes filling up.

"Me, too."

Stanley climbed behind the wheel and started the engine.

"Drive carefully."

Stanley smiled. "Will do."

Mabel watched them drive off, her chest aching from an overwhelming feeling of love and sadness. Liv laid her head on her mother's shoulder. Mabel hugged her tight. "You have a wonderful daddy," she whispered.

"Hello. Where is everyone?" Ed said, tossing his keys on the table.

Lily ran into the kitchen. "How did it go?"

Ed smiled. "Everything went very well. Where are the kids?"

"Rory and Rachael are on the shore, and Laura's down for a nap." She pulled a chair away from the table and sat down. "So, don't leave me hanging. Tell me everything."

Ed grinned. "Honestly, it couldn't have gone any better. Victoria is anxious to meet you and the kids, and your parents want to have everyone over for lunch on Monday."

Lily looked surprised. "And they want me to come?"

"Of course."

Lily stared at the floor. "I can't believe it."

Ed laughed. “Well, you should. Lily, your father became very emotional when he heard you were home. He cried. You could tell he missed you. He asked all sorts of questions about you and the kids. Your mother was more reserved, but she certainly didn’t object to the meeting.”

Lily sighed. “She might not have objected, but I bet she wasn’t enthusiastic.”

Ed sat down beside her. “Maybe not. But it’s a start, isn’t it? A good start. And, Lily, she was wonderful with Victoria. You could see how proud she was to discover she was her granddaughter.”

Lily smiled. “And Victoria…she’s happy about everything?”

“Absolutely. Like you and your parents, I’m sure she’s a little nervous. But, yes, she’s looking forward to getting to know everyone.” Lily rested her folded hands against her chin, grateful her prayers had finally been answered, but terrified about what Monday would bring.

Ed touched her shoulder. “Why the long face? I thought this is what you wanted?”

She smiled. “It is. I’m just worried about my mother. And I still haven’t told the kids about their sister and grandparents.”

Ed stood up. “Don’t worry, everything will be just fine.”

Lily suddenly grabbed his hand. “Oh, my God. I’m so sorry. How did things go with Amour?”

Ed grinned. “Good, I think. We had a good talk and we’re going to continue to see each other. No wedding bells in my immediate future, but I didn’t have the door slammed in my face, either.”

Lily smiled. “Give it time. You’ll hear those bells soon enough,” she said, a lump rising in her throat.

Ed opened the fridge. “I’m having a beer. Would you like one, or would you prefer a glass of wine?” He turned toward her. Tears were streaming down her face.

“I’m sorry, I’m just a little overwhelmed by everything,” Lily said hoarsely.

Rory and Rachael ran in the back door. Lily walked to the sink to hide from the kids.

“We picked the names,” Rory said excitedly.

Rachael jumped up and down, clapping her hands. “Inky and Binky. Inky is the one that’s all black.”

Ed laughed. "I like those names."

Lily glanced over her shoulder. "They're perfect names."

"Let's go tell them," Rory said, running into the living room.

Ed put his hand on Lily's back. "You okay?"

Lily nodded and smiled. "Yes, I'm fine. I think I'll have that beer now."

Ed was passing Lily her glass when Rory walked in cradling one of the kittens. "I think something's wrong with Inky." He looked at Ed with tears in his eyes. "I think he might be dead."

"Luke, it's Mabel. Good, thanks. Look, Stanley took JC and Mary Margaret to Pleasant Bay for the night and I'm here alone with the baby. No everything is fine. I just need to speak with Mark, and since he has no phone, I was hoping— Oh, he's with you. Yes, thanks…that would be great." Mabel wasn't expecting to speak with Mark so soon. She closed her eyes, trying to quickly collect her thoughts. "Hi, Mark, how are you? Yes. I'm very sorry. I'll miss her. Actually, Toni's the reason I called. I don't mean to upset you, but I called her home and her mother said she's not there. No, I'm sure there's a good explanation. Maybe she's visiting a friend. No, I called this morning. No, she said she hadn't heard from her in some time. Anyway, you know me, I'd like to know she's okay. Yes, I know you do, too. I was wondering if she might have stopped into Halifax on the way home…maybe to visit a girlfriend…or someone she worked with at the telephone company? *Betty.* Do you have a phone number? Okay. And what's Betty's last name?" Mabel put her head in her hand. "Okay, if you think of it, let me know. Is there anyone else you can think of? Yes, I know. Stanley always says I worry too much. Yes, goodnight."

Mabel hung up and began pacing, her concern mounting by the minute. She needed a distraction. She lifted Liv out of her playpen, walked into the kitchen, and put her in her highchair. "I need to knead," she said, pulling her ten pound bag of flour from the pantry. She looked at the clock, wondering why she hadn't heard from Amour. She put a handful of raisins on Liv's tray. "I hope things went well. I got enough to worry about," she mumbled. The door opened and Amour entered, shaking her head from side to side. Mabel tossed her dish towel on the table. "That bad, eh?"

"I got back with Ed," Amour said. She started to cry.

Mabel looked baffled. "So why the tears?" she said, taking her by the hand and leading her into the kitchen.

"It was a mistake. I can't marry him."

Mabel hugged her. "Why? What did he do now?"

Ed placed the dead kitten in a freshly dug hole, close to where he had buried Nasty and her kittens. He smiled at Rachael who was crying. "Don't worry, honey, he'll come back as tiger."

Rory put his arm around his sister's shoulder. "Don't cry, sis. He's happy now." He looked up at his mother, holding Laura. "He's gone to the jungle, right Ma?"

Lily smiled. "That's right."

Ed slowly shoveled the earth back into the hole, then placed the sod on top. "I'll make a little marker so you can find Inky whenever you come back."

Lily put her hand on Rachael's back. "Let's go inside."

"Bye, Inky," Rory said.

Ed pointed to the wheelbarrow and shovel. "I'm just gonna put this stuff away and start the barbecue. I'll be in shortly. "So, Rory, whadaya say? Think you and your sisters can do hotdogs two nights in a row?"

Rory rubbed his hands together and licked his lips. "Yes."

"Then grab the charcoal from the shed and set up some lawn chairs."

Lily opened the back door and let Rachael walk in ahead of her. She looked back at Ed, pushing the wheelbarrow across the lawn. God, I love you, she thought.

"Ma," Rory hollered from the shed. "We're having hotdogs again."

Lily smiled. "I heard."

Rory picked up the heavy bag of charcoal and laid it against his hip. The rolled up top came open, spilling a third of the contents onto the ground. Rory quickly dropped to his knees and started scooping the black bricks back into the bag. He looked around to see if anybody was watching, then got up, hoisted the bag up to his chest, and awkwardly carried it across the yard.

Ed watched him struggle under the weight. "Here, give me that," he said, grabbing it with one hand and setting it down. "It's pretty heavy."

Rory shrugged. "Not really."

Ed grinned. "You have a bug on your face," he said. Rory batted at his cheek. Ed pointed. "No, other side." Rory slapped the left side of his face. Ed nodded. "It's gone. Now, how about going inside and grabbing me a beer?"

Rory ran to the house.

Ed chuckled when he heard the gales of laughter coming from the open window.

"What's so funny?" Rory wanted to know.

"Your face," Rachael squealed. "It's all black."

Luke locked up the store and joined Mark and John in the back room.

Mark butted his cigarette and passed a beer to John. "Open this for me will ya?" he said, holding up his bandaged hand. "Sore paw."

"Wonder what James would think if he knew we were back here?" Luke said.

"He'd probably wish he was with us," Mark said.

John shrugged. "Maybe he is." He pointed to Mark. "But, I'm pretty sure he wouldn't be too happy to see you smoking."

Mark shook his head. "What are you talkin about, he smoked like a friggin chimney."

"Yeah, and it killed him," John said.

Mark lit another cigarette. "Don't you have a date or something?"

John looked at Luke, then back at Mark. "No, no date. Marjorie had other plans," he lied, pouring himself a rum.

Mark noisily sucked in the smoke. "So, this Marjorie...ya think she's the one?"

John shook his head. "No, don't think so."

Mark chugged his beer and let out a long, loud burp. "Good. Don't go rushin into things. Women can be nothin but trouble." He took a drag of his cigarette and looked at Luke. "By the way, where's your old lady, tonight?"

"She and Mary Mack went to the show."

Mark pulled his cigarette from his mouth and looked back at John. "Whatever happened between you and Victoria? I always liked her. And she's pretty hot lookin."

John shook his head. "Why does everyone ask me that?"

Luke sipped his rum. "Cause everyone figured you two would end up getting married."

John shrugged. "She only ever wanted to be friends…wasn't interested in me in that way."

Mark scoffed. "Not interested in you in that way. What are you talkin about? Yer a fuckin good lookin guy…the second best lookin guy in the family." They all laughed. "Of course, we all know I'm the handsomest one of all," he slurred. "I gotta take a piss."

"Peek in on Matthew while you're up there," Luke said.

Luke waited for Mark to leave. "By the way, thanks for changing your plans. We need to spend more time with him. He's really hurting…just too proud to admit it."

"He's also very drunk," John said. "I think he was drinking before he arrived."

Luke and John whispered about Mark's drinking and their concern over Toni while they waited for him to return.

Luke looked at his watch. "What the hell is he up to? He's been gone for twenty minutes."

John chuckled. "He's probably passed out on your bed."

"He better not be." Luke downed his drink. "I better go check." He walked through the store and headed up the stairs. He could see the faint light coming from Matthew's room. He stopped at the door, listening to Mark speak to his son. He could tell Mark was crying. "Damn," he whispered under his breath, feeling awful for his heartbroken brother.

"I do love ya," Mark said. "Can't tell ya how much. Ssssh," he said, swaying back and forth and holding his finger to his mouth. "It's our secret. We can't tell a soul. Funny, ain't it…how things turn out. Me, your daddy…but not really your daddy. Don't matter. I'll always watch out for ya. I promise." Mark wobbled as he bent down and kissed Matthew's head. "Love ya, my boy," he slurred. He stood up straight and turned around. Luke was standing inches from his face, glaring at him.

Mark laughed nervously. "Hey, buddy," he said, trying to recall what Luke might have heard. He pointed at Matthew. "He's all good. Sleepin like a baby."

"What did you mean... *Me your daddy, but not really your daddy...it's our secret?"* Luke asked through clenched teeth.

Mark made a face and tried to walk past him. Luke grabbed his arm and spun him around. "Answer me!" he seethed.

Mark stumbled backwards. "I dunno what the hell yer talkin bout."

"I heard you. You said you were Matthew's father," Luke said. His mind flashing back to the day he returned home from the war. Mark was walking backwards and grinning from ear to ear, telling him he had met a girl. *Her name is Alice. She works in the bakery.*

He grabbed Mark by the collar. "Did you sleep with my wife?"

Mark shook his head. "Yer crazy. Of course not! No way."

"I don't believe you!"

Mark pushed him. "Go fuck yourself."

Luke charged at him. "You fucking bastard," he said, punching Mark in the face and dragging him out of the room.

"Let go of me," Mark yelled, trying to escape his brother's grip. He elbowed Luke hard in the gut.

Luke bent over, gasping. Mark tried to run past him, but Luke pounced on his back. They tumbled down the stairs.

"What the hell is going on?" John yelled, rushing toward them as they wrestled on the landing. He finally got between them long enough for Mark to scramble to his feet. "What the hell is wrong with you two?"

"Tell him!" Luke screamed.

John looked at Mark, blood streaming from his nose and seeping through the gauze bandage on his injured hand. "Tell me what?" John angrily demanded.

"Daddy," the small voice called from above. Everyone looked up. Matthew was looking down at them with his face pressed between the railings.

Mark stumbled out the door, falling on the front step.

John looked back at Luke. "Jesus Christ! What the hell just happened?"

Mabel put a cup of tea in front of Amour and sat beside her. "So, you told Ed you'd give him another chance."

"Yes."

Mabel blew on her tea. "Go on."

"Honestly, it was like any doubts I had about him were completely erased. I was all set to forget the whole thing. Then, he started telling Jeanne and Hector about Lily's kids and his face completely lit up. I mean, it's obvious they mean the world to him. That's when I realized I couldn't rob him of the one thing I know would make him happier than anything else…a child of his own."

Mabel smiled. "Amour, what in the world are you talking about? Ed's known forever that you can't have children. That hasn't stopped him. And you must have talked about it?"

Amour nodded. "Sure, it came up. But I don't think he really thought things through. Oh, I'm sure everything would be fine for the first few years, but then he'd start to have regrets. I can't do that to him."

Mabel stared at her friend. "Amour, I'm not saying it can't happen, but I think you have to let Ed make that decision for himself. Don't try and make it for him. Tell him how you feel. He's a smart guy. I'm sure if he has any doubts, he'll tell you."

Amour took a deep breath. "There's something else that keeps nagging at me."

"What's that?"

"Lily."

"What about her?"

Amour picked up her cup. "I just don't understand their relationship." She tilted her head from side to side. "*I know, I know, they're just friends.* But why? I mean, Ed is always going on about how she's so smart …how she's overcome so much…what a wonderful mother she is. And we both know she's beautiful…not to mention still of child-bearing age. So why me and not her?"

Mabel laughed. "Amour, because he doesn't love Lily. He loves you. Look, Ed knows his own mind…his own heart. And I see how he looks at you. He loves you more than you realize. Why everyone else sees it and you can't is beyond me." She stood up and looked down at her friend. "Amour, I know you're feeling guilty. You seem to think that since Michael's not here to experience joy, you shouldn't either. That's crazy. Honestly, Myrtle's right. It's time for you to stop looking for reasons not to be happy and just marry the guy."

Lily sat on the couch with Laura on her lap, and Rachael and Rory at her side. Ed entered and sat across from them. Lily smiled at her son. "So, I have something to tell you guys. Something that I'm very happy about. And I hope it makes you happy, too."

Rachael's eyes widened. "Are you and Ed getting married?" she asked excitedly.

Lily felt her neck get hot. She glanced at Ed, looking over the top of his glasses and grinning. "No," she said firmly. "Ed and I are just good friends."

Rachael's face fell. "*Oh*," she said, the disappointment obvious in her voice.

Lily told them they had a sister and grandparents that they were going to meet for the first time on Monday. There were a million questions from Rory and Rachael about why their sister lived with another family, and why no one ever told them about their grandparents, but Lily, with Ed's help, honestly satisfied their curiosity, without getting into detail about the more painful aspects behind their fractured family.

"So, what do you think about meeting your big sister and grandparents?" Lily asked, looking from Rory to Rachael. They both nodded enthusiastically.

Lily smiled. "Okay, now time for bed," she said, setting Laura down, and guiding her and Rachael down the hall to the bathroom.

"C'mon, Binky," Rory said, cradling the tiny kitten.

Ed picked up a pillow that fell on the floor and tossed it on the couch. "Goodnight, Rory."

"Night, Ed."

Ed felt a wave of sadness, thinking about how much he'd miss Rory and his sisters when they returned to Sussex. He looked at his watch, surprised Amour hadn't called. He dialled the manor. "Victoria, how's your mother feeling? *At Mabel's.* Oh, good. She must be feeling better.

So, we just talked to the kids. They're really excited about meeting you. I bet. No, just tell her I called. Yes, I'll be up for a couple more hours. Goodnight." Ed hung up, disappointed Amour didn't call as promised. He went into the kitchen and returned to the living room with a bottle of wine and two glasses.

Lily entered and plopped down on the couch. "Whew! That went better than expected."

Ed poured the wine and chuckled. "You're going to have to explain the birds and the bees to them before long."

Lily tucked her legs up under her. "I think Rory knows more than he's letting on. But thanks for helping me buy more time."

Ed reached across the coffee table and handed Lily her glass. "They're great kids. I'm gonna miss them."

"And they're gonna miss you." She looked into her glass. "So will I."

Ed put his feet up on the table. "They've become very attached to Binky."

Lily nodded. "Especially Rory."

Ed grinned. "And they're very good with him."

Lily dipped her head. "What are you getting at?"

It took some cajoling, but Ed eventually convinced Lily that the kitten would be better off with the kids than with him. They spent the next hour talking about all that had happened since they first met.

"Would you ever move back home?" Ed asked.

Lily ran her finger around the rim of her glass. "No…too much history."

"But you'd be closer to Victoria and your parents."

Lily shrugged. "They might not even want me in their lives." She held up her glass. "You have no idea what my mother can be like. Besides, the town hasn't always been kind to us. I don't imagine people's attitudes have changed that much."

Ed looked at his watch. "But people change…they can surprise us."

Lily smiled. "Unfortunately, in my case, it's never been a pleasant surprise." She sensed Ed was distracted. "Am I keeping you up?"

Ed shook his head. "No, why?"

She pointed. "You keep checking your watch."

Ed nodded. "I was expecting Amour to call, but I doubt I'll hear from her tonight, it's almost ten. Look, if you want to take my bed, I really don't mind sleeping on the couch."

Lily stood and picked up the empty wine bottle. "Not on your life."

Ed took the bottle from her. "I'll look after this," he said and headed for the kitchen.

"Ed?"

Ed spun around. "Yes?"

"Thank you," Lily whispered.

Ed smiled. "Lily, you and the kids are always welcome here. I hope you know that."

Alice entered the store, turned on the light, and started upstairs. She put her hand on the rail and looked down, her heart quickening when she saw the blood. She ran up the stairs and down the hall to check on Matthew. She opened the door and sighed, relieved he was sleeping soundly. She then hurried down the hall and pushed on her bedroom door. Luke was sitting on the side of their bed with his head down.

"I saw blood on the stairs. Are you okay?" Alice asked. Luke raised his head. Alice rushed to him. "Oh my God! What happened?" She was about to touch his swollen cheek when he slapped her hand away.

Alice stepped back, shocked by his physical rebuke. "What was that for?"

Luke sneered. "You tell me?"

"Luke, you're scaring me," Alice said.

Luke stood and pointed down the hall. "Who's Matthew's father?" he demanded.

Alice's mouth went dry and her legs felt like rubber. "*What?*"

"You heard me!"

"I know you've been drinking and something upset—"

"Who's Matthew's goddamn father?" Luke screamed.

Alice's head was spinning. *How did he find out? Mabel was the only other person who knew. Mark doesn't even know.* "I don't know what you are talking about."

"You slept with my brother, you whore!"

Alice sat down on the bed. "*What?*" she asked, laughing nervously. "Who told you that?"

Luke kicked over a chair. "*Who told me! Who told me!* My brother told me…that's who fucking told me! You know…your secret lover!" he shouted.

Alice wanted to run out of the room, but was frozen in place. Her mind was racing. *How did Mark know? Why would he tell Luke?*

"Mark told you?" she asked incredulously.

Luke ran his hand through his hair. "I heard him talking to Matthew. Saying he was his daddy and it was their secret."

"Luke, you must have misunderstood. Mark's been through so much—"

"Don't lie to me!" he screamed, his spit flying in her face, causing her to flinch. He started pacing around the bedroom, angrily waving his arms about, and clenching his jaw. "What a fool I've been," he said. "Everyone must have been having a good chuckle. And here I was, thinking my big, healthy baby boy came early. Thinking my wife loved me. Now I get why you were so upset with Mark the night of our wedding…why you were always so nervous around him. You're still in love with him, aren't you? That's why you didn't want to have anything to do with Toni."

"No!" Alice shouted. "I love you! I've always loved you!"

"Did you know you were pregnant when we got married?"

Alice realized there was no turning back. "Luke! You have to believe me. It was a mistake," she said through tears. "I don't love Mark. I love you." She put her head in her hands and sobbed.

Luke bent down, his head inches from hers. "Look at me!" He grabbed her hands and roughly pulled them away from her face. "Look at me!" Alice lifted her eyes to meet his. "Did you know you were pregnant before we got married?" he angrily repeated.

Alice nodded slowly.

"So ya didn't just cheat on me…you lied to me… trapped me!" he yelled.

"No!" Alice hollered. "Luke, please! I swear, I've always loved you," she pleaded.

Luke shook his fists in her face. "Then why did you fuck my brother!" He began walking in circles, crying. "My brother," he repeated more softly. He suddenly stopped and stared at her. "Who else knows?" he demanded.

Alice looked at him, her eyes pleading for forgiveness. "Luke, I'm sorry!"

"Who else!"

Alice dropped her head. "Mabel," she whispered.

"And Stanley?"

Alice shook her head from side to side. "I don't know. Maybe."

"You're damn right he knows! If Mabel knows, Stanley knows." He tilted his head back and closed his eyes, thinking he had nothing left. He lost his wife, his child, his brother, and his closest friends. "You lied to me. You let me believe I'm the father of your bastard child?" he said softly.

Alice covered her ears, brought her knees up to her chest, and started rocking back and forth. "Don't call him a bastard."

Luke grabbed his jacket off the bed. "Isn't that what you call the son of a whore," he said, storming out and slamming the door. He was heading for the stairs when he looked up. John was standing in the hall, holding Matthew. "Get out of my goddamn way!" Luke said, brushing past them and taking the stairs three at a time.

John walked to the end of the hall. "Alice, it's John. Are you all right?" He gently bounced Matthew in his arms and kissed the side of his head. "Alice, you okay?"

Mabel was getting ready for bed when the phone rang. She ran downstairs hoping it was Toni. "Hello. Oh, hi John. No, he's in Pleasant Bay with JC and Mary Margaret. Why? What's wrong? What do you mean, a big fight? *Oh no.* Is anyone hurt? And Luke's gone, too?" Mabel put her hand on her forehead. "Was Mark drinking?"

Mabel paced as John told her that after the fight, Luke screamed at him to leave, so he went to Mark's apartment to check on him, but he wasn't there. When he came back, Luke and Alice were screaming at one another. Mabel put her hand to her mouth, fearing the explosive secret was finally out. "Where's Alice now? And she won't talk to you? Okay. Listen...can you come here and stay with Liv while I go talk to Alice? Good. I can be ready in ten minutes," she said and hung up.

Mabel was waiting by the door when John arrived. She looked at the blood on his shirt.

"I tried breaking them up. There was blood everywhere."

Mabel hugged him. "How are you doing?"

"I'm worried. One minute, everything's fine. The next, they're at each other's throats. Mark's hand looked bad. I'm scared he might have wrapped his car around a tree...he hardly had a leg under him."

Mabel forced a smile. "I'm sure he's fine. Any idea where Luke might have gone?"

He shrugged. "That's why I called. I thought he might have come here."

Mabel nodded. "And you don't know what caused the fight?"

John hesitated. "No." Mabel thought he knew more than he was letting on. "We were in the back of the store having a few drinks and Mark went to use the bathroom. He was gone so long, Luke went to check on him. Next thing ya know, they're at the bottom of the stairs, swinging at one another."

Mabel was now convinced Luke somehow discovered Mark was Matthew's father. "I'm sure Liv won't give you any trouble. She usually sleeps through the night. I left a bottle in the fridge just in case. Just warm it up a little. I'll be back as soon as I can," she said and left.

Mabel entered the store and gasped at the sight of the blood trailing from the door and up the stairs. She peeked in at Matthew who was fast asleep, then knocked on Alice's door.

"I told you...leave me alone!" she yelled.

"Alice, it's Mabel." She waited. "Alice, please. I'd like to—"

Mabel was surprised when the door suddenly flew open. "Did you tell Mark?" she angrily demanded.

"So, he knows?"

"Yes, he knows! And *I* didn't tell him. So that only leaves only one other person. You!"

Mabel shook her head. "Let's sit down and discuss this in—"

"Get the hell out of my house," Alice said.

Mabel put her arm out to keep the door from slamming shut. "I'm here as a friend who wants to help. And for the record, I didn't tell Mark, you did."

Alice's mouth fell open. "What the hell are you talking about? I never—"

Mabel brushed past her and pointed to the bed. "Sit down," she said harshly.

Alice glared at her. "I never told Mark he was Matthew's father," she insisted.

"Sit down!" Mabel hollered. She leveled her voice. "Alice, you may not have told Mark in so many words, but you're the reason he knows," she said, telling her that both Mark and Stanley put things together the day Mark unexpectedly showed up at the house when she and Luke were there with the baby. "Remember, Mark had been drinking and calling Matthew, '*his boy?*' It was all innocent enough, that is until you suddenly grabbed Matthew and started screaming at Mark. Remember? '*He's not your boy.*' Alice, if Stanley could put two and two together, you can bet your bottom dollar, Mark could, too."

Alice put her head down.

Mabel sat next to her on the bed. "And let's not forget, everyone was a little surprised when the baby came early." She squeezed Alice's hand. "Mark paid me an unexpected visit in April. He didn't even tell Luke or John he was in town. I immediately knew why he came to see me. Alice, I wasn't prepared to lie. There's been too many lies as it is, and Mark deserved to know the truth. So when he asked me to confirm his suspicions, I did. But, Alice, he also swore he would never do anything to hurt you, Luke, or the baby. That's why I'm so surprised he told Luke."

Alice wiped away a tear. "Luke overheard him talking to Matthew."

Mabel nodded. "So, it was the liquor. I didn't think he would deliberately try and make trouble."

Alice burst into tears. "Luke hates me. He'll never come back."

Mabel held in her arms and rocked her back and forth, letting her cry to the point of exhaustion. She eventually helped her into bed. She was about to shut the bedside lamp off when Alice spoke up. "Do you...do you think John knows what happened?" she asked, her breath catching between sobs.

"No, I don't think so," Mabel lied. She turned the light off and shut the door. *God, I hope Luke took his pills.*

Sunday, August 3

Ed smiled at Lily standing over the toaster. "I like mine burnt," he said, rushing for the phone. "Hello. I was hoping it was you. I thought you were going to call last night? No, that's all right. Victoria told me you were at Mabel's. Anyway, we're talking now. I'm just glad you're feeling better. Actually, I thought I'd take a drive over. What time will you be home? Great." Ed wasn't sure if he detected something in her voice, or if it was just his imagination. "Amour, we're good though, right? Good. See you then." Ed hung up and returned to the kitchen. Rory and Rachael were colouring at the table. He looked over their shoulders. "Nice," he said, nodding his approval. He handed Lily a plate for the toast. "Amour's going to eleven o'clock mass. I'm going to head to town around eleven-thirty."

Lily buttered a piece of toast. "Everything okay?"

Ed smiled. "As far as I know."

Lily added more bread to the toaster. "Actually, I was thinking about stopping by to see Mabel and Stanley."

"Perfect," Ed said. "We'll go together. You can drop me off."

Ed and the kids waited in the car for Lily. "Finally," Rory said, when she stepped outside.

Lily opened the passenger door. "The line is still busy. I hope she won't mind if we just pop by unannounced."

Ed started the car. "I'm sure it will be fine. And if they're not home, you can always go back to the beach."

They pulled into the manor shortly after noon.

"Hey, it's the same castle we saw the other day," Rachael said.

Ed gave Lily a curious look.

"I told ya, it's not a castle," Rory corrected.

Lily blushed. "We drove by after we came from the beach," she said.

Ed stepped out. Lily scooted behind the wheel. "Okay, have fun," he said to the kids, closing the door. He was watching them drive off when Amour came outside.

She pulled on his arm. "Let's take a walk."

"All right," he said, looking at the ground and scratching his head. "Why do I get the feeling I'm in trouble."

Mabel put the kettle on, her mind leaping from Toni, to Alice and Luke, to Amour. She jumped when the phone rang. "Hello. Okay. How is Alice? That's probably for the best. Thank you. Oh, and John, let me know the moment you hear anything. I don't care if it's in the middle of the night." She hung up and looked up to see Myrtle coming up the front steps. "Dammit," she whispered, thinking she'd normally love a visit with Myrtle, but not today, she had too much on her mind.

"Stanley and the kids aren't home yet?" Myrtle asked.

Mabel opened the door and stepped out. "Hopefully soon."

Myrtle held out a jar of jam. "How about some delicious blueberry jam in exchange for a nice, cold beer?"

Mabel smiled and went inside to get the beer. *Hopefully, she'll just have the one and then go home.* When she returned, Myrtle was hanging over Liv's playpen.

"Love watching them sleep," Myrtle said. She sat down in one of two large wicker chairs. "I talked to Amour. She told me about Toni. Hopefully she's all right."

Mabel leaned against the railing. "I've asked Gordon Dunphy to do what he can to track her down. If he doesn't have any luck, I'll have to call her parents back. Not a call I'm looking forward to."

Myrtle nodded. "Terrible situation. But at least things went well with Victoria's grandparents. Amour says everyone's getting together tomorrow."

Mabel sat next to her. "It's such an incredible story. How Lily met Ed, and Victoria met her grandparents. You know, if it wasn't for Ed, no one would know the difference. Everyone would just be going about their business, probably passing each other on the street without a clue as to who was who."

Myrtle nodded. "I like Ed a lot."

"You know he and Amour are talking again?" Mabel said.

Myrtle adjusted her toque. "Yes, she told me."

"Hopefully it will all work out," Mabel said. She gave Myrtle a puzzled look. "You still haven't told me why you thought the wedding wouldn't happen?"

Myrtle took a drink. "I told you…I'm a witch."

"Seriously."

Myrtle shrugged. "I was just in a bad mood." She put her head down. "Still feel bad about how mean I was to Rosie."

Mabel turned down her mouth. "To be honest, everyone was a little taken aback. You usually don't mind a little off-coloured humour."

"I wasn't myself that day." Myrtle took another swig. "I found a lump in my right breast," she blurted.

Mabel let out a heavy sigh. "Oh my God. When?"

"About six weeks ago. Saw the doctor just before I went to club. He confirmed it was cancer. That's why I was out of sorts. Still, no excuse for taking it out on Rosie."

Mabel ran her hand up and down Myrtle's arm. "I'm so sorry, Myrtle. I had no idea. Are you going to have surgery?"

"Yes. Doc said I should have them both chopped off. Said if the cancer's in one, it's just a matter of time before it's in the other."

"And?" Mabel asked.

Myrtle laughed. "Might as well, besides it'll keep me balanced." She cupped her right breast and jiggled it. "Imagine goin round with just one of these."

Mabel's shoulders fell. "I really have no words. But you're strong, and otherwise in good health."

Myrtle shook her head in disgust. "I don't know why God put me on this earth as a woman. He should have saved himself the trouble and made me a man. I'm built like a stevedore for Christ's sake. I'm bald. And, soon, I'll be titless." She hiked her pant leg. "And look at my frigging legs. Wish I had that hair on my friggin head."

Mabel didn't know whether to burst out laughing, or burst into tears. "Myrtle, you should have told me. I would have gone to the doctor with you."

"Rosie came with me," Myrtle said matter-of-factly.

Mabel was glad Rosie was with Myrtle when she received the devastating news, but she was surprised Myrtle hadn't asked either her, or Amour, given their long friendship. "I assume you told Amour?"

Myrtle shook her head. "No."

"Myrtle, you have to tell her," Mabel insisted. "She'd want to know."

"I will. But now is not the time. She's already got so much on her plate."

"Amour, you're scaring me. Am I in trouble?"

Amour smiled sadly and shook her head. "No, you're not in trouble."

"So, what's on your mind?" Ed asked.

Amour leaned into him and held on to his arm. "You… what makes you happy?"

Ed stopped walking and looked at her. "*That's it? What makes me happy?* Well, that's easy. *You.*"

Amour walked in front of him, turned, and pulled on his hand. "Maybe now, while I'm still breathtakingly gorgeous," she said and laughed. "But what about when I'm old and fat?"

Ed wondered what she was getting at. "You'll always be breathtakingly gorgeous."

They reached the bottom of Hillier Street and trod through the high grass to the edge of the cliff. Amour sat down. "Now, *this is breathtaking*," she said, taking in the shimmering, blue waters and billowy, white clouds.

Ed sat beside her and leaned back on his outstretched arms. "It sure is. What is it, Amour? I know you have something to say."

Amour pulled her knees up, turned her head toward him, and smiled. "I saw how you are when you talk about Lily's kids."

"*Oh*? And how is that?"

"Your face lights up."

Ed shrugged. "So, they're great kids."

Amour looked back at the water. "You deserve to have kids of your own."

Ed sat up. "Is that what this is about?"

Amour nodded. "You'd make a wonderful father. And you're still young enough to chase some little ones around...to have your own son or daughter...maybe a couple of each."

Ed plucked a long piece of bearded grass, got to his feet, and squinted into the bright light. "You see, there's just one problem with that theory, it can't happen with the woman I love. And if it can't happen with her, it's not going to happen at all." Ed looked down at her sitting with her knees up to her chin and her arms wrapped around her legs. "Amour, if you don't marry me, trust me...I'll die a lonely, old man."

"You say that now, but what about in three or four years from now? I'm afraid you'll have regrets...blame me."

"I won't," Ed insisted.

"Maybe not consciously, but it's only natural you'd—"

"Amour, I won't. I know I won't. I've known all along you can't have children. Trust me, it's not going to happen."

"You don't know that," Amour said, dropping her head and hiding her face.

"And you don't know that it will." Ed sat back down beside her. "Amour, we have no way of predicting the future. But give me some credit. I think I know my own mind...what's in my heart. And I know what makes me happy. And that's you." He looked up at the sky. "Look, we're not kids anymore. And you know I love you. At least I hope you do. And, I believe you love me."

"I do," Amour whispered.

"Then why delay the inevitable?"

Amour raised her head and rested it on his shoulder. "I don't know."

"Amour, I swear to God, I'm okay with not having children." He tilted his head. "I'm happy being an uncle to my nieces and nephews. And I won't lie, I'll always want Lily's kids in my life. And if you ever marry me, and Victoria settles down and starts a family of her own, I'll be a grandfather. And I'd be happy with that. I know it."

Amour turned down her mouth. "I'm not ready to be a grandmother," she playfully pouted.

Ed kissed the top of her head. "Of course not. You're way too young for that. But hopefully you're ready to be my wife." Ed stood and helped her to her feet. "Seems to me you've run out of excuses. Amour, let's grow old and fat together?"

Amour chuckled. "You'll never be fat."

Ed stepped back, put his hands on her shoulders, and grinned. "Amour, for the second, and hopefully last time...marry me?"

Amour poked him in the stomach. "Actually, it's the third time you've asked."

Ed raised his eyebrows. "Well, there you go. See, I won't take no for an answer." He smiled. "Please, don't make me ask a fourth, fifth, sixth time?"

Amour smiled. "I suppose that wouldn't be fair, would it?"

Ed quickly scooped her up and kissed her.

Amour squealed and started laughing.

An older woman adjusted her clothes prop, lifted the bottom of her damp white sheet, and peered under. "Beautiful day," she hollered to the tall, handsome man plodding through the field with the pretty, young woman in his arms.

Ed grinned. "Best day of my life."

The kerchief-clad women reached in her basket, pulled out a pillow case, and gave it a good snap. "Great drying day. Got a good blow comin in from the north."

Mabel laid Liv on a towel and changed her diaper. "I would have thought your father would have been home by now." She heard a car pull in the yard and looked out the window. "Finally," she said, picking Liv up and going outside.

"We caught some fish," JC said excitedly and placed a small pail at her feet. "See, there's four of them."

Mabel looked at the tiny, green guppies darting back and forth. "I see that," she said, forcing her voice to sound cheery.

"I'm going to show Myrtle," JC said, running down the steps and through the field.

Stanley stepped out and waved.

"You just missed Lily and the kids," Mabel said.

"How are they?"

"Good. Lily looks wonderful. Kids seem happy. They're gonna try and come back before they go back to Sussex." She looked for Mary Margaret. "Where's her nibs?"

Stanley took Liv from Mabel. "Asleep in the back seat."

Mabel nodded, grateful she had a chance to tell Stanley about all that happened before her headstrong daughter demanded her full attention. She quickly filled him in on the fight between Mark and Luke, her late-night visit to see Alice, Myrtle's breast cancer, and her call to Gordon for help in finding Toni. Stanley put Liv in her playpen and went inside. "Where are you going?" she asked.

"After all that, I need a drink."

"I'll have one, too," Mabel hollered.

Stanley came back outside and handed her a scotch. "And I was worried you'd be sitting home alone, bored out of your mind."

Mabel leaned back in her chair. "The situation with Luke and Mark is a mess. I don't see any way to fix it."

Stanley sipped his drink. "It's not your problem to fix."

Mabel looked at him. "I know. But that doesn't mean I shouldn't care. I'm worried sick over Luke. God, to think he and Toni are both out there somewhere, and in such pain."

"And Mark," Stanley reminded her.

Mabel nodded. "Yes. Mark, too. It's just I don't worry so much about him doing anything...you know what I mean." She took a drink. "And you have no idea where Luke would go?"

Stanley shook his head. "No clue. He always stayed close to home. I'll ask John if any of his old airforce buddies are still around."

Mabel put her head down and started to cry. Stanley put his drink down and crouched in front of her. He took her hands in his. "Mabel, I need you to listen to me."

Mabel looked up. "I'm sorry. I just feel so helpless."

"Mabel, what more can you do?"

She stood up. "There is one thing," she said and went inside.

Stanley finished his drink and wondered what she was doing. He opened the door. "Mabel?" He walked down the hall, looking in the living room and kitchen. He went upstairs, checked the bathroom, then pushed on their bedroom door. Mabel was kneeling beside the bed, praying over Father Gregory's maniturgium. He quietly pulled the door over and started down the hall, when he suddenly stopped, a wave of panic washing over him. "Oh, no," he whispered, picturing Mary Margaret's blanket sitting on the kitchen counter in Pleasant Bay. "Please, please, please, let it be in the car," he whispered.

Lily hoped Ed was ready to leave. She pulled into the manor, got out, and walked up the curved, stone steps. She looked at the lush green lawn and the tidy rows of brightly-coloured flowers bordering the white gravel driveway, wondering if Amour paid someone to look after her beautiful property. She tapped on the door and nervously ran her palms down her pale blue, cotton skirt. "Damn," she whispered, looking down at the dark streaks her sweaty hands left behind.

"Come in," Ed said, beaming.

Lily immediately knew he had good news to share. "No, I just wanted to see if you were ready, or if—"

Ed looked past her. "Where are the kids?"

She nodded over her shoulder. "In the car."

"Go get them and come in for a minute. Amour and I just poured a drink."

Lily tried to object, saying she would take the kids to the beach, but Ed insisted. "She doesn't bite. Besides, we're celebrating."

Lily smiled. "The wedding is back on."

Ed winked. "Yes."

Lily fought back tears as she walked back to the car. She took a deep breath and opened the back door. "Okay, guys, we're going inside for a bit."

"Inside the castle?" Rachael asked excitedly.

"Rach, it's not a castle," Rory insisted.

"No fighting," Lily warned, her heart pounding and her stomach in knots. "Be very careful and don't touch anything. And don't forget your please and thank yous." She took Laura by the hand and followed Rachael and Rory inside.

Amour entered the foyer, stood beside Ed, and smiled at Lily. "It's good to see you again."

Lily had forgotten how stunning she was. "Congratulations."

Amour laughed. "He already told you?"

"He didn't have to. I could just tell."

Amour smiled at the kids. "Hi there."

Lily introduced Rory and Rachael. She then bent down and picked up Laura. "And this is Laura." Laura stretched her arms out to Ed. Lily smiled at Amour. "She's developed quite an attachment."

Amour grinned and looked up at Ed. "I can see why." She then looked back at Rory and Rachael. "Do you guys like chocolate cake?" They both eagerly nodded. Amour took Rachael by the hand. "Well, lucky for you, I just happen to have some."

They were walking through the dining room when Lily pulled on Ed's arm. "Is Victoria here?" she whispered.

"Afraid not. She's out with her girlfriends."

Lily knew she would see Victoria the next day when they met at her parents, but she was disappointed just the same. She looked around at the beautiful surroundings and felt totally out of place. I should never have agreed to come inside, she thought. She followed the others into the kitchen, her anxiety growing by the minute.

"We're having a Jack Daniels, but we also have some rum and vermouth," Amour said to Lily. "Of course, we always have tea on the go."

"Thank you, water will be fine."

Ed could tell Lily was uncomfortable. He poured a whiskey and handed to it to her. "You can't celebrate with water," he said.

Lily nervously sipped her drink, watching her kids devour their cake.

Ed topped up his drink. "You kids ever sit in a gazebo?"

"A what?" Rory asked.

Ed put Laura on his shoulders. "C'mon, I'll show you."

Amour sat across from Lily. "How's your drink?"

Lily smiled. "Good." She cleared her throat. "Amour, I want to thank you for making it possible for Victoria to meet us…and my parents."

Amour smiled. "She should know her family."

"Still, not everyone would be so understanding."

"Are you nervous about tomorrow?" Amour asked.

Lily nodded. "Terrified."

Amour leaned forward. "Your parents are lovely. Your father got very emotional when he talked about seeing you after all these years."

Lily wiped away a tear. "We lost so much time." She paused to collect herself. "And we can never get it back."

Amour squeezed Lily's hand. "That's why you need to make the most of what's left." She sat back and looked into her glass. "Ed helped me see that there's no point in dwelling on the past, or trying to change things that can't be changed. He says we need to wring every bit of happiness out of every minute, of every day." She laughed. "Wring it dry, he says."

Lily smiled. "He's a wonderful man. And you're a very lucky woman."

"Hello," Victoria said, surprising them.

Amour stood and hugged her daughter. "Your brother and sisters are outside with Ed." She picked her drink up off the table. "Why don't you two chat a bit, while I go check on them." She put her hand on Lily's arm and smiled. "Take all the time you need."

Monday, August 4

Ed tapped lightly on the bathroom door. "Are you all right?"

Lily sat on the side of the tub, praying her stomach would settle. "I'll be out in a minute."

"Okay, the kids are in the car. And just so you know, Binky is coming with us. They want to show Victoria and your parents."

Lily opened the door.

Ed hugged her. "I know you're scared. Everything will be just fine."

Lily took a deep breath and exhaled. "Let's do it."

Forty minutes later, they passed the sign marking the entrance to town. "Doing okay?" Ed asked Lily.

"I feel like throwing up," she whispered.

Ed smiled. "Remember, they're as nervous as you are."

Lily shook her head. "I doubt it."

"I told Amour we'd meet in front of the pop factory so we arrive at the same time."

Lily nodded. She looked in the back seat. Laura was asleep with her head on her sister's shoulder, and Rory was holding Binky's box on his lap. She smiled. "Remember your manners."

"What do we call them?" Rory asked.

Lily looked at Ed. "I never even thought about that."

Ed looked in the rear view mirror and smiled. "Why not ask them what they'd like to be called?"

Lily smiled at Ed. "I don't know what I'd do without you."

"There they are," Ed said, pulling into the pop factory. He put the car in park and got out.

"Where are you going?" Lily asked.

Ed smiled. "Victoria can take you the rest of the way."

Victoria got in and handed Lily a photo album. "Mom and I put it together."

Lily opened the cover and looked at a picture of Amour and Michael holding Victoria up to the camera, and smiling broadly.

Victoria smiled. "It was the day they took me home." She started to laugh. "Lots of pictures of me as a baby, I'm afraid."

Lily turned another page. "I love seeing them. You were a beautiful baby. And your father is so handsome."

Victoria laughed. "He used to say I got my good looks from him." She looked in the back seat and smiled at Rory. "So, this is Binky."

"Do you like his name?" Rachael asked.

Victoria smiled. "I love it."

"And he's getting stronger every day," Rory proudly chimed in.

Victoria looked at Rachael. "Close your eyes and hold out your hand. Okay, now open them."

Rachael beamed at the lady bug pin sitting in the palm of her small hand.

Victoria smiled "I hear they bring good luck." She turned to Lily. "And I have one for Laura, too."

"That's very sweet of you," Lily said. She looked back at Rachael. "What do you say?"

"Thank you."

"You're welcome," Victoria said. She reached in her pocket. "And this is for you," she said, passing Rory a compass.

"Wow, thanks." He held it up for his mother to see. "Look, Ma."

Lily wiped away a tear, grateful the beautiful, young woman sitting beside her was raised by two loving parents.

Victoria sat forward and started the car. "It's going to be a wonderful day," she said cheerily.

Lily smiled. "It already is."

Hector looked at his watch, then up at the owl clock. "That queer, little clock of yours is running slow again."

Jeanne placed her pork pies on a plate. "How do you know?"

Hector tapped the face of his watch. "It's ten to one, not twenty to one."

"Maybe your watch is fast."

"Nothing wrong with my watch," he huffed, looking out the window for the third time in as many minutes.

Jeanne put the plate in the center of the table. "Hector, a watched pot won't boil any faster. They'll get here when they get here."

"I don't know how you can be so calm. I'm a wreck," he said.

Jeanne took the creamer from the fridge and put it next to the sugar bowl. "It is what it is. It's in God's hands now."

Hector took a deep breath. "It's also in yours. Jeanne, please don't go opening up old wounds. Let's think of this as a fresh start."

"I'm not going to make any trouble. But I'm not going to put up with any, either." She pointed to his belt. "You should let that out a notch, your pants are puckering."

Hector was opening his belt when he heard the car door. Jeanne looked out the window. "They're here."

Hector quickly tucked in his shirt, fastened his belt, and rushed down the short hallway to the front door. "Jeanne, hurry up," he said, waving for her to join him.

"You answer it," she whispered from the kitchen.

Hector opened the door. Victoria was walking up the steps with Rory and Rachael at her side. Lily followed, with Laura asleep on her shoulder. Hector placed his hand on Rory's shoulder and smiled at Rachael, then looked up at the daughter he hadn't spoken to in almost twenty years.

"Hi, Daddy," Lily said hoarsely.

Hector wrapped his arms around her and Laura. "I'm so sorry," he repeated over and over again, sobbing. He finally collected himself and stepped back.

Lily looked down the hall. Jeanne was wearing the mauve sweater with the pearl buttons Lily had secretly left on the doorstep many years ago. She wondered if it was just a coincidence her mother wore it on this day, or if she was acknowledging she knew where it had come from.

Jeanne slowly walked toward her, stopping briefly to acknowledge Rory and Rachael. She placed her hand on Laura's head. "We have a lot to catch up on," she said, her eyes fixed on her sleeping grandchild. Laura lifted her head off of her mother's shoulder and started to cry. Jeanne took her from Lily. "There, there, little one. It's okay," she said, kissing her forehead. "Come with me. You come, too," she said to Rory and Rachael. "Do you like Iron Brew?"

Victoria looked at Lily. "What's keeping Mom and Ed?" She opened the door just in time to see them pull away. "I guess they're not coming in after all," she said.

Lily was about to push the curtain aside to see for herself, when her father flopped down on the couch with his hand over his chest. "Da, is it your heart?" she asked urgently.

Hector coughed. "I'm fine…just not used to so much excitement," he choked, running his hankie under his nose.

Lily looked around the dreary room, thinking it was exactly as she remembered. The same furniture, the same grey doilies, and the same grainy photographs on top of the out-of-tune piano no one ever played.

Rory came in with his pop and sat next to his grandfather. "I saw you before."

Hector smiled "You remember me?"

Lily looked at her father and shrugged. "Rory, what are you talking about?"

"I saw him at my school."

Hector looked at his daughter. "I knew there were some mean kids giving him a hard time. I used to keep an eye on him, from time to time."

Lily teared up. "I had no idea. And you sent us money, too?"

Hector shook his head. "No, dear. I probably should have, but I didn't."

Lily was surprised. She had always assumed her father was her secret benefactor. She closed her yes, it must have been Mabel and Stanley, she decided.

The next two hours were a mix of awkward silences and forced conversations as the family of strangers worked to get to know one another, or make peace with one another. Lily was grateful Victoria was in the room to lighten the mood and keep the conversation going. It was clear she had already won over her grandparents, and that they would have a wonderful future together. Lily smiled as her father studied the pictures of Victoria through the years. What a shame they didn't know you as a child, Lily thought. She looked at her mother sitting with Laura on her lap and felt a sudden wave of sadness. Her mother's face was long and drawn, and her bony, loose-skinned hands, a tell-tale sign of the passage of time. There won't be too many more years for you to be a grandmother, she thought. Lily was relieved her mother was so gentle with the kids, but hurt she took pains to avoid being alone with her. Lily wondered if it was because her mother felt guilty for throwing her out as a penniless, pregnant teenager, or if it was because she was still ashamed of her. She smiled. "That's a lovely colour on you, Ma."

Hector laughed. "That's her special occasion sweater. I keep telling her to go buy herself some new clothes but she keeps wearing the same old things."

"There's nothing wrong with my sweater. It's in perfect condition," Jeanne scoffed. She looked at her daughter. "It was a birthday gift from Dot."

Hector shook his head. "That's not what Dot says."

Jeanne squared her shoulders. "Well, you keep insisting you didn't buy it for me. Who else would have left it on our doorstep?"

Lily thought about telling them it was her, but decided it might seem like she was rubbing salt into the wounds. She looked down at Rory and Rachael playing jacks on the floor. "Thank you for the kids' toys. It wasn't necessary."

"That's what makes giving it so special," Hector said. He smiled sadly. "We missed their birthdays and all those Christmases."

Rory looked at his grandfather. "What's that banging noise?"

Hector went to the window. Tipper was bouncing his ball against the side of the shed. "Damn, I forgot about Tipper," he said, rushing outside and leaning over the railing. "Tipper! I'm sorry. I completely forgot about the ballgame."

"That's okay. We probably only missed a cuapla innings."

"No, I can't listen to it with you today. My daughter and grandchildren are here for a visit."

Tipper threw his ball in the air and caught it. "Okay. Want me to come back tomorrow to start the basement?"

"No, not tomorrow. I'll let you know."

Tipper shrugged and started to walk away. "Ya know my Red Sox are gonna pound your Yanks into the ground."

Hector smiled and waved him off. He was about to go back inside when he stopped. "Hey, Tipper. Hold on a sec. I'll get you the transistor. No reason you can't stay and listen to the game."

Tipper punched the palm of his mitt. "Nah, don't bother. Not the same when I can't make fun of you and your sucky team. Besides, Gran will listen to it with me. See ya later."

Hector closed the door and looked at Lily. "Where's your mother?"

"On the phone."

Hector nodded and pointed over his shoulder "That's the kid I hired to help around the property. We sometimes listen to the ballgames together." He looked at Rory. "Ed tells me you're a pretty good ballplayer."

"I hit two home runs," Rory said proudly.

Hector smiled. "I used to be a pretty decent player in my day, too. I played third base."

"I'm in left field. I like the Cubs."

"The Cubs are playing my Yankees Friday afternoon. Want to listen to the game together?"

"Sure," Rory said enthusiastically.

Lily made a pained expression and touched her father's arm. "I'm sorry, Da. We won't be here." She looked at Rory sitting on the floor beside his sister. "Remember, we're leaving on Thursday."

"You can't stay a few days longer?" Hector asked.

"Please!" Rory said, his hands pressed together as if in prayer.

"I'm sorry, honey. I have work on Monday and a dozen things to get done before then."

Jeanne entered and looked at Victoria. "That was your mother on the phone. She invited us all to supper tomorrow." Jeanne quickly realized what she had said. She put her fingers over her mouth and turned toward Lily. "I'm sorry. I'm not quite sure how to refer to anybody anymore."

Lily smiled. "It's okay, Ma. There's no need to apologize. Amour is Victoria's mother."

Rory dropped the jacks on the floor, passed the small rubber ball to his sister, and shrugged. "I know, I'm as confused as you are."

Mabel was nodding off when she heard her name being called. She eased her arm off of Mary Margaret and slowly got up from the bed. She tiptoed away, stopping briefly to pull Liv's blanket up over her shoulder.

"Hello! Mabel, are you home?" Amour hollered.

Mabel appeared on the stairs and put her finger to her mouth. "Shush. I just got the girls settled."

"Sorry," Amour whispered. "Everything okay? We just came from the bakery, and John said you and Alice both took the day off. Are you feeling all right, cause you look like hell?"

Mabel sighed. "I feel like I've been there and back," she said, telling Amour about her sleepless night consoling Mary Margaret. "Stanley left her blanket in Pleasant Bay and she was distraught. He's on his way there now. Lord knows we won't survive another night without it."

"We won't stay," Amour said. "I just wanted to let you know I took your advice... and, well—" She held out her hand.

Mabel looked down at the ring and hugged her. "Finally, some good news." She peeked out the door. "Is Ed with you?"

"Yes, but—"

"But nothing. I need to congratulate him." Mabel stood in the doorway and waved. "What are you doing out there? Come on in."

Despite the happy news the wedding was back on, Mabel had difficulty following the conversation; her mind drifting to her friends whose lives were in turmoil. She was relieved when Ed suggested he and Amour leave.

"We should get going. Lily and the kids might be waiting for us back at the manor," he said. He smiled at Mabel. "I'm anxious to find out how things went with Lily's parents."

Mabel nodded. "I know she was worried sick about the reunion. Hopefully it went well," she said, walking them out to the verandah.

Amour and Ed were halfway down the front steps when Amour suddenly turned around. "Why don't you and Stanley come to supper tomorrow night?"

Mabel at first declined, saying it was a family gathering, but eventually relented, realizing Amour was not going to take no for an answer. She watched them drive off and closed the door, hoping the girls would stay down long enough for her to grab a quick nap. She plopped down on the couch and was just about to doze off, when the phone startled her. She jumped up, hoping it was Luke or Toni. Her face fell when she heard the voice on the other end. It was Bessie calling to tell her one of the ovens was out and they were behind on the orders. *What else can possible go wrong?* She closed her eyes. "Okay, don't take any more orders for today or tomorrow. What are we short of? Pack up some flour, butter, and raisins, and have Mary Mack come here." She threw her hand up. "Of course her car is on the fritz," she said, exasperated. "Okay, tell her to call Bay Taxi and I'll pay for it when she gets here. Stanley can drive her home." Mabel hung up and was looking for the number for the appliance repair shop when the wailing started. She looked up to see a red-faced Mary Margaret sitting on the stairs, screaming for her blankie.

Stanley was about to unlock the door when he realized it had been jimmied open. He pushed on it and slowly stepped inside. There were empty beer bottles on the counter. He walked into the living room, looked into the backyard for any sign of an intruder, and eased his way down the hall. "Anybody here?" He checked the bathroom, then slowly turned the knob of his bedroom door and pushed it forward. Luke was sprawled face down on the bed.

"Luke," Stanley said, shaking his shoulder. "Luke."

Luke slowly rolled onto his back and opened his eyes. He propped himself up on his elbows. "What time is it?"

Stanley looked at his watch. "Ten to three. I would have given you a key, ya know."

Luke sat on the side of the bed. "I'll fix the damn door."

"That's not what I'm getting at," Stanley said. "Where's your car? I didn't see it out front."

Luke dismissively pointed. "I parked down the road." He squinted as if in pain. "I didn't expect you back so soon."

"So you knew I was here with the kids?"

Luke nodded.

"So why not just tell me you needed a place to stay?"

Luke put his head in his hands. "Cause maybe I didn't want you to know I needed a place to stay."

"When did you eat last?" Stanley asked.

Luke shrugged, got to his feet, and started for the door. "I'll get out of your way."

Stanley grabbed his arm. "Don't be ridiculous. You can stay here as long as you like."

Luke pulled his arm free. "No thanks."

Stanley followed him into the living room and pointed. "Sit down," he said firmly.

"Fuck you," Luke shot back.

Stanley pushed him onto the couch. "Sit down and listen to me," he ordered.

Luke tried to get up, but Stanley pushed him down again.

"You knew and didn't tell me," Luke sobbed.

"That's right, I didn't tell you! Why would I want to do anything to hurt you…ruin things for you! To be honest, Mabel and I prayed you'd never find out. But don't ever think we took any comfort in knowing what was going on. In fact, we hated it. And one more thing, if either Mabel or I thought for one minute that Alice didn't really love you, we would have said something. But, Luke I'm sure she does…I know she does. Yes, she made a stupid mistake. A big one…one that I'm sure both she and Mark will regret for the rest of their lives. And deep down, no matter what you think of them at this moment, they both love you. And so do I. And so does Mabel."

It took a few more angry outbursts and more than a few tears before Luke finally admitted that, if he were in Mabel and Stanley's place, he wouldn't have handled the situation any differently. Stanley opened his wallet and removed all the cash that he had. He placed it on the table. "I won't tell anyone where you are, but you need to get to a phone first thing in the morning and let John know you're okay. He'll tell the others, so at least they're not worried something terrible happened to you."

Luke stared at the floor. "What, like I threw myself off a cliff or something?"

Stanley blanched at the chilling reminder of Luke's father's suicide. "And you swear you've got your pills?"

"Yeah, at least a month's worth."

"So what will you do?" Stanley asked.

Luke shrugged. "Probably head to Halifax…look for work."

"What about the store?"

Luke rubbed his forehead. "I honestly don't care. John can keep it."

"John can't run the store and go back to school."

Luke shot him a look. "Then he can sell the damn thing. I honestly don't give a shit."

Stanley pressed his lips together and raised his eyebrows. "I know you don't want to hear this again, but you need to know Alice really does love you. And Matthew…he needs you in his life. Not easy for a boy to grow up without…well, you know what I mean."

Luke nodded to the cash on the table. "Thanks for the money. I'll pay you back when I get work. And I'll fix the door."

Stanley shook his head. "You don't need to worry about either. I just want you to look after yourself. Promise me you'll call me at the office from time to time, so I know how you're doing?"

Luke nodded and forced a smile. "I will."

Stanley paused at the door. "And remember, call John first thing in the morning." Stanley left, got in his truck, and started the engine. He looked back at the cabin, wishing he could do more for his friend, then put the truck in gear and backed up. "Dammit," he said, quickly shoving it in park, getting out, and going back inside. "Almost forgot Mary Margaret's blanket," he said, quickly grabbing his daughter's cherished ball of wool off the counter. He looked up to see Luke standing at the window with his head down, sobbing. He quietly walked out, heartbroken for the young man inside whose life was instantly shattered by an unforgiveable betrayal.

Mabel looked at the clock. "Where the hell is he?" she seethed. She dropped a bread pan into hot, soapy water and quickly dried her hands in a dish towel. "I'm going to kill him," she said, walking to the bottom of the stairs, hoping the crying finally stopped. Stanley came through the back door with Mary Margaret's blanket. Mabel angrily charged toward him and grabbed it from him. "Where the hell were you! She's been howling for the last four hours."

"I didn't get away until much later," he lied.

"Well you should have damn well told me! I kept telling Mary Margaret you'd be home any minute. I just got her down."

"I'm sorry. I didn't know," he said, looking around for any sign his supper was waiting for him.

Mabel sat down and put her head in her hand. "It was the day from hell," she said, describing the bakery's oven breaking down, and trying to keep up with orders at home while looking after the kids. "I'm exhausted, but I doubt I can get any sleep again tonight. I still haven't heard anything about Luke or Toni. And Alice is frantic. She called three times asking if we heard anything from Luke. And John has no idea where his brothers are...if they're dead or alive."

Stanley walked to the pantry and came back with a bottle of rum and two glasses. He put it them on the table, debating whether he should break his promise to Luke and tell her where he was. He poured a drink and put it in front of her.

Mabel pushed it away. "I don't want that."

"Drink it. It will help you sleep," he said, pouring himself a drink and sitting across from her. *If I tell her, she might tell Alice and Luke would soon find out I broke my word to him. It would just be one more betrayal. If Luke doesn't call John in the morning as he promised he would, I'll tell her then.*

"Oh, and Amour and Ed stopped by. The wedding is back on," Mabel said flatly.

Stanley took a drink. "Well, that's good. In October...at the cabin?"

Mabel reached for her glass. "Yes. They asked us to supper tomorrow night. Lily and the kids will be there with Victoria's grandparents."

"But we're not going, right?"

Mabel sighed. "She wants us there. What could I say?"

Stanley swirled his drink. "You could have said no."

"Well I didn't," Mabel snapped.

The phone rang. Mabel pushed her chair back and stood up. "Now what?" She picked up the receiver. "Hello. Alice, you need to slow down. *What?* When? Male or female?" Mabel plopped down on the chair next to the telephone. "Alice, I'm sure it's not. Who is there with you? I'll come right over. No, I'll have Stanley call Gordon. He'll be able to tell us more. Yes, I'll be there within the half hour," she said and hung up.

Stanley stood beside her. "What's going on?"

Mabel looked up at him with glassy eyes. "That was Alice. Corliss told her they found a body washed up on Lingan Beach."

Stanley closed his eyes. "It's not Luke."

"You don't know that!" Mabel shot back.

"Trust me, *I know it's not*."

"How would you know?" Mabel demanded.

"Because I just left him. He's in Pleasant Bay."

Jeanne entered the living room carrying a shoe box.

Hector looked up from his book. "Whachya got there?"

Jeanne sat down. "Some old photos." She smiled and passed him a picture. "Remember, we were visiting my cousin Sheila in Lake Ainslie?"

Hector nodded and smiled at the photo of him with Lily on his shoulders. "That wasn't yesterday," he said, joining her on the couch. He looked at the box on her lap. "I didn't realize you kept all these."

"They've been in the back of our closet. But, you're right, it's time to put a few of them out. And tomorrow, we'll get some of us with the grandchildren."

"And Lily," Hector said.

"Yes, and Lily, too. And once we paint the living room, we'll get some nice frames and hang them on the walls."

Hector smiled. "So we can put those godawful pictures of your dead relatives in the back of the closet?"

Jeanne looked over her glasses. "They're family, too. We'll make room for new ones."

They looked at a couple dozen more photos, searching their memories for the events of the day that made them special enough to capture on film. Jeanne elbowed him. "Oh my, look at you in this one. You were so young."

Hector looked down at a picture of himself standing at the end of a wharf and grinning into the camera. He flipped the photo over to see if there was a handwritten date on the back. "Swim trunks were a little tight, but look at that incredible physique." He winked. "And I haven't changed a bit."

"No, not a bit. You just lost your mind, your hair, and your waist," Jeanne said and laughed.

Hector smiled sadly, trying to remember the last time he heard her laugh. He closed his eyes, grateful the reunion with Lily went so well and that Jeanne didn't dredge up the hurtful past. He reached over and squeezed her hand. "I missed that," he said.

Jeanne took off her glasses and gave him a bemused look. "*Missed what?*"

"Your laugh."

Jeanne looked down. "I missed it, too. It was like I forgot how." She lifted her head and looked into the kitchen, avoiding eye contact. "I know I haven't always been easy to live with," she said regretfully. "I've been praying for guidance...to be less unyielding...less harsh." She smiled. "The incident with Tipper helped me see how quickly I've been to judge." She turned to face her husband. "I'm going to try my best to do better...to be kinder and more forgiving."

Hector surprised her with a hug. "Thank you," he whispered. "That's all that I can ask." He let go of her and leaned back. "Jeanne, I think God's already answered your prayers. He's given you...he's given *us* a second chance to be a family again...a big, beautiful, happy family with grandchildren to spoil."

Jeanne's chin began to quiver. "They are beautiful, aren't they?"

Hector nodded. "Absolutely. And smart, just like their grandfather."

Jeanne rested her head on his shoulder. "I've been such a fool."

Hector put his arm over her shoulder and kissed the top of her head. "Jeanne, dear, now's not the time to look back. We have too much lost time to make up for. And I don't want to waste a minute of it on regret. I want to make more wonderful memories with Lily and the kids. I want to take a million pictures and cover every inch, of every wall in the house."

Jeanne sat up and smiled. "Hector, I was thinking, school's not going back for another month. Maybe Lily will let the kids stay with us for a while. We can drive them back to New Brunswick, maybe even stay a little while...see where they live. What do you think? C'mon, Hec...there's nothing keeping us here."

Mabel waited for Stanley to hang up from speaking with Gordon. "What did he say?"

"He doesn't know anything more than we do. He said he'd make some calls."

Mabel took the receiver from him. "*Tonight*?"

"Yes. Look, at first you thought it was Luke, now you think it's Toni. You worry too much."

Mabel started dialling. "Pass me my drink," she said, pointing into the kitchen. "Alice, it's me. I won't be coming over after all. Look, it's not Luke. Yes, I'm sure. Stanley was with him this evening. I'm sorry, he doesn't want anyone to know. But trust me, he's alive and doing as well as can be expected." Mabel closed her eyes and tilted her head back. "Alice, I'm sorry, he doesn't want you to know, and it's not my place to tell you. I know you're worried. We all are, but at least we know he's okay. Look, I've got to go. No, I'll tell John. Sorry, Alice, I have to go. I'm waiting on a call from Gordon and don't want to tie up the line. I still haven't heard from Toni. I'm worried sick it might be her. Yes, I'll talk to you in the morning. Try and get some sleep."

Stanley passed Mabel her drink. "I wish you wouldn't tell John."

"He needs to know," Mabel said sharply.

"Okay, but don't tell him where he is. Luke is adamant no one know. Oh, and tell him Luke will give him a call in the morning, but not to let on we told him."

Mabel shot him a look. "Then here, you talk to him!" she said, angrily thrusting the receiver at him and returning to the kitchen. She downed her drink, poured another, and sat at the table, waiting for Stanley to finish up with John.

Stanley hung up and looked at Mabel sitting with her head down. He walked up behind her. "He's glad that I called." He put his hand on her shoulder. "John said he heard that the body that washed up on shore was a female."

Mabel started to cry.

Stanley sat down beside her. "We don't know that it's Toni."

Mabel looked up. "And we don't know that it's not."

Stanley put his arm around her shoulder.

Mabel flinched. "So, if Alice hadn't called about the body found on the beach, you weren't planning on telling me you saw Luke. You would have left me thinking the worst."

Stanley sighed and shook his head. "You would have heard first thing in the morning when Luke called John."

Mabel got up quickly and flung the remains of her drink in the sink. "I'm going to bed."

"Will I wake you if Gordon calls?"

Mabel turned and stared at him. "Oh, don't worry about that," she said angrily. "I won't be asleep. I've got too much on my mind, including how my husband would have left me tossing and turning all night for no good reason."

Stanley's shoulders fell. "That's not fair, and you know it," he said softly.

"Life's not fair," Mabel said dismissively and walked away.

"Are they asleep?" Ed asked.

"Rory is still awake." Lily smiled. "He told me he had a great day. Wondered why he hadn't met his grandparents sooner."

Ed puckered his mouth "What did you tell him?"

"The truth. I said we got mad at each other, then too stubborn to admit we made a mistake."

"Not exactly the truth," Ed corrected. "Seems to me your parents bear the lion's share of the blame."

Lily sat across from him. "I don't know about that. If I had listened to them in the first place, things would have been a lot different."

Ed sipped his tea. "Funny, isn't it...how one bad decision as a teenager impacted so many lives...yours, your parents, your kids."

Lily nodded. "Even yours. Let's face it, if I hadn't gotten pregnant, I would never have ended up at the Roachville Pines and we would never have met."

Ed smiled. "And I would never have met Amour. So I guess some good has come from an otherwise bad situation."

Lily leaned back. “I think you’re right, it’s gotta be fate. There are just way too many coincidences to think it’s all random.” She waved her arm in the air. “Must be some strange, unknown force out there in the universe, guiding us along.”

Ed raised his eyebrows. “*God, perhaps?*”

Lily raised her eyebrows. “If it is God, he sure hasn’t made things easy for me, or for my God-fearing parents for that matter. You’d think he’d at least give *them* a break.”

“Maybe he knew you were all strong enough to survive whatever he threw at you.”

Lily gave him a puzzled look. “See, that’s what I don’t understand. Why make anyone suffer?”

Ed shrugged and put his cup down. “If we didn’t have pain and suffering in our lives, I wonder if we’d be able to truly appreciate happiness and joy.”

“I guess.” Lily smiled. “Rory was right, today was a good day. A really good day. I used to feel like my kids would grow up without a single, fond memory of their childhood. I mean, with the constant bullying after their father went to jail, then our time in Roachville living with that goddamn monster. I honestly thought we’d be stuck with him forever. And I certainly never thought they’d get to meet their big sister or grandparents…*or you.* God, I hope you know they think the world of you.”

Ed smiled. “And I think the world of them.”

Lily brushed away a tear and chuckled. “Maybe the worst *is* behind us. And maybe we will make more happy memories…like we did today.”

Ed nodded. “You will. I know it. And I hope I’ll be a part of them.”

Lily put her fist to her mouth, struggling to keep from bursting into tears. “You better,” she managed to choke out.

Ed got to his feet and handed her a hankie. “Well, it’s not like you can get rid of me. After all, I’ll soon be part of the family.”

Mabel was sitting in a chair by the open window when Stanley entered their bedroom. “Gordon said the body was in the water for days. He suspects it’s an old woman from New Victoria who wandered away from home. He'll know more when he talks to the medical examiner in the morning."

Mabel nodded and blessed herself.

"I'm sorry," Stanley said. "I didn't think a few hours would make that much difference."

Mabel looked out over the black water, thinking about the time Stanley was upset with her for not telling him why she was so cool toward Mark. As much as she had wanted to end the friction it had caused in their marriage, she held firm and honoured her promise to Alice to never tell a soul that Mark was Matthew's father. Mabel turned to face him. "I overreacted," she said, realizing she couldn't very well fault him for doing something she was also guilty of. "Too many people to worry about, and not enough sleep," she said wearily. "In the morning, I'll pack up some food and fresh bedding for you to take to Luke. Obviously, he's welcome to stay as long as he likes, but you better tell him about the wedding. Amour was talking about taking a drive to Pleasant Bay so Ed could see the place."

Stanley sat on the side of the bed. "I don't think Luke intends to stay long. He said he'll likely head to Halifax and look for work. Hopefully, he won't cross paths with Mark."

Mabel reached up and pushed the window down. She was disappointed but not surprised Luke was planning to move on. "So many broken hearts. I feel so awful for everyone, but especially Matthew. He did nothing wrong, yet he'll be the one who suffers the most."

"Kids are resilient," Stanley said.

Mabel shook her head. "That's just a lot of bull. Kids scar just as easily as the rest of us. And when they do, they bear them a lot longer. God forbid if it ever gets out what happened. Matthew will be treated like an outcast, even though he did nothing wrong. Just like Lily's kids. God, Matthew adored his—" She paused. "Luke."

"And Luke adored him," Stanley said.

"But somehow he can still walk away, like he wasn't a huge part of his life for the past two years."

"Mabel, Luke is devastated."

"I know. Still, it's not fair." She started to stand, then sat back down. "If Luke goes to Halifax, who's going to look after the store?"

"He said John could take it over."

Mabel frowned. "Another innocent victim. That's not what John wants. He wants to go back to Dal."

Stanley unbuttoned his shirt. "He can always sell it."

"And how would that work with the bakery? Luke was always more than happy to give us lots of leeway with our comings and goings...not to mention the window space for our display. I doubt a new owner would be so generous."

"Of course they would. We both know the bakery brings people to the store. They'd be a fool to say no to you for anything you requested. Besides, we could always buy it."

Mabel stood up. "*The store!* I don't think so. Who'd run it?"

Stanley kicked off his shoes. "We'd hire someone to help Corliss. God knows, there's lots of people desperate for work."

Mabel shook her head. "Still, it's managing everything. I've got enough to worry about. I'd sell the bakery before I'd ever buy the store."

Stanley tossed his shirt on a chair in the corner. "You'd never sell the bakery."

"*Oh, yes I would.* As a matter of fact, I've been giving it a lot of thought. Pretty soon we'll be losing our sitters, with Myrtle having her surgery, and Victoria starting her teaching job. And now...Luke giving up the store and the oven on the fritz...maybe someone's trying to tell me something. Maybe it's a sign."

Tuesday, August 5

Mabel heard the phone and opened her eyes. She was surprised Stanley was already out of bed. She rolled over, looked at the clock, and bolted upright. "Ten after eight," she muttered, whipping the covers aside. She threw on her robe and rushed into the hall, pushing open the doors and looking at the empty, unmade beds. She was at the bottom of the stairs when Stanley hung up.

"That was Gordon. It was the old woman from New Victoria."

Mabel blessed herself and sighed. "I can't believe I slept this late. You should have woken me up."

Stanley headed down the hall. "You needed the sleep. Kids had their breakfast, so you can take over from here."

Mabel followed him into the kitchen. Mary Margaret was sitting on the floor trying to tie her shoe laces, and Liv was sitting in her highchair clawing at a piece of toast. "Where's JC?" she asked.

"Myrtle's."

"*This early*?"

Stanley shrugged and took one last sip of his tepid coffee. He poured the remains in the sink. "I'm off."

"But I haven't packed the stuff up for Luke."

Stanley pointed to a box near the front door. "I pulled some things together."

Mabel smiled and nodded. "Don't forget we're going to Amour's for supper."

"Dammit! What time?" he asked impatiently.

"Five."

Stanley shook his head. "There's no way we can get out of it?"

"No," Mabel said firmly.

Mabel was on her knees helping Mary Margaret remove a knot in her shoelace when the phone rang. "Hello. Oh, hello, Mr. Bruffatto. No, he just left. *Mark*? I'm not sure. How much? No, I can look after that. Actually, I'm pretty sure they won't be returning. No, I'm sorry. Yes, they should have let you know. I understand. *Today*? What time? Yes, I suppose I can meet you there. Of course. I'll stop by the bank on my way. Thank you." She hung up and returned to Mary Margaret who was lying on her back and angrily writhing on the floor, frustrated her laces weren't cooperating. Mabel picked her up, put her on her lap, and eased a shoe off her small foot. "Let's take a deep breath and count to ten," she said, as much to calm herself as her red-faced daughter. She looked at her youngest, quietly sitting in her highchair, her face and hair smeared in butter. "I think it's gonna be another one of those days," she muttered, wishing she could crawl back into bed.

"Hello," Victoria called out.

"Thank God," Mabel said. She looked up to see Victoria coming down the hall holding Matthew's hand. Mabel was suddenly struck by his resemblance to Mark. She wondered how long it would be before others noticed and began to put two and two together. She put Mary Margaret down and smiled at the young boy. "Hello, Matthew."

Matthew looked down at the floor.

Victoria gave Mabel a pained look. "I'm afraid we have a sad little boy on our hands. He's missing his daddy." Victoria bent down to be at eye level with the two-year-old. "But it's going to be okay, cause we're gonna go to the park with Mary Margaret and JC, and have lots of fun, *right*?"

Matthew didn't look up.

Victoria smiled at Mabel. "Where is Luke, anyway? I asked Alice, but she tore off without giving me an answer. Said she was late for an appointment."

Mabel ran a damp cloth over Liv's greasy face. "I think I heard him say something about going to see the surgeon in Halifax...a follow-up visit about his leg," she lied.

"See," Victoria said to Matthew, "your daddy will be home before you know it."

Alice sat with her head down. She couldn't shake the image of Luke wildly pacing around their bedroom, calling Matthew a bastard. *Isn't that what you call the son of a whore.* She clasped her hands and brought them to her mouth, thinking about what she would tell her father. Telling him that she and Luke had a fight, and that he just needed time to cool down wouldn't hold up for much longer; Corliss' questions were becoming more pointed, and his patience, more thin. Alice wondered if his love for her and his grandson would be strong enough to withstand the truth, or if he would be so ashamed he'd disown her. She heard the familiar clickety-clack of high heels on the wooden steps and raised her head. Lizzie MacNeil was walking up the long, steep stairway with one hand on the railing, and the other wrapped around the arm of a young man.

"Thankyou, darlin," Lizzie panted. "Yer a life-saver...and handsome to boot. Got a girlfriend?" She laughed. "Just kiddin. I might be a little too... mature for a young man your age." She let go of his arm and pulled her short, teal blue sweater down over her black, tight-fitting skirt. She looked around the crowded waiting room for anyone she might know and smiled; her bright red lipstick smeared across her teeth. "Minnie!" she said, waving. She clattered across the room and sat beside the frail woman with the grey beehive. "Haven't seen you in a dog's age. I imagine ya heard about my dear friend, Gladys Ferguson. Poor thing. One minute we're chattin about gettin together for lunch; the next, she's on her kitchen floor, dead as a doornail. I'm gonna miss her. Heard it was a massive heart attack. At least she went quick," she said, snapping her fingers. "Not like your friend, Josie. I heard she was beggin to be put outta her misery. Musta been in some godawful pain, lingerin on like that for so long." Lizzie reached in her handbag and passed Minnie a tissue. "God love her. At least she's finally at peace. So how are you, dear? Everything good?" she asked, looking in Alice's direction.

Alice quickly turned away, hoping Lizzie didn't recognize her.

"Mrs. Toth?" Dr. Murray's secretary called out. "You can come in now." She held the door open for Alice. "Dr. Murray will be with you shortly."

Dr. Murray's secretary smiled as Alice walked past. "He won't be long," she said and closed the door.

Alice sat down, scanning the pamphlets tacked to the bulletin board. *Gonorrhea, Signs and Symptoms. Adolescents and Sex...talk to your child. Heart Disease...it can kill you.*

The door suddenly opened and Dr. Murray breezed in smiling. "Good morning," he said warmly. "Sorry about the wait. I had to duck out on a house call."

"That's all right," Alice said flatly.

Dr. Murray leaned against the examination table and grinned. "So, you were right. Congratulations."

Alice closed her eyes and slowly nodded.

Dr. Murray was surprised by her reaction. He expected her to be jubilant, yet she seemed downcast. "Alice, I thought you would be more... enthusiastic. I thought you wanted a second child?"

Alice forced a smile. "How far along do you think I am?"

Dr. Murray tilted his head and turned down his mouth. "At least three months...maybe four. Do you still have morning sickness?"

Alice shook her head. "No."

"Good." He patted the table. "Jump up and I'll do a quick examination."

Alice teared up. "Do I have to?"

Dr. Murray saw the distress on her face. "No, you don't have to. We can wait a week or two. Just check with Shirley on your way out for a time that works for you. Of course, if you have any issues in the meantime, you know how to reach me."

Alice stood up. "Thank you," she said weakly.

"Are you sure you're okay?" he asked.

Alice nodded, burst into tears, and stormed past Shirley, startling concerned onlookers in the busy waiting room.

"Wasn't that Alice Toth, who works at Cameron's Bakery?" Lizzie asked Shirley.

"Yes. Her husband, Luke, runs the store."

Lizzie nodded. "Poor thing. She obviously got some terrible news."

Shirley put her hand on Lizzie's arm and leaned into her ear. "Oh no, dear. On the contrary. I'm sure it's just her hormones. She's pregnant."

Mabel left the bank and walked down Commercial Street. She turned down the dark alley alongside the Co-op and climbed the stairs, praying Toni was in Waterville with her parents. She looked up to see Mr. Bruffatto standing on the landing. "Sorry I'm late," Mabel said. "The bank was much busier than I expected."

"No worries. I just got here myself." He waited for her to join him. "Sorry about the stink in the alley. Goddamn cats. Anyway, it's good of you to come and look after things. Kids these days are so unreliable. I thought your friends would be different."

Mabel smiled. "They've had a hard go of things lately."

Mr. Bruffato dipped his chin and smiled. "I hear that a lot. Anyway, they must have took off in a hurry. They left a lot of stuff behind. Didn't even bother to lock up. I'll take the garbage out, but the fridge needs to be cleaned out and all their personal belongings removed." He pointed. "I brought some empty boxes up from the Co-op. They got plenty more if you need them."

"What about the furniture?" Mabel asked.

"Up to you. If you want to leave it, I can always find someone to put it to use."

"That would be great." Mabel opened her purse. "Fifty-five, right?"

Mr. Bruffato watched her count out the bills. "I appreciate you takin care of this. Can't tell you how many times folks take off and leave me high and dry. Anyway, I'll let you get to it. Don't worry about locking up. I'll be back this evening."

Mabel put her billfold back in her purse. "Thank you." She waited for him to leave, then entered the kitchen and opened the fridge. She shook her head at all of the spoiled food she and her friends sent over while Toni was in the hospital. An hour later, with the kitchen thoroughly cleaned, she started tidying up the living room. She bent down to pick up an empty whiskey bottle and spotted a folded sheet of paper sticking out from under the couch. *Payment Due.* It was a bill from the hospital. She checked the date, thinking it likely hadn't been paid. She was about to put it in her purse, when she noticed the handwriting on the back.

Dear, Mark: I know you tried. You deserve more. You deserve to be a father. I'm going home. I have only one thing to ask of you. Please buy a headstone for our son and tend to his grave. I wish you a lifetime of happiness. Love, Toni.

Mabel stared at Toni's note, sat down heavily, and wept for baby Duncan and his devastated parents.

"Mabel! You here?"

Mabel quickly wiped her eyes and ran the back of her hand under her nose. "*Mary Catherine*? What are you doing here?"

"I stopped by the house and Victoria said you were here. Oh, my God! What's wrong?"

Mabel passed her Toni's note.

Mary Catherine read it and looked up. "It's so heartbreaking," she said, gently folding it over and passing it back to Mabel. "Any word from Toni?"

Mabel shook her head. "Afraid not."

Mary Catherine sighed. "It's like the whole world has been turned upside down. And what the hell is up with Alice?"

Mabel was sure Mary Catherine wouldn't have heard about the fight between Luke and Mark. She gave her friend a curious look. "What do you mean?"

"I just saw her out front. She was running down Commercial Street like she just robbed the bank. She looked upset. Wouldn't stop when I called out to her...and I know damn well she heard me."

Mabel shrugged. "I have no idea."

Mary Catherine removed her sweater. "So, what can I do?"

"How about packing up whatever's in the bathroom."

Mary Catherine grabbed an empty box and headed down the hall. "I was thinking," she hollered, "summer will be over before we know it. Why don't we have Victoria stay with the kids so the four of us can go to Pleasant Bay for a weekend? We could even ask Alice and Luke...have a barbeque. I can bring my Rummoli board."

Mabel looked around at the happy faces, grateful for a reprieve from the sadness that had been weighing her down for most of the day. Ed passed her a glass of vermouth. "Cheers."

She smiled and lifted her glass. "Cheers to you and your beautiful bride-to-be."

Ed looked at Amour sitting next to Lily and Jeanne. "She *is* beautiful," he said, grinning proudly.

Mabel took a sip. "And very lucky to have found you."

Ed laughed. "Not so sure about that."

"I am," Mabel said. "You are a good man. I never mentioned this to you before, but I want to thank you for being so kind to Lily and the kids. They certainly didn't have an easy time of things. Honestly, if it weren't for you, God knows, they might be still caught up with that horrible Dan McInnes."

Ed titled his head. "And if it weren't for Lily, I would never have met Amour or Victoria." He pointed. "Or your handsome husband." He turned to her. "*Or* my favourite baker."

Mabel chuckled. "Looking for a discount, are you?"

"It's true. Ask Amour. I told her the only reason I agreed to sell my place and move to town is because I'd be closer to the bakery."

Mabel playfully nudged him. "It's nice…isn't it…seeing everyone together… so happy?"

Ed took a drink. "It sure is."

Lily approached. "What are you two up to?"

Mabel smiled. "We were just saying how nice it is everyone is together."

Rory and JC tore past, with Mary Margaret and Rachael chasing after them. "The kids are getting along great," Lily said to Mabel.

"We'll have to arrange a day for you to bring them to the house. When are you heading back?" Mabel asked.

"Laura and I are heading back on Thursday. Rory and Rachael are going to stay with my parents for a couple of weeks."

"That's fantastic," Ed said.

Amour joined them and looped her arm around Ed's. "What's fantastic?"

"Lily was just saying that Rory and Rachael are going to stay with their grandparents for a bit."

Amour smiled. "I know. I was just telling Jeanne that if they get to be too much, Victoria and I can help out. And, of course, Myrtle is always around."

"Have you spoken to Myrtle lately?" Mabel asked.

"No. Why?"

Mabel shook her head. "Just wondering," she said, thinking Amour had no idea what her friend was going through.

Hector held his Brownie Hawkeye up and called for everyone's attention. "Let's get a picture," he hollered.

Stanley insisted on taking the picture and herded everyone into the foyer, lining them up at the bottom of the stairs. Despite Mabel's objections that it should be a family photo, Amour insisted that she and the kids join in. Stanley attached the flash and looked through the viewfinder. "Lily, can you move a little to your right. And, Ed, scoot in closer to Amour. Great. On the count of three everyone say *cheeeese. One. Two. Three.* " He snapped the picture. "Okay, one more for good measure," he said, quickly replacing the bulb. He raised the camera back up, once again peered through the small hole, and took a step back. He then took another step back, this time ensuring Michael's portrait was within the frame. "Perfect. But this time, instead of saying *cheese,* everyone say… *family.* Okay, on the count of three. *One. Two. Three.*"

"Family," everyone called out as a second bright flash signalled the happy moment was memorialized for future generations to look back on.

Stanley handed the camera back to Hector. "I hope they turn out okay."

"I'm sure they'll be just fine. I'm gonna pick up a cupula nice frames at shedden's...give one to Lily and keep one for myself. And I know just where I'm gonna put it."

Mabel handed Liv to her father, charged up the front steps, and burst through the door. She ran for the phone. "Hello." She put the receiver down. "Dammit."

Stanley came up behind her. "Didn't make it in time?"

"No."

Stanley looked at JC and Mary Margaret. "You two head upstairs and get ready for bed." He put Liv on the living room floor. "They'll call back if it's important."

"It might have been Toni or her parents. Do you think it's too late to call them now?"

"Yes."

Mabel removed a notepad from the drawer and dialled the number scrawled across the page.

"Mabel, they're farmers. They go to bed early," Stanley warned.

"It's not even eight-thirty," Mabel said defiantly. She let the phone ring a dozen times and was about to hang up when she heard the groggy voice on the other end. "Oh, hello. It's Mabel MacIntyre...Toni's friend. Yes, from Glace Bay. I was just wondering if you heard from her, or if you had a chance to pass on my message?" Mabel brought her hand to her mouth. "I'm so sorry. Yes, of course." She looked up at Stanley hovering over her, looking concerned. "I know. I'm very sorry. Yes, I understand. No, thank you. I'm very sorry. Goodnight." Mabel hung up and put her head in her hands.

Stanley brought her to her feet and cradled her in his arms. "What happened?"

"She's fine. She's at her cousin's in Dartmouth," Mabel said.

Stanley broke their embrace and held her at arm's length. "Then what the hell was that all about? Why were you saying you were *so sorry*?"

Mabel started to laugh. "I got Toni's father out of bed. He chewed me out for calling so late. Told me to never call again at such a late hour."

Stanley wagged his finger at her. "I told you."

Mabel smiled. "At least, now, I have one less person to keep me up at night."

"Funny, she didn't call you," Stanley said.

Mabel shrugged. "For all we know, she tried. Or maybe she just wants to put everything behind her...get on with life."

Stanley walked into the living room. "Where'd Liv go?"

Mabel ran to the kitchen. "She's not in here."

Stanley looked behind the couch. "She's not in here, either."

Mabel ran back down the hall and looked up. "Found her," she said, rushing up the stairs to pick her up. Stanley appeared at the landing. Mabel looked down at him. "She almost made it to the top this time."

Mary Margaret came out of her room crying.

"What's wrong?" Mabel asked.

"I lost my blankie," she pouted.

Mabel turned to Stanley. "Check the car. If it's not there, it's gotta be at Amour's."

Wednesday, August 6

Mabel entered the bakery, surprised to see Alice at her station. She walked up beside her. "I thought you were going to take some time off," she whispered.

"I need to keep busy."

Mabel smiled at Bessie. "Where's Mary Mack?"

Bessie looked up at the clock. "She should be here any minute."

Mabel laughed. "She should have been here twenty minutes ago," she said, looping her apron over her head. "How's the oven working?"

"Good as new," Bessie said.

Apart from the noisy greetings and the anticipated sympathies extended to Mary Mack for whatever unfortunate reason held her up, the four bakers quietly went about their business of creating mouth-watering aromas and eye-pleasing pastries worthy of the cover of the Canadian Home Journal. Mabel looked around and wondered if she really could give it up. Ever since she had walked through the doors as a hapless seventeen-year-old, and James Cameron offered her a job making bread, the bakery was like her second home. She smiled when she thought of how good the Camerons were to her and the Toth boys. *It was like we were the children they never had.* She felt herself well up, knowing how heartbroken they would be to see what was happening between Luke and Mark. She glanced up at Alice and suddenly stopped kneading. Alice was standing over her table with tears rolling down her cheeks. Mabel quickly wiped her hands in her apron and approached her friend. "Alice, go to the apartment. I'll join you in a bit," she whispered.

Alice nodded and quickly left.

Mabel briefly returned to her kneading, before leaving to join Alice. She was cutting through the store on her way to the apartment when she saw John sitting behind the counter. "How are you doing?" she asked.

He shrugged. "All right, I guess." He gestured to the apartment above. "Better than her," he said icily.

Mabel was now sure he knew more than he was letting on. "So, you talked to Luke?"

John nodded. "Says he's not coming back. Told me to do what I want with the store."

Mabel nodded. "Any word from Mark?"

John shook his head. "No, but I'm not surprised."

"It's a difficult time for everyone. You know Stanley and I are here for you…if you need anything…or just want to talk."

"I know. Thanks."

Mabel went upstairs and knocked on Alice's bedroom door. "It's me."

"Come in."

Mabel entered, sat next to her on the bed, and took hold of her hand. "Alice, I'm not sure what to say. I was afraid it would come to this. It's not going to be easy. You're gonna have days you won't want to get out of bed. You're gonna have to dig down and find the strength to go on. Remember, you have Matthew to think about. Things will get better in time. In the meantime, you're going to have to force yourself—"

"I'm pregnant," Alice blurted.

Mabel closed her eyes. "Jesus. Does Luke know?"

"No."

"How far along are you?"

"Three, maybe four months."

Mabel exhaled heavily. "You need to tell him."

Alice scoffed. "Yeah, and how the hell am I supposed to do that!" She jumped up and waved her arm. "I have no idea where he is. And even if I did, it's not like he's gonna talk to me. He made it clear he doesn't want anything to do with me. He called me a whore."

"But he doesn't know about the baby. He's angry. Alice, he's not the kind of man to abandon his child. He's just not. I know it," Mabel insisted.

"*Matthew was his child!*" Alice screamed. She plopped down on a chair and leaned forward with her head down. "It's no use, he doesn't want to have anything to do with us," she cried.

"Still, he has to know. I'm going to have Stanley reach out to him."

Alice wiped her face. "Go ahead. It's not going to make a damn bit of difference."

Stanley's heart sank when he drove past the knoll and saw no sign of Luke's car. "Dammit," he muttered, putting the car in park and getting out. *Maybe he drove to Baddeck for some groceries.* He walked up the steps and entered. The place was as neat as a pin. "Luke, you here?" He opened the fridge. Apart from a block of butter, it was bare. He walked into the living room and spotted the note on the mantel.

Dear Stanley,

Thanks for giving me a place to lay my head and get my thoughts together. You and Mabel have always been like family to me. I apologize for how I reacted when I found out you knew Alice had betrayed me. I would have done the same. It's time for me to move on. There's no future for me here. I'll write once I get settled. Give my love to Mabel and tell her not to worry. And please keep an eye out for John. He's a good kid and doesn't deserve any of this. Take care, Luke.

Stanley locked up and got back in the car, wondering if Luke would keep his word and write, or if he would put the past behind him and move on. He turned the ignition, thinking Mabel was going to be distraught. She was sure that the moment he heard Alice was pregnant, he'd swallow his pride and return home. *It was just wishful thinking.* He put the car in gear and drove down the dusty road, past the cherry trees. He arrived home an hour and a half later to see Mabel sitting on the verandah with the kids. He stepped out of the car and shook his head.

Mabel stood. "He won't talk to her?"

"He wasn't there." He walked up the steps and passed her Luke's note. "He's gone."

Mabel read the note and leaned into him. "So many lives in turmoil," she whispered.

Stanley wrapped his arm around her. "I know."

Mabel looked up at him. "Can you handle things here for a while?"

Stanley nodded. "Are you going to talk to Alice?"

"Yes."

Stanley passed her the car keys. "Good luck."

Mabel hugged him. "I don't say it often enough, but I'm a very lucky woman and you're a wonderful man."

"No, Mabel, I'm the lucky one," he said, leaning forward and kissing her forehead.

Two Weeks Later

Tuesday, August 20

Tipper and his friend, Joey, leaned their bikes against the Commercial Street Bridge and began spitting hawkers over the side.

Joey laughed. "See that one?" he asked, punching Tipper's arm. "Go ahead. Beat that!"

"Yeah, well watch this," Tipper said, taking a loud, deep sniff and noisily bringing the salty, wad of phlegm to the back of his throat. He tilted his head back, then quickly leaned forward, hurling it into the air.

"Whoooa!" Joey said laughing. "That was the best one yet."

Tipper grabbed his handlebars. "So, what now?"

"Ballgame doesn't start till three...wanna go to Bicycle Hill?" Joey pointed. "Hey, ain't that the old guy you used to work for?"

Tipper turned and looked across the street. Hector was standing at the window of the chip wagon with a young boy.

"Yeah."

"What happened, anyway? Did he fire ya?'

"I guess he ran out of jobs for me to do," Tipper said, turning his bike around.

"Watcha doin?" Joey asked.

"I think I'm gonna skip the hill and just head home."

"But you promised ya were comin to my place to listen to the game," Joey pouted.

Tipper shook his head. "Nah. I'm just gonna head home...listen to the game with Gran. See ya," Tipper said, walking alongside his bike.

"So, we gonna meet at the church tomorrow and play shinny?" Joey called out.

"Yeah."

"How bout givin me back my goalie stick?" Joey hollered.

Tipper kept walking. "Mine now," he said, giving his friend the middle finger.

Tipper pedalled down Seaview Street, trying not to cry. It wasn't the same listening to the game with Joey. *He don't know dick all about baseball. Not like the old man, he knows every player...all their stats.* "Fuck you," he muttered. "Dropped me like a dirty habit. Just like my good-fer-nothin mother." He was passing Holy Cross Church when he saw the familiar car in front of his house. He stopped momentarily. The car began to pull away. "Hey!" he hollered. "Wait!" He pushed forward and began pumping, faster and faster.

The car suddenly stopped and the driver stepped out. Hector put his hand up to his forehead to block the sun and watched as the bike wobbled from side to side, eventually straightening out as it picked up speed.

Tipper slammed on his brakes, sliding sideways and stopping within inches of the back bumper. "Hey, old man. What's up?"

Hector nodded to the car. "My grandson, Rory, is with me. We're gonna listen to the game. Thought you might wanna come along?"

"Yeah, I guess I could do that. Long as ya don't mind me givin you a hard time when your team goes down and starts bawlin like a bunch of crybabies."

Hector laughed. "We'll see about that."

Tipper leaned his bike against the side of the house. "I just need to tell Gran." He opened the screen door. "Hey, Gran. I'm gonna listen to the game with the boss. I won't be too late," he hollered, letting the door bang shut and heading to the car. He was about to get in the back seat.

Hector ducked his head out the window. "Get in the front with us."

Tipper jumped in next to Rory.

"This is Rory," Hector said. "He's a Cubs' fan."

Rory held his grease-stained box of hand cut fries out to Tipper. "Want one?"

Tipper took a fry. "Cubs' fan, eh? Me...I'm a Sox man...all the way."

Kenny stood in the doorway with his hockey bag slung over his shoulder.

Father shook his head. "Mother, come see who's at the door."

"Who is it?" Mother called from the living room.

"It's the prodigal son," Father said. "Lookin a little sheepish."

Mother entered the kitchen. "You and Tommy have a fight, or did ya finally get tossed out on your ass?"

Kenny dropped his shoulder and let his hockey bag slide to the floor. "Both."

Father opened the fridge. "So I suppose ya think ya can just waltz right back in here and enjoy free room and board?"

Kenny looked at his mother. "I got no place to go."

Father sighed. "No, I don't suppose ya do. Word's out about all yer wild parties. Oh, and that little two alarm fire ya started."

Mother's eyes widened. "*What fire*? Nobody told me about any fire!"

"It was just a small grease fire," Kenny said.

Father popped the cap off a beer. "Little grease fire my arse! I heard the walls in the kitchen are as black as the inside of a cow."

"Well, get your sorry ass in here," Mother said.

Kenny sat down at the table.

Mother whipped her dish towel off her shoulder. "If you plan on staying here, there's gonna be some new rules. If you've got money enough to pay rent, you've got money enough to help at home."

Kenny thought of the money he owed for damaging the rental property, and Tommy and Vinny's cars. "I got no money. I still gotta pay for the damages from the fire."

Father shook his head. "Once you pay off Bruffatto, you can start paying us. What do you think Mother, twenty dollars a month sound fair for room and board?"

Mother nodded her approval. "A deal at twice that amount."

"But what about college?" Kenny whined.

"Oooh, so all of a sudden you're worried about college. Ya weren't so worried about yer schoolin when ya were horny for a place of your own," Father said.

"I blame that Doreen one," Mother huffed. She glared at Kenny. "Don't think for one minute you can bring that...that girl round here."

"Fat chance of that," Kenny said under his breath.

Father flicked his beer cap into the garbage can. "Game's about to start," he said and walked away.

Mother put the kettle on. "Are you hungry?"

"Starvin."

She smirked. "That makes two of us. I bought fresh calves liver for dinner."

Kenny screwed up his face and gagged.

Mother pointed to the potatoes and onions on the counter. "You can get started on the potatoes. Make sure ya peel enough for leftovers. Oh, and cut the onions into rings. Not too thick."

Kenny closed his eyes and nodded.

"And when yer finished with that, ya can fold the wash and put it away."

"Can't that wait till after the game?"

"No, because after the game, you'll be doin the dishes."

Kenny got up slowly, walked to the counter, and picked up an onion.

"Oh, and Kenny...I'll look after the liver. Don't need ya burnin the place down your first night back home."

Mabel was putting her groceries away when Amour entered crying. She didn't need to be told why. "She told you?"

Amour nodded. "I'm scared for her."

Mabel smiled. "Me, too."

Amour wiped her eyes. "She's known for weeks. I can't believe she didn't tell me."

"She didn't want you to worry...with everything else you had going on in your life."

Amour pulled a chair out from the table and sat down. "I talked to Ed. He agrees we should delay the wedding."

Mabel put a quart of milk in the fridge. "Myrtle wouldn't want you to do that...and you know it."

"But she'll still be in the hospital. She'll miss everything. And I was hoping she'd sing at the wedding."

Mabel began filling the kettle. "It's up to you and Ed, but I honestly don't think that's what—"

"Hello!"

Amour turned around. "It's Mary Catherine. Does she know about Myrtle?" she whispered.

"Yes, Myrtle called her after she spoke to you," Mabel said.

Mary Catherine looked at Amour. "It's terrible, isn't it?"

Amour started crying again.

Myrtle suddenly appeared at the back door. "Ya can save yer tears for my funeral. I ain't dead yet."

Mabel shook her head. "Myrtle, nobody makes an entrance like you," she said, opening the cupboard and removing two teacups. "Who's for tea?"

Myrtle put her hand in her pocket. "To hell with the tea," she said, holding up a pint of whiskey.

Mabel put the tea cups back and returned with four glasses.

"So, Mabel," Mary Catherine said, "what the hell is going on with Luke and Alice? I heard they split up. And don't tell me you don't know, cause I know she tells you everything. I'd ask her myself, but she keeps avoiding me...won't return my calls."

"I was gonna ask the same thing. I heard she and Luke had a big fight, and that Luke packed up and went to Halifax to live with Mark," Amour said.

Mabel picked up her grocery bag and placed it on the counter. She closed her eyes and took a deep breath. "I'm no sooner gonna talk to you about Alice's private life, than I'd talk to Alice about yours. If Alice wants you to know what's going on, she'll tell you."

"So, she has talked to you," Mary Catherine said.

Mabel gave her an exasperated look. "Ladies, we're all friends. Good friends. And good friends don't pry or gossip about each other. Good friends listen when asked and support each other when needed. If you want to be a friend to Alice right now, respect her privacy...give her some space."

Myrtle began handing out the glasses. "Mabel's right. Here's to being good friends and minding our own goddamn business. If we're going to gossip, let's gossip about everybody else."

Two Months Later

Friday, October 3

Mabel put her tea on the table, sat down, and sifted through the mail. She stopped when she came across a small envelope addressed to her. She didn't recognize the handwriting, and it was missing the street address. *That's strange.* She slid the letter opener under the corner flap, tore it open, and removed a small folded note.

Dear, Mabel:

I'm sorry for taking so long to write and thank you for being so kind to me. At a time when I was at my lowest, you were like an angel at my side. What makes it even more special is you hardly knew me. Mark told me you were a special lady, but I got to see it for myself.

I'm back in Halifax and working at The Lord Nelson Hotel. I started as a maid, but I'm now working in the office, helping in the accounts department. I share an apartment with my cousin, Eunice. Anyway, I'm doing better. I still think of Duncan every day, just not every minute of every day. As they say, time heals all wounds.

If you see Mark, please give him my best. It hasn't been easy for him, either. Hopefully he is keeping well and finding comfort in being close to Luke and John.

Anyway, thanks again for opening your home and heart to me, and all the best to you, Stanley, and the kids.

Sincerely, Toni

P.S. I heard you called home and my father tore a strip off of you. Sorry about that. He's really a good guy, but he can be pretty crotchety if he doesn't get his sleep.

Mabel turned the note over, hoping to find a return address, but there was none. She folded the note and put it back in the envelope. She sipped her tea and thought of her own angels. She got up, grabbed her coat, and walked out. She smiled when she pushed on the freshly-painted gate and it swung open without the usual harsh squeak. She walked down the narrow gravel path, stopped under the Red Maple, and got down on her knees. "Where do I start?" she whispered. *So much has happened. Unfortunately, not all of it has been good. Luke and Mark have had a falling out that I'm afraid is beyond repair. And Luke has left Alice and Matthew. Not sure where he is. Probably Halifax. He promised to write, but we still haven't heard from him so he has no idea Alice is pregnant. And God knows where Mark is. And poor John. He put off returning to college, trying to figure out what to do with the store. If he decides to sell, I'm thinking about closing the bakery. But don't worry, James, I'll always make melt-in-yer-mouth bread…but just for family and friends.*

The wind picked up. Mabel looked up at the rustling leaves and watched as several drifted down and onto the ground. She leaned over and brushed them away from Margaret's headstone. *Stanley is doing well. The business is thriving...which is just one more reason for me to sell the bakery. And the kids are all good. JC is in grade three and Mary Margaret grade primary. And Liv is into everything. I can't take my eyes off of her. I don't know where the time goes. It seems like it was just yesterday when I walked into the store hoping to get a job. Remember, I thought Stanley was creepy. Who would have thought we'd be married with three kids. All n' all, I have nothing to complain about. Lots of worries…but no complaints. Things turned out pretty darn good for me, and I have you to thank for that. As my mother would always say, count your blessings. I try and do it every day, and when I do, you're both at the top of my list. I'm going to Pleasant Bay tomorrow. Amour is getting married, so I'll have a visit with Ma and my baby brother. I often wonder what life would be like if they were still alive. I know Ma would adore the kids. And God knows I could use her help in managing Mary Margaret. I love her to death, but sometimes she can be a handful.* Mabel wiped away a tear. *I can barely remember what Ma looked like. If it weren't for the photos you gave me, I would have forgotten how beautiful she was. But sometimes, I'm sure she's with me... like you're with me. I'm never really sure. Maybe it's just that I miss you all so much, I convince myself you're nearby...guiding me... protecting me.* Mabel removed a few more leaves from their gravesites. *I better go. I promised Mary Catherine I'd help her make perogies for the wedding. I'm sure she's wondering where I am. I'll be back before too long. Love you and miss you."*

Mabel blessed herself, got to her feet, and walked to the far end of the graveyard. Once again, she got down on her knees and blessed herself. *Dear Lord, bless this child whom you have welcomed to your eternal home. May his soul, the soul of my beautiful boy, Gregory, and those of all of the small, earthly bodies that lay at my feet, rest peacefully in your heavenly kingdom. And, Lord, please heal the hearts of those who mourn the loss of a child. Give them the strength to accept your infinite wisdom and to accept that, one day, they will be joyfully reunited with those they love.*

Mabel kissed her finger tips, pressed them against the cool, granite face of Duncan Alexander Toth's headstone, and got up off her knees. She looked down at a several rows of small, wooden crosses and thought about the parents of the children who lay below. *There's nothing more painful than losing a child. It's something you never get over.* She wondered if it was overwhelming grief, poverty, or indifference that resulted in so many of the gravesites being neglected. She bent down to straighten one of the wooden crosses and noticed there was no marking to identify the deceased child. *It's not right. You deserve to be remembered and cared for. You deserve a name...a headstone.* She looked around. "You all do," she whispered sadly. She walked away, vowing to do whatever she could to see that no child, no matter how brief their time on earth, would be forgotten.

Saturday, October 4

"We got this. You go and get ready," Mary Catherine said.

"Are you sure?" Mabel asked.

Mary Catherine passed a tray of sweets to Charlotte. "Yes. Now go!" she said, shooing Mabel off.

Mabel stopped on her way to her room and smiled at Jeanne reading to JC and Mary Margaret, then looked out the bay window. Ed, Gordon, Hector, and Sam were huddled together, laughing. She looked skyward at the thick, menacing clouds. *If only the weather would cooperate.* She went to her room, changed into her dress, and stood before the mirror. "Dammit," she muttered.

"What's wrong?" Stanley asked, entering with a glass of vermouth.

Mabel was standing sideways and looking over her shoulder. "I must have put on weight. My dress is too tight," she said, running her hand over her belly.

Stanley raised his eyebrows. "*Really*? Looks good to me. The Justice of the Peace is here."

Mabel sat on the side of the bed and slipped on one of her pumps. "How is Ed doing?"

"Cool as a cucumber. Frank Miller, his buddy from the RCMP, just arrived. Here, thought you could use this," he said, passing Mabel her drink.

Mabel took a sip. "Still no sign of Lily?"

"Not yet."

"I was thinking," Mabel said, "I'd like to stay a couple of extra days. Just to relax and put our feet up."

Stanley looked in the mirror and undid his tie. "But what about work...and school?"

"We could take a couple of days off work. Things won't fall apart. And JC and Mary Margaret can miss a couple of lessons. Weren't you the one saying we needed to spend more time together as a family?"

"Let me give it some thought," he said, turning to face her. He dropped his arms in frustration. "Can you please fix this damn thing? Whoever invented the tie should be shot."

Mabel shook her head. "Yes, you men have it so hard. Imagine wearing a bra or a girdle all day long." She began knotting his tie, stopped, and dipped her head towards the door. "I think that's Lily and the kids now. But who's that with them?" she asked, unable to place the voices. Stanley shrugged. Mabel pulled her husband's collar down in the back and patted his chest. "Done. Now let's go see who's here."

They entered the living room to find Ed excitedly introducing the unexpected guests to the gathering. "Mabel! Stanley! Come meet my friends, Giles and Yvonne LeBlanc," he said. He turned and hugged Lily. "You knew they were coming all along and never said a word."

Lily smiled. "They wanted to surprise you."

"Here they come!" Charlotte hollered from the kitchen window.

Mabel went outside to greet Amour and Victoria. She opened the passenger door and beamed at the bride in her camel-coloured Chanel suit. "You're absolutely beautiful. Ed's going to die when he sees you."

"Let's hope not," Amour laughed.

Mabel ducked her head inside and smiled at Victoria. "And you, too, young lady. You look amazing." She looked back at the cottage. "Everyone is here, so, if you're ready, I'll get everyone situated?"

Amour took a deep breath. "I'm ready."

Mabel ran back inside and ushered everyone into the backyard. She looked up to see the clouds breaking apart. "Please, please, please," she muttered. She quickly herded the guests into place, then stepped back to survey the gathering. She placed her hand on Ed's arm. "All set?"

Ed smiled and nodded. "Since the first day I laid eyes on her."

Mabel turned to face the small gathering of friends and family, and held up her pointer finger. “Okay, nobody move,” she instructed and went back inside. Amour and Victoria were standing by the front entrance, holding their bouquets. Mabel hugged Victoria and then the bride. “Your groom is anxiously waiting.”

Amour smiled and nodded. “I wish Myrtle was here,” she said with tears in her eyes.

Mabel squeezed her hand. “She’s here in spirt,” she said, reaching for her own bouquet and leading Victoria and Amour through the cottage to the back verandah. She glanced overhead. The thick, dark clouds were beginning to thin out, leaving a grey, wispy veil over the white, afternoon sun. She then gave Jeanne her cue to start signing.

Tell me it’s true, tell me you see
I was meant for you, you were meant for me
My darling, my love, how clearly I see
Somewhere in Heaven you were destined for me
Nothing could save me, fate gave me a sign
I’ll always be yours, come rain or come shine

The sun broke through just as Jeanne took her seat, casting a bright, warm glow upon those assembled below. Mabel dipped her head and whispered, “Thank you,” picturing another beautiful, sunny day many years ago. Her mother had lifted her up to the kitchen window and pointed to the spot she had hoped to plant cherry trees. Mabel felt a sharp pang of sadness, cursing the cancer that ravaged her mother’s young body, robbing her of so many simple pleasures, so many special moments. She lifted her head at the sound of chuckling. Liv was awkwardly running through the grass to her father when she fell headfirst into the grass. Stanley was about to go to her rescue, but Mary Catherine beat him to it, taking Liv by the hand and turning her around.

Mabel glanced at Stanley, then smiled at Amour. If you are half as happy as I am, you’ll be a lucky woman, she thought.

“Well, then…I guess that’s it,” the Justice of the Peace declared. “I now pronounce you man and wife.”

Ed was about to kiss the bride when Yvonne yelled something in French. "You be quiet," he playfully chided to laughter. He then kissed his wife and pumped his fist in the air. "It's official! We're married!" he hollered to applause and whistling.

Mabel waited for Victoria to hug her mother, then stepped forward. "I wish you and Ed a lifetime of happiness," she said, kissing Amour's cheek. She stepped back as Mary Catherine and the other well-wishers rushed forward for their turn to congratulate the bride.

Stanley appeared at her side and nodded toward the colourful autumn hills in the distance, painted in red, gold, and orange leaves. "Look," he said, grinning.

"Kids!" Mabel excitedly hollered. She pointed. "Look! Look up! A rainbow!"

Ed ran through the grass, scooped up Laura, and put her on his shoulders. "Go ahead, touch it." He laughed as Laura held her small arm up. "Come on…stretch. Higher. Keep stretching."

Mary Catherine and Lily began passing out flute glasses, followed by Sam who poured the Champagne.

Gordon called for everyone's attention. "Everyone have a glass?" he asked, waiting for Sam to fill his own. He turned to face the newlyweds. "Ed, we haven't known each other very long…in fact, it's only been for a little over two years." He pointed to Frank. "From the moment Frank introduced us, I knew you were a good man, with a big heart…someone who cared deeply about the welfare of others." He smiled at Lily. "Even strangers. But I certainly never expected that as two grown men in our forties…early forties…" he added to laughter, "I certainly didn't expect our friendship would grow so close…so quickly. Hell, you're a farm boy from Bathurst and I'm a cop from the Bay. You're a baseball fan. I like hockey. We honestly don't have a lot in common, but in the end, I guess it really didn't matter, fate had other plans in mind for us. Cause, here I am making the toast at your wedding. So, thank you for the great honour of being your best man, and thank you for your wonderful friendship. Charlotte and I look forward to many more evenings of love and laughter with two of our dearest friends." Gordon raised his glass. "To my good friend, Ed. And to the love of his life…his beautiful bride, Amour. May your love continue to grow and sustain you for many years to come. To Amour and Ed."

"To Amour and Ed," everyone said in unison.

"Before we dig into all of the delicious food the ladies have set out, Stanley has something to say," Gordon added.

Stanley stepped forward. "I'd just like to echo what Gordon said. It's a real honour for me, as I know it is for Mabel and Victoria, to be a part of this great day and to witness the union of two of my favourite people. For a while, there, I wasn't sure this day would ever come," he said to laughter. "But I'm not here to give a speech." He pulled several telegrams from his breast pocket and held them up. "I'm here to read these." He put on his glasses. "Ed, we are so sorry we are not there to witness your special day. We wish you every happiness and look forward to meeting your bride. Love and miss you. Blessings, the Baxter clan." Stanley looked up and smiled at Ed holding Amour's hand. "I guess they couldn't list all of the names. I hear the Baxter clan makes up half of Bathurst."

"Just about," Ed said to laughter.

Stanley reordered his papers. "Amour and Ed. Gloria and I are thinking of you on this special day. We will stop by the manor when we return home from Boston to properly toast your union. Love, Ted and Gloria. And this one," Stanley said, "has travelled quite a distance. Dear Amour and Ed. We are deeply disappointed that we are missing this wonderful day. We send our love and best wishes from foggy London. Look forward to hearing all about it when we return to Halifax. Love and happiness, always, Owen and Clair."

Stanley took off his glasses. "Owen and Clair flew to London last week to visit Owen's twin daughters."

Ed smiled at Amour and squeezed her hand. "You okay?" he asked, knowing the last telegram would trigger memories of Michael.

Amour looked up with tears in her eyes. "Yes," she said, resting her head against his shoulder. "Why wouldn't I be? I'm Mrs. Edward Baxter."

"What the hell are you doin here?"

"What do you mean?" Amour asked. "We came to see you."

"Shouldn't ya be in a motel somewhere, pawing at each other?"

Ed laughed. "My thoughts exactly."

Amour shot him a look. "You look better. How are you feeling?"

"How do you think I feel? I feel like someone just chopped my tits off. How was the wedding?"

"It was very nice. But we missed you." Amour said.

"And did ya miss me, too?"

Amour and Ed spun around to see Rosie coming through the door. Rosie winked at Ed. "Well, now, don't you look dapper in your fancy duds. But I bet ya can't wait to get outta them, can ya?" she said and laughed.

Amour shook her head. "Yes, Rosie, we missed you, too." She reached in her purse. "I brought you both a piece of wedding cake," she said, placing the napkin-wrapped fruit loaf on Myrtle's bedside table. "Your flowers are beautiful," Amour said. "Oh my, what a gorgeous arrangement. Who are these from?"

"Kenny."

"Kenny...the same Kenny who used to date Victoria?"

Myrtle nodded. "The same."

Amour looked impressed.

"Did ya get lots of pictures?" Myrtle asked.

"Of course," Ed said. "Hector was there with his Brownie."

Myrtle tried to adjust her pillow, but became frustrated.

Amour rushed to her aid. "Are you in a lot of pain?"

Myrtle shook her head. "I'm fine," she said, tilting her head back and closing her eyes.

"She's too damn stubborn to admit it," Rosie said, pouring a glass of water and putting it on Myrtle's tray.

Amour thought back to the night Myrtle and Rosie first met. She was sure the two would never speak again, let alone become so close. Rosie's a wonderful friend, she thought, knowing how much she looked forward to the wedding, opting instead to keep Myrtle company. "You're a good friend," she said to Rosie.

Myrtle scowled. "She's a pain in the ass...that's what she is. Hoverin over me like I'm about to take my last breath." She looked at Ed and Amour, and waved them off. "Why don't you two lovebirds get the hell outta here and go do whatever it is yer supposed to be doin on yer honeymoon." She pointed at Rosie. "And take her with you."

"Oooooh, now that's an interesting proposition," Rosie said. She elbowed Ed. "So whadaya say, handsome...think you can handle the both of us?"

Amour chuckled. "Okay, time to go." She leaned down and kissed Myrtle's forehead. "I'm glad you're feeling better. You'll be back to club before you know it."

"Take care," Ed said, leading Amour to the door.

"Hey," Myrtle called out. They both turned. "I'm really happy for you."

Amour smiled. "We know," she said, linking her arm through her husband's and walking out.

Ed shook his head and chuckled. "You've got some pretty interesting friends, that's for sure."

Amour tugged on his sleeve. "*Oh yeah*? Well so do you."

Ed screwed up his face. "*I do*?"

"Uh-huh. I think Frank is pretty interesting...don't you?"

Ed tilted his head to the side. "*Frank?* I guess, if you say so."

"*Oooh, I do.* But it's just not me who thinks so. Just ask Lily. Didn't you notice, she and Frank could barely take their eyes off one another?"

Monday, October 6

"Hello! Anyone home?" Victoria hollered, placing a book on the coffee table.

"I'll be right down."

Victoria turned to John. "C'mon in. Oh, look. Granddad hung the picture."

John looked over her shoulder and laughed. "Looks like Mary Margaret's picking her nose."

Victoria swatted his arm and pointed. "That's my little brother Rory. And that's Rachael...and there...that's Laura. Look, Stanley even got my Dad in the picture. See, that's his portrait."

Jeanne came downstairs. "Hi, dear. How was school today?"

"Hi, Nan. School was good. This is my friend, John Toth."

"Hello, John. I've seen you at the store. It's nice to finally meet you."

"Nice to met you, too."

Victoria pointed. "I wanted to drop off that book I was telling you about."

"Thank you, dear."

"Where's Granddad?" Victoria asked.

"He and Tipper went to buy more paint. They're going to freshen up the spare bedroom for when Lily and the kids come home."

Victoria looked around. "The living room looks great. So much brighter. Anyway, we can't stay. We're going to the rugby game. Glace Bay is in the quarter finals."

Jeanne smiled. "When will the newlyweds be back?"

"Not until next Tuesday." Victoria leaned in and gave her a quick hug. "Gotta run. I'll see you on the weekend." She and John were heading to the car when Jeanne called her back.

Victoria ran back up the steps. "Yes?"

"I was just thinking, if you'd like, you're welcome to ask your young man to Thanksgiving dinner," Jeanne said.

Victoria looked at John leaning against the car.

"Thanks, Nan. I'm sure he has plans. And he's not my boyfriend. Just a good friend, that's all. We've known each other forever. But thanks anyway."

"Oh," Jeanne said. "I just assumed. He seems very nice."

Victoria grinned. "He is," she said and bounded down the steps. She looked at John. "All set?"

"Yep," he said, climbing in and starting the car. "I'd like to take her up on her offer."

"*What?*" Victoria asked, laughing.

"I'd like to come for Thanksgiving dinner."

Victoria was surprised. "*Really?*"

"Yeah, really."

"Great, I'll let her know. Sorry, I just thought you wouldn't want to —"

John backed out of the driveway. "Ya know where else I'd like to go?"

Victoria could feel her heart race. She laughed nervously. "No."

"I'd like to go to the show on Friday night. *Decision Before Dawn* is playing."

"*Oh?*"

"You like war movies, right?" he asked.

"Yes, of course," she lied.

John smiled. "Thought so. I remember seeing you and Kenny at *Hour of Glory*." He glanced in her direction. "So, it's a date?"

Victoria smiled and nodded. "It's a date."

"Mr. Toth, you can go in now."

Luke walked past the short, stout woman and entered the small, cramped office. "Thank you."

She smiled. "Have a seat. Mr. Thompson will be with you shortly."

Luke sat down, opened his wallet, and counted his few remaining bills. He had thirty-six dollars to his name and still hadn't paid his landlady. If he didn't get this job, he didn't know what he would do.

Mr. Thompson breezed in and tossed a folder on his cluttered desk. "Nasty day out there."

Luke stood and shook his hand. "Yes, it's pretty miserable. Thanks for seeing me."

"Well, hopefully it will be a good use of our time," the Supervisor of Port Operations said. He put on his glasses, opened the folder, and quickly scanned its contents. "I see you were overseas."

"Yes."

"Airforce?"

"That's right. I was a gunner."

"See lots of action?"

Luke nodded. "Too much."

Thompson picked up a pen. "I was too young to enlist. I was pissed at the time. Now, I'm grateful. I see from your application that you ran your own retail business."

"Yes, a store in my home town of Glace Bay."

Thompson looked over his glasses. "So what brings you to Halifax? More to the point, why would you want to give up being your own boss to work for someone else?"

Luke shrugged. "Long story, really. Just needed a change of pace." He sensed his answer wasn't satisfying the man who'd determine if he'd get the job or not. "To be honest, my marriage fell apart. I needed a change of scenery...a fresh start. We both did."

Thompson pressed his lips together. "I get it. It's no bowl of cherries, that's for damn sure. Any kids?"

Luke felt a lump rise in his throat. "No," he said hoarsely.

"Well, that's good. Believe me, it's a lot harder when kids are involved. Sooo—" he said, quickly double-checking the application for the name. "Luke. Looks like it's your lucky day. I just happen to have an opening in the warehouse and a soft spot for veterans. You can start on Monday...

eight on the dot. Forty hours a week. Four thirty-five an hour. If you don't have your own safety gear…hard hat, boots, gloves… we can sell them to you. You can either buy them outright, or if you don't have the cash to pay up front, we can deduct the cost from your wages." He scribbled a note on the top of the application and handed it to Luke. "Take this to the Personnel Office, four doors down on your left. They'll give you the rundown…get you squared away."

Luke stood and shook Thompson's hand, relieved he now had a steady job with a decent wage. "Thank you so much. I really appreciate it. Means a lot."

Thompson smiled. "Good luck."

Luke was at the door.

"By the way, you're not related to a Mark Toth are you?" he asked.

Luke stopped in his tracks, turned back, and shook his head. "No, I don't think so," he lied, his heart pounding.

Thompson stood and nodded. "Oh, okay. It's just that it's not a common name in these parts. And we hired a Mark Toth to work inventory about a month ago. He's supposed to be a pretty decent boxer." He shrugged. "Who knows, maybe you two are distant cousins."

"Maybe," Luke sad sadly. He walked down the narrow hallway past the Personnel Office, dropped his application in a garbage can, and walked out into the pouring rain.

Stanley slammed the trunk down and got behind the wheel. He laid his hand on the ignition and looked at Mabel. "You sure we have everything?" he asked.

Mabel pointed to Liv, dozing on her lap, then to JC and Mary Margaret in the back seat. "One. Two. Three. Everything we need."

"You're sure?"

"I'm sure," she said. "I went through the place from top to bottom…twice."

Stanley started the engine and drove down the driveway, past the cherry trees and the grassy knoll where Mabel's mother and infant brother were buried.

Mabel blessed herself. "I hate to leave. The air is so fresh and the trees are so beautiful at this time of year. Maybe we should come back for Thanksgiving?"

"I just drained the pipes and shut the water off," Stanley protested.

"I know. I should have thought of it sooner. I'll have to get the turkey in the next day or two. Just a small one this year, for the five of us."

Stanley smiled. "I like that…just the family."

"I'm thinking six or seven pounds will be plenty big. Oh, wait. Myrtle will be home. I can't have Thanksgiving dinner and not ask her."

Stanley nodded.

"And what do you think about asking Alice? God love her. She's having such a rough go of things." Mabel shook her head. "I don't know how she does it. Working long hours, raising Matthew on her own, and six months pregnant. And then there's all the ugly chatter about why Luke ran out on his wife and son."

"Of course, invite Alice and Matthew," Stanley said.

Mabel smiled. "Great. But, ya know, if I ask Alice, I'm going to have to ask Corliss."

Stanley cocked his head. "Yes, I suppose you do."

"And what about John? We can't leave him out."

Stanley glanced at his wife. "So what are we up to now?"

Mabel counted in her head. "Ten. But that's it."

"Where are you going to put everyone?"

"We'll eat in the living room. Remember that year we had everyone over for Christmas…the year Mark surprised us…we managed. It'll be tight, but we can fit everyone around the table. And it's really no more work. Ya just peel a few extra potatoes and throw a few more carrots in the pot, that's all."

Stanley looked bemused. "We'll be up to twenty before you know it."

Mabel swatted his arm. "We will not." She chuckled. "But now that I think of it, if we have Myrtle over, I really should invite Rosie. I'd hate to think she'd be spending Thanksgiving home alone."

"Mabel!" Stanley said, sounding exasperated. "Just get a thirty-pounder. You know damn well the numbers are gonna keep going up." He shook his head. "So much for just the family."

Mabel looked out at the lush, colourful leaves, then down at Liv asleep on her lap, and felt an overwhelming wave of emotion wash over her. She turned toward Stanley. "All those people I just mentioned… Myrtle. Alice. Matthew. John. They're all family, too, ya know."

Stanley nodded. "I know."

"And James and Margaret, two of the most important people in my life, we weren't related, but they loved me. And they loved Luke and his brothers…just like they were their own." She turned and looked at JC with his eyes closed and his head resting against the back door. "And what about JC? He and Myrtle are practically inseparable. God, at times I think if we left it up to him, he'd just pack up and move in with her. And what about Victoria's grandfather. Victoria says he and that young boy are as thick as thieves."

Stanley smiled. "Tipper."

"Yes, Tipper. And look at Ed…how he is with Lily's kids. Anyway, my point is family is a lot more than being related by blood. So, as far as I'm concerned, if I have to hang from the ceiling to make room for everyone to come together so we can give thanks and count our blessings, I'm damn well gonna do it."

Stanley reached across and squeezed her hand. "You're right." He smiled. "You okay?"

Mabel pulled a tissue from her purse and wiped her eyes. "I'm fine." She laughed. "Actually, I am so much better than fine. I am a very lucky woman who has been blessed beyond measure," she said, tilting her head back and closing her eyes.

Stanley looked at her, then down at the sleeping child in her arms. And I am one lucky guy, he thought.

"Stanley," Mabel said.

"Uh-huh?"

"I don't remember packing Mary Margaret's blanket. You put it in your bag, *right?*"

Until We Meet Again

CPSIA information can be obtained
at www.ICGtesting.com
Printed in the USA
LVHW111708280322
714548LV00022BA/56

9 780228 863854